Estelle Ryan

The

Braque Connection

The Braque Connection
A Genevieve Lenard Novel
By Estelle Ryan

First published 2013

Acknowledgements

Writing is an isolated and humbling profession. Isolated, because so much of it happens in my head, and alone with my computer. Humbling, because of the honour to have so many amazing people supporting me. This book might not have been written, had it not been for the support, love, understanding and help I received from the extraordinary people in my life.

Charlene, for your never-ending interest, unconditional love and support. Anna, for your support. Moeks, for your faith in me, and your love. Wilhelm and Kasia, Ania B, Krystina, Maggie, Julie, Jola, Alta for your interest and support. Ania S for being a resource. Jane, for your interest, love and unwavering support. Maja Dziurosz for your friendly help regarding the underpaintings. Any mistakes made are mine, but I'll blame it on artistic licence. R.J. Locksley for editing. Mary Guhin for your sharp eyes that helped polish my book.

This time my special thanks goes to those readers who allowed me to use their names in this book. My deepest apologies that I killed so many of you! Your support have been, still is, invaluable to me. It was an honour and fun to write some of you into *The Braque Connection*. Please stay in touch.

Dedication

To Linette.

Chapter ONE

"Jenny, wake up." A warm hand was rubbing my shoulder a bit too vigorously. "Wake up, honey-buns."

I bristled at the term of endearment. I had heard it used recently and it had offended me deeply. I considered such saccharine terms disparaging, something I couldn't associate with the voice calling me. I tried to open my eyes, but my eyelids would not respond to the message sent by my neurotransmitters. My cognitive function appeared to be impaired. Not even a frown formed on my brow as I attempted to ascertain where I was. It was disconcerting that I couldn't place the voice calling me, even though it sounded familiar.

A slow panic started to creep through me. Why could I not move? Why could I not remember things? I swallowed and tried to call up Mozart's Piano Concerto No. 27 in B flat Major. Mentally writing any of Mozart's compositions always calmed me. For the first time in my life, I couldn't recall one single concerto, étude, sonata or opera. Dread settled heavily on my mind. Forcing my thoughts away from not being able to move or remember, I focussed on what I could feel.

Pain. Intense, overwhelming pain. My head felt like it was twice its size and filled with wet wool. Had I been imbibing? I had not been drunk before, thus my knowledge was purely academic. What I was experiencing would seem to fit the symptoms of *veisalgia*, or in layman's terms, a hangover.

I continued my self-examination, ignoring the incessant voice calling me. Had my muscles not been so unresponsive,

I would have been much more tense as my situation revealed itself in disturbing fragments. I was naked. Naked, on a bed and curled up against another naked body. My heart rate increased exponentially with this awareness. I had no recollection of how I had come to be here. My head was on a man's shoulder, my right hand resting trustingly over his heart. He was lying on his back, his right arm holding me against him, still rubbing my shoulder. I was on my side with my one leg thrown over his. I was cuddling. I never cuddled.

"Jenny, please wake up." Concern strained the familiar male voice.

I groaned. The deep voice vibrating against my ear increased the pain throbbing against my cranium.

"Honey-buns, wake up."

"Don't call me that." Forcing all my annoyance into my vocal cords resulted merely in a hoarse whisper. The chest under my head heaved with a deep breath.

"Oh, thank God." His chest shuddered. "How're you feeling?"

Darkness pulled at me and in my weakness I surrendered to its lure. The insistent shoulder-rubbing and irritating voice dragged me back to painful, paralysed consciousness. After a few seconds I realised I was keening. I swallowed the next monotone sound, but couldn't stop the groan. My head was pounding.

"Who are you?" I asked.

He drew in a sharp breath and slowly released it. "I'm your sugar-bunny."

Without the headache and worrying weakness in my limbs, I might have punched the chest I was resting on. As it was, it took immense effort to merely open my eyes. Pain that I had only read about stabbed at my eyes. I breathed through the nausea and looked beyond the naked chest under my hand.

We were in a bedroom, the bed comfortable yet firm under me. I was facing a wall, mostly taken up by a large window with the curtains drawn open. In front of the windows were two wingback chairs separated by an antique-looking coffee table. Elegant. The glass panes behind the leather chairs did not quite reach the floor or ceiling, but were large enough to afford me a full view of our surroundings. The pastoral landscape outside in the waning light of day was in sharp contrast to the turmoil in my mind. And it did not look familiar. In fact, it didn't look like anything I had seen in France. Where were we? Who was I with?

"Honey-buns, you need to get up."

I gritted my teeth and pushed myself up on shaking arms. I only managed a few inches, hoping it was enough to find out who was insulting me with such endearments. My eyes travelled from my hand to the muscular chest, neck and higher. Above the strong jaw with a few days' worth of stubble was a familiar mouth with uncommon depressed angles. I studied the *depressor anguli oris* muscles by his mouth for a few moments to determine whether the corners of his mouth were downturned in pain or distress. It was distress.

"Jenny?"

I raised my eyes and recognition slammed into my throbbing brain. I was naked in bed with Colin, the thief and art forger everyone called my boyfriend. His slow blinking and the elevation of his medial eyebrows evidenced deep concern.

"I am not your honey-buns." With great strain I moved my fingers, managing only a light pinch to his pectoral muscle. "And you are not my sugar-bunny."

His expression relaxed slightly. "We are naked in a strange place and that is what you want to argue about?"

"Colin." I collapsed back onto his chest when he smiled his relief at hearing his name in my still-hoarse voice. "Where are we?"

"Um, England?"

"Why are you questioning your own answer?" I wished I had the strength to look at his face. My expertise was in nonverbal communication, a skill I had learned out of necessity. Reading and interpreting body language did not come naturally to me. I relied heavily on my training to understand people's communication beyond their words. Being as weak as I was now, I only had Colin's words. "Why do you think we are in England?"

He sighed. "We're in my cottage in England."

I had not expected that answer. There were a few important questions I knew I had to ask, but couldn't reach them in my mind. My neocortex seemed capable of only the simplest of reasoning. "Why did you bring me here?"

"Can you sit up?" He shifted under me. "We need to move. It might help."

I lifted my hand. Ten centimetres above Colin's chest, it fell back. I had limited control over my muscles. Dark fear entered my peripheral vision.

"Jenny, you have to try and stay with me." He turned, and I rolled away from him onto my back. My breathing was erratic, my heart racing. Colin leaned over me. "Come on, Jenny. Stay with me. We have to get you moving. Maybe it will get this crap out of your system. We have to be ready to go. I don't know what kind of danger we are in."

The moment I heard the word 'danger', the darkness swallowed me. As a child I had succumbed to the warm safety of that darkness more often than my parents had appreciated.

Not even the best doctors or therapists had been able to stop me hiding there, away from reality. Shutdowns had been a haven from reality. It was only when I realised that my life, my childhood, would be exponentially easier if I pretended to be normal that I had made an effort to not give in to the allure of that safe place. I had spent the rest of my youth and most of my adulthood training myself and controlling my environment to not evoke such a reaction to stimuli.

Then, a year ago, Colin had entered my life. As an art thief he represented everything I had fought against—chaos, grey areas of morality, friends of dubious character and a non-systematic approach to life that had challenged my carefully constructed and disciplined world. It didn't matter that he had been working undercover for Interpol all along. He called his profession retrieval specialist. I called it being a thief, which placed him in the darker shades of grey. Six months ago the dynamics in our relationship had changed and we were now considered a romantic couple. Daily I struggled with the differences in our views on life. Recently I had been doubting the durability of such a relationship.

As the darkness abated and awareness of my surroundings returned, once again I heard myself keening. I hated this weakness in me, but had come to tolerate it. I concentrated on my breathing. The keening stopped at the same moment Colin grunted in annoyance close by. This brought me fully back to consciousness and I opened my eyes. I assumed it was night, because heavy curtains covered the windows, two lamps providing light in the bedroom. Colin was sitting in a chair next to the bed. He was dressed in black jeans and a long-sleeved black shirt, unbuttoned and not tucked in. On his lap was a funny-looking telephone, but he wasn't looking at it.

"Hey." His eyes narrowed in evaluation. "How're you feeling now?"

I took a moment to take full inventory of my body. "Still weak, but much better. What is that?"

"A sat phone."

"Sat for satellite?" I slowly pushed myself onto my elbows. A soft, beige sheet covered me. "Why do you have a satellite phone?"

"We have to contact Vinnie." He looked back to his lap and finished reassembling the instrument before attaching it to an electrical cord. It looked like an advanced smartphone. I had imagined satellite phones to be bigger and bulkier. "There was something wrong with the battery, but it should charge now."

"What can Vinnie do if we're in England and he is in France?"

Colin answered me by lifting one eyebrow. I hated when he did that. I might be an expert in nonverbal communication, but words went a long way to lend context to body language. Although this one was clear in its message. My question had been rather naïve. Colin's friend and flatmate Vinnie was much more a criminal than Colin. He wasn't working for Interpol, but helped Colin and me solve complex art fraud cases in any way he could. That usually involved him using his contacts from the crime world.

Despite Vinnie's extensive criminal resume, I considered him my friend. It was a friendship that was not easy to reconcile with my strict definitions of acceptable behaviour. He was, however, a good person to know if found in a situation such as ours.

"What happened to us?" I asked as Colin placed the phone on the bedside table. My eyes widened at the other object on the table. "A gun? Where did you get a gun?"

"This is my cottage, Jenny." He pulled back his head a centimetre and blinked slowly, indicating his unwillingness to elaborate. "I only ever came here in times when things were dire. I've set this place up as my safe house."

"A safe house that no one was supposed to know about?" I held the sheet against my chest and sat up with difficulty. I was hurting everywhere.

"Exactly. No one, except Vinnie, knew about this place."

"And me." In an attempt to win my trust when we had first met, he had given me the addresses of his five homes.

"And you." He leaned forward, his elbows resting on his knees and his hands clasped. "Do you remember how we got here?"

"No. The last thing I remember is sitting with you in the viewing room, talking about going home." To help me in my work, my viewing room had been specially adapted by Phillip, the owner of Rousseau & Rousseau, an upmarket insurance company. In the soundproof room I watched recorded interviews with suspects of art crimes to determine their truthfulness by observing and analysing their body language. Recently Colin had been spending more time there with me. I thought back to my last memory. "We were arguing."

"I remember that." He shook his head. "Now it seems like a really silly argument."

"It wasn't. I still maintain that breaking through the wall to join our two apartments is a bad idea." Without my knowledge, Colin had bought the apartment next to mine nine months ago. The last few weeks he had been pushing me to join the two apartments. I didn't like change. This was change.

"A silly argument that now is unimportant." The slight contraction of his *orbicularis oculi* muscles around his eyes alerted me that he was about to reveal something of significance. "We've lost three days, Jenny. It's three o'clock, Monday morning."

I closed my eyes against this information and called back the piano concerto. To my relief, the balanced blend of piano and orchestra came to mind, and I mentally wrote the first eight bars on music sheets. When I opened my eyes, my hands were fisted in my short hair. I let go and pulled the sheet back up to cover my bare chest. "We were drugged."

"That is also the conclusion I had come to. What I don't understand is why? And who? And why here? God, I have too many unanswered questions and I still have a hell of a headache."

"Are you sure it's been three days?"

He nodded and immediately winced. If his headache equalled mine, any movement should be attempted with great care.

"That means whoever drugged us had to keep on drugging us." Fear of the unknown things that were done to us tightened my throat. I had an unfortunate knowledge of medication that could result in the loss of consciousness. And the loss of memory. My parents had often agreed to prescriptions in the hope of curbing my disorder.

"They had full access to this place. Jenny, I swear to God I had the best alarm system installed here. It is a complex system that is still fully functional. I checked it while you were sleeping." His expression changed to deeper concern. He swallowed twice. "I think we were given the date-rape drug."

"A benzodiazepine?' Dismay flooded me. This was what I had suspected, but hearing it made it real and terrifying.

"If that is the date-rape drug, then yes."

"That would explain the anterograde amnesia." In my case, memory loss was the only side-effect that could remotely be considered beneficial. My experience with benzodiazepines had not been positive at all. I was in the one percent of paradoxical patients who experienced the opposite effects to the intended purpose of these drugs. The general public did not know their treatment value beyond Rohypnol, famed for its use at parties.

He swallowed again. "Do you feel… um…"

"I've not been raped."

Colin's head dropped into his hands as a trembling breath left him. "Thank God."

"You were worried."

He lifted his head, his eyes wide. "No, Jenny. I was terrified. You were on the bed keening and rocking, and I didn't know if it was a usual episode or because of something much worse."

"I'm okay." I caught myself as I lifted one shoulder in a half shrug. I wasn't convinced of what I had just said. "I'm not really okay. When I was a child, my parents tried to put me on various benzodiazepines."

"Why?"

"For some people they are effective in treating obsessive compulsive disorder and acute anxiety, to name only two. I exhibited those behaviours and my parents wanted to fix it with drugs, but it didn't work. I suffered from seizures and became more aggressive. Fortunately, that particular period of experimentation only lasted a few months." I shifted and felt all the aches on my body. It made me angry. "No, I am not okay at all. My body wasn't raped, but someone violated me, violated us. They took us without our permission, undressed us, drugged us and took us to a different country. In that sense, I do feel raped."

Colin's *masseter* muscles bunched as he clenched his jaw. "Yeah. Me too."

"I want to have a shower." I wanted to wash other people's hands off me. I wanted to wash this fear off me.

"Not a good idea." He looked contrite. "We might be

carrying evidence on our bodies. We'll have to be processed."

"No." I shook my head vigorously. "No, no, no. I'm not letting anyone else touch me. No."

Colin lifted his hands in a pacifying gesture. "Okay. Let's not talk about that right now. We need to figure out why we are here."

"Yes." A rational discussion would help to push the dark panic away. I inhaled deeply to focus my thoughts. "If we were drugged, it must have happened at Rousseau & Rousseau."

"Not necessarily. I don't remember anything after your threat to create a spreadsheet with all the reasons why we should not break through the wall." His lips twitched. "I remember saying something funny in return, but I can't remember what."

"You didn't say anything." The corners of my mouth turned down with the memory. "You smugly handed me a spreadsheet with reasons why you should break through the wall. You had anticipated my reasoning and were arrogant about that."

He attempted to hide his smile, but gave in. "God, I'm good. I remember creating the spreadsheet, but not handing it to you. What else do you remember?"

"I fed the papers into the shredder." An uncomfortable emotion tugged at me. I was feeling guilty about my pertinacious unwillingness to listen to his arguments. "You laughed at me and handed me another copy. That one I put in my handbag. I shut down my computers and we left."

"Was there anyone else still in the office?"

I thought for a moment. "No. Vinnie had only been there until lunch. Francine had left an hour before us. Oh, wait! Angelique was still in the office. We walked past her on the way out. She didn't look up when you greeted her."

Phillip's personal assistant was a dedicated woman and

fiercely loyal. Recently she had been less successful in her attempts to cloak her discomfort around me.

"Was Phillip still in the office?"

My eyes flashed wide open in shock. "Phillip would never do something like this. Why would you even suggest it?"

"He's friends with Millard," he said as if that would explain everything. Manfred Millard worked for Interpol, and on request of the president headed our team as we worked to find the man who had tried to kill the president and his family six months ago. Colin and Manny had a history and a deep dislike of each other.

"We should phone Manny."

"Later. First we need to speak to Vinnie. Don't argue with me on this one, Jenny. Rather tell me what else you remember."

"We didn't see anyone else, only Angelique. We took the elevator down, left the building, found the car where you had parked it and got in." I frowned. "I don't remember anything after that. I don't know whether you even started the car or drove home."

"Was there someone in the car?"

"I don't know." My hands fisted on my lap. My whole life I had worked with single-minded determination to have and maintain full control over my life. Not having any control, not having any memories was causing me severe psychological distress.

"Hey." Colin reached over and took one of my hands in his. "It will be okay. We'll find out what happened."

It was hard to believe him. How could we find out what happened if we couldn't remember anything? I pulled my hand back, only to experience a blitz anxiety attack when I saw the inside of my forearm.

On the pale skin was a tattoo. There was no scabbing or other signs of healing, indicating that it was not done with a needle. Knowing that this was just a henna tattoo brought only a small measure of comfort. It was an intricate design of curls, twirls and whorls, beautiful only in its decorative purpose. There was no picture. I rubbed the centre of the tattoo even though I knew my skin would be stained for at least a week. I rubbed harder.

"Get it off me. Get it off."

"Jenny, stop." Colin took my hands in a firm grip. "I thought you weren't going to like this."

"Did you do this?" Before I finished my irrational, impulsive accusation, I was shaking my head. "I know you wouldn't. Why would somebody do this? What is this?"

Colin exhaled heavily. "I think all of this is a message. Being drugged, kidnapped, taken to my unknown safe house and your tattoo."

I saw it in his face. He had the same suspicions that had entered my mind. I closed my eyes against these thoughts and wrote a few more bars of the piano concerto. When I opened my eyes, he let go of my hands. "Why don't you go find some Mozart to put on the sound system?"

The thought of Mozart's music surrounding me lifted some of the anxiety. "I need my clothes first."

"I looked through the whole house and couldn't find any of our stuff. Not your handbag, our clothes, shoes, nothing."

"What am I going to wear?"

Colin got up and walked to a beautiful dark wood chest of drawers against the wall. "You can wear my t-shirt and sweatpants. The pants will be too big for you, but you can tighten the drawstrings."

"No, I can't wear your clothes. I want my clothes. I can't wear someone else's clothes. They're not my clothes."

Halfway to the chest of drawers Colin stopped and turned back to me. He looked tired. "My clothes are clean, washed and ironed. At the moment, you are wearing a sheet that was washed and ironed in the same way. I know this must be very difficult for you, Jenny, but I need you to work with me, not fight me on everything."

My shoulders slumped. "I'm sorry. I don't know how to handle this. You are the only familiar element in this situation, which makes it easier to fight you. It doesn't justify my behaviour. I'll try harder."

He nodded and turned back to the tall piece of furniture. Two minutes later I was dressed all in black. I had to roll up the legs of the sweatpants, and the soft t-shirt was two sizes too large, the sleeves falling below my elbows. I felt much less exposed and vulnerable. The thick black socks were also too large, but made me feel protected against whatever could be lurking on the floors. I now had the confidence to take in my surroundings. Colin had returned to the chair next to the bed and was monitoring the satellite phone.

The bedroom was spacious and elegantly decorated. The oriental rugs, the heavy wooden furniture and the paintings were the epitome of understated wealth and elegance. Knowing Colin's masterful skills at forging art, I was not surprised that even a place he only used as a safe house would be tastefully decorated. I took my time absorbing all the details. Above the chest of drawers was a Picasso painting. Whether authentic or expertly forged, it perfectly fitted the theme of the room.

I turned towards the bed and gasped. "You stole my painting!"

Colin looked up from the instrument in his hands and followed my accusing glare. He laughed softly. "I had that before we met, Jenny."

Above the bed hung my favourite painting. I could never afford the original, so I had saved until I could buy the best reproduction Phillip could recommend. Jacques Braque's

Harbour in Normandy had appealed to me from the very first moment I had seen it. Something about the fragmented forms and geometric shapes resonated with my neuro-patterns. Looking at this painting in Colin's bedroom, I felt my mind agreeing with the cubist rendition of that scene.

"Did you forge this?" I stepped closer and Colin stood up, looking at the painting.

"Yup. This is one of my best wor..." He leaned in and narrowed his eyes. "This isn't right."

"Do you see a mistake?"

Colin's body language had frozen into an alertness that worried me. It was the kind of physical reaction exhibited moments before an attack, when the aggressor studied his prey.

"Bastards!" Colin grabbed the painting off the wall and angled it toward the light. "This isn't mine."

"Whose is it?" I walked to stand next to him. No matter how hard I looked, I couldn't see what was wrong. It looked like my reproduction, which looked like the original. "What's wrong with it?"

"These aren't my strokes."

"You can see the individual strokes?" I had known Colin had a good eye for art, but seeing this at a glance was a unique skill.

"Of course I can." He shook the painting. "This is not my frigging painting. Someone stole my painting."

"Why would someone do that?"

His anger seemed disproportionate to the theft of a forgery. He shook his head. "I don't know. It doesn't make sense to replace my forgery with another forgery."

"Are you sure this is also a forgery? You aren't maybe being set up for the theft of the original?" That certainly would explain our presence and the loss of days.

"No, this is a forgery and a very good one at that. Not as good as mine though."

I didn't know what to make of this. There seemed no rationale behind such an action, except for Colin's earlier suggestion that this was a message. "Is anything else out of place here?"

"I didn't look for things like this." He carefully placed the painting on the bed. "I'll check the rest of the house while you put on some Mozart."

By definition, I would believe a cottage to be small. Not in this case. Colin's safe house had two floors, three bedrooms and a bathroom on the top floor. I followed him down the stairs to the living areas on the ground floor. He stopped at each painting, glaring at it first, then inspecting it carefully. I left him at a Rembrandt that truly looked like an original to my untrained eye.

The ground floor had been altered to be a large open space with stone pillars informally creating separate spaces. I easily found the sound system and the selection of CD's next to it. No sooner had Mozart's Flute Concerto No. 2 in D Major started to fill the cottage than Colin appeared next to me, holding a statue with the sleeve of his shirt. I assumed that was to preserve possible fingerprints.

It was a smooth, cream-coloured lion, worn from many years of touch. Working in an insurance company that often dealt with art cases, I had learned that these kind of statues were usually marble, jade or bronze. This statue didn't look like it was made from any valuable material.

"Another forged forgery?" I asked. The tension lines along his mouth and eyes worried me.

"No, this is not mine." He put it on the seventeenth-century side table. "I once had my hands on it, but it never belonged to me nor have I ever reproduced it."

"There is more to your history with this statue." I could see it written all over his face.

"This is a Tang Dynasty marble lion."

"It doesn't look like marble."

"It isn't. It feels like plastic." Colin's jaw worked while he stared at the curtains covering the windows. His lips formed a thin line as he turned to me. "This was the piece I was reappropriating when Manny arrested me."

"Oh. Oh my." I knew my eyes were wide from shock. "I think it's time to call Vinnie."

Chapter TWO

"Now we wait." Colin placed a cheap-looking cell phone on the coffee table next to the satellite phone and the gun. We were in the bedroom, seated in the wingback chairs.

"Why didn't you just phone Vinnie?" I had quietly watched Colin remove the new cell phone from its box, turn it on and send an SMS. "And why did you take that cell phone apart?"

"Vinnie and I have a system. I use an untraceable phone to send him a coded message. In this case, I sent him an offer for a penis enlargement drug. Now he knows I am going to phone him in fifteen minutes on an untraceable phone." He smiled at my confused expression. "In our line of work, in our lives, it is better to take precautions. Phoning Vinnie on his usual line runs the slight risk of someone tracing the call."

"But all of you are disproportionately paranoid about these things. Francine runs antivirus software on your phones and computers at least twice a week." Francine was a computer genius who always looked like she had stepped off a Paris catwalk. She was an exotic beauty who had totally disregarded my social awkwardness and resistance to friendship. The fifth member of our unique group, she was also the only female friend I had.

"That is true, but I don't want to take any chances. Especially since we don't know how we got here or why we are here." He nodded at the dismantled instrument. "I took it apart so it cannot be traced. I will phone Vinnie from the sat phone to a brand-new cell phone that will be destroyed after this conversation. That way we stay safe."

Part of me considered this to be excessive vigilance, but another part of me agreed with Colin. The mystery surrounding our current situation warranted caution. I hated everything about this. Not knowing how we got here, what I had been drugged with, where the henna tattoo had come from and who had touched me constricted my throat.

"I really want to shower."

Colin took a deep breath. "You're okay now, right? No episodes?"

"What does that have to do with taking a shower?" I wasn't going to panic washing this experience off my body.

"Did you look at yourself when you got dressed?" he asked softly, carefully.

"No." I glanced at my forearm and grimaced. I had purposely avoided inspecting my body—a cowardly attempt to avoid looking at the tattoo. "Why? What's wrong?"

"Lift up your shirt, Jenny."

My eyes widened and I crossed my arms over my chest. "This is not the appropriate time for sex. Frankly, I'm surprised that you would even suggest this. You're usually much more sensit... oh, that's not what you meant."

His eyes had softened and the corners of his mouth had twitched at my outraged reaction. He turned serious again. "Just lift your shirt, Jenny."

I took the hem of the T-shirt and lifted it to reveal my abdomen. I groaned with the effort and saw why it had hurt. On my stomach were two large bruises, each the size of a fist.

"Why did I not feel this?"

"Push up your sleeves."

I swallowed and pushed both sleeves up to my shoulders.

My upper arms were black and blue. Some places I could see individual finger marks where a hand had gripped me. I stared open-mouthed at these. On the outside of my forearms, where I wouldn't normally look, were also dark bruises. I recognised them for what they were. Defensive injuries. I had been so concerned about the tattoo and my pounding headache that I had not noticed these horrid marks. How could I not have felt these bruises that were now sensitive to my probing fingertips?

"Jenny?" The tone in Colin's voice drew my eyes away from the discolouration on my skin. I looked up. The *procerus* muscle contracted his brow into a frown of concern. "You okay?"

"What happened to me?" The question came out as a whisper.

"I don't know." He leaned closer and took my hands in his. "There might be evidence on our hands, in our hair, fingerprints on our skin that can help find the guys who took us. I know you don't want anyone else to touch you, but your injuries need to be documented."

"What about you? Do you have bruises?"

"I have a knot at the back of my head. I assume some arsehole hit me. And a few scratches on my arms. Nothing else."

"So why do I… I must have had a meltdown." I flinched at the realisation.

"A meltdown?"

"You've only ever seen me shut down." Going into my head was embarrassing, but it was only one type of reaction to external stimuli. "A meltdown is… it's not pleasant to witness. I also lose awareness of what is around me, but I act out."

"How?" he asked quietly.

"Everyone is different and every meltdown is different,

but it can become very violent, physically aggressive. If indeed I was given a benzodiazepine, it would explain a meltdown." That had been the result when those drugs had been administered to me before. Restraining me even at such a young age had brought a lot of damage to those attempting to hold me, as well as to myself.

"For what it's worth, I hope you kicked their arses." Colin squeezed my hands. "Will you hold out on that shower until after the call?"

I nodded.

"Okay, let's hear what Vinnie has to say. I'll put it on speakerphone." He picked up the satellite phone and dialled. The tinny ringtone sounded only once.

"Dude!" Vinnie's voice boomed over the phone. "Where the fuck have you been?"

"Hey, Vin." Colin smiled. Me too. Vinnie was not only tall and built like a warrior, he had a personality to match. "We're okay."

"Where have you been? We've been worried… wait. Is Jen-girl with you? Where is she? Is she okay?"

"I'm here, Vinnie." I leaned closer to the phone. "I'm well."

A rush of sound came over the phone. I assumed it to be Vinnie loudly sighing in relief. His often unwanted affection towards me now brought stinging tears to my eyes. Another rustle sounded over the phone, followed by two male voices arguing and an impressive use of expletives. Colin's shoulders stiffened. He had also recognised the other voice.

"Frey, where the bloody hell are you and what the holy hell have you done with Doctor Face-reader?" Manny always sounded annoyed, his crisp British accent lending it a stronger sense of superiority. What I heard now was anger masking concern. My eyes started stinging again.

"You're on speakerphone now, dude." Vinnie's voice was dark. "The arsehole insisted."

"You're the one who phoned me fifteen minutes ago and told me you'd found them."

"You phoned Millard?" Colin didn't hide his shock. I was also taken by surprise. Vinnie and Manny had a tumultuous relationship at best. For reasons I didn't know they continued to antagonise each other, often with personal attacks. Fortunately, I had witnessed in both of them the ability to move past their deep dislike of each other when we had been faced with crises. Then they had worked together. Then, and apparently now.

"None of us have slept in three days, dude. Millard has been turning over all kinds of rocks looking for you two." Reluctance entered his tone. "He deserves to be in on this call."

Colin's eyes widened and he took a sharp breath. He schooled his face into a neutral expression. "Do you know who took us?"

"You don't get to ask questions first, Frey." Manny's tone was clipped. "First you answer my questions."

"Colin didn't do anything wrong, Manny." I couldn't let them start an inane argument. We had more important issues to discuss.

"Don't you start with me, Doc. I have quite a few things to say to you once you get back." He huffed a few times. "Looking into bloody thefts without discussing it with me."

"Ask your questions, Millard," Colin said, preventing me from giving Manny an annoyed reminder that it was my job to analyse data and inspect anomalous cases.

"Where are you?"

"England."

It was silent for a moment. "*Where* in England, arsehole?"

"In the countryside, in the northeast."

"You're in your safe house?" Shock added a strained quality to Vinnie's words. "Dude! How the fuck did he know?"

"How did who know?" I spoke directly into the phone. "Do you know who took us?"

"How did you get there?" Manny asked, ignoring my question.

"We don't know." Colin impressed me by stopping the deluge of unanswered questions to give a concise report of everything we had concluded so far. "Jenny has some serious bruising. I think she put up quite a fight, so there might be some evidence under her nails."

I gasped, brought my fingers right up to my face and stared under my nails. The thought of someone's skin under my nails made me want to not only shower, but scrub in scorching hot water. I shuddered and mentally wrote another four bars of Mozart's piano concerto.

"I know someone in Scotland Yard we can trust."

"Millard, you can't trust just anyone." When Colin wasn't purposefully baiting Manny, he treated him increasingly more often with respect. Like now. "You need to be sure about this person. Someone managed to find out the highly protected location of a place I only use in dangerous situations. If you weren't… well, *you*, I wouldn't even trust you right now."

That was the only compliment I had ever heard Colin give Manny. Coming from him, it was the highest praise he could bestow on anyone. This served to emphasise the dire situation we found ourselves in.

"Rhodes can be trusted. I won't let just anyone close to Doc."

Colin glanced at me. "You okay with this?"

"He's not touching me." I couldn't tolerate the thought of another stranger touching me. It took great restraint to not react in revulsion whenever Vinnie hugged me. I trusted Vinnie with my life.

"I'll be with you all the time. Between you and me, we can do what needs to be done and give the evidence to Millard's guy."

I closed my eyes when another shudder shook my body. Allowing myself to focus solely on the half-written mental music sheet, I continued writing the piano concerto. When I opened my eyes to agree, the telephone discussion had moved on.

"What kind of drug do you think?" Manny asked, all business.

"I reckon it was the date-rape drug," Colin said.

"It's a benzodiazepine," I added. "It's a psychoactive drug, which interferes with forming and consolidating memories of new material. That is why we can't remember what happened."

"So Rohypnol is a benzo-thingie?" Vinnie asked.

"Benzodiazepine, yes."

"Rohypnol is easy enough to buy on the street." Manny stayed quiet for a few seconds. "Give me your address or co-ordinates, Frey. I'm going to see how soon Rhodes can be with you. We need all the evidence before it metabolises even more."

"There goes my safe house." Colin sighed and rattled off the address and the GPS co-ordinates.

For two minutes we listened to Manny make a phone call and confirm with someone the sensitive nature of this case. Once he had received a vow of silence, he gave a brief description of the situation and the address.

"Twenty-five minutes. I'll tell them. Thanks, Rhodes."

A few beeps sounded over the phone, probably Manny turning off his cell phone.

"Doc?"

"I'm here."

"Rhodes will be there in twenty-five minutes. He said you shouldn't pee until then. Or shower."

I groaned.

"Frey, we have another problem." The reserve in Manny's voice sent a spike of adrenaline through my body. It made me feel cold. "You're wanted for murder."

"I'm what?" Colin's question was lost in Vinnie's loud expletive-filled expression of shock.

"I knew you were hiding something from me, old man." Vinnie only spoke softly and slowly when angry. "Dude, I knew this arsehole was up to something. Yesterday morning he suddenly went from concerned about you guys to secretive. I even told Francine that I wished Jen-girl had been here to read the arsehole's body language."

"Vinnie," I interrupted his tirade, "let Manny speak. This could give us insight into why we are in England right now."

"Oh. Yes. Okay, speak, old man."

There was a short silence. "One of my old colleagues at Scotland Yard phoned me yesterday when an interesting case came across his desk. When I was looking for you fifteen years ago, we were working in the same department. He was there when I arrested you, so he knew my interest in you."

"Obsession, more like," Vinnie said. For years Manny had been looking for Colin, never finding enough evidence to locate or arrest him. Colin had known this and had done his own detailed investigation into Manny.

Colin and Vinnie had been on a job stealing an artefact from a museum when a middle-aged security guard had had a heart attack. He had made an unscheduled walk-through of the museum when he ran into Vinnie. It had been too much for his unhealthy heart.

Colin had sent Vinnie away, phoned Manny and tried to keep the guard alive with CPR. The guard hadn't made it and Manny had arrested Colin at long last. A few hours after Manny had booked Colin, he was released on orders from Interpol. They had recruited him to work for them on cases that could not be handled the usual legal way.

"When he saw you as the suspect in the murder," Manny continued, ignoring Vinnie, "he immediately phoned me. Apparently, you killed someone in England the day before yesterday."

"I didn't do this."

"Here's what the evidence tells us. You picked the lock of the French doors leading to the library of a large mansion on the outskirts of Maidenhead, Berkshire. In case you don't know, it's twenty-five miles outside London. Once inside the mansion you broke into the safe and stole a few documents, which the owner claims are worthless. You also stole an original Braque painting, worth more money than I make in a decade. The butler must have heard something, came into the study and surprised you. There was a struggle, you picked up some ridiculously expensive statue and knocked him out. While the fifty-eight-year-old male was lying helpless on the expensive Persian carpet, you shot him three times in the chest and left with the painting."

"No fucking way!" Vinnie's voice boomed through the room. "My man would never shoot anyone."

A long silence followed Vinnie's outrage. I stared at the gun lying on the coffee table. It took less than a second to dismiss the direction of my thoughts. Empirical evidence counted in Colin's favour. I knew him. I could read him. He might be a thief, but he would never kill anyone. I also took note of the stolen painting being a Braque and wondered about the connection.

"There must be a mistake, Millard." A series of expressions flitted over Colin's face as he processed this information.

"No mistake. Sorry." Manny sounded genuinely contrite. "I asked Smith to double-check the evidence. It was your fingerprints on the door handle, the safe and the statue. Your skin cells were also found under the butler's nails."

"I have scratch marks on my arms. That must be where they got the skin from." Colin leaned closer to the phone. "You know I'm being set up, right?"

"As much as I would like to see you behind bars, Frey, I don't want you to go for something that you are not guilty of."

"Does that mean you believe Colin?" I asked. People can be extremely unclear in their communication. I wished I could see Manny. By the tone of his voice and his words alone, I couldn't tell if he was convinced of Colin's innocence.

"Yes, Doc. I believe him. Unfortunately. You forget that I followed him for years. I know his MO. Firstly, he doesn't kill. He's a thief. I also know that he would never break into a place without using gloves. The photos they took of the crime scene did not show the level of... holy hell, I hate saying this." It was quiet for a few seconds. I imagined Manny scowling and rubbing his hand hard over his face. "It didn't show your level of professionalism."

"Colin, don't." I reached out with my hand as if to physically stop him from baiting Manny. His intent was in every muscle movement of his face.

"Come on, it's so easy." His expression lightened for the first time since I had woken up. He shrugged when I shook my head. "I suppose I should thank you, Millard."

"Oh, don't hurt yourself, Frey. I'm still waiting for the moment you slip up, so I can throw your arse in jail."

"Let's stay on topic," I said. "Tell me more about the house that was broken into. Who owns it and where were they?"

"Give me a sec, Doc. I've got the case file here on my tablet. Let me just get to it."

A few months ago, Francine had convinced Manny to become more technologically updated and to give in to the pressure from Interpol to get a tablet. Her method of persuasion involved preposterous flirting and threats to catch him unawares with a kiss that would rock his world. Those had been her exact words. It had worked. Manny often scowled and swore at the tablet as he swiped and stabbed at it with his strong fingers.

"Got it." Manny's voice broke into my thoughts. "Okay, here it is. The owners were at some society dinner when this happened. They got home around two in the morning and found their house broken into and their butler dead on the library floor."

"Who owns the house?" My words were clipped. Why did people not answer questions concisely? There was always an irrational need for excess information.

"Kathleen McCarthy. She is the—"

"—sole owner of Windsor stables. She is worth over forty million pounds," I said. A surge of adrenaline caused my stomach to feel hollow. "She also owns a vineyard in France and a few other interests in most European countries."

"How do you know this, Doc?"

"Rousseau & Rousseau handles her insurance. And her house in France was broken into a few weeks ago."

"Is this one of the thefts you were looking into?" Colin asked.

"I knew it!" Manny's exclamation came over so loud the phone distorted the sound. He had to be very close to the instrument. "When I found out that you were looking into some thefts, I knew it was going to bring trouble. Thefts that had nothing to do with any of our cases. And now a man is dead and Frey is as good as guilty."

I flinched as if Manny had punched me. "This is not my fault. I was just doing my job, looking for anomalies or patterns in art crimes."

"Damn it all to hell. I know, Doc." Manny sounded tired. "I shouldn't shout at you. Not yet anyway. Oh wait, Rhodes is calling."

I glanced at Colin while Manny spoke to his Scotland Yard contact. Every muscle in Colin's body was tense, his lips tightened into a thin line. The more stressed a person becomes, the less you see of his or her lips. With Colin's past, it would be difficult to convince anyone of his innocence. His, and my, lack of memory would add to the mounting evidence against him.

"He's five minutes out." Manny's voice dropped a tone. "Frey, do whatever he asks. We need the evidence. Especially any DNA that can be recovered."

A shiver went through me at the reminder that someone else's DNA might be under my nails. My breathing became shallow and it required hard concentration to not give in to my desire to rush to the bathroom and spend an hour under hot water, scrubbing.

"We'll do what we decide." Colin was being obtuse, but I knew he wanted the evidence just as much. "Vin?"

"Dude?"

"Can you organise a lift home?"

"Whoa there, cowboy," Manny said. "Don't give me a reason to really throw your thieving arse in jail. I'll handle your transport home. Have you forgotten that you are working on a team directly under the president? Everything you do will affect him, idiot."

Colin closed his eyes and shook his head. I was too distracted by whatever was under my nails to give appropriate attention to this new argument. Having spent the last six months working with them had desensitised me to their constant bickering.

"You are twisted, old man," Vinnie said. "Colin was asking me if I could ask my cousin, who owns a legit chopper service, to get them across the pond."

"Without papers? Without any documents? That's not legit, arsehole."

"Whatever, old man."

I once read a study revealing all the microorganisms residing on our skin, better known as skin microbiota. A percentage of the average one trillion microbiota living on human skin could be under my fingernails at this very moment. My empty stomach recoiled. A second later, Colin twisted and looked out the window. "Your man is here, Millard. Just organise to get us home."

Without waiting for a response, he disconnected the call. There was so much more that I wanted to ask, but knew it would have to wait. No matter how much I rationalised the need for being processed, I knew that the next hour or so I would have to rely on Mozart more than usual. At least I was going to get rid of whatever was caught under my nails and I could focus on the hot shower I planned to have.

Chapter THREE

"There we go. Scrape it all onto the paper. That's it." Ben Rhodes was a jovial, overweight man who had been in awe of meeting me. I had to admit being taken aback by his star-struck greeting. It appeared he had read most of my articles and had even attended a seminar I had presented at Oxford University a few years ago. I guessed his age to be in the mid forties, which made his blushing when he greeted me charming.

As soon as Ben had recovered from meeting me, he had given us plastic containers for urine samples. That done, we were now sitting at the kitchen table, scraping possible evidence from under our nails. I didn't know if this was worse than Ben drawing enough blood to fill three small little vials. The more blood they had, the more tests they could run, he had said while I had tried to not give in to panic. Colin had insisted on doing the rest ourselves without explaining why. Ben had been very accommodating, which led me to believe that Manny must have given him some background on me. All but my left pinkie nail had been scraped.

"What else do you need from us?" Colin asked. He had scraped his fingernails much faster than I did. I was making sure to get any and all foreign skin microbiota and other elements from under my nails.

"I would like to photograph your injuries." Ben nodded in approval when I finished my pinkie nail. He carefully folded the paper and placed it with all the other evidence.

"But first I need you to brush your hair onto another sheet, Doctor Lenard."

"Call me Genevieve, please." I was still looking at my nails when his request registered. "Oh God, there is evidence in my hair?"

I closed my eyes and focussed on Mozart until my heart rate slowed down. When I was able to ignore the images flashing through my mind, I looked at Ben, ready. The movement around his mouth, but especially around his eyes alerted me to more than mere patience. He was showing empathy.

"Who is it?" I asked softly.

"My son." His smile conveyed deep affection. "He was diagnosed with autism at the age of three. He's now thirteen and is driving us crazy with his latest music choices. It's been a hard, but interesting road."

"How severe is he?" There was no evidence of shame or regret in Ben's nonverbal cues. For that alone he gained my respect.

"Pretty high-functioning. His biggest problem is socialising." He placed a large sheet of paper on the table. "It is something we're working on all the time, teaching him to better understand social cues and structures. Your lectures on non-neurotypical behaviour helped us a lot. It also got him to take an interest in body language. Now he interprets every single bloody movement we make."

The *orbicularis oculi* muscles around his eyes relaxed completely while he was talking about his son. His mouth softened and he became much more animated. The love he had for his son was evident. My childhood had been filled with emotional distance, pressure to be normal and ultimately rejection from my parents.

"Your son is a very lucky young man," I said.

"No, we are the lucky ones. He keeps us on our toes and

helps us appreciate every small step, every special moment." He handed me a fine-toothed comb, wrapped in plastic. "If you could brush out your hair on this sheet, it would be great."

The reprieve our conversation had brought disappeared. I took the sterilised comb from the plastic cover, angled my head over the sheet of paper and started combing. No matter how much I combed, it didn't take away the feeling that I had to comb harder.

"Jenny, stop." Colin's hand folded over mine. "I'm sure you got it."

I swallowed and focussed on the hot shower that I would soon have. Carefully I put the comb on the sheet and watched Ben fold the corners of the paper over the comb and any particulates I had managed to get rid of. Colin combed out his hair, but was much more efficient at it. He winced a few times as he touched the knot at the back of his head.

The next twenty minutes were uncomfortable as Ben took photos. He first photographed the scratches on Colin's arm and the knot at the back of his head, showing me how it would be done. When it was my turn, I lifted my shirt to just beneath my breasts and closed my eyes. The discomfort I felt was not because a stranger was looking at my bare abdomen. It was the reminder of unknown assailants touching me, hitting me, that had me reaching for Mozart yet again.

My life had never been without challenges. During my formative years it had been fighting the stigma attached to anything and anyone deviating from society's definition of 'normal'. University had been a challenge in itself—a new social environment with many unknown factors, all of which had sent me into countless bouts of panic, resulting in shutdowns sometimes lasting for days. But I had fought my way through my fears, constantly tightening my control, and dealing with challenging situations.

I had not been born with skills like most neurotypical people. The field I had graduated in was chosen with the utmost care. Typically, people on the autism spectrum did not read and understand body language. I was now one of the world's leading experts. My further education in psychology aided me in a better understanding of neurotypical behaviour, most of which I considered irrational and nonsensical.

Despite all my education, my analytical skills and exceptional IQ, I failed to find enough rationalisation to calm myself. This situation and all it encompassed was becoming more overwhelming by the minute. Observing Ben's fleeting micro-expressions of horror, anger and sympathy while documenting my injuries exacerbated my blooming panic.

"We have given you all the symptoms we have so far experienced." My voice was strained. This was an attempt to change my focus while Ben took close-up photos of my arms. I needed my mind to become immersed in analysis or problem-solving. That would keep the panic at bay. "In your experience, do you agree the drug could be a benzodiazepine?"

He briefly looked up from zooming in on four dark marks next to each other. Fingers from a large hand, a man's hand.

"Yes, unfortunately." He frowned. "But it should've had a calming effect on you."

"It doesn't." Briefly I told him about my experiences with benzodiazepines.

"Are you using any other medication at the moment?"

"Only vitamin supplements when needed." I had vowed to wean myself off medication as much as I could. As long as I focussed on my physical and psychological health, I was able to avoid having to use pharmaceutical help. "It has been a long time, but sometimes I need SSRIs."

"What's that?" Colin asked.

"Selective serotonin reuptake inhibitors." Ben looked back at me. "Do you often suffer from depression?"

"Not as much anymore. I have managed to find a good balance in my life." It was strange that I talked so easily with this man I had never met before. Maybe it was the knowledge that he understood on an uncommonly deep level.

"Do you think the benzodiazepine will have an adverse effect on you in the long term?"

"I hope not. It has been more than twenty years since I last had anything like it. Once it had metabolised, there weren't any aftereffects. I hope it will still be true."

"What aftereffects?" Colin asked.

"There is a lot of disagreement about long-term effects and frankly, I don't think that a few days' use qualifies as long-term use. We would have to use it for longer than three days to see definite effects in our cognitive functions." One look at his face and my eyebrows lifted. "You are scared?"

"I'm not scared." He tried to relax his facial muscles, but the fear was still visible. "I'm just concerned about all these side effects. Wait. Why are you not freaking out?"

I stiffened. "What—"

"Sorry, Jenny." Colin knew I was sensitive about the word 'freak'. "'Freaking out' usually means becoming hysterical."

"It doesn't make sense."

"I know." He sighed. "What I want to know is why you are not more concerned with everything he's just said."

"May I?" Ben looked at me. I nodded, curious to hear his reasoning for my behaviour. I assumed he felt he had personal insight. He turned to Colin. "Knowledge makes her feel safer. The more she knows, the more empowered she feels.

It is the strangeness, the lack of information making her feel powerless and therefore uncomfortable. How did I do?"

"You're mostly right," I said when he looked at me, expectation around his eyes. "Especially about my need for information."

"The first few years with Tommy were really difficult." Ben's voice softened as he spoke about his son. He was photographing my back. Colin was holding my shirt up, his hands warm where he touched me. "He wouldn't accept a simple answer to a question. He wanted an encyclopaedic answer even for the simplest of questions. It used to drive us nuts. Then we got him an iPad. Honest to God, that was a gift. He has two sets of encyclopaedias on it since he doesn't believe in the reliability of information from the internet. Now we know when he has a question. He stops talking and starts tapping away on his iPad. It's brought us all quite a lot more breathing space."

"You seem to have found a good compromise." A hitch in Colin's tone made me turn to him. What I saw on his face took me by surprise. Envy was an emotion closely related to regret. We felt envy for things we didn't have, regret for things we had or hadn't done. A stabbing pain hit me in my chest. I didn't hear Ben's reply, wondering what Colin felt was missing. Was it related to our relationship? To date I had not seen any nonverbal indicators that he regretted being with me or that he envied other couples. Indicators of impatience, yes. But not envy or regret. This was a first.

As I inhaled to ask him, Ben's cell phone rang. Since it was ten past six in the morning, I suspected the call came from Manny rather than from Ben's friends. I could hold my questions for Colin until another time. This took precedence. Ben listened to the caller and responded with monosyllables. A soft thudding coming from outside drew my attention to the window and the large meadows visible in the early morning light.

"Your ride should be here any minute," Ben said as he placed the phone on the table. "Manny sends his regards and wishes you happy travels."

"That arsehole would never say that." Colin got up and walked to the kitchen window. "They're landing."

The thudding had increased exponentially. With disbelief I watched a sleek, black helicopter land in the meadow about a hundred metres from the cottage. The efficiency with which Manny had called in Ben's help and now our transport was impressive. The knowledge that I had to travel in a helicopter for an undetermined distance, not having showered and not wearing my own clothes, sent a rush of adrenaline through my system.

"Jenny? Jenny, I need you to stay with me." Colin was rubbing my arms, his voice insistent. "Jenny?"

I took a few breaths into the silence. No more thudding. "Is the helicopter gone? Can we drive back to France?"

I was still in my chair at the table. Colin had pulled a chair closer to sit facing me. He was very close, his thighs on the outside of mine, worry clear on his face. We were alone in the kitchen. "The pilots are set to take off as soon as you are ready. This is a special helicopter—it can fly long distance, is quite comfortable and will be the quickest way for us to get home. Once we're home you can shower, use your own products and wear your own clothes."

I smiled. "You're an exceptional manipulator."

"Other people might call it negotiation." He took both my hands in his, the muscles around his eyes relaxing, softening his expression. "And I know you. As much as you hate wearing my clothes and not having showered, you would rather wait another few hours and shower in your own home than lose another thirty minutes here just to wear my clothes again."

It was difficult to speak past the muscles in my throat tensing up. "You don't know me as well as you think. Wearing your clothes is not as disconcerting as the thought of not showering. But I can't get into the helicopter."

"Why not?" No censure, only curiosity and concern.

"I'm not prepared for it. I don't know the safety features, the statistics on accidents and survival rates." My voice rose in pitch and volume. "I don't know the experience of the pilots or whether the current fuel levels will be sufficient for the fuel consumption to take us all the—"

"Hey, it's okay. Take a breath." He waited a few seconds for me to compose myself. "You know this is the fastest way for us to get home, right?"

"Rationally, yes."

"Is there any way that you can Mozart your way into the helicopter?"

"How many times do I have to tell you not to use Mozart as a verb?"

He smiled at the old argument. "Well, can you?"

"I would rather not." My intense fear of change, of the unknown had been the reason I constantly pushed myself, wanting to move past the many limitations my mind placed on me. I had travelled to all the continents on the planet unaccompanied. I didn't want to be a prisoner to my own fears. Despite everything in me screaming in horror, I straightened my spine, lifted my chin and inhaled deeply. "After the pilots assure me that they are qualified and we have enough fuel, I will board."

As soon as I said it, panic punished my body. I thought back to all those times I had been convinced I would not be able to get onto the plane. Like then, I now focussed on my end destination. A hot shower in my apartment. I pulled my hands out of Colin's and stood up. "Let's go."

"Wait." I looked around the kitchen. "Where's Ben?"

"He left soon after the helicopter arrived. He told me to give you his regards."

I nodded. It was a pity. I had liked Ben and would've liked to thank him for his patience. There wasn't time for pondering on this. I had to get into that helicopter.

It had been a long time since I had needed to practice such unyielding control. Through the short conversation with the pilots, getting into the helicopter and wondering about all the unknown bacteria in this aircraft, I held myself together. Changing focus made it easier to control my stress levels. I observed, questioned, analysed and processed. I noticed sadness flash over Colin's face as we took off. His safe house had been compromised and would most likely never be used again. The sadness led me to believe that he had valued this specific home.

When turbulence made the flight uncomfortable, I asked the pilots more questions. I learned about all the instruments they were using to keep us safe. Once, the younger pilot lied when I asked about emergency landing statistics. I pointed out what an incompetent liar he was and explained how he could improve that skill. His colleague laughed and gave me the correct statistics. Throughout the whole journey, Colin said very little, watching me with a foreign intensity or looking out the window.

By the time we landed in an empty parking area quite close to my apartment, my muscles were trembling. I believed part of that to be caused by hunger, but mostly this was due to the tension of holding myself up, maintaining my defiant posture. It was exhausting. When Greg, the incompetent liar, opened the door for us to exit the helicopter, I realised that I was clutching Colin's hand. My fingers were white from the strength of my grip. Consciously, I relaxed my hold and wondered why he had not said anything. I stared at our joined hands.

Colin's smile was gentle when I looked up at him. Expressions I did not often observe around his eyes now had my full attention. For a few seconds he sat quietly, allowing me to study him. I wanted to ask why I saw pride and respect when he looked at me, but he shook his head. "Let's go home. We can talk there. The car is waiting for us, but we're going to have to walk there. Will you be okay walking only in socks or do you want me to carry you?"

Walking across a meadow in Colin's thick socks had not been too difficult. Nature's dirt was acceptable to me. A glance at the paving brought information flooding into my mind. Statistics on bacteria and organic matter caused my blinking to increase. I forced my thoughts away from that and looked at Colin.

He was already moving past me to climb out. He stood tall at the door and held out his arms. "In my arms or a ride on my back?"

"Your back." It would make me feel less weak.

He turned around and presented me with his strong back. I had never been carried on anyone's back before. I had seen this on television and in parks when parents, usually fathers, carried their tired children to the car after a day of fun. This was a first for me. It took a few tries before I clung onto Colin like a baby monkey. Twice he had to tell me to ease up around his neck, I was choking him.

The pilots found this amusing, but I could not see the humour in this. With every passing second my desperation for the safe haven of my apartment increased. Transferring from Colin's back to the town car was awkward, only to repeat the exercise when we arrived at the front door of my apartment building. I wouldn't even get down from Colin's back when we were in the elevator. I had seen a neighbour's dog urinate in excitement one day. I shuddered.

"You all right back there?" Colin's voice vibrated where my chest pressed into his back.

"I will be soon." One more floor, the hall and I would be in my sanctuary. A soft ping announced that we had arrived, the doors opened and Colin walked to the front door. He let go of one of my legs and lifted his hand to knock, but the door swung open. Vinnie's large frame filled the door to my apartment. He was wearing his usual combat pants and black T-shirt, stretched over muscles that belonged on a wrestler. Whenever he experienced intense emotions, the long ragged scar down the side of his face became more prominent. Like now.

I expected an outburst filled with expletives, but Vinnie merely stood there staring at us. After two seconds of observing him, I tapped Colin's shoulder. "Let me down."

I slid down his back, preparing myself for the next few minutes. In the year that I had known Vinnie, I had discovered that despite his criminal background, his size and demeanour, he was sensitive. Of those I counted to be my friends, he needed the most reassurance. I stepped around Colin and stopped in front of Vinnie. He was ignoring Manny's irate insistence for him to move out of the way and had his attention solely on me now.

"We're here, Vinnie." It had become easier, but I still found friendship difficult. Comforting a friend was not a skill I excelled in. Logic and rationale were my fortes. Reassuring someone wasn't.

Vinnie didn't respond verbally to my attempt at reassurance, but his micro-expressions told me everything I needed to know. Our disappearance had affected him deeply. The relief on his face warred with fear and anger. After a year of friendship, I knew what he needed. It came at a great personal cost, but I had learned that friendship meant being selfless even at trying times. I sighed, bracing myself as I stepped closer and opened my arms.

Strong emotions washed over his face before he lifted me and enveloped me in an embrace gentle enough to not cause me too much discomfort. He buried his head in my neck, his whole body trembling. My feet were dangling, my arms loosely draped around his large shoulders. Behind him Manny had grown quiet. I awkwardly patted Vinnie's shoulder. "I'm okay, Vinnie."

He shook his head and held me tighter. I looked over his shoulder into my apartment. Manny was standing a few feet behind Vinnie, scowling. He looked even more rumpled than normally. Dark rings under his bloodshot eyes showed that he too had suffered. His unshaven jaw was not the usual lazy one-day stubble. It was a few days' growth. He looked exhausted.

"Come on, big guy. Let's go inside." Colin's hand rested lightly on Vinnie's arm and pushed him into my apartment. "Jenny's been wanting to be in her own place since she woke up."

Still Vinnie would not let me go. He turned around and took a few steps towards the sitting area to the left. The living area of my loft apartment was one large space, strategically divided into the sitting area to the left of the front door, my library and reading area to the right. Deeper into the apartment, after the reading area, was the kitchen—across from it, the dining area. Vinnie stopped next to one of the two large sofas.

I heard him swallow, and allowed him a few more seconds

to compose himself before I would start squirming. My dislike of being touched was not nearly as important as assuring Vinnie that I was here and mostly unharmed. A strong tremor shook his body before he released his hold on me. He lowered me to the ground, but anchored me with his hands on my shoulders.

I was the one studying people, analysing the expressions on their faces. Being on the receiving end of such a scrutiny from Vinnie was a novel experience. I waited him out.

"Jen-girl." He cleared his throat. Bending slightly at the knees, he peered into my eyes. "Are you sure you're okay?"

"I will feel much better once I've had a shower, but I'm operating just fine, thank you."

"Did those fuckers hurt you?"

"Yes, but I didn't feel it." My half-shrug was unsuccessful. His hand on my shoulder was too heavy. "It hurts a little now, but the bruising will disappear in another few days."

The scar on the side of his face became pronounced as his lips compressed. "I will get those bastards, Jen-girl."

"No, you won't." Manny stepped closer, but was wise enough to not be within punching distance. "I want you to be in jail, but for some reason Doc likes you, so you will let us do this the right way." Manny looked at me. "We will get these sons of bitches the legal way and make sure they never see the light of day again."

I gasped. "You can't kill them, Manny."

"I'm not going to kill the… ah. That saying means they will never leave prison, Doc. Not that I will kill them." The small smile my misunderstanding brought to his face was worth my annoyance at yet again lacking knowledge of common lexicon. He inhaled deeply and let it out on a loud sigh. "I'm glad you're home, Doc. I'm even glad to see the thief."

Colin pushed past Manny, purposefully bumping him out the way. He held out his hand to greet Vinnie. My shoulders felt much lighter as Vinnie lifted his hands and used Colin's outstretched hand to pull him into a man-hug. At least Colin's height was near enough to Vinnie's to not necessitate being lifted off the ground. Manny looked at the two friends with disgust curling his top lip.

"Genevieve?"

I turned around to see Phillip and Francine quietly waiting to greet me. They too wore the stress of the last two days on their faces and bodies. Francine was dressed like a supermodel, her exotic looks enhanced by the cream dress and designer jewellery. Her eyes were void of the usual dark eyeliner and mascara she used to draw attention. A few dark stains under her eyes were evidence of tears having washed away her makeup. I liked Francine being my only female friend. She was not overly emotional like most women. Therefore I was taken aback at the fresh tears in her eyes.

"I'm really happy you're here." She took a step closer. Uncertainty halted her movements, her need undisguised.

"Oh, for goodness' sake." I took a few annoyed steps towards her. "Give me a hug then."

Relief, but mostly gratefulness drew her mouth and eyes into a smile. Logically I understood people's need for physical closeness and hugging during times of distress. Practically, it overwhelmed my senses. Francine's subtle, and undoubtedly expensive, perfume surrounded me as she gave me a strong hug. I had become more accustomed to Vinnie's embraces and Colin's romantic affection. Being hugged by a woman was a new experience for me. She was soft, yet strong. I found myself returning the hug. Soon enough she let go of me, wiping at her eyes.

I turned to Phillip. He took both my hands in his and pressed them against his heart. "Don't ever do this to me again."

"I didn't…" My voice was so full of tears I had to stop talking. Phillip was the first person who had faith in me as an individual. My professors had had faith in my academic abilities, others had had faith in my expertise, but it was Phillip who had shown trust in me as a person seven years ago. For no logical reason he had taken me under his care after an accidental meeting in an art gallery. He had given me a job, given me carte blanche to do my job in my own way. He was a father to me.

I swallowed hard, but a few tears rolled down my cheeks. I was not only feeling my own relief at being home, but observing the deep affection and relief on Phillip's face elicited a fierce emotional response in me. He brought a warm hand to my cheek, gently wiping away tears. "We'll leave you to shower and eat. Vinnie prepared a cold breakfast for you. We wanted to be here to greet you, but will give you time to regroup. As soon as you are ready, we will meet in the office to debrief. Is that acceptable?"

I nodded, still not confident in my voice.

Of everyone in my apartment, Phillip had known me the longest. It had only been in the last three years that our relationship had moved from strictly professional to a more personal level. In hindsight, I knew it had all been dependent on me. He had given me the time and space to come to him when I was ready. After seven years, he knew me well, but I knew him just as well, if not better. And this was why I knew that he had arranged this welcoming party to be short.

A quick glance at Manny's discontent confirmed my suspicions. Manny would have wanted to debrief us immediately, Vinnie would've wanted to get names to hunt down, and Francine would've wanted data to start an immediate online assault. Phillip was the one who knew I needed time to go through my familiar routine, to later meet in a familiar professional setting in order to regain my equilibrium. I squeezed his hands long and hard, knowing he would understand my unending gratitude.

Chapter **FOUR**

"Ah, you're here." Phillip pushed away from the large, round table and stood up. It was strange to see him in the team room. I usually met with him in his office or he came to my viewing room. He lowered his head, studying me. "Are you refreshed?"

"Yes, thank you." It was only an hour and fifteen minutes since everyone had left my apartment. I had spent longer than usual under the shower, scrubbing with the strongest soap I had. Colin and I had quickly eaten, not speaking much. Both of us wanted to get to work and solve our mysterious abduction.

"I'll get Manny." Francine's make-up was perfect, no evidence of tears. She winked at me. "He went to make himself that horrid tea with milk."

When the president had asked us to form a special investigative team, Phillip had not only agreed, but had insisted on his high-end insurance company's offices housing our activities. Within three weeks he had converted the two rooms next to my specialised viewing room to a large open workspace. Separating my viewing room from our team room were two glass sliding doors that sealed to afford me the soundproof silence I sorely needed on a frequent basis.

In the team room, Phillip had installed a computer system to Francine's exact specifications. Her work station took up almost as much space as my long desk and the ten computer monitors mounted on the wall above it. Manny had a large desk, overflowing with little pieces of paper. Vinnie had no desk and spent minimal time in the team room. Most of his time was spent socialising with his criminal acquaintances, keeping contact in the hope to find information that could aid us in our investigations.

After three weeks of Colin using the far corner of my desk and leaving his files in my cabinet, I had insisted on him moving to the team room. He had refused and successfully convinced me that sharing a room with Manny for any length of time was not wise. That had resulted in a smaller desk against the wall to the left behind my workspace in the viewing room. Colin had proved to be a quiet worker, not disturbing me when I was analysing footage or doing research. The space he would've taken up in the team room now had a dark wooden table with chairs. It was here we had team meetings and this was where Phillip had been waiting for us.

I sat down in my usual seat, hanging my handbag over the back of the chair. I moved with care, every twist of my body reminding me of the numerous bruises marring my torso. Vinnie was already seated, his legs stretched out in front of him. "How're you doing, Jen-girl?"

"I feel much better, thank you." I had chosen my outfit deliberately. My summer trousers were light and fitted comfortably around my hips. When I sat down, the material didn't press against any of the dark bruises. The patterned blouse was dark, but of a light material. The long sleeves hid not only the tattoo, but also the bruises on my arms. Knowing that nobody else would see proof of my abuse made me feel more confident. I had not felt comfortable with Ben's anger and pity at witnessing the injuries. Vinnie and Manny's anger would overwhelm me.

Francine came back into the team room, followed by

Manny, who looked as tired as before. His stride was purposeful, his eyes set on me. He put his mug of tea down on the table as he stopped next to my chair. "Doc."

I looked up at the proud man, who was impatient with psychology, seldom understood me, yet treated me with an odd kind of respect. His military training and years in law enforcement had made him less inclined towards emotions and always looking for reasons to imprison Vinnie and Colin. In his late forties, on days like today, when stress became visible around his eyes and his unshaven beard showed greying hair, he looked closer to his retirement years.

He glared at me, his emotions carefully hidden behind his usual mask of annoyance. On a deep inhale, he relaxed his face and allowed me to study his true expressions. I knew when we had met a year ago, he had been suspicious of my skills and uncomfortable with me. Over time, his acerbic attitude had not changed, but he had become more protective of me. It didn't take my three doctorate degrees to know that it was the most comfortable way for him to show affection. And that was what I saw in his expression right now. That, concern, and unsurprisingly, anger.

"I'm okay, Manny."

"Ben Rhodes sent me the bloody photos, Doc."

I closed my eyes for a second. My careful choice of clothes had just become a moot point.

"What photos?" Vinnie asked.

"They had beaten Jenny while she was out." Colin had taken a seat next to me. Anger was evident in his tone. "You can see the shape of their fists, Vin."

Vinnie got up so fast his chair fell over and landed with a thud on the heavy carpeting. Now I had two irate men towering over me, glaring at me as if I had been the one injuring myself. At least Colin was glaring at me sitting down.

Were it not for my background in psychology, their behaviour would offend and intimidate me. It merely irritated me.

"A few days and the bruising will be gone." It was most inconvenient reassuring people. "It hurts a little, but that too will fade."

"Should you not go to the doctor? What about internal injuries?" Francine asked.

"The bruising would look different," I said. My voice was less calming, more defensive. I did not want a doctor examining me. It would mean more strange hands touching me. "This is muscle damage only. They didn't break anything. I will be fine."

Vinnie made a sound of disgust, picked up his chair and sat down hard on it. "Let's get those fuckers. Francine, have you got any video yet?"

"I'm still looking." Francine was reputed to be one of the world's best hackers. "I didn't find anything on public sites, now I'm looking to the other places."

Manny groaned. "Can't we try to keep this above board for a change?"

"You want to get court orders for all security cameras of all the companies in all the cities from here to England?" She lowered her eyelashes, her voice turning sultry. "Not even your animalistic sex appeal would be enough for all that, handsome."

Manny should have been used to Francine's outrageous flirting by now. He wasn't. His already tense body language tightened up even more. "Watch it, little girl. I told you before, you go up against me, there's not a chance you will win."

Francine gave him a slow wink and looked at me. "When you didn't show up at home on Thursday evening and we realised you were gone, I immediately started searching for you. The security cameras in this street were supremely inadequate."

"We've installed more," Vinnie said, nodding for Francine to continue.

"I couldn't find you guys anywhere. When you phoned this morning, I hacked into all the transportation points' video feeds." She ignored Manny's pointed cough. "Nothing. You weren't taken there by train, air or across the Channel by registered ferry or any other way. It must have all been private. Cars, planes or boats from places with no or limited security."

A soft knock at the door interrupted our conversation. The door whooshed open and Angelique entered carrying a tray. She had been Phillip's personal assistant before I started working here. It had been seven years and still she looked at me with fear. I had briefly attempted being friendly, but that had frightened her even more. I kept our contact to a minimum and she avoided me as much as possible. That was why her presence and the tray filled with refreshments got my attention. She placed the tray between Francine and Manny, where there was more space between the chairs. Manny had shifted away from the ever-flirting Francine.

"I brought some coffee and croissants." She looked at me. The fear was evident, but I also saw regret. Odd. "Are you well, Doctor Lenard?"

"Yes, thank you, Angelique."

No matter how many times Phillip had told her to fit in with the rest of the more informal atmosphere in the office and call everyone by their first name, she insisted on titles. I narrowed my eyes and studied her. Something was different about her behaviour. It was entirely possible that she was empathising with Phillip and the others' concern. She had never before indicated any concern for my well-being. My scrutiny brought more fear to her body language and she took a few steps to the door. "If you need anything else, let me know."

"Thank you, Angelique." Phillip's deep, calming voice drew her attention away from me.

"Sir." She nodded at him and hurried from the room. The door closed quietly behind her.

"Tell me about the murder," I said to Manny. Without any video or reasonable suspect, I needed more information.

"Oh no, missy." The corners of Manny's mouth turned down. "I haven't even started asking you questions. Once I'm satisfied, you get to ask me questions. Here's a question for you, Doc. Why were you investigating those thefts?"

I knew which thefts he was referring to. "I was bored."

"And?" Manny waved his hand in a fast rolling gesture when I didn't continue.

"And when I'm bored, I start looking for anomalies in the investigators' reports, in reported art thefts, in police reports."

"We're supposed to look for Kubanov, missy."

"And we're not finding him." My tone was as argumentative as Manny's. This was the case that had brought Manny and the rest of the team into my life a year ago, also introducing us to Tomasz Kubanov, a rich and powerful philanthropist in Russia. Numerous law enforcement agencies across the globe were looking for evidence to convict him of a long list of crimes ranging from art fraud to arms trafficking to human trafficking. He was considered a dangerous and evil man.

Twice we had almost caught him. It was after the last event that the president had formed this team, our main goal finding and capturing Kubanov. Kubanov had formed an unhealthy obsession with me since I had destroyed a lucrative art fraud ring a year ago, and then foiled his plans to destroy the president's family six months ago.

"Seriously, no one is going to say it?" Francine threw her

hands in the air. She enjoyed being melodramatic. "Fine, then I'll say it. This thing stinks of Kubanov. We might not have found him, but he has come looking for us. Well, for the two of you."

Colin tensed next to me when everyone turned their attention to us.

"There is absolutely no proof that this is Kubanov." Only my suspicions.

"Oh, come on, girlfriend." Francine started counting on her manicured fingers. "In an amazingly well-organised attempt, you and sexy over there are kidnapped, drugged and shipped to a location no one knows about. Sorry, Colin… no one *knew* about. Then in another amazingly well-organised event, Colin is set up for the murder of the butler. That butler is connected to you because of your snooping through some burglary files. Who else do we know capable of orchestrating something this complex? Huh?"

"We have no evidence," I said. Even I could hear the lack of conviction in my voice. I had to agree with Francine. The events of the last few days were very indicative of Kubanov's *modus operandi.*

"And you have still not told me why you were looking into those burglaries." Manny tapped one foot, waiting.

"In the last four months a few homes with exceptional security systems had been burgled. I thought that it might be related to the last time Kubanov had shown himself, and I looked into it. The afternoon we were taken, I realised that they were not related at all. I watched the interviews with the homeowners and saw that two of those were lying when they swore they had switched on the alarm systems before they had left. One owner was lying when confronted with his financial situation and whether he would use the insurance payout to cover mounting debts. That is why I said it came to nothing."

"So it's pure coincidence that Colin is being set up for the murder of a person connected to one of those cases?"

"I can't answer that question. I don't have enough data."

"You think it is connected?" Manny's voice rose in frustration. I often had that effect on him.

"I can't answer that—"

"Bloody hell, missy." Manny rubbed his face with both hands. With closed eyes, he breathed deeply twice before looking at me. "Okay, what do you want to know?"

"Tell me more about the murder."

"There's not much to add to what I told you this morning. The full report is on the system, so you can read the detail. One thing that I didn't mention and that is a bit of a mystery is the ballistics."

"What about the ballistics?" Vinnie knew people in the arms trade. The illegal arms trade. Of our team, he carried the most knowledge about weapons.

"The scientists in Scotland Yard are stumped by the evidence," Manny said. "They recovered the bullets from the butler, none of which had any striae. There were none of the usual identifying marks on the bullets to help the lab find out if the gun had been used in any other crimes, who it is registered to and whatever magic they can pull from a few lines on a bullet. They also found traces of a waxy residue and alcohol."

"What are they thinking?" Vinnie asked.

"Oh, there's a whole lot of speculation going on." The smile Manny aimed at me was genuine. He enjoyed irritating me with unsubstantiated conjecture. "But let me tell you more before I share their theories. The stippling found on the body indicated the gun had been shot at close range, at most two metres. The depth of the penetration and the angle indicated the gun was shot from a minimum of fifteen metres."

"Is that possible?" I asked.

"The shooter would've had to stand outside, behind the house and on a garden wall. So no, Doc, it's not possible."

"But how can the evidence be this contradictory?"

"Ah, and that is where the speculation comes in. The lab guys think it might be a homemade or a modified weapon of some kind that uses nine-millimetre bullets. There have been cases of bullets fired from a modified pipe with a firing pin of sorts."

"I assume that to not be a smoking pipe."

"It's called a zip gun, Jen-girl," Vinnie said. "To have a crude firearm, you need a barrel and a chamber. The barrel can be any kind of pipe. What the old man is talking about is something like that."

"So it is nothing like the bore lapping we found in the first Kubanov case?" I asked. A cache of Eurocorps weapons had been stolen over a long period of time, all identifiable features removed. The numbers had been filed off the guns and the insides of the barrels smoothed by a method called bore lapping.

Manny shook his head. "It is unlikely. If shot from a normal handgun, the velocity of the bullet would have been much higher than the lab guys have estimated. When I spoke to them, they were all excited about the mystery. They re-checked their evidence and it confirmed the shooter was standing almost two metres from the victim. This was doubly confirmed by a slight void in the gunshot residue and blood spatter on the carpet. A void in the shape of two shoes."

"What size?"

"Smart, Doc. You really want to prove your boyfriend's innocence." He looked at Colin, his *risorius* muscles turning his smile into a smirk. "It's your birthday, pretty boy. Those were British size thirteen."

"A large man." My thoughts immediately went to the men who had broken into my apartment a year ago and attacked me. They had been big men. Colin was one point eight metres tall, but I was sure his feet were not that large. I looked at him. "What size shoe do you wear?"

He smiled. "Ask Millard. He should know."

"Depending on his designer, he wears an eleven or eleven and a half. Never a twelve. He's a tall criminal without big feet to brag about." Manny looked proud that he knew that much detail about Colin. When he had investigated Colin, it had been much more in-depth than I had been led to believe. A slightly disturbing discovery, but upon consideration it made sense. Such information could help if ever there were footprints logged as evidence in an art crime. Despite knowing that Colin was working for Interpol and cooperating with him in the last year, Manny still wanted to see Colin incarcerated.

A stray thought took my attention away from Colin's feet. "What about other cases?"

"What other cases, Doc?" As Manny asked the question, his eyes flashed with understanding. "You mean cases with similar ballistic evidence to this case?"

"Yes. Have you found any?"

"Doc, I've been a bit busy looking for you and bloody Frey."

"I'm sure Genevieve is not criticising you, Manny." Phillip laid both hands flat on the table. "We all know that finding them took priority."

I sighed when Phillip looked at me, waiting. Tiptoeing around people's emotions was exasperating. I looked at Manny, but he waved his hand at me. "Don't apologise, Doc. That will really piss me off. You are right. I should've thought about this, but I was worried about your skinny arse. I will get onto this ASAP."

"If we find more cases, we might find out what kind of weapon was used. That will bring us closer to finding out who killed the butler and then set it up so that all the evidence points to Colin."

Colin turned to me. "Are you conceding that our kidnapping and this murder are connected?"

"Of course." I frowned at the obviousness of it. "Why wouldn't I? A murder committed while you were not conscious and while you have no proof that you were unconscious is convenient. Being forced into unconsciousness, taken to the country of the murder, and having all the evidence point to you is not convenient. It is suspicious."

"Sometimes your logic isn't my logic," Francine muttered while tapping away on her tablet computer. She stopped and slowly looked up. "Did I just say that out loud?"

Vinnie chuckled. "Jen-girl knows that her logic is much better than our logic."

"Speak for yourself, big guy." She looked at me with an apologetic smile. "You know I didn't mean it badly, right?"

"I don't know why you are worried. Of course my logic differs from yours. My brain functions differently to yours." I tilted my head. "Although your reasoning skills are superior to most. It must be the neuropaths created from your hacking work and imagining all those conspiracy theories."

"Um. Thank you?" The humour in her voice lightened the atmosphere around the table. I assumed her question to have some positive nuance and didn't pursue the rationale of it. There was something else in Francine's demeanour that was more interesting.

"What are you hiding?" I leaned closer, narrowing my eyes

when she shifted in her chair. "Your eyes just flashed to your tablet. What do you have there?"

She put the tablet on the table and put both her hands over it, unconsciously covering whatever information she was withholding. Her gaze had turned serious. "Genevieve, this is one of those times when you should think of the bigger impact of revealing what you see."

"Why? What illegal acts are you busy with now?" Manny tried to lift her hand to get to the tablet. She pressed down harder and caught him by surprise with a kiss on his cheek. Manny jerked away and glared at her. "Bloody hellfire, working with you people is making me old before my time."

"You were old before you met us, old man." Vinnie emphasised the last two words with a malicious smile. "And stop wrestling with Francine before I come over there and beat you senseless."

With the exception of Phillip and myself, everyone got involved in an argument about Francine handing her tablet over to Manny. Phillip looked at me. "Is it always like this? How do you ever get anything done?"

"Antagonising each other serves as a form of relieving stress." After six months of daily being exposed to this behaviour I was used to it. Phillip seldom spent time with the team, his experience of the inner dynamics limited. I lifted one hand loosely, palm up. "As long as I don't hear them in my viewing room, I don't care. Even while looking for Kubanov, we have solved more art fraud cases in the last six months than the FBI art crimes unit in the same period of time. We're an effective team."

Phillip blinked slowly at my last statement and looked at Francine and Manny threatening each other, almost nose to nose.

"It's only a bloody list, you big British bully." Francine lifted the tablet and shook it at Manny. "A shopping list."

"Whose shopping list?" I asked into the sudden silence.

Francine glanced at Colin, guilt changing her body language. It was difficult to achieve mental and physical comfort while carrying and concealing distressing knowledge.

"Colin did not kill that man," I said. Even with Phillip here, I found myself mediating. It was most wearisome. "Manny is being obtuse, but he will not send Colin to prison for something he didn't do. The evidence is strong that Colin is being set up, so whatever information you have there will only help us find the person setting him up. It won't give Manny power to arrest Colin."

The slight relaxation of the *orbicularis oculi* muscles around her eyes proved that I had interpreted her concerns correctly. I ignored Phillip's surprised inhalation and the speculation in his eyes. I had no desire to become more adept at negotiation and mediation.

"It's a shopping list of goodies bought by one of Colin's aliases," Francine said.

"What did I buy?" Colin asked. "Wait, which credit card did they use?"

"Sydney Goddphin, but it wasn't from your account. Someone opened a new account using your Sydney ID, address and other personal information. With that card you bought wood glue, a few wires, duct tape and seventeen pagers." She winked at Manny. "I hacked that bank account to get this valuable information."

"The same identity your safe house is registered under." Vinnie whistled. "Dude, someone's really got it in for you."

"The things you bought make no sense." Francine swiped the screen of her tablet computer. "It's useless stuff. Pagers are so last century. You would never use these things for a heist."

"What could it be used for?" I asked.

No one answered for a long while. I took the time to observe their nonverbal cues. Manny was angry, but as usual was using it to mask deeper emotions. Worry being the most apparent. Colin was not as worried as would be expected with evidence mounting against him. Whenever he was plotting out a strategy, his bottom jaw would move while he tilted his head slightly to the back. Right now he was staring at the ceiling, his jaw busy as if he was chewing gum.

Both Francine and Vinnie had expressions revealing that they had theories as to the use of the products bought with Sydney's credit card. Most likely Francine's theory involved government cover-ups, if not an invasion by extraterrestrial beings. I was surprised she had not brought up alien abduction as a theory about my and Colin's recent experience.

"Only three people knew about my safe house. Myself, Vin and Jenny." Colin dropped his chin and stared at Manny. "Did you know about my place in the UK?"

"You really think I didn't do my homework on you, Frey?" Manny's *risorius* muscles contracted in a micro-expression of a smirk. "I knew about your place in the UK, your place in Italy, and I know your parents' place in Long Island."

Anger flashed over Colin's face at the mention of his parents' residence before he marginally relaxed. When we had first met, Colin had given me the addresses to five of his homes across Europe. Manny had only mentioned two. I suspected Colin had a few more residences registered to other pseudonyms.

"How did you find out about my place in the UK?"

"When Doc found out about your use of seventeenth-century poets as false identities, I had myself a little look around. Turns out that Sydney Goddphin had bought his rustic home through a lawyer and the locals seldom saw him.

The lady at the local grocer was most taken with the charming young man who had shopped only three times in her humble store. You had made quite an impression. But she preferred you without the beard. The photo I had was much more becoming, she told me."

In an unconscious reflex, I extended my arm in front of Colin, preventing him from getting out of his chair. He frowned at my arm for a second, then looked at me, one eyebrow lifted.

"Manny wouldn't have kidnapped us and set you up for murder. You know this."

"I don't know this, Jenny. The arsehole's been after me for decades. Who's to say he hasn't been planning this all along?" He leaned back in his chair, his glare at Manny filled with malevolence. "If you knew about my safe house, why did you ask for the GPS co-ordinates to send your Scotland Yard friend?"

"I wasn't going to take a chance that my intel was faulty. Not when Doctor Face-reader's life was on the line. Why the bleeding hell am I explaining this to you, cretin?"

I looked at Phillip, irritation tightening my voice. "Why aren't you calming everyone down and mediating as usual?"

He lifted both hands in surrender. "I don't want to interfere. You are doing exceptionally well."

"No, I'm not. They're not using logic." I realised my arm was still in front of Colin. I pulled it against my torso and turned to him. "You are far too intelligent to assume that Manny would murder someone to accumulate evidence to have you imprisoned. Murder, Colin. Murder!"

That was it. I stood up and grabbed my handbag.

"I think I have been handling the last few hours extremely well. Your need to lash out at each other, and Phillip, your lack of intervening is exasperating. I'm going to my viewing room. Don't even consider entering unless you have started using real logic and not immature, fearful verbal attacks on each other."

I slung my handbag over my shoulder and walked to the door, ignoring the shocked looks. The control I conducted myself with was slipping and noticeably surprising everyone. On an intellectual level, I understood the need people had to attack. It created a false sense of proactive behaviour, a reflex reaction to counteract the feeling of powerlessness. On a personal level, I found such behaviour to be counter-productive.

After waking up in a strange country and expending copious quantities of energy on holding black panic at bay, I did not have the mental wherewithal to tolerate neurotypical reactions to fear. I needed to analyse, process and focus on work, on data. I needed to watch footage. I needed to be alone.

Chapter FIVE

"Jenny?"

A warm hand squeezed my forearm, bringing me back to my viewing room. I opened my eyes to find myself huddled on my large office chair, clutching my knees to my chest. Colin had swivelled my chair and was sitting across from me, watching me with great intensity.

"What time is it?" My voice sounded far away. I had worked through a few files on my computer before mentally writing Mozart's Clarinet Concerto in A Major to put some order to my thoughts. The strain in my muscles indicated that I had been in this position for a lengthy period.

"Just after three." Gently, Colin uncurled my fists and held my hands in his. "Are you okay?"

I nodded. Once I had started writing Mozart, the full impact of what had taken place, of what I had seen on the monitors must have overpowered me. I had been in my head for four hours. If I were sitting with my feet on the chair, curled up in a protective position, it was safe to assume that I had also been keening. I cringed.

"No one else has been around." Colin must have seen some nonverbal cue to my thoughts. "It's only us."

He nodded towards the thick glass doors. In the team room, Manny was sitting at his desk, Francine and Vinnie at the square table with two computers open in front of them. All three were looking at me. Were it not for the sincere concern dominating their expressions, I might have been much more ashamed of my show of weakness.

"Is this from being kidnapped or something else?"

I assumed he was referring to my shutdown. With a grimace, I dropped my feet to the floor and pulled my shoulders back to stretch my back muscles. It was a mistake. Stretching made me feel the bruising on my stomach. I hunched my shoulders. "Both. I think you had better call the others."

No sooner had Colin turned to the glass doors and gestured with a nod than everyone got up and hurried across the team room. Manny entered the code in the keypad to open the doors and came through first. He pulled closer the third chair in my viewing room, placing it on my other side. For once he didn't need reminding to keep at least fifty centimetres between us. Francine pressed a button to keep the doors open, preventing my room from feeling crowded. She stayed close to the door, Vinnie next to her.

"Have you got something for us, Doc?"

"Emails."

"What emails?" Colin kept his attention on me. "Who sent you emails?"

"I did." I turned to my desk, control over the internal turmoil returning to me in increments. "At some point during our abduction, I must have managed to get a hold of a device with internet connection and send myself a few emails."

"And you remember this?" Manny moved so close I felt his body heat against my arm. "Does this mean you remember more? Do you remember who took you?"

Too sensitive to stimuli and no longer willing to be an altruistic friend, I leaned away, my shoulder touching Colin. "Move back. Please."

"But you're touching *him*." Manny's lip curled in disgust

and he shook his head. With a glare at Colin, he pushed his chair away. "Talk, missy."

I brought my email inbox up on one of the large monitors in front of us. "I don't know how or where I was able to send emails, but I did."

"To which email account?" The disbelief in Francine's voice caught my attention. "I checked all your accounts while you were away, hoping to catch something that might help us find you guys."

It took me a moment to answer. "I don't know why I'm feeling apologetic. I really shouldn't. I have a right to my privacy."

"Jenny?"

I caught myself crossing my arms and immediately lowered them. "I lost my privacy when all of you entered my life. After the last fiasco and all the hacking, I knew I had zero privacy online. None of my observations, analyses, article outlines were private thoughts anymore. I need my privacy. I need to have something that belongs only to me."

"So you opened a private email account." Francine's smile held pride. "Good for you, girl. I had no idea."

I knew this was high praise. Francine was far superior to anyone, including me, in acquiring hidden data and information online. I didn't feel complimented. It was rather resentment at my need for subterfuge to maintain minimal privacy which dominated my emotions. I pushed it back, focussing on the case.

"The effects of being drugged are clear in my emails. Most of this doesn't make sense. If I had the context within which I had written these emails, it would be much easier to interpret."

"Just show us, Doc."

I opened the first email. "This was sent on Thursday evening twelve minutes past eleven."

An image filled the monitors. Two large shapes separated by a dark gap were badly out of focus. The photo was dark, any images beyond the blurred shapes impossible to identify.

"I have no idea what this is supposed to be. The second email is more telling, but still nonsensical." I clicked and the next email opened. "I sent this email on Friday afternoon at twenty past five. There are only these words: 'hypertrophic', 'hexahedron', '*Homme a la*', 'halo die'."

"You were creating quite the rhyme there, Doc."

"Not a rhyme. An alliteration. Without the context it is difficult to interpret my reasoning for any of these words."

"What do you think it means?" Francine moved closer, staring at the monitor.

"I don't know," I said. I hated speculating. "'Hypertrophic' usually refers to an abnormal enlargement or excessive growth. It could be of an organ, it could be scarring that is red and raised above the skin."

"Maybe you described one of the kidnappers."

"I really don't know." I didn't like this feeling. "The second word, 'hexahedron', is a solid figure with six faces, and the next looks like the beginning of a phrase. It is in French, a language in which I would never write notes to myself. It could be the title of a painting or a book, or maybe I overheard someone say this."

"What's 'halo die'?" A small smile lifted the corners of Vinnie's mouth. "It sounds like you're predicting the death of an angel."

For a few seconds no one spoke. I didn't have any theories to put forward on the last entry.

"Yup, that email makes no sense." Vinnie lifted both shoulders. "You are difficult enough to understand when you are not drugged, Jen-girl. Who knows what your mind was doing while high. What other emails did you send?"

"The third email makes even less sense. I sent it on Friday just after six in the afternoon." It was extremely frustrating that I couldn't make sense of my reasoning when I had sent this to myself. I opened the second email.

Manny chuckled. "'Big boom'? Were you thinking about evolution, Doc?"

"I keep telling you I have no idea what I was thinking. Clearly, my neurological paths were impaired by the drugs. Everything is pure speculation. It could be evolution, it could be a volcano."

"Or an explosion, a bomb." There was no more laughter in Manny's voice. "I hope we're not going have a repeat of the last time. Bloody hell. What do the other emails say?"

I was a bit embarrassed to open the next one. I looked at the words, finding it difficult to believe I had written it.

"Oh, you were high, girl." Francine laughed softly. "'Frame… of reference. Hahahahahaha.' How many ha's did you write?"

"Too many."

"Again this could be that you overheard a conversation," Colin said. "You knew they were trying to set me up for that murder, to frame me."

"Which then leads me to ask if 'reference' has any relevance. Whether the written laughter has any relevance. Whether the ellipses have any relevance. Even worse, if these emails have any relevance."

"I'm sure it does, Jenny. You wouldn't have gone through the trouble to send something to yourself if you didn't think it would help."

"Is there more?" Manny asked.

"Only one more and this one is the biggest mystery." I opened the email. "I sent this photo at ten to five, Saturday morning."

Everyone leaned towards the monitor. I clicked on the photo to open it up in full screen.

"What is that?" Vinnie squinted and walked closer. "Jen-girl, you need to work on your photography skills."

"What do you think that is, Doc?"

"Blueprints," Colin said softly. I looked at him in surprise. When I had opened my email account earlier and this photo had been there, I would never have guessed it to be a blueprint. I had stared at the monitor for a long time, trying to figure out what image I had attempted to capture. All I still saw were some out-of-focus lines on white. The confidence in his knowledge was clear on Colin's face.

"How can you be so sure?"

"He's a thief, Doc." For once Manny didn't look at Colin with intense dislike. "Of course he's going to know what a blueprint looks like. He would need those to plan all his heists."

"Is this for a building?" I asked Colin.

"There's no way to tell. The photo is badly out of focus, which hides whatever detail there is to clue me in on what this plan is for."

"I'll clean up the image," Francine said. "Forward it to me. I promise I won't go into your system to retrieve it."

I studied Francine's nonverbal cues for a few seconds. My need for privacy was not borne out of a distrust of the people in this room. It was a simple desire to have something exclusively to myself. In this current situation, it would be unwise to cling on to that. "I think it is better if you get into my system and into this email. Not only to see if you can get a clearer image of this photo, but also to find whatever other clues you can from my emails."

"Done." Her facial muscles relaxed, softening her expression. "Thank you."

Manny sat up and looked at Francine, his eyes bright with intent. "Find us a smoking gun, supermodel. I want to know who these idiots are who dared kidnap Doctor Face-Reader."

"But it's okay for them to kidnap me?" Colin asked. "I'm deeply hurt, Millard. Deeply hurt."

I saw a goading response form on Manny's lips. I wanted to stay on topic, not mediate between them. There were too many things that still needed to be explored. "There's something else."

Everyone turned to me, the change in my tone drawing their attention. I pushed up my sleeve to reveal the tattoo. My breath caught again at the violation of my skin.

"Oh my God." Francine stepped closer and looked between my arm and my face. "You refused to get a sexy little tat with me. When and why did you get this?"

"I didn't get this." I desperately wanted to pull my sleeve down and remove this desecration from my sight. "This was done to me while I was drugged."

"What is it, Doc?"

Manny had known about the tattoo. It would have been on the photos he had received from Ben. I wanted to declare my gratitude to him for not pushing me about this earlier. Uncomfortable with displays of emotion, I chose to not thank him. "I don't know. Looking at it like this, it seems to only be twirls and whorls, but I'm sure there is more."

I decided that everyone had had a long enough look at my arm. I pushed my sleeve down and felt a small measure of relief. The door to the hallway whooshed open and Phillip walked in, his eyes widening when he saw everyone gathered in my viewing room. "Is everything all right? Genevieve?"

"I'm fine, thank you."

He lowered his chin, giving me a stare filled with scepticism. The only way I could convince him I was managing was by focussing on work. I did that. Ten minutes later, Phillip was up to date with my emails and my tattoo.

"I sent you an email earlier, Doc." Manny shifted closer, but quickly leaned back when he saw my expression. He scowled. "Just open the bloody email."

I wasn't surprised by his annoyance. Manny was an interesting example of the male psyche. One day I was going to delve deeper. At the moment I didn't want to risk his ire. I opened his email and scanned through the content.

"Eight cases?"

"That I could find while you were faffing about." Manny waved an impatient hand at Phillip when my boss inhaled to comment. "She's not offended. Right, Doc?"

"Offended about what?" I didn't understand his triumphant smile following my question, and didn't want to ask. "Tell me about the cases."

"All eight are unsolved cases with similar ballistic profiles as the murdered butler. Some of these could very possibly be false positives, but as far as I could see from the ballistic reports, none of the retrieved bullets had any striae. In most cases there were disparities between the evidence from the stippling and the velocity of the bullet when it entered the body."

"Is there anything connecting these victims?"

"Not much." Manny shook his head. "I managed to get twelve of the twenty-eight EU countries' cooperation. The others will get back to me. The eight cases come from six of these countries. I'm sure there are more such cases, but I don't know if they are connected at all. The victims have varied profiles."

"No similarities in social standing, economic position, career or any other field?" Phillip asked.

"Not enough to establish a pattern," Manny said. "There are working-class victims, two rather wealthy victims, men, women, killed at home, killed in a park, killed on the street. Nope, nothing to say that there is one killer targeting specific people."

"In your opinion, would you say that these crimes were all committed by different people?" I asked.

Manny took some time to think about this. He looked at the list of names on the computer monitor. "Yes, eight murders committed by eight different killers."

"Then we should look at the element connecting the killers, not the victims," I said.

"Mind explaining, please?" Phillip asked.

"Well, it's logical. The only thing connecting these eight victims of violent crime is the weapon of choice. The questions we should ask are who owned the weapons and where they obtained those weapons. If these weapons were supplied by the same arms dealer, it might take us closer to–"

"Kubanov," Colin said. "Maybe we should start the investigation with the assumption that everything is connected to Kubanov and look for his connection to the weapons."

"A valid point," I said. "The main problem is that in the last six months we have found no concrete evidence pointing to Kubanov being involved in the arms trade. All we have is anecdotal proof. I need more data."

"The search for cases with similar ballistic profiles is still fresh," Manny said. "I should get more results today and tomorrow. Then we can separate the wheat from the chaff and get to those cases which are really connected. I'll have you drowning in data by tomorrow afternoon, Doc."

For a moment no one spoke. Knowing Manny, his thoughts

were consumed with the case. That was why he used two phrases I was not familiar with. I assumed he spoke metaphorically when he promised to drown me in data. I hoped he would keep true to his word.

"I'm going to get started with tracking those emails." Francine straightened to her full model height. Her standard high heels made her even more eye-catching. "Does anyone have anything else to add? If not, I want to get to my computers."

"You might want to hear this." Tension in Phillip's tone caught my attention. He clenched and unclenched his hands, but caught himself and flattened his palms against his thighs. "I just finished a video conference with Kathleen McCarthy."

"The owner of the butler house?" Vinnie asked.

"Yes." Phillip nodded.

"Did you record it?" I asked.

"Already emailed it to you," Phillip answered. Many times a recording like that had rendered suspicious contradictions in the client's account of events. Such inconsistencies were easy for me to notice by analysing their body language while being questioned. "For what it's worth, I don't think she was hiding anything."

"What did she say?" Manny asked.

"The Braque painting that Colin had stolen from her house—"

"—allegedly stolen," Colin said, his voice low.

"Allegedly stolen," Phillip said with a nod. "That specific painting was a forgery."

"How is that possible?" I asked, ignoring the sharp inhalations of those around me. "The painting was vetted before Rousseau & Rousseau insured it."

"Apparently, she was in need of some cash flow three months ago, and decided to sell the Braque. She had an interested buyer who insisted on authenticating the painting using his own people. They said it was a brilliant forgery, maybe the best they had ever come across. It was quite a challenge for them to prove that it was not the real Braque."

"The question is then whether she bought the forgery or whether someone had broken into her house and had replaced the original with the forgery." Colin frowned. "That also means the butler was killed for a forgery."

"I looked at her file and went over the provenance information and the authentication certificates." Phillip pulled at the cuffs of his suit jacket, a gesture belying the confidence in his tone. "I'm as sure as I can be that we insured the original Braque."

"Which painting of his?" Colin asked.

"The Harbour of Normandy."

Colin's expression mirrored mine. Disbelief.

"Just like your Braque." No sooner had the words left my mouth than Colin's eyes narrowed. He caught his sharp inhale quick enough to make it almost imperceptible. His exhale was controlled. He was displeased.

"Your Braque? Since when do you own a Braque, Frey?" Manny sat up, his eyes narrowed.

"I'm sorry." I leaned slightly towards Colin. "I didn't know you didn't want me to say anything."

"Say anything about what?" Manny's voice raised. "Start talking, Frey."

"Back off, Millard. I was going to tell you in any case." Colin gave me a half smile. "No harm done, Jenny. After what Phillip just told us, it would've been stupid to not consider that painting part of this... I don't know what this is. A case? A conspiracy? A setup?"

"What about your painting?" Manny enunciated each word as if it were a separate sentence.

"Years ago I painted Braque's Harbour in Normandy for my safe house. It was one of my best reproductions ever." There was pride in Colin's tone. "It had been in my safe house for eight years. Until yesterday. When I saw the Harbour of Normandy hanging in my bedroom, I knew that it was not mine. Someone had replaced my forgery with a lesser forgery."

"Oh, wow," Francine said. "Now we have the stolen original, the McCarthy forgery and the safe house forgery. Ooh, it sounds like a delicious conspiracy."

"Dude, none of this makes sense." Vinnie's face twisted in confusion. "Someone breaks into your place to replace your forgery with another forgery. The butler gets killed and a forgery of the exact same painting is stolen. What are the odds?"

"I don't think such odds are calculable, Vinnie," I said. "But I think it is safe to say that it is extremely unlikely. This definitely draws a connecting line between the butler and Colin. What that line implies is unclear to me at this moment."

"Where's the painting?" Manny asked. "The safe house forgery?"

"With a friend." Colin's lips compressed into a thin line. "I'm not telling you where that painting is, Millard. I'm having it checked out. Jenny might not like that we don't have irrefutable proof, but I'm convinced Kubanov is behind this. That leads me to think that there is a reason he put that forgery in my home and I intend to find out why."

"Your friend bloody better not be destroying evidence, Frey."

Colin's laugh and expression communicated disdain. "I assure you, he's more skilled than most of your ham-handed

CSI-wannabe scientists. If there is any code, any hidden message, anything on that painting, he will find it. He might not be able to interpret it, but if something is out of place, he is the one who will notice it."

I was leaning back in my chair. Already I had inadvertently broken a confidence. I didn't want to say anything about the statue that Colin had brought back. It was now up to Colin to share that information with Manny.

Watching Vinnie and Francine's reactions was interesting though. The lack of surprise and their attempts at looking disinterested indicated they knew who Colin had taken the painting to. I thought it prudent to not verbalise my observations.

"You will keep me updated." Manny didn't ask, he ordered.

"Only because you ask so nicely." Colin's smile carried no hint of sincerity. "But I do have another little gift for you."

"I'm listening."

"Remember the Tang Dynasty marble lion?"

"Of course I do. If the ugly thing was not an antique and out of my price range, I would've bought it and put it on my mantelpiece." Manny looked at Phillip. "Frey had that statue in his hands when I arrested his sorry arse. It was like being handed a trophy."

"Only to have it taken away, old man." Vinnie shifted against the doorframe. "How did it feel to lose your big prize?"

Manny ignored him. "What do you have for me, Frey?"

Colin swivelled his chair and pulled open one of my drawers. I bit down hard to not lecture him on allocated spaces. We'd had that conversation numerous times, yet he still ignored my requests and used my drawers to store his things. At least he was neat.

"Did you steal that?" Manny's accusation snapped me out

of my irritation. He was staring at Colin holding the statue he had brought from England. It was in a sealed plastic bag.

"I found it in my safe house." Worry lines formed next to his eyes and on his brow. "As much as we have been investigating Kubanov, he has obviously also been investigating us. He knows more about me than I thought possible. My safe house was a closely guarded secret. Yes, I know you found it, but it wasn't easy, right?"

Manny nodded.

"If you were able to locate my safe house, I suppose Kubanov could as well. What really chaps my arse is how he knew about this." Colin shook the statue. He was becoming more agitated. "I certainly never told anyone that I had this in my hand when you arrested me. Can you see where I'm going with this, Millard?"

The tension in the bodies occupying my viewing room elevated to an uncomfortable level. Manny blanched at Colin's question, his face losing colour. "As much as you annoy the living tar out of me, Frey, I would never sell you out to someone like Kubanov."

"Oh, I know that." Colin wasn't trying to bait Manny as usual. He was controlled, his tone smooth yet threatening. "What I'm wondering is how careless you have been with the information you gathered on me. And don't pretend that you don't have a file on me."

For a long while Manny didn't answer. His internal struggle was mostly controlled, but I caught glimpses of the micro-expressions revealing the choices he was busy making. I knew he had come to a decision when the *orbicularis oculi* muscles under his eyes contracted and he gave a curt nod.

"I have two files on you." Gone was the irritation and sarcasm. This was Manny at his professional best. "One is on the Interpol system. It has mostly generic information on you, but nothing that would lead back to your connection to Interpol or to Doc. The other file is only on paper. Those are my notes, newspaper clippings and copies of suspicious reports that I had gathered in the last fifteen years. Some of it might not relate to you, but most of it I've come to know was my gut telling me the truth. That file is in a place no one will find or have access to."

The significance of this moment was not lost on me. Nor on Colin. Manny had surprised us all with this level of trust.

"Have you shown the second file to anyone?" Colin asked after a few moments.

"To me," Phillip said. A wry smile curved his mouth when everyone turned to him. He looked at me, an unfamiliar apologetic expression lingering. "I pressed Manny with everything I had, even our friendship, to get information on Colin. I knew there was no way to persuade you to not go after that first case with the murdered students. I was horrified when Colin had first broken into your flat and you showed an uncommon interest in working with him. Once Manny knew that Colin was in on the case, I pushed him for assurance. I needed to know you were safe. Seeing the file on Colin satisfied me."

"Even though you didn't know he was working for Interpol?"

"I just needed to know there was no violence connected to his crimes."

"Well, I don't know what to say." I really didn't. I was deeply offended that everyone constantly felt the need to protect me. Yet on an academic level I understood the motivations for their actions were concern and affection. It left me conflicted.

"It was an irresponsible move, Millard." Disapproval depressed the corners of Colin's mouth. "Who else had access to this file? Someone must have seen your personal notes and used this against me."

"No one else ever saw that file and we both know that Phillip would never put Doc's life in danger by revealing my notes. But let's not continue arguing this point. What do you want me to do with that statue?"

Colin stared at Manny until the slight relaxation of his mouth told me he had decided to not pursue this issue any further. "Give it to your forensic guys to analyse."

Manny cleared his throat. "My ham-handed CSI-wannabe scientists? Why won't you give it to your criminal friend?"

"Firstly, he's not a criminal. Secondly, he owes me only one favour. And lastly, his forte is in paintings, not sculptures." Colin handed the statue over to Manny.

"It looks like the real thing." He turned it over and weighed it in his open palm. "This doesn't feel like it. I'll get it to the lab."

Colin, Manny and Phillip started discussing the different forensic tests needed to analyse the statue. I lost interest and turned to my computer. I wanted to analyse the information Manny had emailed me. I had an overwhelming number of questions and limited information—information that only led to more questions.

Chapter SIX

"Twenty-seven? In the last twenty months? Isn't that a lot?"

"I won't be surprised if there are more, Doc."

I had spent the rest of yesterday afternoon sifting through the information from Francine, Manny and Phillip. I had also spent an inordinate amount of time staring at the tattoo on my arm, hating the violation of my person. I had barely sat down with my coffee five minutes ago when Manny had barged into my viewing room and ordered me to open a folder on the server our team shared.

I lifted my coffee mug and took a blissful sip. With Colin's influence, Phillip had invested in a new coffee machine. Not only was the machine superior, but the coffee beans Colin brought were of the highest quality.

"Doc, are you listening?" Manny hovered next to me, agitated. He pulled a chair closer and fell into it. Only now did I see him holding a few printed pages. "I need your full high-IQ attention here. I got most EU countries to cooperate. I even got the FBI to hand over files on cases with similar ballistic evidence. I spent the whole evening eliminating cases that were not related."

"How sure are you they are not related to the butler?"

"I've been doing this job for longer than you've been alive, missy."

"That is a gross embellishment. If you have been working as a detective for thirty-four years, then you must be at least fifty-three. You are forty-eight, far too young to make an outrageous statement like this." My voice tapered off at the end. Manny's expression was informing me that I had overstepped the line. "You were just trying to make a point that you have much more experience than me and therefore are more equipped to make informed judgements on the relevance of a case."

"Now she's telling me what I was saying," Manny said, looking at the ceiling and breathing heavily through his nose. He dropped his head and glared at me. "Hellfire, you can test a man's patience. May I continue now with the cases, missy? Good. As with the first eight cases I had found, these are different in most ways. The demographics of the victims vary far too much to find a pattern. Most of the victims are from a lower income class."

The glass doors between my viewing room and the team room whooshed open and Colin walked in, followed by Vinnie. The latter stopped just inside my room and leaned against the door. It always appeared as if he wanted as much distance between him and Manny as possible. Colin walked closer, carrying his coffee mug. "Morning, Millard."

"Frey. I was just telling your girlfriend here about the twenty-seven cases I think are related to the butler's case. It's on the server, so you can read all the details, but the gist of it is that there is no connection. These victims are worlds apart. There are three unemployed men, two of whom are suspected to have organised crime ties. Julie Sim was a woman who owned a small bodega in Miami and had no criminal ties at all. She wasn't Hispanic, so I don't quite know how she came to own a bodega."

"My God, you are small-minded." Colin sat down on his chair, shaking his head. "Being Hispanic is not a requirement for owning a store."

"Hmm. Well, Lesley Roberts and Rita Freudenberg were working-class people without any direct connection to any criminal activities. Jason Brat, Kenny DuRand and Alex Reed were US citizens with close connections to the drug world. Apart from the butler, there were only three others from the shiny side of the tracks. That would be the rich neighbourhoods, Doc. There was J Conner Beatty, a plastic surgeon, Jennifer Hymes, an executive, and Susan Kadlec, a professor of art history from a university in Prague."

Had I not grown bored with the recital of names and looked at Colin, I might not have caught the micro-expressions tightening the muscles around his eyes and mouth. First there was shock, immediately followed by deep grief. He had known Professor Kadlec. After yesterday's mistake of speaking too fast, I bit down on the inside of my lips to prevent myself asking him about it.

Manny hadn't noticed anything, still looking at the list in his hands. "Then there was Dakhota Wilson living in Spain. The detectives were convinced that her spouse had her killed."

"A spouse assassination?" Vinnie's tone indicated humour. "What did she do? Burn the rice?"

"She married a much younger man, then lost all her money in a bad investment the young gent had suggested after they immigrated to Spain." The corners of Manny's lips turned down. "He most likely told her he loved her and that she was beautiful no matter her age. She desperately wanted to believe him and gave in to that need. He used her for her money and just before she went bankrupt had her killed. The insurance payout was over three million dollars."

"Why so sour, old man?" Vinnie's smile attempted innocence. It failed. "Did one of your previous wives try to off you?"

Manny glared at Vinnie. "I don't have time for you today, criminal. One of these days though. One of these days it will be you and me."

"I still maintain that we have to find the murderers," I said, hoping to avoid another one of their petty arguments. "The strongest common factor here is the ballistic evidence, the weapons they used. It is therefore safe to infer that the supplier of these weapons might be someone we would do well to find. The best way to do that is to speak to the killers. But first we have to find them."

Manny snorted and lifted the printed pages. "Seriously, Doc? You want us to solve twenty-seven murders?"

"Yes."

Manny waited. When I didn't elaborate, he rolled his eyes. "These cases have been thoroughly investigated. They are unsolved cases because there was not—"

"Did you only look for unsolved cases?" I asked, not caring about his weak arguments.

"Yes."

"What if a case with ballistics like this was solved? What if more than one case were solved? What if these killers are in prison? We will be able to interview them immediately and possibly find a link. No, not possibly. I'm convinced we will find a link."

Manny was quiet for a moment. "You are right, Doc. I will get onto that right now. Although I don't have high hopes. I had put out a request to the law enforcement agencies for cases that fit our profile, and I only got cold and unsolved cases."

"Look again. I don't have as many years' experience as you, but one thing I do know is that there are many simpleminded criminals. It is unlikely that if we have twenty-seven unsolved crimes committed with these types of guns, there aren't at least three or four killers from other cases who got caught."

"Right. I'll get onto that."

"Was there anything in these cases that had a connection to Kubanov or any of his people?" Colin asked.

"I ran all of the names we found in the last six months against these cases and came up empty. Nada. Nothing. No connection."

"We have to find the killers." Even though I hated repeating myself, this was one instance when it seemed necessary. "If you don't have anything else of value to add, leave me alone to look into these unsolved murders. I'm confident I will find something the detectives have missed. Something that will lead us to the killers."

"Go nuts, Doc. It's your party."

I frowned. "There isn't a party. I never have a party. I prefer to celebrate my birthday quietly."

"Wait. What?" Francine stormed into the room. She must have been listening from the other side of the open door. "You never have a party? Never? Not even for your birthday?"

I slowly moved my head from left to right in negation. Her strong reaction and the expressions of sadness and pity surprised me. "Why does it matter so much to you?"

"Everyone should celebrate their birthday with their friends and family."

"My parents wouldn't agree with you." It had only taken one disastrous birthday party at the age of five for my parents to declare an embargo on future celebrations. "They believed one should never show such narcissism."

"Is that what you believe?" Francine demanded.

I gave it some thought. "No, I suppose not. Since I didn't grow up celebrating my birthday and never had friends, I just never had the need for something as frivolous as that."

"Frivolous? Frivolous?" Francine flapped her manicured hands around. "This cannot be allowed."

"Do you have something to report, supermodel?" Manny's exasperated question thankfully interrupted her rant.

"As a matter of fact, I do." Like a chameleon, she changed from dramatic woman to sleek hacker. I recognised that look. "I managed to track the emails Genevieve sent to herself. It was done from a 4G device. The good thing about 4G is that it is IP-based. The bad thing about this specific 4G device... well, they managed to mask their IP address."

"Can you trace the device?" Manny frowned. "Do you know what device she used?"

"I can't tell if it was a laptop, tablet or smartphone." Francine uttered an unfeminine, but decidedly frustrated sound. "The other bad news is that the device is no longer switched on. I can't trace it."

"So you have squat."

"No, I don't. Okay, maybe I have squat from the emails, but I did clean up the photos Genevieve took." She nodded at my computer. "I emailed it to you."

I opened my email, clicked on the attachments and brought both photos onto the monitors. I squinted at the photo with the two out-of-focus shapes, then the one with the blueprint. "It still looks like nothing."

"That's not nothing, Jen-girl." Vinnie stepped away from the door and walked closer to the monitors. "That is a blueprint for a gun."

"What kind of gun?" Manny asked.

Vinnie took his time to answer. "I can't tell. The photo doesn't give enough detail. It is definitely a handgun."

"Bloody hell." Manny rubbed the back of his neck. Any further comment was interrupted by the ringtone of his smartphone. He took it from the inside pocket of his jacket and scowled at the screen. "I have to take this outside."

Without waiting for a reply he left through the wooden door to the hallway. If he avoided the team room, this call had to be confidential in nature.

"Girlfriend, you and I are going to sit down and have a good talk about parties. Don't think I'm going to forget about this." Francine muttered a few more things under her breath as she folded her arms across her chest.

I knew she was going to follow up on this topic. I was not looking forward to it. I turned to Vinnie, who was still studying the blueprint photo. "What else can you tell me about the photo?"

"Not much." The micro-movement of the muscles around his mouth and eyes and the slight lifting of his shoulder alerted me to the lie. He had a suspicion, but didn't want to share it. After some thought I decided to give him the time or space he needed to process his thoughts. I knew he would share important thoughts or findings.

"Was this the best you could do with the other photo?" Colin asked, looking at the two indistinct shapes. "Any idea what this is?"

"To be honest, I spent more time cleaning up the blueprint photo. I might be able to clean this one up some more. There seem to be some shapes far in the distance."

I turned to her. "Please try to get as much as you can from this photo. I don't know if I took the photo because there is significance in it, or because I had some other reason in my drugged state."

"I'll get right on it." She winked at me and walked to the team room with strides that had turned many heads in the streets. Vinnie mumbled an excuse and followed her, the doors sliding shut behind him. He was planning something.

I knew him well enough to recognise the signs. I could only hope he would remember to stay safe.

The sudden quiet in my viewing room was welcome. Colin was busy with an instant messenger chat at his desk and I had time to think. I looked down at my arm, considering my next step. It was hard to look at the intricately drawn symbols on my skin and not give in to the almost crazed compulsion to remove it. Even if it meant removing my skin.

At least twenty minutes passed as I stared at my arm until my eyes lost focus. And that was when I saw it. Cleverly hidden in the whorls were numbers. I grabbed a pen and wrote down the numbers in the order they appeared on my skin.

"What have you got, Jenny?" Colin sat down next to me and put his smartphone on my desk. For once I didn't complain. This was more intriguing.

"Numbers." I wrote down the last two numbers and shoved my arm at him. "Look."

He took my arm with both his hands, tilting it back and forth. "I don't see it. Show me."

With my index finger, I followed the lines of each number as I pointed them out. "See, this is a five, this a seven, this nine."

We looked at my arm in silence. Altogether there were twelve numbers.

"Another code?" Colin asked, still holding my arm.

"Undoubtedly."

"The results are in." Manny came in from the team room and stopped when he saw Colin and I bent over my arm. "I hope you two are not snogging. Please tell me you are inspecting that tattoo."

"We are." I pulled my arm free from Colin's hands and showed it to Manny. "There are numbers here."

A few long strides and Manny was in front of me. He made a growl-like noise when I wouldn't let him touch me. He leaned in to look as I showed him the twelve numbers.

"Any idea what this means?" He pulled a chair closer and sat down hard.

I pushed my sleeve back down and cradled my arm. "Not yet, but I'll figure it out."

"I'm sure you will, Doc." He lifted the phone in his hand. "I got a call from the lab. You were most definitely drugged."

"Was it a benzodiazepine?"

"Yes. The lab guys said that they identified it as Lorazepam." Manny glanced at Colin. "Your results are the same, by the way."

"Gee, thanks, Millard. At least now you have proof that I was too drugged to kill someone."

"Ah, not that simple, my criminal friend." A malicious smile lifted the corners of Manny's mouth. "They found the Braque painting."

"Which one of the many?" Vinnie asked from the glass door. He looked less stressed than after initially seeing the blueprint photo. Francine joined him, also waiting for Manny's answer.

"The one stolen from the McCarthy house."

"How can you be sure that it was the one that was originally there? If the original had been replaced by a forgery, who's to say that the painting found isn't another forgery?"

"Whoa there, Doc." Manny lifted both hands. "They know it's the McCarthy forgery because it has traces of the butler's blood on it. It also has Frey's fingerprints on it."

"Not possible. I was not there."

"I know, I know. Don't get your panties in a twist."

"Um, Colin doesn't wear panties. They are called boxers. Panties are only for females." I thought about this for a moment. "And maybe for male cross-dressers. Or men with a fetish."

Everyone laughed, even Manny. I didn't know what they had found humorous. I was feeling a bit defensive. "Cross-dressing is a strongly developed subculture. Men who prefer to wear women's clothes are not necessarily transgender. There is a rich history of men dressing as women as far back as in Greek and even Norse mythology. As for men with a fetish, this is generally a well-hidden subculture. Anthropologically speaking, this is a rather interesting topic."

"Moving right along." Manny shook his head, still smiling. "Frey's fingerprints were found all over the painting. A significant find was his prints overlaying the butler's."

"Meaning that Colin had touched the painting after the butler," Francine said. "There is no way that any good thief would touch an item without gloves on. Colin uses gloves."

I watched Francine's statement impact Manny and the others. A realisation had just registered with them and did not sit well—regardless of the posturing between them, these people had begun to trust each other. Three people always in the grey areas of legality, and Manny ever the law-abiding and law-enforcing individual.

"I think we need to move on here as well." Colin's soft suggestion was met with a lot of nodding. "If my prints were all over that painting, it is very possible that it is the Braque I had painted for my safe house. How my prints got to be on top of the butler's is only a guess. It could be that they copied my prints and used a thin rubber cast to press over the butler's. Most likely, they pressed his fingers on the painting after he died."

"That sounds like a viable explanation," I said, suppressing a shudder at the violence of this act. "What else did they find on the painting?"

"My guys had some expert look at it and the guy is convinced it is the original. I'm not convinced. I think it's Frey's handiwork."

"Why do you think that?" Colin asked.

"A hunch. You've fooled experts before."

Colin nodded, then pushed his hands through his hair. "Why does Kubanov have such a hard-on for me? Can you get that painting here?"

"It will be here. I knew you would be the best person to identify it as your own work. Or tell us if it is the original." The change in Manny was miniscule. As usual, he was scowling and speaking to Colin in a manner the elite would use to address someone of a much lower echelon. Yet the change was there. He was showing empathy, but attempting to hide it.

"I will definitely know if this is my painting." Colin thought for a moment. "This is a really elaborate setup. For Kubanov to have gone this far is quite significant, right, Jenny?"

"Definitely, but something is off." I didn't know what or how, but my mind was telling me this was not like the cases we had before. "Something is different this time."

"What?" Francine asked.

"I'm not sure. What I have now, what *we* have now, is his behavioural history." I counted on my fingers. "He always uses a third party through whom he executes his plan. There is a strong motive acting as a distraction to his true motive. He uses that third party's criminal system to overwhelm us with events and data to investigate so we can't see his end plan."

"And you want to get to his end plan first?" Colin asked.

"I would like to. But if I go on our experience with him, we won't have any clue as to what he plans until we've solved the puzzle of the third party."

"And that means you want to start with solving twenty-seven murders." Manny shook his head. "You are light years ahead of us, Doc."

"I'll help," Colin said. "Vinnie will also help to look through these murders. Between the two of us, we have enough knowledge of the crime world to spot things. You can then analyse it."

"It might be more prudent if you tell us who would hate you deeply enough to assist Kubanov in killing you."

My question startled Colin. His eyes flashed and then narrowed in thought. It only took a couple of seconds before Colin, Vinnie and Francine were looking at Manny, similar expressions of accusation on their faces.

"Oh, fuck off, you lot." Manny returned their stares until all four chuckled.

"You know, old man," Vinnie straightened away from where he was leaning against the wall, "this would make you the perfect patsy. Personally, I like the idea. You and Colin share a history that Kubanov knows about. He even got you that little statue to show you just how much he knows. He's toying not only with my man here, but also with you."

"Hmm. I hadn't thought about that." He looked at Vinnie. "See what you can find out about this gun blueprint from your buddies."

Vinnie only stared at him. I would've been surprised if he hadn't already contacted someone in the industry to inquire about his suspicions.

When Vinnie didn't answer, Manny grunted. "You criminals are going to drive me crazy. I know you are already paranoid, but it might be wise to watch your backs."

"Aw, Manny." Francine dropped her voice to a sultry tone. "You really care about us. Will you be watching my back for me? Or even better, will you be washing my back for me?"

"You wouldn't know what to do with me, little girl." Despite Manny's scathing words, a slight redness coloured his cheeks. He got up and rolled his shoulders. "I have to go pick up that McCarthy forgery with Frey's prints all over it. I don't know how long I'll be out. If you find anything significant, let me know, Doc. And before you ask, anything significant to this case. I really don't care about any other interesting discoveries you make."

"A bit testy, isn't he?" Vinnie said as the wooden door to the hallway whooshed closed behind Manny. "I think he's really disappointed that he can't arrest you, dude."

"Manny is working hard to exonerate Colin," I said. "You're quite mistaken, Vinnie."

Vinnie uttered a rude sound. "I'll be in the team room checking out those murder cases. Holler if you need me, Jen-girl."

"I'll join you," Francine said and followed Vinnie into the next room. The glass doors slid closed, making my viewing room soundproof again.

"Vinnie knows something, doesn't he?" I had observed only a few micro-expressions, but my suspicion was confirmed by Colin's stronger reaction.

"What makes you think that?"

I lifted an eyebrow and waited.

"Okay, fine." He glanced at the glass doors. "You know he has connections with gun runners."

"Illegal arms traders?"

"Yes. The ballistics are making Vinnie very suspicious. He plans to speak to his contacts about this, to find out what they are thinking. Maybe they've heard about these guns that leave no traceable evidence. It would be a very hot commodity in their business."

"Tell me about Susan Kadlec." Remembering the pain on his face, I kept my voice low and soft.

Colin gave a humourless laugh. "Of course you caught something. What gave me away?"

"Your eyes. There was a lot of grief there. Did you know her well?"

"Yes. I met Susan when I was stealing my education." He leaned back in his chair, his eyes losing focus on the present. "When I was sneaking into the university to learn about art and other subjects, Susan was only an assistant professor, but everyone knew that she was going to be the top of her field one day."

"What was she teaching?"

"Art history. It was her passion and she was good at it. Good at teaching, good at connecting with the students and even better at restoring artwork." He paused for a moment. "It was her restoration work that gave her away."

"What do you mean?"

"After four months of my never missing a class, Susan got suspicious of me. None of her students were as dedicated. She tried to find me on the register and couldn't. That was when she realised that I was attending her classes illegally. Well, as illegal as getting an education can be. She called me to her office and scolded me for not getting a formal education. She was convinced that I had greatness ahead of me and squandering it by fooling around was a crime in her opinion.

"While she was ranting at me, I had a look around her office. There were two impressionist paintings leaning against a filing cabinet. When she noticed my interest, she asked my opinion of her restoration skills. I got up to look more closely at them and told her they were exquisite forgeries. To this day I will never forget her shock. At one point I thought she was going to faint, especially when I told her that I had seen her work at an auction just the previous week. It had been an amazing Monet forgery that had passed all the vetting. You see, the really good art restorers are at heart forgers. She was good, really good."

"She taught at a university. The ethical and moral conflict is too much for me to imagine."

Colin smiled. "If only life was as black and white as you see it, Jenny. No, Susan lived in so many shades of grey that I don't think she ever saw black or white."

"Even more than you?"

"She's the one who taught me most of what I know about forging and fencing. She took me under her wing and I even did a few forgeries for her once she was satisfied with the quality of my work."

"I don't understand how you can sound proud. It was—it *is*—a crime what you did."

"Grey, Jenny. Grey." He shrugged. "She changed later on. It wasn't long after I stopped attending university that I started reappropriating art that was illegally acquired."

"You were stealing back stolen artworks." Why the need for euphemisms?

"Yeah, okay. That. Well, Susan was confused by this. She had found in me a protégé of sorts and had thought us to be kindred spirits."

"Criminals?"

"Master forgers," he corrected. "We had long philosophical debates about my work. When Manny arrested me, things changed even more. I was then unofficially officially hired by Interpol to continue what I had been doing."

I tried, but simply couldn't let it go. "You can't be unofficially officially anything."

"I was on Interpol's payroll, Jenny. That made it official.

No one apart from four men at the very top of the agency knew about my involvement, knew that I was stealing for them. That made it unofficial. Ergo, unofficially official."

"That's just wrong." I waved my hand around. "Tell me more about Susan."

"In the last six years she stopped forging altogether. Instead, she"—he smiled—"officially started doing reproductions of famous masterpieces. Nothing illegal about that. She put her name on it right underneath the artist's forged name. She wasn't particular about the paints and canvasses, using newer materials. That made it nigh on impossible to trace any of her earlier forgeries to her more recent works. Not that any of her earlier forgeries had ever raised any suspicion. Like I said, she was really good."

"And her connection to you?" Kubanov and his apparent vendetta against Colin came to mind. Was he looking for people from Colin's past?

"Oh, we kept in touch." Colin tilted his head to the side. "You're thinking about Kubanov, right? I have no idea how he would connect us. This might be a coincidence. I know you don't believe in that, but maybe Susan got involved in something that she couldn't control and it got her killed."

His voice stumbled over the last few words. He rubbed the heel of his hand on his sternum. He had lost a friend, a colleague and someone he had respected. I had never faced a situation such as this and had no idea what to do or say to someone mourning a dear friend. I awkwardly patted his hand, then decided to rather take his hand in both of mine. For a few seconds, he only stared at our hands. When he looked at me, his eyes were shiny.

"We'll find her killer, Colin. I will make that a priority. Then we will find Kubanov. He will no longer be allowed to take away people we care about."

"Thanks, love." Only in very private moments did he call me that. It felt good. "Thanks for understanding."

I nodded stiffly, wishing there was more I could do to ease the sadness in his eyes. The one thing I could do to show Colin how much I wanted to help him was to investigate the twenty-seven cases. I could only hope that Manny would find some solved cases with similar ballistic reports. It would help greatly to speak to those killers. Also on my list was solving the mystery of the numbers on my arm. But first I was going to start with Professor Susan Kadlec's unfortunate murder.

Chapter SEVEN

"Did you know that Professor Kadlec had lost most of her savings two years ago?"

I knew from the surprise on Colin's face that his friendship with this woman had not extended to financial discussions.

"No." He pulled the chair from his desk closer and sat down. After this morning's revelations, he had given some excuse about meeting a source and had only returned five minutes ago. It was two minutes to three. He was visibly still shaken by his friend's death. "The last time I saw her, I got the impression that everything was fine. She had even insisted on paying for an exuberantly expensive dinner."

"When was the last time you saw her?" I asked.

"About five months ago. Remember that short trip I took to Prague? Well, I stopped over to spend some time with her."

The glass doors slid open and Vinnie stepped into the viewing room, as usual not allowing the doors to close again. "Howdy, Jen-girl. What's cookin', good-lookin'?"

"I know you are using an expression, because it is very clear that I'm not cooking." I was too distracted by the smug look on Vinnie's face to concern myself with understanding his greeting. Something had happened while he and Colin had been away. Something that caused his *occipitalis* and other muscles to put the triumphant look on his face. I turned to Colin. "Did you get any impression that she was stressed about something?"

He thought about it. "No, I really didn't. She was relaxed and was excited about the summer holidays. What did you find out?"

"While you were away, Francine helped me and we found a lot of information. I'm no longer surprised at how much information people put on social media and other public places. Yet it still amazes me. Most of our discoveries were done this way, the legal way." I was extraordinarily proud of this. For Susan's financial information, Francine had had to access her bank account. Of that I wasn't as proud. "Susan Kadlec didn't lose her money through some irresponsible investments or fraud. She lost it in a very traditional manner—recession."

"When the global economic disaster struck the first time, she was financially still very strong," Francine said from the team room. She must have been listening in on the conversation. A few quiet footsteps and she appeared in the door next to Vinnie. "As the years went on and global finances failed to recover, her savings became increasingly depleted. She was granted a large loan just before the worst of it hit, which made her vulnerable to bankruptcy. I didn't know her, but I can only imagine that she was going to do whatever she could to not lose everything she had worked for her whole life."

"She took on extra work." Colin's voice was strained, the muscles next to his eyes tense. "Please tell me she didn't get back into forgeries and she got killed for that."

"She did get back into forgeries." I lifted my hands. "Wait, before you jump to conclusions. She was offering her services to authenticate artworks, not to forge them. This is where Francine's research became a little less legal. I didn't ask and don't want to know how she did it, but she found out that Susan had been looking into authenticating a Degas for a museum in Madrid. This museum was acquiring the piece through an art dealer."

"That painting the prof was checking out," Vinnie said, "does it have any connection to Colin?"

"Not as far as we could find. The painting, the museum and everyone else seem to be quite separate from this case." I lifted my index finger. "With the exception of the ballistic evidence of the weapon used to kill her."

"What I found related to this case is that the dealer was selling the Degas for Tall Freddy."

"No fucking way!" Vinnie stepped away from the door and towered over Francine. Francine was taller than the average woman, but at just over two meters in height, Vinnie had no problem looking down on Francine. "That guy is brutal."

"How do you know him?" I asked.

"Freddy Gagliardi is a vicious Italian bastard. A tall, ugly bastard. He runs one of the last organised crime families still standing in southern Italy. He specialises in cocaine and small arms. He brings that shit into Europe, spreads some of it around and sends the rest to the US."

"Why don't the police arrest him?" If Vinnie knew this much, surely the police had enough evidence to incarcerate him.

"Because he's a slimy, slippery, sneaky son of a bitch," Vinnie said. "He has a lot of the older politicians under his control. He's a land developer with this stupid reputation of being a kind businessman, looking after his community. Lying bastard."

"Sounds like Kubanov." I thought about this for a second and looked at Colin. "He would be the kind of person Kubanov would use to get to you. Do you have any ties to this Tall Freddy?"

"Nothing. I didn't even know about this guy until now.

My field of expertise is art, Jenny. Not organised or violent crimes." He nodded at Vinnie. "No offence intended, Vin."

"None taken, dude."

"Francine found out Tall Freddy wanted to sell the painting to the museum," I said, getting back on topic. "They wanted to have it vetted by some respected authority."

"Susan," Colin said softly.

"Her authentications have become increasingly more respected in the last two years. She was really good at catching the forgeries."

"It takes one to know one. Okay, so what did she find?"

"Francine found emails from Susan to the art dealer warning him to stay clear of Tall Freddy. When he didn't respond to the first email, she sent another one. That was the one revealing the probable motive for this crime." I could only hope that I had adopted the right tone and was using the right words to not add to Colin's sadness. "Susan discovered that the painting was one of those looted by the Germans during the Second World War. It had never been recovered and to this day is on the FBI's list of missing artworks."

"Stolen by the Nazis? My God, Susan would definitely have reported that. Even in the best years of her forgeries, she never had any tolerance for war crimes."

"It would seem that Tall Freddy didn't have any tolerance for honest people," I said. "Have you read the case file?"

Colin shook his head.

"Please do so. Since you knew Susan rather well, there might be something that would help us connect Tall Freddy to other elements of this case."

"Where was she killed?" Colin's lips were thinned, a sign of distress.

"In her home. They successfully made it look like a burglary that went awry. He had stolen all her electronic devices, her television and a few other things. It is all listed in the report. She had insured her house and had kept up with the payments, most likely because of the art in her house."

"Were those things real?" Vinnie asked.

"As far as the report goes, they are authentic, yes." The *levator labii superioris* muscles raised my top lip in disdain. "Even the smallest painting is worth more than all the large things he stole. He also didn't even go through her handbag. I'm sure the engraved cigarette box would've brought him a large sum. And it would have been easier to sell."

"What cigarette box?" Colin's muscles had frozen into an alert stillness. "Do you have photos of that?"

I studied him for a few seconds, then turned to my computer. "It's all in the file that Manny had sent. I'll bring it up."

There was silence in the room until the photo of the silver cigarette box filled one of the ten monitors in front of us. It looked like an antique with intricate engraving on the lid and sides. A beautiful and elegant piece. I did not miss Colin's gasp, nor did I miss the slight collapse of his torso. "You gave this to her, didn't you?"

"After she told me that my work with Interpol had inspired her and she had decided to go straight." For a few seconds he looked away and focussed on the empty wall to our right. "She was a social smoker, only smoking one cigarette a week, maybe even less. Keeping an ugly cigarette pack in her handbag for that purpose was something she refused. So she bought a pack every time she wanted to smoke one. When I gave her this box, she was crazy about it. It was elegant and large enough for five cigarettes."

"Think hard, Colin. Are you sure there is nothing that connects you and her to this case?" There was too much coincidence for my liking.

"I'll read the case file and think about it, but I honestly cannot think of anything that would've led Kubanov to her."

"Tell me about this connection you have with Susan Kadlec." Manny stepped into the viewing room, his brow lowered into a scowl.

"She was my friend." There was no confrontation or apology in Colin's tone or body language.

"Sorry to hear that, Frey. Care to tell me why you didn't disclose this earlier?"

It didn't take much debating for me to convince Colin that Manny needed to know everything we knew. Reluctantly he relayed his history with Susan Kadlec. I added a few facts Colin had left out as his emotions caused him to become more withdrawn.

"We definitely need to see if there is more of a connection than ballistics."

"As soon as we can speak to some of the killers from the other cases, we should ask them about their weapons *and* about the cocaine."

Manny's nostrils flared. "Firstly, missy, there will be no 'we'. You will not be going anywhere near these people. Secondly, why do you want to ask them about drugs?"

"We've told you about Tall Freddy's involvement in Susan Kadlec's murder. I'm wondering if he might be a connecting factor between all these cases."

"Hmm. Well, let's just first find some killers to interrogate, shall we?" Manny looked at Colin and nodded towards the team room as he sat down in the chair he always claimed in my viewing room. "I brought the McCarthy painting. Now you can tell us if it's the original or yours."

"Ooh, I want to see it." Francine's enthusiasm startled everyone. "Where is it?"

"On my desk." Manny had barely finished his sentence when Francine left the room. She returned seconds later holding the painting away from her body, looking at it with the most beautiful smile. A genuine smile.

"It's stunning." She handed it over to Colin. "I totally get why you wanted this in your home. Isn't it just supercool that Genevieve also has this in her apartment?"

"Explain." Manny glared at me as if I had committed a crime.

"If you are such a great detective, you would've seen this painting in my bedroom." I lost some of my annoyance watching Colin. He was turning the painting in all directions and studying the frame. "I love Braque's work, but this one especially. Since it was not for sale, and even if it was I could not afford it, I had a reproduction made by a reputable artist."

Everyone stared at me. Even Colin looked away from the painting to stare at me. "Jenny, there is no such thing as a reputable reproduction artist. What that person is doing is forgery with his name on it. If he or she can do that, they can also paint it without their name on it."

I took a moment to consider this. After working with these people, I truly should no longer be this naïve. "You are right."

"Aw, Jen-girl, don't look so sad. At least you got yours the legal way. My man here didn't even put his name on the painting he did for his safe house. The one that was stolen. Hey, dude, is this baby yours?" Vinnie forgot about my discomfort and turned to Colin.

"The painting is mine, the frame not."

I looked at the frame around this forged masterpiece. It was a large dark wood frame with gold plating on the inside, the wood itself approximately twenty centimetres wide and easily ten centimetres thick on the outside. I wondered why there was a need for such an elaborate frame. The painting's beauty was enough for me to have chosen a simple frame. This one had to be very heavy if it was solid wood.

No matter how interesting the frame was, my eyes kept straying back to the painting. It was by far one of my favourite artworks. What sent a small shot of adrenaline through my system was the tiny rust-coloured spots on the left-hand side of the painting. My stomach felt hollow at the remnants of such violence. It was hard to tell if there was dried blood on the wooden frame.

"What was wrong with the frame you had?" I asked.

"I suppose they had to change the frame to match the one in Kathleen McCarthy's house." The lack of confrontation in Manny's conduct was odd. I was watching him for more cues as to ascertain intention. "The lab did all the tests they could—"

"Why didn't they remove the painting from the frame?" Colin turned the back of the painting towards Manny. "My God, your people really are CSI wannabes."

The *masseter* muscles controlling Manny's jaw tightened. When he spoke it was through his teeth. "If you'd allowed me to finish my sentence, you would've heard that I had asked them to only do topical tests. I didn't want to remove anything in case you could see something they didn't know to look for."

"Oh." Colin looked chagrined. "Well, I doubt there would be much evidence on here in any case."

"What do you suggest we do with the painting now, Frey?"

"I'll take this one to my friend as well."

"The friend who owes you only one favour? You lied, didn't you?"

"He did," I said. "It was very clear in his body language. I was surprised you didn't catch that, Manny."

Both men turned to me.

"You shouldn't have said that," Francine whispered loudly. Her dramatic delivery lessened the tension, and I renewed my concentration to not speak my thoughts.

"FYI, he does owe me only one favour," Colin said to Manny. "If I take this painting to him, I will be in his debt. Something I can't say I'm excited about."

"Just give me the evidence and I'll arrest him, Frey." Manny shrugged as if he didn't care. I knew that wasn't true. "Easy solution. You won't be indebted to this criminal and I'll have another notch on my belt."

"He's not a criminal. You'll have to get your rocks off arresting someone else, old man." Clearly Vinnie knew this enigmatic friend of Colin's.

"Ah, now that you've joined the conversation, want to tell me if you've found out something from your crime buddies about the guns?"

Vinnie lifted one shoulder. A half shrug. He was going to lie. "I haven't found out much. Tomorrow I'll meet up with some guys and will possibly have something more to tell you. Maybe. Or not."

"I would have thought you would work harder to help your buddy out of this mess he's in."

"Oh, I'm doing what I can, old man. Don't you worry." Vinnie was still leaning against the wall, looking nonchalant, but he had taken offence at Manny's insinuation.

Manny got up and walked to the team room. "Do more. We need to put this whole craziness to bed before it turns into the same things we had previously with Kubanov."

Francine followed Manny to the team room, teasing him about his sexy three-day-old stubble. I didn't know how Francine saw that as sexy. It made Manny look older and even more tired than usual. Colin's torso turned to the team room as well.

"Where are you going?" I asked.

"I'm going to drop the painting off and I'll be back." Colin turned back to me and stared at me for a few seconds, allowing me to read his expression. The deep gratitude I saw made me feel uncomfortable.

"It's my job," I said. "I'm good at it. And I promised you I would find Susan's killer. I hope it makes you feel a bit better."

"It does." Breaking his usual behaviour, he leaned over and kissed me. It wasn't a quick peck. He conveyed not only his affection for me, but also his relief through the passionate kiss. I kissed him back.

"Get a room, dude. Seriously, man." Vinnie sounded so disgusted that both Colin and I laughed. With a final goodbye, Colin left through the wooden door leading to the hallway.

"Please come in, Vinnie. Let the door close." I was convinced he didn't want Manny to hear what we were going to talk about.

Vinnie stepped away from the wall and pressed the button on the keypad behind him. "What's up, Jen-girl?"

"What have you found out about the guns?"

"Shit, you saw that?" He walked over and sat down in Manny's chair. "Jen-girl, you can't tell anyone. This dude is bad news. He's extremely smart, which is what makes him dangerous."

"Is this the man you are meeting tomorrow? Is he the same guy you talked about before? Hawk?"

"Of course you would remember that. Damn it, when did I talk about him?"

"A year ago." I smiled at his grunt. "You should know that I don't often forget names or details. I also remember Manny asking you then to help him catch Hawk."

"As if." Vinnie snorted. "Mind you, after this I might just give him up to the old man. Hawk has recently been up to a lot of shit and he needs to be stopped."

"Yet you feel confident enough of your own safety to visit him with questions about his business?"

Vinnie shifted in his seat. "I am not going to tell you how this happened, but Hawk owes me big. Really, really big. Me and mine are safe from him."

Although all cues pointed to Vinnie being sure of his safety, flutters of fear moved around my stomach. "Promise me you'll be careful."

Vinnie smiled at me. "Of course, Jen-girl. I want to get information so that we can clear Colin."

"Have you told anyone else? Do you have someone who will go with you?"

His eyes shifted. Avoidance. "I have a plan."

"Vinnie?"

"It's safe, Jen-girl. Don't worry."

I did. "Maybe we should tell Colin. And Manny."

"No!" He sat up. "Don't tell Colin. He'll worry and would want to come with. The old man will follow me there and lock everyone up. Including you if he finds out you knew anything."

"Manny is not that old." I waved away the irrelevant topic. "I don't know anything important. But I do know that I don't want you to go alone."

"I won't be alone. As I told you, I have a plan."

I stared at him for a full minute until I was convinced of

his truthfulness. It was an unfamiliar and extremely inconvenient feeling to worry so much about one's friends.

Vinnie took a few more minutes to convince me how badass he was. His words. I sent him away when he started talking about cooking dinner. I needed to focus on the twenty-seven cases. Hopefully worrying about Vinnie wouldn't distract me too much.

Chapter EIGHT

"This is a crap idea." Vinnie's voice was low and remorseful. "An epically crap idea, Jen-girl."

"So you've said before." I had not been counting, but I estimated in the last fifteen minutes Vinnie had told me ten times that he regretted this idea. "It is Francine's idea and you told her it was brilliant."

"Well, I made a mistake. This is going to end badly, I just know it." We were in Vinnie's black pickup truck driving to the outskirts of Strasbourg. I had gone to bed late last night after studying the cases and woken up early this morning. To my surprise, Colin had left a note for me next to the coffee machine that he had to meet someone and would see me in the office.

No sooner had I made coffee than Vinnie and Francine had come into my apartment. That was how this new situation had developed. To be truthful, I couldn't believe I had agreed to this. "I thought you said Hawk trusted you. Why would it end badly?"

For a moment Vinnie took his eyes off the road to glare at me. "Because."

"That is not an answer, Vinnie. You went out of your way an hour ago to convince me how safe I would be if I went with you."

It had taken Vinnie more than an hour to persuade me to join him. When he had told me what his original plan had been, I had admitted its genius. He had arranged for a female colleague to go with him to Hawk, pretending to be his psychologist. She was also supposed to be the psychologist to a range of other criminals and had seen an opportunity to make her sessions more lucrative. A few of her patients had told her about their crimes and their needs for untraceable weapons. She wanted to be the one supplying them with guns.

That was where Vinnie came in. He was to introduce her to Hawk in an attempt to gain some insight into these weapons. Unfortunately, Vinnie's colleague was in hospital after being arrested for being in a bar brawl last night. Vinnie had spent the whole night looking for someone who could take his colleague's place, but no one was available. Francine couldn't play this role because Hawk had met her once. Since Francine was a memorable person, they didn't think it wise to even consider her for this role.

Three more factors added complexity to the situation. Firstly, it had taken a lot of convincing for Vinnie to set up this meeting with Hawk. Vinnie didn't want to cancel the meeting in fear that Hawk would never agree to another time. Secondly, Vinnie knew Hawk well enough to be convinced the arms dealer would become suspicious if Vinnie showed up without the psychologist and started asking questions about untraceable handguns.

Lastly, Hawk had told Vinnie that this morning was the only time he had available for a meeting. Apparently he had something very important happening in the next few days that would take up all his time.

Francine had thought I would be perfect for this ruse. There was logic in her reasoning, but it had taken a lot of convincing to sway me. If not for Vinnie's plea that doing this could help clear Colin's name from any suspicion, I would now be in my viewing room. Safe.

"You promised no harm would come to me."

"Not from Hawk." Every time Vinnie said this, I couldn't find one single deception cue. "It's the others I'm worried about."

"Which others?"

"Colin. The old man."

Understanding filled my mind. "You know they are going to be furious with you for taking me."

"Colin still thinks you are falling apart from the kidnapping. The old man would love using this opportunity to arrest me."

I bristled at Vinnie's first sentence. My whole life I had to fight against myself, my own weaknesses. To have people I valued treating me as weak offended me greatly. It made me obstinate. The more I thought about this, the more determined I became. I didn't even need Mozart. "Do you value our friendship?"

"Of course I do. What the hell kind of question is that? If I didn't think you were the smartest and most reliable person I've ever met, I would not have asked you to come with me in the first place."

"Do you want me dead?"

"Jen-girl, now you're seriously pissing me off." His bottom jaw protruded and his lips were thin lines.

"Good. I depend on you, Vinnie. You will keep me safe. We will deal with the others after we've gathered information from Hawk. Why do you trust him so much?"

"Firstly, thanks. Secondly, never make the mistake of thinking that I trust him. Hawk is known throughout the arms trade to be a ruthless son of a bitch. He didn't become the best by being a nice, kind, generous person, Jen-girl. He is a killer first, a businessman second. I know Hawk really well and, well, he owes me big time."

At eight in the morning, the traffic was getting heavier by the minute. We were going to an address in the industrial area Vinnie had told me, but it had no meaning to me. Not that it mattered. I had never been to any industrial area in or around Strasbourg. Or in any other city for that matter. My travels had been to museums, galleries or remote villages untouched by industry.

After I had agreed to go with Vinnie, Francine had insisted that I wore a disguise. She also equipped me with appropriate technology to record the visit to Hawk's warehouse. Everything had happened so fast, I'd needed to mentally write the Adagio and Allegro of Mozart's String Quartet No. 1. It had soothed my nerves some, but hadn't alleviated an overwhelming concern I had.

"Jen-girl!"

"Don't shout, Vinnie. I'm right next to you."

"You're not listening to me."

"I want to phone Colin again." It worried me that I had not been able to speak to him. This had been the one point I had been adamant about. If I were to join Vinnie, Colin had to know. The problem was he wasn't answering his phone.

"On it." Vinnie pressed a few buttons on the steering wheel and a ringing tone filled the cabin. It rang twice before going to voicemail. Vinnie waited for the signal. "Dude, phone Jen-girl as soon as you get this. It's important."

I rolled my head and unclenched my hands. Not discussing this with Colin was more stressful than normal. I mentally scoffed at the word. Nothing about this situation was normal.

"Jen-girl." Vinnie was speaking loudly. "You're doing it again. Stay with me. We're about twenty minutes out and I want you to go over the plan with me."

"I wish I could speak to Colin." Often I had to fight my

proclivity to become obsessed with an idea. Usually I had better control than now. I simply couldn't let go of my need to hear Colin's voice, his reassurance.

"I know. Although I think he would be seriously pissed."

"I think so too." Despite the many unanswered calls to Colin earlier this morning, I had agreed to accompany Vinnie. Now I was suffering from cognitive dissonance about my decision.

"Can we please go over the plan again, Jen-girl?"

"Why?"

"Because I want to know that you remember everything."

"I have an exceptional memory, some might call it eidetic. I remember the finest detail of what we talked about. You know this."

"Please just do this for my sanity." He was gripping the steering wheel so hard his knuckles were turning white. If reciting our strategy would appease him, I could do this. I had nothing else to do while we were travelling. It might also keep me from paying attention to the panic threatening to enter my consciousness. The longer I thought about this, the more flaws I was finding.

"I am Doctor Ingrid Sebastian, your psychologist, treating you for severe anger control issues. You have been my patient for the last year, and have been confiding in me about your criminal activities for the last four months. A few weeks ago I told you that I have patients who also function in the crime world. Some of them have mentioned their frustration at not finding weapons that cannot be connected to someone or some crime. Then I approached you with a business proposal."

"And since I don't sell weapons, I offered to introduce you to Hawk. That way you have direct access to the main supplier and you will give me a discount on future sessions."

What I could read from Vinnie's nonverbal behaviour was that it had been a stressful night for him. Asking me to take part in this ruse had caused him to frequently rub the back of his neck in a pacifying gesture. He had stopped the moment I had pointed it out to him.

"The old man must never find out about this, Jen-girl. He'll lock me up just for taking you." Vinnie mumbled something more. I only caught a few words, but it sounded like he wouldn't fight Manny if he arrested him for this transgression.

"It would be naïve to think that Manny wouldn't find out about this." He would be livid and would most likely act on his threats to arrest Vinnie. Yet I knew I was going to tell him. After I told Colin. I shuddered at the thought of their reactions.

Vinnie turned into a property with rows of large warehouses. Each one looked impenetrable, walls without windows and the doors shut. There were no cars, only trucks, SUVs and larger vehicles. We drove past the buildings and I only caught glimpses of men loading or unloading boxes and other items that no doubt were being put in storage until they had to be shipped to their new owners. None of the buildings had logos, only large letters on each corner. We stopped at R.

"This is it." Vinnie cut the engine and turned to me. "I know you'll be fine. I'm more worried about me."

"Myself. It's worried about myself." I shrugged when Vinnie looked at me with incomprehension. "It's not relevant. Let's go and find out if you can control your anger while introducing me to my new gun dealer."

"I can control my ang... oh, cool. You're getting into character." A genuine smile crinkled the corners of his eyes. "I knew you would be fine."

We got out the car and I had to grab onto the door when my legs got entangled in the long skirt Francine had given me to wear. It was a soft green material that flowed to my feet, the skirt mostly shapeless. With that I wore a colourful shirt that I would never even take off a shop hanger. It was equally shapeless, the two items combined adding at least eight kilograms to my frame. If Francine had not brought the clothes in sealed plastic covers from the dry cleaner's, I would not have worn them.

I had tenaciously refused to wear someone else's shoes, and Francine had reluctantly given in. The sneakers she had taken out of my wardrobe clashed with the outfit, which she had maintained added to my makeover. She completed this image with an overabundance of jewellery and subtle, but strategic make-up. When I had looked in the mirror, a hippie with gaunt eyes and prominent cheekbones had looked back at me.

Vinnie stepped around the pickup truck and stopped next to me. "Ready?"

"Yes."

"Remember about the glasses."

"They're on my face, Vinnie. They're irritating me. How can I forget about them?" This was Francine's final but most important touch. Not only would they further obscure my profile, but these glasses were equipped with a micro-recording device. The hinge of the left arm was a small switch if touched on the inside. It would record everything I looked at. If Hawk hadn't been scrambling all signals around this warehouse, it would also have transmitted the images to Francine. Now it was merely a recording device. One I planned to study in depth as soon as I was in the safety of my viewing room.

"Just wait to see if Hawk decides to have us scanned for transmitting devices before you switch it on."

"This is the fourth time you've told me this. I remembered it the first time."

Vinnie responded with a snort and shook his head. "Come on then, Nancy Drew."

I didn't know who this was, but saw his attempt to lighten the moment with a jocular reference to someone he had a fondness for. I followed Vinnie to a smaller steel door inside a door large enough for trucks to enter the solid steel structure. It was a beautiful summer morning. The temperature had not climbed yet, but would soon. I wondered if there was adequate air conditioning in these structures.

The door opened before I could ask Vinnie the inane, yet interesting question. A woman stepped out and squinted into the sun. She was wearing fatigues similar to Vinnie's. Over her sleeveless T-shirt was a leather holster with a large gun under her left arm. She was right-handed. Her posture was one I'd seen only in soldiers. This small woman was a warrior and protector just like Vinnie. It was in her body language and her muscle development.

"Rhonda Smothers, you sexy beast." Vinnie's tone held warmth and familiarity. "How's it hanging?"

The woman nodded to the gun. "Still to the left, Vinster. How are you?"

They hugged briefly, Vinnie nearly lifting her off the ground. There was none of the gentleness I had observed in his physical affection towards me. He was treating her similar to Colin, with less trust, but equal regard. Their crushing hug ended and Vinnie stepped back, half in front of me. "I'm well, as you can see. How's Hawk?"

"Pissed at you."

"Because of her?"

Rhonda looked at me, evaluating. "Oh yes. You know he doesn't like visitors. And now you're bringing in a civilian? Not wise at all."

"Rhonda, I would like for you to meet my shrink." He stepped to the side, allowing Rhonda access to me. "This is Doctor Ingrid Sebastian. Doc, this is Rhonda, a very good and long-time friend of mine."

Knowing my role, I held out my hand. "Pleased to meet you, Rhonda."

"Doc." Rhonda took my hand in a crushing grip. She was establishing dominance and I allowed her to. I pulled my shoulders slightly towards my ears in a typical tortoise pose and lowered my eyes. This pleased her and she let go of my hand. "Let's get this party started then."

She held the door open for us, allowing us to go in first. I did not see it as a gesture of hospitality. This enabled her to shoot us in the back if we became a threat. Logic dictated that somewhere in the building was a person with a weapon trained on the door, covering us from the front. I swallowed and touched the inside of the left arm of my glasses.

Rhonda led us deeper into the large structure. I pretended to look without really seeing anything. It wasn't difficult. All I had to do was make sure that the glasses got as much view of the warehouse as possible. I moved my head slowly enough to not create a visual blur, but not so much as to be noticeable.

We passed crates stacked in rows reaching as high as eight meters, but still very far from the ceiling. Aware as I was of Hawk's main business, it was difficult for me to process that these crates might all contain weapons. At the end of one of the many rows was a man working on a tablet computer while looking at the crates. When we got closer I noticed how much shorter than Vinnie he was. I estimated his age at mid-forties, yet he had the kind of look that would ensure graceful aging. Fortunate genes, despite the height disadvantage. He was elegantly dressed in black trousers and an expensive beige silk shirt, contrasted by heavy boots.

"Vinnie, you ugly bastard." The man put his tablet on an unopened crate and gave Vinnie a back-slapping hug. "It's been too long, eh?"

"Hey, gotta make you miss me some, H." The nonverbal cues on Vinnie's face were not what I had expected. Their relationship meant more to Vinnie than he had led me to believe. Vinnie had not trusted me with their history, but something had to have happened to make my paranoid friend feel affection towards a man he had labelled as a ruthless killer. His smile was genuine. "Whatcha up to?"

"Checking inventory. I had an arsehole stab me in the back two weeks ago. Can you believe it, Vinnie?" Hawk's *risorius* muscles moved the corners of his mouth towards his ears. A contemptuous smirk, often mistaken for a smile. "I welcomed this jerk into my business, into my home and he sold me out to the police. What is the world coming to when you can't even trust those around you, eh?"

Vinnie chuckled. "You don't trust anyone, in any case, H."

"True, true, true." Hawk looked at me, his eyes narrowing. "So, this is your shrink, eh?"

"H, I would like you to meet Doctor Sebastian."

Before Vinnie could introduce Hawk to me, the short man stepped closer and held his hand out to me. "Any friend of Vinnie's is a friend of mine. Please call me Hawk."

"Pleased to meet you, Hawk." I offered my hand and he took it in a firm, but respectful grip. A man confident enough in his position that he didn't have to posture or intimidate.

"You have a beautiful smile, Doc." He held my hand for a moment too long. I longed for my hand sanitizer.

My smile dimmed a bit at his over-familiarity, but I recovered by lowering my eyes and making my smile shy. "Thank you."

Hawk turned to Vinnie. "You sure she's only your shrink? A pretty thing like her would distract me too much to talk about my emotions, eh?"

"Careful, H." Vinnie's tone was still friendly, but had lost some of its warmth. "I respect what she's doing. She's really helping me and I promised her complete safety."

"Safety, Vinnie? You brought her here to discuss business." All friendliness left Hawk's body, replaced by an alertness only noticeable to the practiced eye.

Vinnie didn't answer. I saw an opening and took it. I placed my hand on his arm and ignored his surprise. "It's okay, Vinnie. Tell your friend."

For a few seconds Vinnie stared at me, his expression shuttered. Yet I could see him fluctuating between amusement and concern. "If you think so, Doc."

"I think so." I pulled my hand back, resisting the urge to wipe it on the skirt that wasn't mine.

Vinnie looked at Hawk. "There's another reason she's here. Doc reckons I would make faster progress if I trusted more people. I told her you are one of my oldest friends and she suggested I trust you more."

There was a moment of silence before Hawk burst out laughing. Vinnie joined him.

"Um, how much does she know about you?" Hawk asked as he wiped tears from his eyes and gave a few more chuckles.

"Everything." Vinnie lifted a hand to stop Hawk's response. "I need help, H. Things were turning into a complete fuck-up fast. I knew it wasn't long before I lost it and did something I could not get back from. She's helped me a lot in the last year.

A few months ago I realised that she could be trusted with my life and I told her everything."

"You gave her names?"

"When you agreed for her to join me was the first time I gave any name. The things I've told her have been without names and places."

"Most of what he has told me related to his reactions in different situations." I knew I wasn't supposed to talk, but Hawk was the kind of man who needed more than the usual reassurances. "I know he told you that I have other patients like him. Vinnie is not the only person trusting me with sensitive information."

Hawk studied me for almost a full minute. He must have seen something he approved of. "Tell me about doctor-patient confidentiality."

"In my personal practice I take it further than the law requires." I had thought about it this morning and discussed it with Vinnie while Francine had worked on my make-up. "By law I cannot disclose any information about a patient unless he is a danger to himself or society. In my personal practice I will only report a patient if he is an immediate threat to children. My patients know that from the first meeting. So far, it's worked for all of them."

"And I have some dirt on her." Vinnie's smile was filled with retribution. I didn't understand why he would feel the need. I thought I was doing great in solidifying our cover story. "I managed to find some stuff on Doc Sebastian that she agreed shouldn't be public knowledge. We're good, H. She's safe. Else I would never have brought her here."

"You are the most paranoid bastard I know. If you say she's good, I believe it." Hawk nodded. "Well, okay then. Let's have tea, eh?"

He turned away from us and walked even deeper into the building, Vinnie next to him asking Hawk about his family. Just because criminals could coldly execute plans, and people, didn't mean they didn't have the same emotions when it came to family. There was pride in Hawk's voice when he talked about his daughter Monique, getting ready to go to university in America. He didn't want his world to taint her and he was pleased with her American education.

From his chatter I heard his affection as he talked about Monique having been in US schools since the age of eleven. There was also a lot of pride in his voice. He took a photo from his wallet and showed it to Vinnie. I caught a glimpse of a happy teenage girl. He believed she was going to be the best in whatever field she studied.

I followed them, making sure to slowly look from side to side, again as if I was looking, but not absorbing. It was Hawk's admission that he was hoping to take it easier that greatly interested me. He wanted to spend more time with his daughter. From the rest of their conversation I surmised that Hawk was planning to exit this line of business. Although I saw only the left side of his face and his back, it was enough for me to read him. He was deeply concerned about something. Maybe his retirement was forced.

We stopped in front of two large steel cabinets, used in most offices for filing. Hawk looked at Vinnie. "You're sure you trust her, eh?"

"With my mental health and my life, H." His tone and every nonverbal cue agreed with the statement. My carefully constructed mask crumbled for a moment. Despite the many layers that made up Vinnie, and his vast and rich criminal history, he had grown very dear to me.

"Tea it is." Hawk held a key-card to the side of one of the

cabinets and a few short beeps filled the air. The cabinets silently rolled sideways along the wall to reveal a large door that looked like that of a walk-in safe. Hawk leaned close and a retina scanner confirmed his identity, asking in an automated voice for his code. That was entered with one hand covering the other. He seemed to equal Vinnie in paranoia.

"Please, come in," Hawk said when the door silently slid open. The room it revealed was in complete contrast to the warehouse at our backs. I joined the two men in the room and slowly turned around to take everything in. And to record what I was looking at. The walls were filled with paintings that looked authentic to me. Most of the masters were represented on the walls, showcasing the major eras in art history. A glaring omission was the cubist masters. I made a mental note of it. Later I would examine all my observations, as well as carefully studying the footage.

"Doc, green, white or black tea?" Hawk had turned on a kettle and was standing in front of an impressive collection of glass containers filled with tea leaves. My recent poisoning flashed into my mind and I hesitated.

"Doc Sebastian is scared she's going to offend you, H." Vinnie's laugh was derisive. "She's done a lot for me, but she's one of those health nuts. Vegan, can you believe? And she doesn't drink any kind of tea or coffee."

"Really?" Hawk looked at me as if he saw me for the first time. "Not even rooibos tea? Its health benefits are many."

"No, I don't drink rooibos tea." It was the truth and I felt relieved to not have to lie about my beverage preferences. Once I had tried this apparently wonderful tea, but the taste did not please my palate. "I'm well aware of its highly regarded health properties. I just don't drink it."

"May I offer you anything else?"

I knew my refusal would be considered an insult. "Bottled water, if you have any."

"Only the best." He opened a small built-in fridge and took out a bottle of expensive imported water. I didn't care as much about the purity of the water as I did the sealed top. When I heard the crack of the seal breaking, relief rushed through me. He poured the water into a sparkling clean crystal glass. It was no guarantee, but much better than taking a chance with tea leaves.

Vinnie had no such problems and easily accepted the white tea Hawk brewed for them. Two hardened criminals drinking tea out of fine china was another valuable piece of information I stored. I had come to learn Francine's sense of humour and predicted she would find this highly entertaining.

For the next twenty minutes I quietly watched Vinnie and Hawk chat. There was an easy camaraderie between them borne from years of friendship and shared experiences. It made me more curious about Vinnie's past, something I had never asked him about. I wasn't one to pry, believing people would share what they were willing to share when they were ready. Maybe I was mistaken and should ask more intrusive questions.

"So Doc, you want to step into the shadows with us, eh?" The change in Hawk's tone and body language announced the true conversation was about to start.

"Yes." It took monumental effort to lie about my greed for more money. It took no effort to appear nervous and uncomfortable in a new situation. "In the last week alone, I listened to three patients expressing interest in finding untraceable weapons."

"I don't know if I should laugh or shoot both of you." Hawk's micro-expression confirmed his indecision. I hoped he would laugh.

"I told you I trusted her."

Hawk took a long time to reach a decision. I watched the process unfold on his face. He sighed and looked at me. There was not a single sign of deceit. "If I ever so much as get a hint that you spilled a word about this, I will find you. And I will kill you."

"I believe you." I did.

"Good. What are you looking for?"

"When I spoke to Vinnie, he told me there have been guns on the streets for a few months now that left no traceable evidence on the bullets. No striae, nothing whatsoever. That's what I'm interested in."

"What makes you think I will have one of those, eh?" He laughed softly when Vinnie looked at him in disbelief. "Sure, I've also heard of those."

"Do you have any of those?" I asked.

"Nope. I am trying to source it. You are not the only one interested in this, eh?" Hawk stood. He was announcing the end of our meeting. "I will remember to let you know as soon as I find those guns myself, eh?"

Vinnie stood as well. "Thanks, H."

"You know you're welcome here any time." Hawk watched me get up from the sofa. "I like you, Doc. You are also welcome here any time."

"Thank you." That was the only safe answer I had for his lie.

Hawk led us out the warehouse, chatting to Vinnie about inconsequential things. Five minutes later we were in the pickup truck driving past the other warehouses to the main road. Vinnie was very quiet. I waited. When he was ready, he would talk. It took ten minutes.

"He was lying about not knowing about the guns, wasn't he?"

"Yes."

"He made me, didn't he? He made us."

I remembered this expression from Colin's last experience with Kubanov. Vinnie had lost his cover with Hawk. My voice was quiet with sympathy. "Yes."

"Fuck." Vinnie hit the steering wheel hard with his fist. "Fuck, fuck, fuck!"

Chapter NINE

The wooden doors to my viewing room whooshed open, drawing my attention away from the monitors. Before anyone stepped into my room and saw what I was doing, I switched screens. On the monitors now were the list of products bought with Colin's credit card and photos of my tattoo.

Phillip stepped into the room, pulled a chair next to mine and sat down without saying a word. He looked at me for a few seconds. "Genevieve, what is the point of having a cell phone if you never answer it?"

"It didn't ring."

"Is it switched on?"

"Oh. No." I cringed. In the pickup truck, Vinnie had asked me to turn off my phone and I had. It was still in its designated pocket in my handbag, not functional. "I will switch it on now. Did you phone me?"

"Manny did." Phillip seldom smiled. The closest expression was a slight tightening of the corner of his mouth. Like now. "He was highly put out that you didn't answer your phone."

"Was it an emergency? Should I phone him?" I hated talking over the phone.

"No, please don't phone him." Phillip's mouth twitched again. "He's in a meeting with Interpol and I don't think he will survive the aggravation."

I quietened. "I don't mean to be aggravating, Phillip."

"I know. Manny is more on edge when he's meeting with

what he calls the pen-pushers. Despite a direct order from the president, these guys still try to get as much information about what we do here from Manny as they can."

"Why? Shouldn't the president's order be enough?"

"Yes, and Manny takes great pleasure in telling them that." Phillip glanced at the monitors. "What are you working on?"

"The credit card purchases."

"Oh, Genevieve." His head tilted to the side and his eyes narrowed. "You are such a terrible liar."

"Not always." I had been quite adept this morning in Hawk's warehouse. Phillip waited and I knew from experience that I would have to answer him. Honestly. "I can't tell you. Not yet."

"Because it is a huge government secret or because Manny is going to be angry?"

I bit down on the insides of my lips to prevent the full truth of what had transpired this morning spilling from my tongue.

Phillip sighed. "Manny will find out, you know."

I nodded.

He got up and looked down at me, making sure I saw the severity of his concern. "Be careful, Genevieve. Rather face Manny's anger and be safe than do something you will not come back from."

Without waiting for my response, he left. I sat for a few minutes debating whether I should phone Manny and tell him about my visit to Hawk. It didn't take long to reach the conclusion that it would indeed be an unwise decision. If a mere phone call would irritate him during his meeting, revealing this information to him would surely cause rage. I would tell Manny as soon as I saw him.

But first I would have to tell Colin. I was not looking forward to that conversation. On our way back, Vinnie had phoned Colin a few more times with no results. I was now waiting for him to return our calls or come to the office. I hated that, for a moment, I wondered if he was avoiding me.

With all the events taking place around us, I still hadn't had time to ask him about his expression of envy I had seen in his safe house. I was also scared to ask him. Despite not seeing any nonverbal hints of him growing weary of me, that flash on his face had been very disturbing. Had I not been paying attention? Had he been losing patience with me?

I shook my head at this unproductive speculation. Colin knew better than anyone that I needed full verbal and nonverbal truth. Hints and metaphors didn't work with me. I trusted him enough to relax in the knowledge that he would address an issue if there was one. Satisfied with that thought, I switched monitors to return to the warehouse footage and pressed the play button. I had gone through the whole video once before at normal speed. I was noticing more things this time around. I knew what to be looking for.

Vinnie and I had just stepped into the warehouse with Rhonda. I changed the settings on the player software to play at a slower speed. My focus with this viewing was everything in the background. I wanted to see what I hadn't seen before. I paused the shaky image before we turned into the first row of crates. To the left were three men offloading a large delivery truck. I zoomed in on the boxes being carefully loaded onto a forklift. Three large boxes were stacked on the forks with room for only one more.

It was easy to identify the content of these boxes. There was a huge picture of a television on each box. It looked different from the large-screen television I had in my apartment and I wondered if it was one of the newer-generation sets. Or did those boxes indeed contain televisions?

Since that was not my concern at this moment, I clicked on the play button again and watched as the image turned to the right. We were following Rhonda to meet Hawk.

I paused every few steps to zoom in on the stickers identifying the content of each crate. They were mostly electronic devices. The stock in the warehouse had to be worth a few million Euro if all those crates were filled with what was on the stickers. Vinnie was right. Hawk was a good businessman. Nothing on the stickers stood out or made me suspicious. I ignored the conversation with Hawk to focus on the background.

For a few moments Vinnie's back filled most of the monitors when he had moved in front of me in an unconscious gesture of protection. He didn't trust Hawk. Not with me. I moved out from behind his back and the image showed more of the warehouse. The room with the large glass windows caught my attention and I waited until we were walking to Hawk's den to get a better image. I paused and zoomed in.

I was astounded that I had not noticed this before. What had attracted my attention before were the large barrels, some with identifying stickers, others without. Not anymore. I stared at the back of the room, perplexed. Why would a businessman, who mainly dealt in electronics, and an arms trader need carpentry equipment? I zoomed in even further, allowing the software to clear up the image.

I wasn't looking at just any kind of carpentry equipment. These were the kind of tools an artisan would use. I only recognised a few of the tools, all of which looked of the highest quality and new. They had been used, but there wasn't much evidence of long-term use. The large, foot-operated joiner was still shiny. There was a clamp and other equipment I could not name. On a large workbench, I saw hammers, tape measures, craft knives and more common tools, most of which were used for woodwork.

Was Hawk a master carpenter at heart? An artisan? Was it someone else in his organisation? I made a note to ask Vinnie if any of these tools and equipment could be used in building bombs.

My thoughts were rudely interrupted by a commotion loud enough in the team room to filter into my room through doors that had not been closed completely. The glass doors slid open and loud voices preceded the two angry men into my room.

I quickly switched off the monitor and swallowed my panic when Vinnie and Colin stopped in front of me, Vinnie preventing Colin from coming too close.

"Get out of my fucking way, Vin."

"It's not her fault, dude. I made her do this."

Adrenaline shot through my system, making my heart race and my mouth dry. Dark edges entered my vision. I knew there were times Colin found me trying. Not once had he lost his temper with me. His patience and understanding had at first been a surprise, but later became expected. I had seen him annoyed, frustrated, in physical pain, but never enraged. His body had gained an uncommon rigidity, his feet planted wide apart, the corners of his mouth turned down and his lips in thin lines.

"Did he?" Colin looked around Vinnie to catch my eye. "Jenny, I'm asking you a question. Did Vinnie force you to go with him?"

"Don't do this, dude. Don't take this out on her."

"Get out of my way, Vin. You've done enough damage as it is."

I couldn't speak. My mouth felt frozen, the muscles in my body not responding to any signal from my brain. I had never been in a situation like this. The worst confrontations I had ever experienced were with my parents and theirs were silent acts of disapproval. I had no frame of reference for such aggression between friends.

"Dude, calm down and let's talk about this." Vinnie was talking fast, his hands at his sides, but slightly lifted in an unconscious stop gesture. "Our trip wasn't wasted. We found some interesting information. We even have video. Jen-girl recorded the whole thing."

Colin pulled his arm back and punched Vinnie full and hard in the face. He had reacted so fast, I hadn't seen it coming. Not while trying to slow down my breathing. The attack had taken Vinnie by surprise too. His head snapped back and he stumbled a few steps back, into my chair. He stepped forward, lifting his hand to his cheek. It came away bloody.

"You put a fucking camera on her?" Colin's voice was distorted and loud from his irrational anger. A glance at his face told me he was fast losing perspective, losing his ability to stop. "Do you want her to die? Or do you have a fucking death wish?"

Vinnie's expression went from contrite to irate in a second. "How dare you? I've done everything to keep her safe. You're fucked up, dude."

Just like that, the last of Colin's rationality fled. It might have been interesting to observe such behaviour had it not been almost on top of me. And had it not been two people I had come to care for.

Colin attacked Vinnie with the fervour of one of the wrestlers they liked to watch on my large-screen television. They fell over the chair at the end of my desk and landed on the floor, fists thudding into flesh. Despite the size disadvantage Colin had to Vinnie, he managed to do a lot of damage. There was blood spatter on my desk and on my carpet. I looked down and saw a tiny drop of blood on my foot, just above my shoe.

"Do something!" Francine rushed into the room. Her accusing look brought the dark edges closer into my sight. "Genevieve, say something! Don't just sit there. Make them stop!"

I couldn't. In front of me were the three people who had made an exceptional effort to become my friends and to teach me about friendship. Yet I was immobile in my chair. It was too much for me. There was nothing I could do to stop the blackness taking over my body. At least the blackness was safe and without friends hitting each other.

It was a cramp in my lumbar muscle that pulled me back into my body and into the present. I was curled up in my office chair, a soft groan leaving my throat. I had been told that sometimes I keened, sometimes I groaned and sometimes I was so completely still it was worrying. Momentum kept my body rocking and it took a few seconds of concentration to stop.

"You're back." Colin was sitting next to me, presumably in the chair he and Vinnie had knocked over in their scuffle. I was reminded why I had disappeared into my head and I inspected Colin's face.

"You're hurt."

"It's nothing." His tone and body language belied this. "Just a few scrapes."

"You're holding an icepack to your eye and your hand is wrapped in another icepack. That doesn't qualify as nothing." I lowered my legs to the floor and shifted closer. When Colin leaned away from me, I blinked, dumbfounded. That had never happened before.

"Yeah, well. Vinnie's face is as hard as a frigging rock."

"Did you break something? Maybe you should go to the

hospital." My voice faltered on the last part of my suggestion. His glare was filled with fury. My throat was dry, the muscles tense. "Colin. I'm sorry."

"Why didn't you tell me?"

"I tried to phone you the whole time before we went." My tone was filled with a plea for understanding. "You can check your voicemail. I phoned you at least twelve times. Vinnie also phoned you."

"That's it?" He lowered the ice pack to his lap. "That is your reason for making such a stupid decision? For not waiting to speak to me before you went to a criminal internationally notorious for torture?"

Anger was understandable, but it was his other micro-expressions that pressed into my chest until it felt as if my heart was hurting.

"I'm sorry," I said softly. "I don't know what to do."

"I'm so angry right now, Jenny. No, it's not anger I feel, it's fury. Fury that you could've been killed by a stupid, stupid decision. I try. God, I really try. It's not always easy, but I try. You want to know why?" He waited until I nodded. "Because I trust you, Jenny. Not only to keep your word or to not reveal my confidences. I trust you with my psyche. I know you will never use anything against me. I trust you with my life. I also trusted you with you. I thought you were much smarter than going into a situation like this."

His anger towards me was a horrid experience. But it was the thought that I was responsible for a rift in Vinnie and Colin's friendship that burned at the back of my eyes. I blinked at the tears which had filled my eyes, obscuring my vision. "I don't know what to say."

"What? No arguments of logic and indisputable rationale? What a surprise." He leaned back in his chair, looking at the ceiling.

The depth of my emotional connection to this man became clear to me when it proved to be extremely hard to remove my feelings from this situation and look at it objectively. I had thought agreeing to accompany Vinnie would help Colin. This was proof of my inexperience with interpersonal relationships. Colin had said he was furious, but what I saw on his face was something else. Something I would never have predicted. "I've hurt you."

"No, Jenny. This is not hurt." His sigh was deep and heavy. "This is me being tired of giving you everything and getting very little in return."

His statement caught me by surprise. Was this related to the envy he had felt at Ben's relationship with his son? I felt weak with the powerlessness I was experiencing. "I don't know what you want from me. This is uncharted territory for me. I don't have a frame of reference to work from."

Colin pushed the fingers of his healthy hand through his hair to grip it hard. "I know, Jenny. I know."

We sat staring at each other for what felt like an hour. It was three minutes. He dropped his hands to his lap. "You were looking at the footage you had recorded. Did you find something interesting?"

His expression warned me that we were not going to resolve the situation here and now. I was aching with the need to know what it was he felt he didn't have in our relationship, but I didn't want to do more damage by insisting. I tightened my jaw muscles and turned to the ten monitors against the wall.

Instead of telling Colin my findings, I ran through the forty-seven-minute video with him. It was normal speed and I said very little, observing him. I clicked on the stop button when Vinnie and I left the building.

"He did this to help you," I said. "*We* did this to help you."

Colin inhaled deeply and exhaled slowly. "Jenny, I can't remember ever being this angry. I'm too angry to talk about this. We'll shelve this, okay?"

I nodded stiffly.

"Good. So now that I've seen the whole thing, what did you find?"

I spent the next half an hour showing him the crates with electronics and the woodwork equipment. "Why do you think he has this?'

"There could be a very nefarious reason or something as benign as his hobby. Aren't you the one always resisting any form of speculation?"

"Of course." This was not our usual work dynamic. A large chasm had opened between us. "Would any of these tools be used for making or altering guns?"

"Aha, I see where you are going with this." He thought about this for a moment. "You would have to ask Vinnie, but I'm pretty sure these tools could be used for bore lapping."

"Where is Vinnie?"

"He left." Colin's lips compressed and the corners of his mouth turned down.

"Is he okay?"

"Francine went with him. He's fine."

"Like you?"

"Jenny, drop it." He looked away for a second, shaking his head. "It means you should stop discussing this topic."

"I know what 'drop it' means. Vinnie says it to Francine all the time when she insists on adding more spices to his cooking." My emotions were hurting more than anything I had experienced before. I tried to compartmentalise and dissociate as much as possible. It helped very little. "I entered the numbers on my arm into Google."

"Did you get anything?"

"Nothing."

"Have you tried any other decryption methods?"

"Francine has, but I haven't had time yet."

As we had done on a previous case, Colin and I worked through a few ciphers until we found the key. Each number multiplied by two and replaced by that letter of the alphabet resulted in a surprising code.

"'rousseaus.hin.org'. He's using the plural of Rousseau in an inarticulate manner, but he's giving us a website."

"This feels too easy." Colin looked at the scribbles on his notepad. "We didn't even have to scramble the letters."

I agreed with him. Had Kubanov become lazy? "Do you think it is safe to open the website?"

"Francine's antivirus programmes will catch any virus he might have put in there." Colin leaned forward. "Let's check it out."

I entered the letters into the address bar and pressed enter. It took my computer less than two seconds to open the webpage. I gasped and barely paid attention to Colin using Vinnie's swearwords. On the monitors in front of us was a slideshow presentation, moving from one photo to the next. Each photo was of me.

Taken with a zoom lens, a few photos were of me in my apartment. One photo was of Colin and me walking across one of Strasbourg's beautiful bridges. On another photo, I was having lunch with Francine, and another showed Vinnie and Colin in conversation on a street while I stared off into space.

"Jesus." Colin's voice held a quiet note of fear.

"I've been stalked." I was stating the obvious. "This is something Kubanov would do. This is him hunting me and letting me know that he could've had me any time."

I felt another shutdown closing in on me. Already I had lost two hours due to a lack of emotional control. I didn't want to lose any more time. I didn't want to give Kubanov that kind of power. I exited the website.

"It's too much for me. I need to focus on something else for a while."

Colin studied me for a moment, and nodded. "Let's look into those unsolved murder cases. We'll get back to this later."

Relieved, I opened the first file on the list and noticed my unsteady hands. I was on emotion overload. Colin's anger and hurt, fear from this stalker website, but mostly the fear of Colin losing regard for me made it difficult to breathe. He started talking about the case now up on the monitors and I forced my attention to it. The longer we worked on the case, the more I was able to distance myself from my chaotic emotions.

Colin insisted we took a break after a few hours, but agreed to have a short lunch in the viewing room. By half past five we had solved another two cases. I had sent a detailed email to Manny in both cases. His response had been 'Good' both times. Nothing more, just one word.

"Only one more case, then we're going home, Jenny." Colin lifted his arms towards the ceiling, stretching his back. "God, I can't sit in this chair for the rest of the evening. Only one more case. We'll worry about the website tomorrow."

"Okay." I was scared I would widen the chasm between us by demanding to stay longer and look into the website. The initial shock of seeing photos taken of me without consent had worn off. Curiosity had set in. If Kubanov had designed that slideshow, there was an underlying message or code in it.

Of that I was sure. The look on Colin's face was enough to ignore my curiosity though.

I opened the case of Ilse Smith, an apparent drive-by shooting in Aberdeen. I stared at the information on the monitors until I couldn't bear it anymore. This uncomfortable atmosphere between us was exhausting me. I looked up at Colin. "Promise me something."

He raised one eyebrow. "What?"

"You will always be honest with me." I lifted both hands when his brows drew together. My chest was hurting with all the unsaid words. "Please let me finish. This is not easy to say. Um, if you get tired of me, I want you to promise me that you will end our relationship."

"Oh God, Jenny." All his anger was back. "I can't talk about it now. I'm going to get us some coffee. I won't be long."

He shoved his chair back and left the room with long strides. The doubt I had seen on his face exacerbated my emotional disquiet. I barely heard the doors open and close. This was one of the few times in my adult life that I had felt at a complete loss. Facing the turmoil in my psyche was something I wanted to avoid, so I turned back to the case I had opened on the monitors.

Before long I was engrossed in the case. Ilse Smith had worked in a women's boutique. She had been single, living on her own, but with close relationships with her family. Her funeral had been attended by more than three hundred people. She had made friends with all her customers, volunteered at a local community centre, babysat for her friends and tutored a neighbour's son when he'd had problems with his English classes.

When Colin placed a coffee mug in front of me, I started.

"Interesting case?"

"Sad." I looked at her photo on the monitor. She was

slightly overweight, giving her features a distinct softness, befitting the accounts I had read about her. "And senseless. The only mildly controversial thing she ever did was to head up a petition against land development in her neighbourhood. The development would've resulted in the local community sports grounds being turned into a shopping mall. None of the neighbours wanted more shops to spend their meagre earnings in. They wanted the sports grounds to spend their leisure time in. She had led a campaign successful enough that the local council rejected the developer's application."

Colin took a few sips of his coffee, sighing with pleasure. "Why did the police dismiss the developer as a suspect?"

"Every person on the developer's payroll had an alibi for the night of the murder." I lifted my coffee mug and inhaled. Colin had used the special blend he insisted was the best. He was right. The coffee was delicious. I took a sip and put it on the desk. Colin was drinking his coffee as fast as usual, not savouring it.

"Well, that is the most likely suspect. What about friends and family?"

"They were all devastated by her death. The Aberdeen police did a really thorough investigation from the look of this report. It is one of the most comprehensive reports so far."

"Hmm." He frowned and rubbed his eyes. "Anything connecting her, her family or the developer to any of the other cases?"

"The first thing I did when Manny emailed me all the reports was to run a comparison between the cases. If there are connections, it is in the scanned documents, not the data that they put in manually." I had told him that before, but he asked me with each new case. It wasn't in me to be impatient and remind him how much I hated repeating myself. The fresh bruising on his face and the way he cradled his hand prevented me. I lifted my cup and sipped.

"Damn, I'm tired." Colin stretched his eyes as if it was difficult to keep them open. "Why don't we just shut this down and take it up again tomorrow?"

"After I put the names of all the friends, family, co-workers and everyone connected to the developer in the system. And then check it against the other names we have so far." I felt the pull of fatigue, but the intrigue of this case was too strong. I took another small sip of coffee and was surprised to see my hand shake. I put the mug on my desk, a feeling of dread settling deep in my stomach. What I was feeling wasn't fatigue.

"Colin?"

It felt as if someone had drained all my energy at once. Expending more energy than I felt I had, I turned to Colin. He was slumped over the side of his chair, unconscious. I didn't know if the blackness coming over me was my unfortunate coping mechanism or the drug that somehow had made its way into our coffee. We were drugged. Again.

Chapter TEN

Unlike three days ago, I came to with an immediate awareness of what had taken place. My brain was alert, but my body still lethargic from whatever drug hadn't fully metabolised yet. My eyes were closed, and for the moment I thought it prudent to maintain the pretence that I was still unconscious while I attempted to gather more information about my condition and environment.

I was lying on my back on what felt like a tiled floor. It was cool where my skin touched the floor. At least I was still fully dressed. Checking from my toes up, I could not feel any damage to my body other than the heaviness preventing me from jumping up and running away. The only sounds I could hear were night insects and the ticking of an analogue clock in the distance. This led me to believe I was in a building with multiple rooms.

Adrenaline entered my blood, activating my sympathetic system with the immediate result of increased respiration. It took a few seconds of concentration to slow down my breathing in case someone was watching. The longer I was lying here, the angrier I became. Having my free will taken away from me once was unacceptable. Having it happen a second time was infuriating. I'd had no power to defend myself against whoever this enemy was. I strongly doubted Kubanov had done this himself. Again he had found someone willing to run his errands for him.

For a few more minutes I didn't move, not until I was

totally satisfied I couldn't hear another person moving around the building. I opened my eyes and frowned. This was not what I had expected to see. At an estimated ten metres directly above me was the biggest crystal chandelier I'd seen. The balcony under it flowed on both sides to an elaborate rounded staircase winding its way down to me.

I was lying in the foyer of a mansion. To the right in front of me was the front door flanked by narrow windows. Outside it was dark, explaining the sounds of the night insects. It had to be between ten and five in the morning to be this dark during this time of the season. Assuming I was still in France, of course. That thought sent another shot of adrenaline through my system and I closed my eyes for a few seconds. Five bars of Mozart's Oboe Quartet in F Major later, I started focussing on my body. I needed to get my muscles moving, find Colin and get out of here.

Colin. Where was he and why hadn't he woken me up like before? My eyes shot open at the same time as I became aware of my fingers lying in water. I lifted my left hand, a high-pitched groan leaving my throat. My hand wasn't covered in water. It was red and sticky. Blood.

I frantically wiped my hand on my shirt to get the blood off. It took immense willpower to calm myself and find the strength to lean up. I looked at the body of the man lying next to me in a large pool of blood. I couldn't see his face, but this wasn't Colin. He would never wear scuffed work boots.

From the amount of blood on the floor, this man had been fatally wounded. No one would survive such a loss of blood. What had happened? Who had shot him? I looked down at my body to double-check that I had not also been wounded. The only blood on me was where my jeans had been obstructing the blood pool from spreading. And the blood on my hand. I wiped my hand again on my shirt as I looked around the affluently decorated foyer. Colin was not here. I was alone.

The man's one arm was out of my view, his other lying in his blood, reaching out to me. Just as I thought I recognised something about him, his hand twitched. How this man was still alive after such severe blood loss was beyond me. If he was conscious, he might be able to tell me where I was, what day it was and where Colin was. I got onto my knees and crawled to the other side of his body. I didn't want to have any more of his blood on me.

When I reached his thighs, my weak muscles were trembling from the strain. I nearly collapsed when I got a good enough view and recognised Hawk's face. I had watched it so many times on my ten monitors, I would've recognised him anywhere. I stopped next to his chest, exhausted.

Out of curiosity I had read four books on first aid, but had never put any of my knowledge into practice. Touching another person was something I avoided as much as possible. Touching someone covered in blood was not an experience I was prepared for.

"You look... Doc Sebasti..." Hawk barely managed a whisper. His face was pale, but interestingly was void of any expressions indicating pain. His eyelids flickered as he fought to stay conscious, to stay alive. "You... woke..."

"Where are we? Where is Colin?"

"Who?" The question was recognisable from the shape of his mouth rather than from any sound he made. A small exhalation accompanied his rounded lips.

A soft electronic ping preceded a louder ping and the sound of a cell phone vibrating came from his trousers. The strangeness of Hawk receiving a call while he was lying in a pool of his own blood distracted me for a moment. Only for a moment. I ignored the relentless pinging and vibrating sound and leaned closer to Hawk. "Colin. Where is he? Who brought us here? Who shot you?"

"Bastard—" A violent convulsion interrupted him.

"Who brought us here? Who is it? What is his name?"

"Ask... printer."

"What printer? Who is he?" Was it someone who owned a printing business? A person who made prints of paintings?

"Help... me." He frowned. "Don't want... die."

I looked at his torso. The beige silk shirt he had been wearing at the warehouse had two small tears in it as if projectiles had entered through it. One tear was in his abdomen, the other his shoulder. His shirt was dark and wet with his blood. I knew there was nothing I could do to help him. In Colin's words, this man was the most notorious crime lord in France, yet it made me feel sad to watch the life drain from him. It was not a good feeling. Shouldn't I be happy that he would no longer put weapons into the hands of criminals and child soldiers?

"Where are we?" I asked again.

"Home." He coughed softly, but it was enough to send blood running from his mouth. I shuddered.

"Your home?"

He grunted and gave a small nod.

"Who shot you? Who brought me here?"

"Blow... all."

"Blow what?" This was most exasperating, worse than trying to understand Vinnie's euphemisms. "Blow something up like a bomb? Blow something away like the wind?"

"So pretty." Another micro-smile. "Doc, you... pretty."

The hand lying in the blood pool lifted and I saw the damage for the first time. A bullet had gone through the palm of his hand. I could only imagine that he had held up his hand to appeal to the shooter to stop. It had been an ineffective gesture.

"Big blow… printer." He coughed again, this time a lot of blood ran down his chin. "So cold."

He was dying. It was only minutes before he would breathe his last breath and I still didn't know anything.

"Who did this, Hawk? Who shot you?"

"The Printer… he…" His eyes shot wide open. "Doc, promise me."

"What do you want me to promise you?"

"Monique."

It took me a moment to place the name. "Your daughter?"

With his uninjured hand, he grabbed my wrist so quickly, I couldn't avoid it. His grip was surprisingly strong for a dying man. It was hard to not give in to the blackness calling me. This was fast becoming too much for me to handle. I pushed out my bottom jaw and tried to sit straighter. Hawk squeezed hard around my wrist. "Promise, Doc. Keep… safe. Protect."

"You want me to look after your daughter?" What an absurd request.

"Promise." His hand slipped from my wrist, but his eyes pleaded with mine. There was no disguise in his expression, only pure honesty. I remembered the unadulterated adoration in his voice when he had spoken about his daughter. The fear I saw expressed on his face was not for himself. "She… good person. Better…"

"Than you?"

He grunted.

"I will ask someone I trust to make sure she is okay."

"No. You… you must…" His eyes begged me for

something I wasn't eager to give. But how could I deny a dying man a request like this? Even if he was an evil man?

"I will make sure she is well."

"Thank y…" His last breath left him on those words. I was not to get another answer from him. I stared at the carotid artery in his neck for a minute, looking for any indication of blood flow. There was none. I didn't want to touch this man to confirm his death. I knew he was no longer a threat to society. That realisation was immediately followed by the fact that I was kneeling next to a dead man and had his blood on me.

It took mentally writing another page of the Oboe Quartet to gain control. I regained the acuity of my mind, but my muscle strength still had not returned. I leaned back on my heels to take a more careful look around. I had no reason to doubt Hawk that I was in his house. As was often the case with people coming into money very fast, everything I saw in the foyer was bought for its boast value. There was not much personal taste involved, nothing reflective of a specific personality.

At the sides of the foyer where each staircase landed were doors leading to other rooms. The one closest to me was dark and uninviting. A soft light gave me a dimmed glimpse into the room opposite and farther from me. Part of the inside wall I could see was covered in paintings, a few of which I recognised as masterpieces. Even though out of my line of sight, I was sure the wooden floors of that room were covered in more than one Persian carpet. Only the best for new money.

My eyes followed my inane line of thought to the expensive wooden flooring. I wasn't ready for what I saw in the doorway. The dreaded blackness rushed into my vision powerfully enough that it took more than a few minutes of

Mozart to fight it back. The moment I felt I could handle what I had seen, I scrambled on my hands and knees to the familiar-looking legs stretched out on the floor of the other room. I didn't attempt to stand, knowing my muscles would not carry me fast enough.

I reached the room and had to force myself to enter, to confirm whether it was Colin lying in that room. As I crawled closer, I recognised his strong hands first. Artist hands, but calloused from not living a soft life. I liked that about him. His upper body was lying on a dark blue Persian carpet, clashing with the light green dress shirt he wore. There was a lot of blood on his shirt. Distress tightened my throat, making breathing difficult. I stopped next to him, a soft moan escaping from my dry lips.

"Colin?" Only the third time I called his name did I manage to make a sound. It was scratchy and filled with fear. I touched his hand and immediately dropped it, glared at it. His hand was cold. As if there had been no blood flowing to his hand to warm it up. Was the blood on his shirt his? The thought of not having Colin in my life filled me with such deep dismay, I forgot about all other dislikes.

With shaky fingers I unbuttoned his shirt to look for injuries. Halfway down I realised I should first check his pulse, his breathing. There was complete disarray in my thinking. Gone was my normal systematic, analytical and distant observation and processing of a situation. I was filled with emotions so strong, they paralysed my thinking and caused me to act ineffectually.

"Come on, Genevieve." I made my voice strong and hard. "Think."

I took a few focussed breaths and gently touched the side of Colin's neck. The common carotid artery was the one most easily allowing us to feel a heartbeat. I held my fingers against Colin's shaved skin, chanting, "Come on, come on, come on."

I couldn't feel anything. I took another few breaths and pressed my fingers a little harder against his throat. He was lying deadly still, his strong features unmoving. The first flutter I dismissed as my imagination and hopefulness. I held my position and waited for another five weak, but steady heartbeats before I allowed relief to overwhelm me.

Tears streamed down my face as I continued unbuttoning his shirt. I found no injuries. Whose blood was staining his shirt? And why wasn't he waking up? I rubbed his sternum hard with my knuckles. "Colin, wake up. Please. Come on. Wake up."

Distress, but mostly fear heightened the pitch of my voice. Combined with the tears, I sounded like a stranger to myself. Colin didn't respond to any of my attempts to wake him. With every minute I was moving closer to the dark depths of panic. I continued begging Colin to wake up, but to no avail. Not even when I uncharacteristically raised my voice and punched him on his thigh did he react.

"Oh God, oh God. I have to do something." A phone. I needed to phone Manny. He would help. I frantically looked around the room for a phone, but could see none. Then I remembered the annoying pinging and vibrating from Hawk's trousers. I didn't want to go back into the foyer. I didn't want to see all that blood again. But there was no phone in this room, on me or on Colin. Our pockets were empty and no matter how hard I looked, there wasn't a phone in this room.

I didn't want Colin to die because of my unwillingness to look at blood. I touched his face while taking a few deep breaths. "I'll be back. I'm just going to get a phone."

I tried to stand up, but my legs still didn't want to carry my weight. Not wanting to waste any more time, I crawled back into the foyer and to Hawk's dead body. I forced myself to only focus on the pocket of his trousers where the pinging had come from. As fast as I could and without unnecessary touching, I removed Hawk's smartphone. Gripping it tightly, I made my way back to Colin.

"I got it." Speaking to Colin was unproductive. He was still non-responsive. I was scared enough to admit that the reassurance was for me. "I'm going to phone Manny."

He would be furious with me, but he would help. And his was the only number I could recall at the moment. I swiped the touch screen only to smear blood all over it. A high-pitched whine pushed past my teeth. There was still blood on my hand. I wiped my hand furiously on my trousers and did the same with the phone. To my relief, no password was required when I swiped the screen again. Within three seconds the phone was ringing. I held it to my ear and looked at the wall across from me.

"Who the hell is phoning me at two in the bleeding morning?" Manny's sleepy, but agitated voice caused tears to fill my eyes. I focussed on one of the paintings to calm myself, but it had the complete opposite effect. How many more times was I going to see something that rendered me paralysed with trepidation? Manny continued to rudely insist on knowing who had the audacity to phone him in the middle of the night. All I could do was try to prevent a shutdown while staring at Braque's Harbour in Normandy hanging on Hawk's wall.

"Help." I still stared at the painting, irrationally wondering if it was following me. "Help."

"Who's this? Speak up, I can't hear you."

I cleared my throat and looked away from the painting. "Colin won't wake up."

"Doc?" Manny's voice was fully alert. "Doc, is that you?"

"The painting is here." I was trying to pull myself together, but found it very hard. Looking at the painting, I felt myself being drawn into its mystery. I looked down and debilitating fear rushed through me as I looked at Colin's prone body.

"Genevieve!"

In the year that I'd known Manny, he had called me by my given name no more than five times. It was this that brought me to a higher level of consciousness.

"It's me." My voice was trembling and soft, but audible. "I don't know where we are. Hawk is dead and Colin won't wake up. Manny, I don't want him to die."

"No one's going to die today, missy." The sounds of movement came through the phone as if he was running. "Is Frey still breathing?"

"Yes, but he won't wake up." I was repeating myself.

"Doc, stay on the line. I'll come get you." Scratching noises came through the phone, followed by Manny's muted voice. He must have pushed the phone against his chest, but I could hear him shouting at someone. When he called the person 'criminal' a second time, I knew he was bringing Vinnie. I exhaled loudly in relief.

"Doc, is there anyone else there?"

"I don't think so. It's just me." My voice broke. "And Colin. Hawk is dead."

"What the fuck are you doing with Hawk?" There was a lot of noise, shouting and a car racing coming through the phone. It was interrupted by beeping. "Bloody hell, my battery is going. Doc?"

"I'm still here."

"Doc, I need to know where I'm driving. Somewhere in Strasbourg, in France, to the airport? Where are you?"

"I told you I don't know." I felt smothered by the panic bearing down on me. There was no greater torture for me than the lack of information and knowledge. "Hawk said we're in his house."

"But you said he's dead."

"He said that before he died."

There was another muted conversation, cut off when Manny's phone disconnected the call. For a few minutes I hadn't felt utterly alone. Without the telephonic connection I felt isolated and powerless. It was the latter combined with knowing nothing of my location or how we had arrived here that pushed me even closer to the edge. I put the phone on the carpet, next to Colin's head.

"Manny and Vinnie are coming." I awkwardly touched his cheek with my fingertips. He was comfortable with physical affection, whereas I didn't know how to do this naturally. My movements were stilted and uncoordinated. "I don't want you to die. Please don't die."

Colin had been the one pursuing a romantic relationship with me. Before him, I'd had a few short-term affairs, connections I would not even qualify as a relationship. It had merely been for mutual sexual satisfaction. Francine called that 'fuck buddies'. I didn't like the term.

The man lying in front of me did not fit into that category. He had shown me more patience, understanding and tolerance than anyone before. In the last six months, Colin had cajoled laughter out of me. I was not known for possessing a cheerful disposition. He had brought a lightness into my life which, I realised sitting here, I didn't want to be without. I might have told him earlier that he should end our relationship if ever he got tired of me, but looking at him lying in front of me, I wanted to retract my words.

"I don't want you to end it. Don't give up on me." I put my one palm flat on his chest, the other against his cheek. My voice was not my own. To my ears it sounded thick with unspoken emotions. "Don't leave me. I don't want to go back to living the way I did before you broke into my flat. Please don't go."

I picked up the phone and redialled Manny's number. It went to voicemail. I trusted him to keep his word and find us, but I needed reassurance. This was the first time in my life that I had considered someone else's safety and life before my own. I couldn't allow myself to give in to the tempting blackness and leave Colin without any defence. Not knowing how else to stay calm, I started going through all the different aspects of this case. Out loud. I talked to Colin as if he was aware of every word I said. The irrationality of it was not lost on me, but it seemed the only prevention for my pending panic attack.

I didn't know how long it took me to discuss the tattoo on my arm. I described the website in every detail I recalled. The angle of the photos, the order of the slideshow and the people with me when the photos had been taken. I described the colours of the website and the strangely ornate frames used around each photo. As I spoke, loose bits of information congealed into something more substantial, but my thinking brain was still too occupied with everything that surrounded me to allow it to filter through.

Sounds outside stalled my monologue. Someone was at the front door. If it were the Printer, I didn't want to give away that I had survived. Until this moment I hadn't given any thought to the possibility that he might return. If the Printer was indeed a man. I grabbed Colin's cold hand in both of mine and fixed my eyes on the door. I didn't have a view of the front door, and was overcome with the deep discomfort of not knowing who was going to come through that door.

Scratching noises at the door indicated the door was being opened by a key or lockpick. I hoped it was Vinnie and his expert lockpicking skills. It felt like an eternity before the door opened to allow the night in. The insects sounded closer. I would've preferred to focus on their night sounds, but careful footsteps were coming my way.

I held my breath and huddled closer to Colin. Once I'd read a story about a man who had wrapped his waterproof watch in a handkerchief to put it in his jacket pocket as his little sailboat was sinking. Huddling close to Colin held the same lack of logic, yet it made me feel better. Safer. A few whispered words reached me, but were too quiet to identify the speakers.

The barrel of a hefty handgun came into view, followed by Vinnie's large frame. Relief flooded through my body, making my muscles weaker than they still were. I didn't stop the involuntary cry of recognition and collapsed onto Colin's chest.

"Jen-girl! They're here, I have them!" Vinnie shouted over his shoulder as he took two large steps to reach us. "Are you okay? What the fuck happened? Is Colin okay?"

Manny came running into the room, concern all over his features. As if through water, I heard them asking me one question after the other. Vinnie tried to lift me away from Colin, but I clung to him, unwilling to move from his chest. Now that these two men who would do anything to keep me safe were here, I could let go. I wrapped my arms around Colin and allowed the blackness to take me away from this horrid place. Manny and Vinnie would take care of everything. They would make sure Colin didn't die.

Chapter ELEVEN

It was the vibration of Colin's voice against my back that brought me back. My breath caught as I opened my eyes and saw the same room Colin had been lying in. The early morning sun was shining through the large window. I was on the sofa, hugging my knees tightly to my chest, my back warm against Colin's chest. He was sitting at an angle, both arms around me, holding me to him. Any other person and it would have sent me into a shutdown or possibly a meltdown. Being surrounded by Colin made me feel safe.

"Jenny?" He stretched his neck to look around at me. I turned my head, an unpleasant warmth colouring my cheeks. I didn't like being so vulnerable. "How're you feeling?"

I patted his arm stiffly and moved away to sit next to him. I couldn't get myself to move too far away from him. I studied him until I was satisfied with what I saw. "You didn't wake up."

"I'm awake now."

"He took his sweet time too." Vinnie was sitting on an antique chair. His lounging pose and large body looked incongruous with the fine design and thin legs of the early nineteenth-century chair. He had a cut above his eyebrow and a lot of bruising on one side of his face, the discolouration indicating it was recent. It had to be from his physical altercation with Colin, yet there was no animosity between them at the moment. For that I was grateful. His smile was genuine and relieved. "Hey, Jen-girl."

"Hey." I had learned to greet like this, but it felt improper. I turned back to Colin. "Are you well now?"

"I have one hell of a hangover, but I've survived worse."

I knew this to be true. Soon after our first case a year ago, Kubanov had lured Colin to Russia. There he had captured Colin and had tortured him for days until Vinnie had found and rescued him. It had taken Colin months to recover. He still had the deep, ugly scars on one leg as a reminder.

"How long have I been out?"

"Three hours," Vinnie said before Colin inhaled to speak. His *corrugator procerus* muscle contracted to form a deep frown. "You scared the living shit out of me, Jen-girl."

"You've seen me like this before, Vinnie." Much to my chagrin. "Why did it scare you?"

"No, not that. Being woken up by the old man in the middle of the night and hearing him panic." He lowered his head and looked at me from under his eyebrows. "That is what scared me. I seriously don't know how I got dressed and downstairs so fast, or how he got to the apartment that fast, but we were driving here before I was awake."

I doubted that. Vinnie had the ability to go from a deep sleep to fully alert in a heartbeat.

"How did you find us?" I wanted to apologise, because I was sure Colin had asked all these questions before, but I knew Vinnie didn't mind telling the same story numerous times. His repetitive anecdotes bored me at times.

"Manny got Francine to track the phone you used to call him. Stupid arsehole didn't charge his phone and we lost contact. By the time she came through with the location, we were already on our way here. When he said that you told him you guys were in Hawk's house, I was sure you were here."

"You've been here before?"

"Nope." A calculating smile lifted one corner of his mouth. "I just like to know everything I can about the people who might be a threat to me."

Colin's breathing changed. More audible, harder. He was getting angry again.

"Dude, I don't know how many more times I have to apologise. I didn't think he would be a threat to Jen-girl."

"Clearly you didn't think."

"Please don't argue now." I felt raw from all the emotions. "Vinnie lost somebody he cared for."

"Who?"

I looked at Vinnie. "He might not have been a good person, but you shared some kind of bond."

"Yeah, some kind of bond is how I would describe it, Jen-girl. We've known each other a very long time and we have helped each other out of a few scrapes. In this line of work, I knew he was going to meet his end soon." There was more acceptance on Vinnie's face than sadness. "It's better this way."

We sat quietly for a few seconds, reflecting.

"Why's that there?" I pointed at the Braque painting leaning against the legs of Vinnie's chair.

"You wouldn't let go of Colin, so I had to bring it to him."

"What do you mean?"

Colin put his hand on my clutched fists. "Apparently you wouldn't allow anyone to move you, so the medics had to work around you to get to me. When I came to, you still wouldn't let go, so I moved us to the sofa to be more comfortable."

"You've been sitting like this for three hours?" I felt the heat crawl into my cheeks again. It was hard to not drop my head and round my shoulders in defeated shame.

"The paramedics thought it was sweet." Colin squeezed my fists.

I closed my eyes and groaned. The embarrassment was uncomfortable and I was desperate to change the topic. I straightened and looked at the painting. "Is it real? Is this the original painting that was stolen from the McCarthy house?"

"I'm pretty sure it is the original Braque, yes. The angular and shaded brushstrokes in this painting are unique to Braque. I was very close in reproducing this. The artists who did the other forgeries didn't fare all that well. The more I look at this, the more sure I am it is the original."

"How did it get from Kathleen McCarthy's house to Hawk's? What is his connection to her?"

Noises from the foyer caught my attention. A familiar voice reached me before Manny walked into the room. He looked at me, frowned and walked faster.

"You here, missy?"

I looked at him, not understanding his question. I was sitting right in front of him.

"Jenny, he wants to know if you're awake."

"Oh." I frowned at Manny. "Why didn't you say that? Asking me if I am here is redundant."

"You're back, all right." Manny swung around and pointed his finger at Vinnie. "And you. I told you to call me the moment she came to. What part of that sentence didn't you understand, criminal?"

"The part where you ordered me around like one of your mindless underlings." Vinnie's top lip curled, adding to his belligerence. "And she just joined us a few minutes ago. Keep your hair on, old man."

"You people…" Manny's nostrils flared, his body tense. "Missy, would you care to tell me how the bleeding hell you came to be in Hawk's house?"

"I don't know." I watched the *supratrochlear* artery on Manny's forehead become more pronounced. The redness in his face was not from embarrassment like mine. His anger was escalating. I started speaking very fast. "What I mean is that I really don't know how we got here. The last place I remembered being was in my viewing room."

"Do you remember leaving the office?" Vinnie asked. He had his smartphone in his hand. When I answered in the negative he started tapping on the screen. "I'm asking Francine to check all the video from the office last night. Maybe she will find out what happened to you guys."

"It would be a relief to know how we left. One moment I was in the viewing room, the next thing I remember is waking up next to Hawk." I recalled my last thoughts. "Our coffee was drugged."

"What coffee?" Colin and Manny asked at the same time.

I turned to Colin. "Don't you remember?"

"Frey here doesn't remember anything." Suspicion was clear in Manny's voice. I didn't need to see his body language.

"You really don't remember?" I asked, ignoring Manny.

"The last thing I recall is our discussion."

"Which one?" We'd had many during the day. Had he taken a higher dosage of the drug that it had impaired his memory much more than mine?

"The one where you told me to break up with you," Colin said fast, in a low voice.

"I don't want you to do that." I was shaking my head. "At the time I said it, I believed it to be true. I don't want that anymore."

"Frey! Missy!" Manny's frustrated yell stopped even the muted conversations in the other rooms. "What fucking coffee?"

"The coffee Colin made for us." All eyes were on me. "As usual he drank his very fast. I took a few sips, maybe drinking one third of my mug. By the time I realised the feeling I had wasn't fatigue, but the effects of a drug, Colin was already unconscious."

"You did this?" Even though Manny was furious, his question didn't convey any accusation.

"Fuck you, Millard."

"Thought so." Manny nodded. "Then who put the drug in your coffee? How did they get into the office? Oh hellfire, wait."

Nobody spoke while Manny pulled a cell phone from his coat pocket. I bit the inside of my lip to prevent myself from asking him if that one was charged in case he went into an uncontrolled rage. We listened to two conversations. The first was a quick one with Phillip, asking him to secure the offices and not allow anyone in until Manny sent people to go through Rousseau & Rousseau, looking for the drugged coffee. That needed another short explanation and assurance that I was fine. He nodded once and agreed with Phillip that all evidence might already have been removed, but he wanted to make sure.

The next call was longer and more detailed as he gave orders on what to look for and where. It afforded me time to take notice of the people moving around the other parts of the house.

"Are these people police?" I nodded towards the entrance.

Vinnie glanced at the door, his lip curling. "Crime scene investigators. They've already taken Hawk's body to the morgue for an autopsy. Now they're crawling around the house, looking in every nook and cranny. The old man says they're the best."

"They are." Manny put the phone back in his coat pocket. "If Hawk had anything in this house implicating him in some crime, they will find it."

"Why don't you just go to his warehouse?" I asked. "I'm sure you will find lots there to connect him and possibly other people to crimes."

"What warehouse?" Manny's glare carried a lot of anger.

I took a moment before I answered. First I studied Manny's body language, then Vinnie's.

"You didn't tell him," I said to Vinnie. "Why not?"

Vinnie only lifted one shoulder again. His attempt at nonchalance didn't convince me. His other nonverbal cues revealed his true motivation for withholding the truth. Loyalty towards me. He was protecting me from Manny.

"He has to know." I hoped Vinnie wouldn't expect me to continue the deception. Again he lifted his shoulder.

"Of course I bloody well have to know." Manny took a step closer to me. "What warehouse, missy?"

I had known telling Manny wasn't going to be easy. But facing him while he towered over me was more disconcerting than I had anticipated. I turned my hands over and held onto Colin's hand.

"I went with Vinnie to Hawk's warehouse… yesterday morning." My grip on Colin's hand tightened as Manny's hands fisted at his sides, his lips pulled back to bare his teeth, and his nostrils flared. He stormed away, walked back, glared at me and walked away again. He repeated this a few times, even shaking a fist at Vinnie once.

At last he stopped in front of me, his body tense. "Talk. And tell me bloody everything."

As fast as I could, I told him everything. He listened quietly, his anger visibly increasing. When I finished, he turned to Vinnie, disgust curling his upper lip. "Bloody fucking criminal. You took her into the lion's den and look what it got you. This is your fault, you realise that, right?"

"Leave him alone, Manny." I couldn't bear to see the self-blame in Vinnie's eyes.

"No, he's right, Jen-girl." Vinnie sat up. "I fucked up. I don't know how I'll make this up to you, but I will. I swear I will."

"I could've said no." And he would not have been able to sway me.

"Is that where the two of you got your latest war badges?" Manny's nod towards the bruising on Vinnie's face helped me understand his expression. Neither Vinnie nor Colin answered, but their body language was becoming more hostile.

"Regret and accusations are not productive," I said. "Why don't we work with what we have now? Like a recording of that whole event."

"What? You recorded the whole time you were there? Do you have a bleeding death wish?" Manny's eyebrows rose high on his forehead. He turned his anger on Colin. "And where were you while your girlfriend was playing superspy, Frey?"

"He didn't know," I said quickly. "Stop with all the accusations, Manny. Vinnie and I apologised to Colin. Now I'm apologising to you. I planned to tell you, but I should've phoned you before I went."

"You shouldn't have gone at all, missy."

"But I did and now we have more than forty-five minutes' worth of video footage to analyse. You also have an entire warehouse to go through and find some more clues to help us solve this."

Manny stared at me, the *orbicularis oris* muscle compressed his mouth into an angry line, his eyes clear and boring into mine. He was communicating with the sole use of nonverbal cues. It was very effective. I swallowed.

"Manny, I give you my word that I will not do something like this again."

"You put your life in danger, missy." He nodded to Colin without taking his eyes off me. "And Frey's life."

Cold dread filled me.

"Enough, Millard." Colin's hand tightened on mine. "Let's move past this."

"No. Not this time, Frey. You people play fast and loose with rules. You don't respect team work and do just what the hell ever you want. If you don't start working according to some regulations, I will disband this merry group of ours and actively investigate you. All of you. Don't think for one minute that I will not lock you up. And that includes you, missy." Manny had been angry, scathing and even insulting, but seldom grim.

"I already gave you my word," I said. "You need to phone more of your people now, and go to Hawk's warehouse."

Manny didn't follow my lead and changed the topic. "Missy, I will hold you responsible for any future illegal acts of the three criminals we're working with. It's time you people start acting more like a team working directly for the president."

He walked out of the room and returned a few seconds later.

"You will allow the medics to do whatever tests they need to do, missy. None of your nonsense. We need to know what they pumped into your system and how much of it. Got it?" He waited for me to nod, then called towards the door for someone to enter. "Hug Frey or sing a Mozart ditty. We need your blood. I'm going to get a team over to Hawk's warehouse. To do something legally for a change."

He ordered Vinnie to go with him. It was obvious that everyone understood the severity of Manny's ire. And the justification thereof. Vinnie didn't argue with him, just quietly got up and followed Manny out the room. A medical professional approached me like one would a wild animal.

"Oh, for goodness' sake." I held out my one arm, away from me. "Just do this. I'm not going to attack you. Make it quick."

I caught the surprise and relief on the medic's face, but I turned away from him to face Colin. I didn't need to see someone drawing my blood. This was different than sitting in the kitchen of Colin's cottage, the amiable Ben joking while taking blood samples. This time I was concerned about more than just being drugged, abducted and not having yet solved this case.

"Did I do irreparable damage?" My voice was quiet and shaky.

"Oh, Jenny. You have much to learn." Colin put his hand on my cheek. "I was—still am—furious with you and Vinnie. But being angry doesn't mean that I want to leave you. It only means that I'm supremely pissed off. I can't believe I'm saying this, but Millard is right. Most definitely regarding your and Vinnie's visit to Hawk's warehouse. I'm angry because it terrifies me to think of all the things that could've gone wrong."

His hand dropped to his lap, the anger returning to his features.

"How can I make your anger go away?" My parents used to leave me with caretakers for weeks when I had done things to induce their anger. At university, so-called friends had completely cut off contact when I had offended them. It had happened often. I didn't know what to do.

"Give me time." He shook his head. "No, first give me

your word that you will tell me everything from now on. Every decision you—"

"That's impossible. You would have to reside in my cerebral cortex for that."

The medic behind me snorted, but quickly grew quiet at Colin's stern look.

"Yes, of course." Colin's eyes went up and to the right. "Let me say this another way. You are smart enough to know which decisions you should include me in."

"That is true."

"I want your word that you would talk to me."

"Whenever it is possible, I will do this."

"Done." The medic's soft announcement interrupted us. "Thanks, Ms Lenard."

"Doctor Lenard to you, laddie." Manny stepped back into the room, followed by Vinnie. Their body language didn't reveal any animosity. Manny appeared less agitated, which was interesting. Usually spending any amount of time with Vinnie ended moments before a physical altercation. Both men sat down, Vinnie in his previous chair, Manny in a matching chair.

"Okay, Doc. Hopefully you won't throw many more surprises at me, and we can actually finish one topic. Tell me why you think your coffee was drugged."

"It's like I told you before. Colin made us coffee. After he drank it so quickly, he lost consciousness before me. I think I regained consciousness sooner because I didn't ingest the same quantity of the drug as he did."

"And you really don't remember making the coffee, dude?" Vinnie asked.

"No. If they used the same drug, the fact that I took more might be why my memory is affected differently than Jenny's."

"Hmm." Manny tapped his bottom lip with his index finger. "You two are the only ones in the office drinking that coffee. Everyone else drinks coffee from those little capsules. You also use the same cups all the time."

"Mugs," I said. "They are ceramic mugs, not cups."

"Same thing, Doc. Same thing. So, who did you piss off in the office so badly that they would want to hand you over to Kubanov?"

"I don't interact with people at Rousseau & Rousseau." Most people actively avoided me. When the others had joined and we had had the team room made, I had become even more distant from the rest of the employees.

"Well, the crime scene people should be there now bagging the coffee. We'll have to interview the staff." Manny shifted in the antique chair. "Tell me everything from the moment you woke up."

I did. Manny had asked me to tell him everything, so I even included the sounds of the insects I had heard. Manny wasn't interested in that part. It was Hawk's last words that caught his attention.

"Printer? What bloody printer?"

"I asked him, but he didn't say."

"Could it be a thing and not a person?" Vinnie straightened in the chair. "One of those printers he imports and that sits in his warehouse?"

"How can a printer be dangerous?" Colin shook his head. "Apart from the pen being mightier than the sword, I can't see how a printing machine could have drugged and kidnapped us. And killed Hawk."

"And what about the big blow part?" I asked. "Does this imply an explosion?"

"Blow is the street name for cocaine." Manny looked at Vinnie. "Did Hawk deal drugs as well?"

"No, he strictly dealt in arms only. He believed in keeping things simple. Drugs were too messy, he said. Too many people being killed."

"With the guns he supplied." Disgust was evident in Manny's tone and expression. "How could you be associated with someone like that?"

"Above your pay grade, Millard," Colin said. He was defending Vinnie, despite his anger. "This is need-to-know basis only. If you want to know, take it up with the bosses at Interpol. Or with the president."

Manny studied Colin long enough for me to read both. Colin's nonverbal cues were closed, not revealing anything. At least not to the untrained eye. I noticed that he was uncomfortable with having revealed what he had.

Those few sentences implied that Colin had been doing much more for Interpol than merely reappropriating art which had been acquired in wartime or through other nefarious means. It also revealed that Vinnie had been assisting him with the knowledge of Interpol, possibly even on their payroll. Manny's micro-expressions told me that he had come to the same conclusions as I had. I also noticed respect which was quickly tempered. For some time I had suspected Manny enjoyed disliking Colin and Vinnie.

"If you say so, Frey. We still don't know anything. Bloody hellfire, this is frustrating." Manny rubbed his hands hard over his face. "A dead arms dealer, my two best people drugged and taken to his house, a printer and a big blow. Frey being set up, Doc playing Mata Hari and guns that kill people, but can't be traced."

"Can you find Monique?" I asked. "I gave Hawk my word that I would make sure she's well."

"Of course you are going to keep your promise to a dead

criminal." Manny made a disbelieving sound. "You're one in a million, Doc."

"You didn't answer my question."

"Yes, Doc. I'll find her for you. She might be able to give us some helpful information about her daddy dearest."

"I don't think so." Vinnie's lips pursed. "Hawk kept her pretty far away from his life."

Manny frowned when Vinnie's phone rang loudly.

"It's Francine." Vinnie tapped on the phone's screen and held the phone towards us. "Yo, sexy. You're on speakerphone, so hold your sex talk for later."

"Hey, Vin. Is Manny there?"

"I'm here, supermodel."

"Ooh, then I can do the sex talk." Her voice was husky and sensual.

A blush spread just above Manny's collar. "Watch out, little girl. I'm not in the mood for wasting time. Why did you phone?"

"He's being all alpha. Sexy." She laughed softly. "Well, this supermodel found out how Genevieve and Colin were taken from the office. I'm here now and have been going through the CCTV recordings."

"How were we taken?" I asked, leaning towards the phone.

"If Manny remembered to charge his phone and always carry his tablet with him, I would have sent you the footage. Now you'll just have to watch it when you get here. It didn't take me long to find the culprit. Of course, he was very smart and made sure to not have his profile caught on camera."

"It's someone from Rousseau & Rousseau," I said. "Or someone who received this information from an employee. Are you sure it is a man?"

"I'm no expert in body language, girlfriend, but that man

was walking like a man. You'll have to see for yourself, but I know my men. He was dressed as one of the cleaning crew, pushing one of those cleaning trolleys with all their cleaning stuff in little compartments inside."

"I was put in a cleaning trolley?" I needed to shower.

"Isn't this just too cliché for words?" Francine sounded offended. "They could've at least been more original than that."

"Clearly they were very effective." I really wanted a hot shower. "Why be more original?"

"Hmph. Anyway, I have the footage of this guy going into the team room with his trolley. Seven minutes and forty seconds later, he left. He pushed the trolley to the elevator doors and from there went to the basement."

"Where there is a back entrance with CCTV," Vinnie said. I hadn't known there was that much surveillance around the office. These had to be the new cameras they had set up after our first abduction.

"Yeah, but they disabled it," Francine said. "I only have him in the office. He came back and did the same thing a second time. He didn't even pretend to clean."

"What time was that?" I remembered Colin bringing our coffee at around quarter to six.

"He entered the first time at…" There was silence for a few seconds. "Twenty-seven minutes past six."

"The office is usually empty after six," Vinnie said. "Most people leave at five."

"We drank our coffee approximately forty-five minutes before being taken," I said. "Someone must've told them we were drugged. Did you see anyone else enter the team room or the viewing room before or after that?"

"Nobody. The last person in or out before the cleaning guy was Colin. I have him walking out the room and returning with two mugs. Coffee, right?"

I frowned. "Really? Nobody after Colin, not even after we were taken out?"

"Sorry, girlfriend. Nobody in or out."

"Are you sure the footage wasn't tampered with?" Manny asked.

"Of course I checked for that and no, it is the raw footage."

Phillip joined Francine and the conversation. I was not surprised that he was at the office, controlling everything. It took another seven minutes to convince him that I was unharmed, as was Colin. Another ten minutes were spent going over the events and Hawk's last words. Francine posed a hypothesis that Hawk was importing cocaine in the printer cartridges. There was a moment of shocked silence. For a change her theory didn't include government conspiracies or aliens, or both.

I soon got bored with their speculations and insisted on leaving. I wanted to shower and go to the office. Verbalising this thought resulted in a loud and negative response. I was ordered by Manny and Phillip to take the day off to recover from being drugged. Everyone else agreed. Manny's argument won me over. His team was still going through the office looking for evidence and I would not want to be there to experience that. I was tired enough to capitulate after only a few attempts at resistance.

But I was not comfortable with losing time solving this case. If Kubanov was staying true to character, we were working against time. He would have an end goal and that goal would have a date and a time.

Chapter TWELVE

"Who's your daddy now?" Vinnie slammed both hands on my dining room table. I had learned that this phrase was metaphorical, so I didn't answer him. I had made that mistake only once.

"Another one down." Francine rolled her head to stretch her neck muscles. We had been sitting around the table for more than five hours working on the twenty-seven cases Manny had found. We had just solved a seventh case.

After returning from Hawk's house, I'd had a long, hot shower. When I walked out of my bedroom, Vinnie had prepared breakfast, Colin and Francine already seated at the table. They had known I was not going to spend the day doing nothing. Francine had brought my work laptop from the office for us to look into the cases after breakfast.

"I kinda feel like a traitor." Vinnie sat back in his chair, disgust in every nonverbal cue. "I can't believe I'm turning into a Mountie."

Francine snorted. "More like a Bronx cop. You're not polite enough to be a Mountie."

"Not all Canadians are polite." Lecturing at a local university a few years ago, I had met a Canadian anthropologist who had put paid to any preconceived notions I'd had about Canadian stereotypes. "In the east they are less polite than in the west."

"It will be a long walk before you turn into a copper, Vin." Colin was sitting next to me, making notes as we went along.

He was using his own notebook and pencils, my notepad safely in front of me and three pens neatly arranged next to it.

"We still have another eleven cases to go through," I said. "Maybe we will solve a few more to add to the seven we have."

"And maybe I should make dinner so we can refuel, Jen-girl." Vinnie stood up. "We've been at this for hours with only cookies for energy. It's time for my mama's pasta."

"I'll help." Francine got up, ignoring Vinnie's vehement rejection of her offer. I didn't understand the pleasure she gained from teasing him while he cooked. The sound of my doorbell stopped all jesting. Colin and Vinnie glanced at each other and walked to the door together.

The bruising on Colin's jaw and cheek was dark against his skin and he was still careful with his hand, but I knew he would not stand back if it came to our safety. Neither would Vinnie. The two of them appeared to have reached some truce. At the front door, Vinnie leaned forward to look through the peephole. His posture relaxed only marginally as he straightened and opened the door. "Howdy, old man."

Manny grunted something unintelligible and pushed past Vinnie's bulk into my apartment. He frowned at the computer and the notepads on my dining room table. "Are you still working, Doc? You've been sending me emails the whole bloody day."

"You're also working. Why shouldn't I work?"

He stopped next to me, narrowing his eyes. "Maybe because you were drugged and you should rest."

My jaw stiffened. "I'm not as weak as everyone thinks."

"Oh, hell." Manny rubbed his hand over his face. "That's not what I meant."

Colin sat down next to me. "That's not what any of us mean,

Jenny. We're just concerned about you. We're concerned about each other."

"What my man said." Vinnie stood next to Manny, glaring at him. "We got each other's backs."

Manny turned to face Vinnie head on. He was at least a head shorter than Vinnie, but no less of an alpha male. He lifted his chin. "What are you saying, criminal?"

Francine stepped closer. "You might be a handsome beast, but threatening all the time to throw us in jail is not winning you any brownie points. That and fighting every single idea we have. We need to know if we can count on you, Manny."

A combination of the tone of Francine's voice and her body language led me to believe she, Colin and Vinnie had been discussing this.

"Yes, Millard. Can we rely on you?" Colin asked softly. "You know you need us more than we need you."

Manny looked like he had just finished a long, tiring day. This was his normal look, the difference now being the dark circles under his eyes. At Colin's question, his posture changed, the irritability he normally used as a shield no longer evident. It made him look younger, stronger and more formidable. This was more pronounced as his back slightly straightened, his head lifted and his shoulders pulled back. He even looked bigger and stronger.

Manny made unflinching eye contact with Colin, undoubtedly knowing where Vinnie and Francine's loyalties were. If he convinced Colin, the others would follow.

"Ganging up on me, are you?" The lack of Manny's usual derision got everyone's attention. "I would still prefer it if you people kept the law. We have a certain leverage because of our direct orders from the president. But I will not allow for us at any point to overstep boundaries. All you have to do is watch the news to see what happens when governments and other institutions start to freely look into their citizens' private data."

"Well, thank God for whistleblowers." Francine sighed, a small smile lifting her red lips. "I would so totally do Snowden or Manning any day. They are heroes."

"Francine, not now." The look Vinnie gave Francine communicated more than just a warning.

"Why not now, Vin?" Francine asked. "Manny knows we can't do our jobs, this job the president wants us to do, without bending the rules a bit."

"I will not aid or abet any criminal action." Only a few times had I seen Manny this serious, this professional. "As long as you lot understand and respect that, I will have your back."

Colin stared at Manny for almost half a minute. He must have seen the same sincerity I had, because he nodded. "I still think you're an arsehole."

"And you're still a thief." Manny walked to his usual seat and sat down heavily. "But I want your word, all of you, that you will not do anything as stupid as this Hawk fiasco again. I can't have your back if you pull stunts like that. I also can't have your back when you do things I don't know about. You have strategies, you run them by me. We work as a team. That includes you, Doc. You are smart enough to see that the cases we handle are increasing in complexity and danger. I cannot have you put your life in danger like you did going to that warehouse. I need to know that you will inform me about any action you consider taking."

I inhaled.

"Any action pertaining to the case, missy." Manny scowled when I narrowed my eyes at his annoyed interjection. "You were going to ask if 'any' meant absolutely any action. I only need to know about the cases we work on, not your dinner plans with Frey."

"That I can agree to."

"Why are you here, Millard?"

"To see what you've been up to, of course." His glance towards the kitchen was telling. "Have you had dinner yet?"

The change on Vinnie's face was comical, even to me. I had not often observed such an incredulous expression on him. He grunted a few insults before turning to the kitchen. "Dinner will be ready in forty minutes."

"Enough time for you to tell me about the solved cases, Doc."

"I sent you the files of each case." With the name of each murderer.

"But no explanation. I want an explanation. I want details."

"Very well." It was arduous to organise my thoughts every time I had to explain myself to others. On a deep breath, I did just that and went into the detail of the first case we had solved. Soon I noticed Manny's nonverbal cues. I exhaled loudly through my nose. "If you didn't want the detail, why ask me about it?"

"Not that minute detail, Doctor Face-Reader. Give me an outline."

"You are contradicting yourself." Did he want detail or not?

"An outline, missy."

I took a moment to think this over. "These seven cases all have one common denominator. Cocaine."

Manny's chin dropped to his chest after a few seconds. He sighed heavily before looking up. "Doc, that outline is too broad. But it's a good start. Were all the victims users?"

"Actually, only one of them was. But the killers of the seven cases were all involved with cocaine at some point. The victims of these cases can be divided into three categories.

Victims of armed robberies which had turned violent, victims caught in some drug-ring dispute, or victims of domestic violence."

"Tell me more about the victims. An outline."

"Paul Daniel's brother killed him in a drug-induced rage and Alta Clout was a pharmacist killed by a man looking for money and drugs. There is no proof that Jim Roberts was involved in drug dealing, but his sister was and her rival killed him. The other cases are the same."

"How the hell did you guys solve seven cases in a few hours when the locals couldn't do it in weeks?"

"Objectivity," I said. "We looked at the facts with an untainted mindset, studied the evidence and added everything together to find the perpetrator."

Manny looked around the table, slowing when his eyes caught something in Francine's expression. I deeply hoped he was not going to ask about her discomfort. In most of the cases, she had ended up accessing information in an illegal manner. After the speech Manny had just given us, I didn't think he was going to take kindly to all the methods used solving these crimes. I relaxed when he rolled his eyes and looked at me. "Okay, Doc, tell me how this cocaine clue of yours is important."

"It is what can be inferred from it rather than the cocaine itself."

"Drugs and guns go hand in hand," Vinnie said from the kitchen. A mouthwatering aroma was drifting from the stove. "Where you find drugs, somewhere close you will find guns. And vice versa."

"Hawk?" Manny asked.

"As I said before, the guy didn't believe in mixing those two. He imported electronics and sold weapons. He did large-scale sales, so it would be no surprise that some of his guns landed in the hands of drug dealers or other small-time arms dealers. But he never dealt with those smaller guys. His market was the big clients."

"Like Third World crime lords." Manny sighed. "That bloody warehouse has given my guys quite a few surprises. Did you know about the basement?"

"No. There's a basement?" Vinnie shook his head. "I only ever visited him in his office."

"That room behind the cabinets?"

"Yup, that's the one Jen-girl also went into. It's on the video."

"Well, there is a basement that is much larger than the warehouse. It is keeping the crime scene guys busy."

"They're watching out for explosives, right?" Vinnie's contempt was not convincing. He was genuinely concerned.

"They're the best, arsehole. They know what they're doing. Already they've retrieved more than two hundred submachine guns and crates filled with handguns. I should have a full report this afternoon on what they've found."

"Would you like to hear more about my thoughts on the cocaine?" I almost smiled when Manny closed his eyes and breathed deeply.

"Hmm…" Manny tapped his index finger on his lips. He was being sarcastic, which meant he was angry. I didn't know why. "Let me guess. You want me to ask these killers you've found where they get their drugs from?"

"I already told you this two days ago. If we know who supplied them, we might find their arms supplier."

He looked at me, his lips compressed. "Any other requests, missy?"

"When you look into the cocaine, make sure to see if there is any connection to Tall Freddy."

"The Mafia guy who killed Frey's friend?" Manny stared at

the ceiling before he nodded. "Okay. I get it. Tall Freddy is involved in Susan Kadlec's murder, which was connected with a mystery weapon. He is also one of the biggest cocaine importers in Europe. Good thinking, Doc. Maybe you've got the right idea here after all."

"Did you look for solved cases like I asked?" I was tired and found it increasingly difficult to contain my impatience.

"I did and I was getting to it." Manny reached into his jacket pocket and brought out the small tablet Francine had given him. He tapped and swiped the screen a few times. "A few of my contacts got back to me. Right now I have four solved cases, the killers in prison as we speak. I will run the cases you have solved and check if any of those killers are also in prison. Bloody hell, I'm going to owe these locals a lot after this case. They will have to interview the guys and ask them about the weapons, cocaine and Tall Freddy, and get back to me. Soon."

I thought about his plan. It was sound. "I think it would be prudent to find out as much as possible about the cocaine, the product itself. From what I have read, law enforcement agencies can identify unique production batches of cocaine by its composition. If it is tested, we will know if those cases are connected despite the different countries."

"Why is the cocaine important?" Colin often asked the right questions.

"Blow. It really troubled me that with his last breath, Hawk decided to use that specific word. I looked for all its different uses on the internet and the only two relevant to this case are cocaine, which has been abundant in the murder cases, and of course explosives. The latter is a different topic and one that is more closely connected to Hawk than drugs."

"You're really on to something here, Doc. I'll get the locals to double-check the evidence in these cases as well to see if there is anything pointing to Hawk or to Tall Freddy." The tablet in Manny's hand pinged. He glared at it while stabbing at the screen. "Oh, you'll be pleased with this, Frey."

"When you say it like that, I don't know what to think," Colin said.

"I just got an email with the preliminary reports from the McCarthy crime scene. They will do more tests, but so far it's been determined that it was your DNA under the butler's fingernails. But that was the only place they found your DNA."

"Wait." Colin's tone held a warning. "Just how is it that they have my DNA to compare anything to? And how did you get those results so quickly? Doesn't it take weeks or months to get a full report on someone's DNA?"

"That is where we benefit from working directly under the president." Manny's smile was insincere. "I ask, they do. That is the orders they have."

"My DNA?"

"I took your coffee mug when we just started working together. But don't worry, Frey. It's registered under William Strode."

"One of my aliases?" Colin gave a reluctant laugh. "I'll have to give this one to you, Millard."

I knew that this was the closest Colin was going to come to thanking Manny for protecting his identity. Manny seemed to also know this. He just nodded. "They also found DNA not belonging to any of the family members, the butler or to you. Since they don't have anything to compare it to, it will take a bit longer to analyse, or whatever science magic they do with it. Oh, and there was a hair found on the McCarthy forgery they are also testing."

"Does this mean Colin is cleared of that murder?" I asked.

"No. It means that Scotland Yard is looking very hard for

William Strode in connection to a homicide. Doc, this is one case you might also want to have a look at to see if you can solve this. It would be the easiest to get your boyfriend cleared if we had the real killer."

I nodded, not knowing where I would start with that murder case. I got lost in my head for a few minutes considering my options. An aromatic plate of pasta placed in front of me brought me back to the table. Dinner was being served. A few minutes later, everyone was served and we were eating Vinnie's delicious pasta, accompanied by sparkling water. After all the drugs in our system, it was agreed that we would be cautious with our beverages for the next few days.

The conversation returned to the protection of privacy and governments spying on private citizens. When Manny and Francine raised their voices, I went back into my head and assessed all the evidence we had so far. As soon as we finished dinner, I was going to get back to working. The next case I was going to look at would be the McCarthy butler.

"Doc!"

I looked up to see Manny standing, his feet pointed to the door. "You're leaving."

"I have to organise interrogations for all these killers. And I have to check on my teams at the warehouse and Hawk's house." He lowered his head and gave me a serious look. "Go to bed early. We can take this up again in the morning. We'll have a team meeting at eight."

I got up and walked with him to the door. "You look uncommonly tired. You should take your own advice."

"As soon as I can, Doc. As soon as I can." He took a deep breath and left with a tired half smile. It had been a long day for him and I was responsible. We all were. Still holding the front door open, I made the decision to try harder at not being the cause of Manny's stress and fatigue. I was going to pay more attention to including him, and also encouraging the others to treat him with more respect.

"We're also off, Jen-girl." Vinnie stopped in the doorway. "The old man gave some good advice. Go to bed early. We can work on this again tomorrow."

"I agree." Francine walked to us, carrying her computer bag. "I'm going to soak in a hot bubble bath now. I can't remember the last time I went to bed before midnight. Today I'm going to do just that."

"Okay. I'll see you in the office tomorrow morning." I watched them leave and was about to close the door when Colin stopped me.

"I'm also going home."

Disappointment created the feeling of my heart dropping a few centimetres in my chest. "Why?"

He pointed at his face. "I have a killer headache and I don't know if it is from Vinnie's steel fists or from the drugs. I just need to lie down and hopefully sleep for eight hours."

I looked at him, searching for any sign of underlying motivation for him leaving me. He must have seen something on my face, a regretful smile pulling at his lips, but not reaching his eyes.

He moved closer and put his uninjured hand on my cheek. "I'm tired, Jenny. That's all. Nothing more, nothing less."

"Okay." My voice was an emotional whisper. I hated it.

He moved his hand to the back of my neck and pulled me closer for a passionate kiss. I really wanted him to stay, but didn't want to cause him any discomfort. I trusted him enough to take his words at face value.

Only when I closed the door after him a few minutes later did I realise it had been days since he had asked to break through the wall of our apartments. My heart dropped even lower in my chest.

I locked all the locks to my front door, straightened my spine and walked to my bathroom. Cleaning the shower with a toothbrush was what I needed right now to kill the time until I went to bed. Hopefully it would take my mind off Colin and clear it for tomorrow. I needed to put an end to this case. To put an end to Kubanov.

Chapter THIRTEEN

I looked up from my notes on the round table when Phillip entered the team room, followed by Angelique. She was carrying a tray with coffee and croissants. I was too relieved at having Phillip in the room to be concerned about the older woman's nervous body language. If after seven years she still found me terrifying, I didn't see the point in appeasing her. As soon as she emptied the tray, she scurried out. Phillip sat down next to me and cleared his throat. "If the rest of you would please be seated, we can start."

"Is the coffee safe to drink?" Vinnie glared at the steaming mugs in the centre of the table. "What about the croissants?"

"All the perishables in the kitchen have been replaced." Phillip added milk and one spoon of sugar to his coffee. "I will drink this first if you need proof that it's safe, but can we please start? I have a full day."

Vinnie and Francine watched Phillip take the first sip of his coffee before they helped themselves. I had been surprised when they had been in the office before Colin and I arrived. We were all seated in the team room, ready for an early morning meeting. Everyone looked much more rested than when they had left my apartment last night. I had also had a good night's rest after scrubbing my bathroom and the guest bathroom.

The one cup of coffee I'd had at home this morning was not enough, but I couldn't bring myself to take one of the mugs on the table. I looked at Manny. "What did the crime scene investigators find yesterday?"

"Where?" He tore the corner off his croissant and put it in his mouth. "I had one team here, one in Hawk's warehouse and one in his mansion."

"I would first like to know about the findings here," I said. "Did you find our coffee mugs?"

Manny shook his head while he swallowed. "Yes, but all the dishes had gone through the dishwasher. We checked Frey's special coffee and that was without any drugs. The coffee machine was checked inside out. Clean. The water, clean. Nothing in the kitchen or your viewing room had any traces of drugs."

"Then how did it get into our coffee?"

"My guess is that your mugs had been laced with it." Manny looked at Colin. "Did you notice anything strange when you made the coffee?"

"I can't remember making that coffee."

"You know what this means, right?" Francine tapped her manicured nails on the table. "This is an insider job."

"This is incredibly hard to comprehend," Phillip said. The *triangularis* muscle depressed the corners of his mouth. "I can't imagine anyone in this office being in league with the likes of Kubanov. Everyone agreed to be double-checked yesterday. This is a team of dedicated professionals."

"What about their financials?" Francine asked. "Have you checked those?"

Manny's expression changed the longer he looked at Francine. He was an astute observer of people, a natural body language reader. "What did you find, supermodel?"

"Whatever do you mean, Manny?" She placed her hand over her heart and fluttered her eyelids.

Manny didn't speak. He leaned a centimetre closer to her

and waited. He didn't have to wait long. Francine waved her hand in the air and pursed her lips.

"Nothing. Yet. I was helping Genevieve yesterday with the cases, so I didn't have a lot of time to look deeper. On the surface everyone looked fine." She started tapping her nails on the table again. "But there is always more. I will be checking today."

Phillip lifted his hand to stop Manny when he inhaled sharply. "Francine was not violating anyone's privacy rights. A condition of employment at Rousseau & Rousseau is complete transparency with personal finances. This is a business where it is easy to fall victim to numerous temptations offered."

"As long as you lot remember our conversation yesterday." His warning elicited a few snorts and grunts, but no objections.

"Have you received the results from our blood tests?" I asked.

"Yup, you and Frey were drugged with Diazepam. The lab guys said that Frey had enough in his system to explain his memory loss. You had much less, just enough for a relaxing nap."

I took a deep breath. Twice in one week my system had been filled with a chemical I didn't agree to. Diazepam, like other benzodiazepines, could affect cognitive function for up to six months after ingestion. The only positive sides were that it had a relatively low level of toxicity in overdoses. Not that we had been overdosed. Just being dosed was bad enough for me.

I brought up Mozart's Piano Concerto No. 24 in C minor in my mind. After a minute of mentally listening to it, I felt calmer, my heart rate no longer elevated. I was ready to talk about the insights I had gained while cleaning my bathrooms.

"I have something else that is not useful yet, but might mean something. Francine, can you open the rousseaus website?" I played with the cuff of my sleeve, not happy to again look at stalker photos of myself. I was still wearing long sleeves to cover the bruises on my upper arms and the fading henna tattoo. My skin had become red and sensitive from the strong scrubbing I gave it at any opportunity.

"Oh hell, I haven't even had time to look at this," Manny said as photos of me filled the monitor. "Too much happening. Explain this, Doc."

"This is a slideshow with photos taken over the last seven weeks. I know this because of the leaves on the trees and my clothes."

"She remembers what she wore on specific days." There was awe on Francine's face.

"The photos are displayed in chronological order and nothing in the photos has been altered." I had made sure of this, but had asked Francine to double-check. The photos were untouched.

We watched as one after another photo of me slid across the screen. Vinnie and Manny's breathing was becoming heavier with agitation. Phillip was paling.

"He's a sick fuck." Vinnie's words were slow and angry. "What's up with the frames?"

I merely glanced at the ornately drawn frames that surrounded each photo. What had started as an awareness while talking to an unconscious Colin had turned into full-blown results while cleaning my two bathrooms.

"Those frames are the most, maybe only, important part of this website." I pushed up my sleeve, drawing everyone's eyes to the light tattoo on my arm. "Do you see the similarity?"

"Holy Mary. Did you find hidden messages on the frames as well, Doc?"

"Numbers. The first photo's number is three-one-zero-three-zero, the second is five-one-one-three-six, and so on. Francine helped me yesterday, but the numbers didn't take us to other websites, GPS co-ordinates or anything else."

"How many photos?" Phillip asked.

"Thirteen photos and thirteen different numbers. I'll keep looking for the meaning behind it." I knew the message of these sets of numbers were within my reach. Firstly, I could feel my mind working at it. Secondly, Kubanov would only send a code he knew I could decipher. His need for acknowledgement overrode the risk of giving away too much too soon.

"I found footage of the kidnapping." Francine lifted the tablet and waved it. "It took days, but I found a small shop with security cameras facing the street that caught some action."

"Which kidnapping?" My stomach felt hollow.

"The first one." She swiped her finger across the tablet screen. "I'll put it up on the projector."

Phillip had had the best technology installed with Francine's guidance. This included a screen that rolled down from the ceiling to cover half of one wall. We turned to the wall and watched as Francine opened a video file.

"I got this footage three towns away from your cottage, Colin. This was last Thursday evening a few minutes before eleven, as you can see on the time stamp. I just got it, so I haven't cleaned up any images. It's not good quality and doesn't give me enough to identify anyone. Apart from you two, of course."

"How did you obtain this?" Manny asked. "And I don't want to know this to prosecute you. I'm really interested."

"I've told you before. There is a network of people willing to do the legwork if you need something. I put out the word that I was looking for a man and a woman who looked drunk and were helped by military-type men dressed in black." Francine tilted her head. "What? Genevieve is not the only clever one here. I was working on the basis of our last cases and used those parameters to create a profile."

"And these people helping you are all hackers?"

Francine leaned slightly back, away from the interrogation. "They are people who helped me and that is all you need to know. I asked specifically for anything in a fifty-kilometre radius around Colin's cottage and this was what I got."

She clicked on the play button and grainy white and black images filled the screen. The view was from inside a shop that looked like it sold everything. On the shelves were toys, electronics, books, even jewellery.

"This is a second-hand shop." She zoomed in on the view of the street, which were quite wide thanks to the shop windows and the angle of the camera. She had been right. The quality of the footage was poor. Few cars were parked in front of the shop. To the left was a large SUV, dark in colour. The movement entering the screen on that side was the only sign of life on the street. Francine paused the film.

"It is difficult to watch." She looked at me. "Really difficult, so be ready."

A drunk man was being helped by a well-built man with military bearing, dressed in black, a cap pulled low over his brow. Francine had been astute in her descriptions of what to look for. I recognised Colin as the drunk man from his shoes. Vinnie frequently teased him that he was a shoe snob. He only wore designer shoes—even his boots and sneakers were only the best brands. He was wearing the Bertuli Oxfords, dark brown leather shoes he had proudly showed me a few weeks ago.

A couple entered the screen behind Colin and the man. It took me a full two seconds before I recognised the writhing woman to be me. My gasp drew everyone's attention away from the screen. I didn't take my eyes off the screen, just weakly waved one hand to indicate that I didn't want their concern. Whether they understood or not was not as important as what I was witnessing.

On the screen was a textbook example of an autistic meltdown. I had only ever seen children behaving in such a manner. I was totally out of control. Even though my movements were highly disoriented and sluggish, I was kicking and punching the man holding me. The more he attempted to control me, the worse I became. Some of my reactions evidenced my seven years of self-defence training. None of it was effective.

Autistic meltdowns were difficult for anyone to deal with. In my case, it had happened a few times as a child when I had been over-stimulated. Too many people speaking to me at once and a new cleaning lady putting everything out of place had been two major triggers. My more common coping mechanism was to shut down, to go into my head and write Mozart. What was taking place onscreen was the first meltdown I'd had as an adult.

It was not difficult to deduce what had triggered the situation everyone was looking at now. The body language of the man trying to control me became increasingly agitated until he backhanded me. My head snapped back and I fell on the pavement. There was no sound to this video, but it was clear that I was screaming. My face contorted as I screamed and continued attacking the man. Watching this felt as if a belt fastened around my chest, constricting tighter and tighter. I looked away from my thrashing image to look at Colin's image on the video. What I saw made me smile and I took note of the time stamp.

The rest of the footage was more of me in a complete

meltdown, the man punching me a few times until he threw me into the back of the SUV. He closed the door and leaned against it, heaving. Unknowingly, that was the one thing he had done right. Each individual deals with meltdowns or shutdowns differently. Being given space, as the man had done by isolating me in the car, was what I had needed. Until Colin, no one could touch me during a meltdown or a shutdown. His presence and touch made me feel safe, calmed me down. In lieu of that I needed space.

The two men conversed with agitated body language for a few minutes before the one dealing with me opened the door to check inside. His body language relaxed and they shoved Colin's limp body in next to me. A few more exchanges and they also got in the car and drove away.

"Is there any audio for this?" Manny asked after a few moments of shocked silence. His voice was low and gruff with anger.

"No, but I know a guy who knows a guy who can lip-read," Francine said. "I already sent him the footage and he'll get back to me tomorrow at the latest."

I didn't realise my hands were clenched in tight fists until Colin put his hand over mine in a firm grip. "You got in a few really good kicks and punches."

"I haven't done that since I was a young child."

"We'll get those fuckers, Jen-girl. They'll get their own."

I gave Vinnie a weak smile. Their anger was better than pity. It didn't make me feel weak and helpless. I was honest enough with myself to admit the deep comfort and relief I felt with Colin's hand over mine. I had missed his presence last night.

"Francine, can you take the video to eleven fifty-four and sixteen seconds?" I asked.

Francine did that and paused it. "Slo-mo?"

"Slow motion, yes, please. Then pause it on twenty seconds." I addressed everyone. "Don't look at me, look at Colin."

It was hard for my eyes to not be drawn to the panicked movements to the left of the screen, but I watched Colin's image in the centre of the monitor. Looking at it a second time, his behaviour became even more obvious. His drunken movements, his relaxed muscles were too relaxed, too directed. He was much more in control of his body than he wanted these men to think. He swayed as the man put his shoulder under Colin's arm and pulled Colin's arm around his shoulders to make it easier to half-carry him. Colin staggered into the man with the momentum created and rested his head on the man's shoulder. Disgust was clearly written on the man's face and his body language.

On twenty seconds, Francine stopped the video. "What are we looking at?"

"Continue playing, but much slower now. Watch Colin's hands." A smile of anticipation lifted the corners of my mouth. Onscreen, Colin lifted his free hand to rest on the man's shoulder so that it looked as if they were almost embracing. The man shrugged his shoulder to dislodge Colin's hand. He rolled his head on the man's shoulder and allowed his hand to drop to the man's chest where he drunkenly patted the man.

"Oh my God, dude!" Vinnie burst out laughing. "Way to go! You're a rock star!"

"What?" Phillip leaned closer to the screen. "What happened?"

Francine paused the video and took it back a few seconds. I got up and stood by the screen, ready with a pen. As Colin patted the man's chest, I pointed with the pen to Colin's hand. Francine had slowed down the replay more, which made it easier to see the dark shape Colin lifted out of the man's breast pocket. The cell phone was visible for only a second when Colin's hand dropped limply to his side. He fiddled with his trousers, his hand empty after the first touch. This time everyone else burst out laughing. Even Manny smiled.

"You totally robbed him." Francine played the clip again, smiling widely.

"Once a thief..." Manny's attempt at hiding his smile turned the words into a proud statement rather than a scathing insult.

I sat down next to Colin and couldn't help my smile widening. He looked bewildered.

"I have absolutely no memory of doing that." This brought more laughter. "But that was so smooth. My God. I really am good."

"There's something else." I nodded to Francine's laptop. "Can you bring up the photos that I emailed to myself? I want to show the first one."

It took Francine only a few second to put the badly focussed photo up on the screen.

"I had no idea what it was supposed to be," I said. "But now it's clear."

"I must have given you the phone," Colin interrupted, excited. "You took photos and sent it to yourself."

I nodded. "I am sure that this is a very bad photo taken from the back of the car. The two large shapes on the sides must be the headrests from the front seats. That photo was taken and sent to my email address a few minutes after this video was taken."

Manny looked like he had won a prize. "Doc, even when you're drugged out of your mind, you're still smart. I could kiss you."

"Please don't." I knew it was a harmless expression, but I didn't like the thought. The nonverbal communication around the table was much lighter and more positive than a few minutes ago. I, too, felt the excitement of this breakthrough. We watched the video twice more in the next twenty minutes, looking for new clues, but found none. I was too distracted by my meltdown and needed some time to put distance between me and the footage. Since there wasn't much else to discuss, our meeting was dismissed and I went to my viewing room. There was so much that still needed to be analysed.

Chapter FOURTEEN

"Maybe we need to look for a government building with six sides," Francine said as she walked into my viewing room. It was late morning and I was feeling agitated. I had not been able to gain any insight into the butler's murder. I had looked at Susan Kadlec's case again, rendering no further clues. The rest of the twenty-seven cases hadn't led us to any suspects either. I felt extremely unproductive.

To exacerbate my discontent, my workspace was crowded with Vinnie and Colin sitting on either side of me and Francine stepping closer. The emails I had sent to myself were on the monitors to the right, the current topic of discussion. On the rest of the monitors were the other parts of this case.

Francine rested her hip on my table, but quickly stood up when she saw my expression. I had spent enough time with her to recognise the look on her face as the beginnings of some wild conspiracy theory. Vinnie and Colin fell into her trap. They found flaws in her reasoning and debated other possibilities, which she vigorously defended.

I ignored the familiar arguing and stared unseeing at the ten monitors against the wall. Each one showed a different aspect of the case. If I were to draw lines between the monitors, there would not be enough lines. I needed more lines.

"How are these things connected?" I verbalised my thought, which stopped the argument next to me. I pointed at the top left monitor, not caring if they were paying attention. "There we have the first abduction, my tattoo and the website, the numbers and the second abduction, then the numerous murders with bullets that have no striae, Colin being set up, Hawk's murder—"

"—and the bloody painting," Manny said from the door. "That frigging painting keeps popping up everywhere."

I stared at the monitor in the centre with a photo of Braque's Harbour of Normandy. It almost felt like an audible click that went off in my head. "Oh. Oh my."

I pulled up a search engine and within a few seconds had another image on the monitor next to the Harbour of Normandy. "This is Braque's Man with a Guitar, or better known as *L'homme à la guitare*, an oil on canvas, currently in the Museum of Modern Art in New York."

"Isn't that one of the phrases you emailed to yourself?" Francine asked, focussing on the monitor with my emails.

"Only part of it. In my email I wrote '*Homme a la*', which could mean anything."

"But you think it's referring to this painting?" Colin's question sounded more like a statement.

I didn't know why I felt this confident in my opinion. "Yes, I think that."

"Why would you email that to yourself?" Manny asked.

"Wrong question," I said. "The right question is where did I see this painting that it made a strong enough impression to motivate me to email this to myself. Another question is what significance does Braque have in this case? Is it Braque or something else?"

"This reminds me, where is the original painting that we got from Hawk's house, Frey?" The look Manny gave Colin had hints of distrust. "Is it still with your buddy or have you fenced it to some black-market buyer?"

"You really are an arsehole, Millard. I would never sell a

painting of such great value. Pieces like that belong with their rightful owners." Colin took a deep breath. "The painting is safe with my friend. He is a respected art dealer whose reputation relies heavily on the legitimacy of his deals."

"And he's your friend because of his honesty? Or because of your honesty?" Manny was rude, but his question had merit.

"What matters more than your quest for justice is that he can be trusted with a piece that valuable. He will never let it go to the black market, and he knows what would happen to him if he did." Colin's argument was a repeat of yesterday morning at Hawk's house. Manny had wanted to take it in as evidence and it had taken a long time and a lot of shouting, but Colin had convinced him the best course of action was to take the painting to his friend. That way, the original and the two forgeries were all in one place. I was curious to know what Colin's friend had found on those forgeries. Or if he had even found anything.

"And when will this friend"—Manny said the word with distaste—"share with us what he learned from the paintings?"

"I'll see him tomorrow morning."

"That original better be there, Frey." Manny rubbed his hand over his face. "I know I'm going to regret this, but tell me more about this Braque person."

"The quick and dirty version?" Colin asked and waited for Manny's nod. "He was born in 1882 close to Paris, first painted some impressionist work before he was influenced by Cézanne's work. That's when he got interested in cubism. Around 1910 he hooked up with Picasso and the two of them started painting together. In that time they produced works so similar that it is sometimes difficult to distinguish between the two artists. Their collaboration stopped when Braque joined the French army in 1914, the beginning of the First World War."

"Maybe Kubanov's granddaddy fought in the Battle of Tannenberg and died at the hands of the French." Francine nodded emphatically. "That's it. He knows Braque fought in that war and blames his granddaddy's death on the artist. Now he's taking it out on us."

"The Battle of Tannenberg was between the Germans and the Russians. Braque wasn't there." Colin smiled at Francine's flight of fancy. "He was injured in France and started painting again. His later work was a milder version of the harsh lines of earlier cubism. He died in 1963."

I couldn't see any useful information in what Colin had just said. Or in Francine's outrageous theory. My mind wandered to the person foremost in our minds. "Even though we have to make allowances for neuroplasticity, a major personality change seldom occurs."

"Um, Doc? You've just totally changed topics on us. What on God's green earth is neuroplastics?"

"Neuroplasticity." I enunciated the world clearly and with annoyance. Did Manny intentionally get these terms wrong? "It means our brains are in a constant state of flux. And even though it can in theory change a personality, it seldom does. There are very few recorded cases of people undergoing a significant change of character. We might modify some behaviour, change some habits, but it is rare to see notable change in a person over his lifetime."

"Where are you going with this, Doc?"

"Kubanov might adjust some behaviour, but his personality will remain unchanged."

"How is this important now?"

"There is a connection. With every case in the past there was a connection between the art and his crimes. This time will be no different. We just need to find the connection between Kubanov and Braque." I looked at Francine. "Not a conspiracy theory. An actual connection."

"And if you're wrong and find out Braque killed his granddaddy, you come with me for a whole day's spa treatment."

A shiver ran down my spine. "I will not be wrong."

"What connection do you think there is?" Colin asked.

"It would be speculation. I have no evidence to make any connections. Have you not been listening?"

"Missy, for once just make some bloody speculations."

"Speculate. We don't make speculations…" I stopped correcting his grammar when the artery on his forehead became pronounced. "If forced to speculate, I would think it might have something to do with Braque's paintings."

"We have two paintings here. The Man with a Guitar and the Harbour of Normandy. What connection is there between them?"

"They were painted by Georges Braque," I said. "That is the obvious connection."

"And they are both amazing works of art," Colin said.

"I don't know if you smart people see it, but I don't." Vinnie sat with his head tilted to one side, his face twisted in an unattractive squint. "Nope, I don't see why you think it's pretty, Jen-girl."

How did I explain that the heavily worked surface and its dense value gradations appealed to me? It soothed my brain.

"Any better speculation than just his paintings, Doc?"

I seldom grew impatient while investigating a case. Analysing everything to its core was pure pleasure to me. It took time and I didn't mind losing myself in it. I used to lose myself to the point of not eating or bathing for days. Nowadays it was not possible, not with all these people in my life consistently breaking my concentration with food and forcing me to rest. It was annoying, but I appreciated its value, their value. Although sometimes they hindered more than they helped.

"Go away." I turned to my computer and waved with one hand. "I need to work and your badgering will not help me comb through everything faster. I will find theories based on facts faster if you don't demand hypotheses the whole time. I will not speculate any further."

"And you accuse *me* of being rude. That's the pot calling the kettle… Ah, hell, she's not listening anymore." Manny's exasperation almost made me smile, but that would have revealed I was listening. On the monitors I replaced the Man with a Guitar painting with the Harbour of Normandy, the painting that was at the centre of this case. I was not quite sure where I wanted to focus next. The connecting factor between all these floating pieces were almost within reach. It was hovering in the back of my mind and I was at a loss how to bring it into my consciousness.

"He's gone and he took Francine with him." There was an audible smile in Colin's voice a few seconds later when the glass doors slid closed. "You can relax now."

"I was relaxed." I looked back at the emails I had sent myself.

He touched my shoulder. "No, you weren't. Your left shoulder moves ever so slightly when you're avoiding something. It's as if you're having a small shiver, but only in one shoulder."

"For reals?" Vinnie leaned forward in his chair to study my shoulder. "I've never seen that. Thanks, dude. Now I know what to look for."

"Can we please get back to the case?" I pushed his hand off my shoulder and decided my next step. "I want to watch the videos again."

"Sure, if you're up to it." His comment didn't catch my attention as much as the concern in his voice. "Will you be okay?"

"Yes." I sighed. Vinnie was sitting on Colin's other side, still looking at my shoulder. "I'm not lying, Vinnie. I'm genuinely okay watching this footage. It's disconcerting to see my behaviour, but I was not in control, so my emotions are not rational."

The last sentence I said to Colin and my voice tapered down to a whisper. I had worked extremely hard at controlling my behaviour to not have autistic outbursts. At first I had been uncomfortable having shutdowns when Colin was with me, but his lack of concern about it had helped me accept it. A shutdown didn't pose any threat to myself or others, whereas a meltdown could cause a lot of harm. I didn't like that I'd had my first adult meltdown in the presence of strange and dangerous men.

"Are you sure about this? We can take a break."

"No." I straightened in my chair and opened the video player. It felt good to move back into our old dynamic. It was a working relationship I had not appreciated until my action and Colin's anger had changed it temporarily. "I know there is more to see in this footage."

I clicked on the play button and was grateful for Colin and Vinnie's silence. Together we watched the nine-minute video until the car moved out of view. I replayed the video twice more before I paused it to give us the clearest possible shot of the man who had carried Colin.

"What do you see, Jenny?"

I didn't answer him, but opened the video I had taken in Hawk's warehouse. I searched for a specific shot and paused the video there. I zoomed in on the background of the warehouse video until I was happy with what was visible on the monitors. There was no mistaking the body language. As humans, we all had several distinctive gestures and habits that together with build, posture and context made identifying a person easier.

"It's the same man." Colin narrowed his eyes and groaned. "This is such a grainy shot, it's difficult to see, but I'm sure he has a scar just under his left ear. It's clearer on the video from the warehouse."

"A scar." I brought up the email with the phrases. "Hypertrophic. An excessive amount of collagen which causes a scar to be raised and often is red in colour. That has to be what I meant when I emailed this to myself. I was identifying my kidnapper."

"Fuck!" Vinnie stood up to move as close to the monitors as he could. "I know this fucker."

"Language, criminal." Manny was standing in the doorway between the viewing room and the team room. "How do you know this man?"

"I saw him a few times at Hawk's place. I know he did work for Hawk, but he hired himself out."

"A mercenary?" Manny asked.

"Not only. He also acts as a negotiator." Vinnie smiled when Manny scratched his jaw. "Yeah, his skills are not Phillip's. He negotiates with fists and guns."

"His name?"

"Dukwicz. Everyone only knows him by his last name. Or this could be his first name. And when I say everyone, I mean not many people. He's a behind-the-scenes guy. The dude has a rep for being evil. Him you can lock up any day and I'll be happy."

Something about the grainy image of the scarred man's

face called to me. I zoomed out of the image on the warehouse video, took note of the angle and zoomed in again, this time as close to his face as I could while still keeping it mostly clear. All warmth left my body.

"What do you see, Jenny?"

"He recognised me. It's hard to be sure with this quality image, but his expression suggests recognition. That ridiculous disguise didn't work." It was improbable that this man had recognised me from that distance, but I was convinced that was what I saw on his face.

"Then a lot of this makes sense," Colin said. "When he saw you at the warehouse, he must have thought he was no longer behind the scenes and was about to be arrested or something. He had us drugged and killed Hawk in the process."

"There are a lot of missing pieces in your story, but it sounds plausible." Manny looked at Vinnie with uncommon severity. "We need to find this guy."

"Done." There was finality in Vinnie's voice as he turned his attention back to the image on the monitors. "Jen-girl, can you zoom in on his belt?"

I did that and saw the butt of a gun. "Isn't it dangerous to put a gun in your trousers, pointing towards your genitals?"

Vinnie laughed. "Supremely stupid, yes. The movies make it look cool, but it's not a good idea. And you really need to make sure the safety is on, else you can shoot your own dick off."

"Why are you looking at the gun, Vin?" Colin was also studying the butt of the gun, but there was no recognition on his face. "What are we looking for?"

"I don't know." Vinnie tilted his head again. "Something isn't right with this gun."

"It looks like a SIG Sauer P228." Manny had also walked

closer. I felt crowded with three tall alpha males surrounding me. "What doesn't look right about this piece?"

For a long while, Vinnie didn't answer. He tilted his head in the other direction, stared at the monitor and sighed a lot. "I really don't know. This SIG looks off."

I twisted to look at the men behind me. "Is this a modified weapon? Could this be the type of gun we are looking for?"

"This is so not a zip gun, Jen-girl. It looks far too real, but it looks like a toy gun that should be a SIG. This is just too far and unclear to get a good look-see."

The redundancy of his expression didn't bother me this time. I was too absorbed by what this could mean. I turned back to study the monitors again, looking for the connection that was eluding me. I knew this gun had significance, but exactly how I didn't know. Not yet.

"What are you all looking at?" Francine's soft question startled us all. She laughed at Manny's rude expletive.

"What do you want, supermodel?"

"Oh, you sexy man. You have such a way with words. The question is not what I want, but what I have for you." She ran her manicured nail along Manny's collar, her full lips in an exaggerated pout. "That little encryption you gave me was no challenge for me. Do you think that little of me?"

"You have it decoded? Great. Doc, put it on the monitors."

"I don't know what you are talking about." I hated it when people included me in a conversation I had not been part of from the beginning.

"She can't put it on the monitors, Manny. I haven't connected that computer to our system."

"What are you two blabbing about?" Vinnie asked the question foremost in my mind.

"The crime scene guys brought Hawk's computer here for her to get into."

"Hawk had used some baby encryption to keep the amateurs out. It took me all of seven minutes to get into his laptop."

"What's on there?" Manny asked.

"A lot of stuff. I haven't even looked at a tenth of it, but there is something interesting. Hold on." She hurried out the room and came back a few seconds later carrying a silver laptop. It was open, a file on the screen. She put the computer down in front of me and waved away my frown. "What does this look like to you?"

I pushed past the disruption to my organised workspace and looked at the laptop's screen. I had seen similar documents when I had investigated the first case involving Kubanov. That case had included cruise ships and art auctions at sea. I had looked at hundreds of similar documents. "This looks like a shipping manifest."

"Exactly! See? Another connection to Kubanov."

"Where?" I asked. "Is his name on this document?"

"No, but—"

"This is not a connection, but we do have a connection between the first abduction and Hawk." I gestured to the monitor with Dukwicz, the scarred man. "Dukwicz worked with Hawk in his warehouse and is the same man who punched me."

"Dukwicz, you say? Do we know where he is?"

"Nope. But I'm going to find out." Vinnie's jaw muscles were tense.

"I'll see what I can find out about him online." She raised one hand towards Manny and turned her head away from him. "This bastard kidnapped and punched Genevieve, then did it again. I will break any and all rules to find him."

"Do it," Manny said softly. "But leave no evidence behind."

"Leave Hawk's computer with me or email me all his files, whichever is better," I said. "With his computer, I am sure I will get more data to work with. If you give me a few hours, I will tell you what I have."

"And I'll nag the crime scene guys to get me my report," Manny said. "I want to know what is in that warehouse."

We agreed to meet in the team room at four o'clock. I exhaled in relief when only Colin stayed behind. Together we went through the footage again, looking for anything I had missed. When I couldn't see anything new, I clicked on the link to the folder Francine had emailed me. She had copied the entirety of Hawk's computer and put it on our server.

Colin and I had a slight disagreement on which documents to peruse first. We compromised by dividing the work. I checked the inventory lists and Colin looked at the financials on his computer. I compared it to the list of products bought with Colin's credit cards. Every one of those items was in Hawk's warehouse.

Too soon, it was four o'clock. Standing up, I felt the effect of not moving out of my chair for hours. I stretched and wished to be home, lying in a tub of hot water.

"Coming?" Colin waited at the door for me. I picked up my notes and walked past him into the team room. Everyone was seated at the table, Phillip included. His interest was not uncommon, but his involvement in this case was noticeable. Nothing he did was without reason. I suspected his reason was concern.

As I sat down, Angelique entered the room with another tray. Apart from the steaming coffee mugs, there were two large bowls. One held fresh berries, the other pralines. Energy food. She nodded stiffly when I smiled my thanks, unpacked the tray and left as quickly and quietly as she came in.

"What did you find, Doc?"

"The shipping manifests and order forms are long and detailed, and will take time to go through properly. Since you didn't give me enough time, I only scanned a few folders and glanced at the shipping manifests. There I saw something interesting." I asked Francine to bring Hawk's laptop and opened the folder with the offending files.

Manny stopped stirring his tea. "Please tell me you found a smoking gun."

"No, there are no guns listed anywhere on the shipping manifests, but Hawk did keep impeccable records. The shipping manifests were catalogued with reference to all other documents individual items appeared on." I turned Hawk's laptop for the others to see.

"This is all very interesting, Doc. But do you have something useful?"

"Two months ago, a large shipment of unnamed electronic devices was delivered to the warehouse. The products were never entered into Hawk's inventory, but there is a note referencing it to a list of names and addresses. This is anomalous. All other shipments have reference notes to orders, but never to an address list."

"Did you find something interesting on that list?"

"I haven't had enough time to look at it carefully. One of the names listed is Freddy Gagliardi." This interesting finding had solidified my suspicion that Tall Freddy was directly connected to our case.

"Tall Freddy?" Colin tensed. "Vin, do you know of any connection between Hawk and Tall Freddy?"

"No, dude. All I can think of is they both deal in guns. Maybe Hawk supplied Tall Freddy."

Manny was leaning over the table, studying the laptop monitor. From his expression I deduced he was seeing something I hadn't. The more he read, the wider his eyes grew.

"Holy hell. This is a who's who list of criminals in Europe." He pulled the laptop across the table and pushed it in front of Vinnie. "There are names I don't recognise, but most of these names have crossed my desk at some point. How many of them are your pals?"

"Never pals, old man." Vinnie sat up and looked at the open file. "Hmm, I know a few of these guys. Some are small-time crooks, some real badasses."

"I searched the rest of Hawk's computer for references to Freddy Gagliardi or even Tall Freddy and found one more document for him." I wanted to show them the document, but Vinnie was engrossed in the list. "Five months ago, Hawk shipped five 3D printers to Tall Freddy."

"What the hell for?" Manny asked. A connection feeling like a low-level buzzing in the back of my mind loomed, ready to click into place and help me make sense of this oddity.

"Those printers have a wide variety of applications," Francine said. "I had this designer print me a pair of killer sandals to fit the exact scan of my feet. Even NASA is printing engine parts for their rockets."

Manny looked at her in astounded silence. When she pursed her lips and winked at him, he grunted and looked at Vinnie. "I'm sure Tall Freddy isn't printing bloody shoes with it. Can you find out what he's doing with those printers?"

"I can try."

"Guns!" The word came out much louder than I had intended. I took a calming breath before I continued. "I've read a few articles recently about the threat of printed guns."

"Holy hell." Manny leaned back in his chair. "Interpol sent us a memo a few months ago about this. A lot of words, but not much information. Basically it said that 3D printers are now able to print all the parts of a handgun, except for a nail which serves as the firing pin. And the bullets."

"Oh, but there is so much more to this." Francine tapped on the table with her nails. "Those guns can be a real threat, but most of the printed guns are useless. They explode with the first use."

There was silence around the table. Streams of data were flowing through my mind, picking up bits of information discovered over the last week, connecting them.

"Okay, one thing at a time. We can get back to this 3D crap later." Manny sat up. "Doc, email me this document with this address list of criminals. Bloody hell, I don't know if Interpol even have all these addresses. If these are correct, it will be quite the career catch."

I wasn't seeing career advancement benefits in the list. Only more questions. 'Why would Hawk have this list?"

"To sell his guns to them? Like a client list." Manny shook his head. "No, that is too strange."

I agreed with Manny. This theory did not fit the limited profile I had created of Hawk. He didn't seem to be the type of person to send newsletters advertising discounts on various products and introducing new ones. I had once made the mistake of giving a service provider my personal email address. After the second monthly email, I had promptly unsubscribed. It had cluttered my inbox.

My inane train of thought triggered another issue. I interrupted Manny asking Francine to find out everything she could on the listed names.

"Where's Monique? You said you would find her."

"I did. She was on holiday with a friend and her family in Miami. The US authorities are helping her get ready to come here."

"Is she well?" I had promised Hawk to ensure she was well.

"As far as I know, yes." Manny picked up a few sheets of paper. "I got a report from the warehouse. The place is huge and they told me that this is by far not a complete report, but we have something. The important things they have found are mountains of weapons from the basement and traces of C4."

"That's no surprise," Vinnie said. "Guns and explosives were Hawk's business."

"I assume C4 is an explosive," I said.

"Yup." Vinnie nodded. "One of the most stable explosives there are."

"It's not finding the C4 that is interesting," Manny said. "It is where it was found."

I didn't know how I knew the answer before Manny spoke, but I did.

"There were traces found in the basement, no surprise there. But they also found traces by the woodwork equipment." Manny's *zygomaticus* muscles lifted his mouth into a rare genuine smile when no one said anything. "I have stumped you lot. Don't worry. I'm also stumped. I've contacted Edward to go have a look at the warehouse. Maybe he'll see something that could shed a light on this."

I had met Edward six months ago when he had disabled a bomb I had stepped on. Since then I had learned he was one of the most respected explosive ordnance disposal technicians in Western Europe. Adding explosives to our case was strengthening the suspicion of Kubanov being behind this. Art, murder, crime and explosives were in all his past cases. If only I could find a solid link between all these elements and the Russian philanthropist.

Chapter FIFTEEN

"What's eating at you, Jenny?"

I liked the expression. It accurately described how I was feeling. I sank deeper into the passenger seat of Colin's SUV and stared at the street ahead of us. We were going home after a few more hours of searching Hawk's computer. "The numbers."

After a moment, Colin huffed a laugh. "You will have to be more specific than that. Which numbers?"

"Oh, sorry." Being distracted did not aid my communication skills. "Those numbers in the frames on the website are troubling me. There is this deluge of new information coming in and I don't have time to process, analyse or make any sense of it. For example, I don't know what to think about the traces of C4 by the woodwork equipment. And Edward wasn't helpful."

"Yeah, Millard wasn't happy about Edward's answer either." He glanced at me and smiled. Manny had cursed excessively into the phone while listening to Edward. "Especially when Edward said there were many other chemicals in the warehouse that could be used to build a bomb."

"And most of it is as harmful as the dishwashing liquid I use."

"Vinnie has been complaining about the industrial-strength stuff you have. You should buy him some pink plastic gloves to protect his hands."

"Why pink?" I looked away from the road and frowned at Colin. "Actually, why should I buy him any gloves? I have never asked him to clean anything for me."

"He likes it. It relaxes him."

"Oh. I understand that." I did. My recent bathroom-cleaning episode spoke of my intimate experience in this matter. Recently it had become inconvenient when Vinnie's constant presence in my apartment resulted in much less cleaning for me to do. In the last six months I had grown used to hearing keys opening my front door at all times of the day.

I looked back at the road, enjoying the familiarity of the journey home. Colin, Francine and Vinnie never abused the liberties they took entering my home on a whim. They didn't leave anything out of place and respected my bedroom as a place sacred to me. With the exception of this week, Colin had spent a few hours every night with me in my room, always returning to his apartment after our lovemaking. It had been at my request. Most times I felt unprepared for the intense emotionality of my relationship with him. The thought of sleeping next to him made me feel far too vulnerable to consider accepting his nightly offers to stay over.

"Jenny?" Colin's voice had the quality of having called me a few times. It happened often.

"Hmm?"

"What else is bothering you?"

"I don't like feeling vulnerable." The truth escaped my mouth before I stopped to think. "Forget about it. I was thinking about something different."

"What were you thinking about?"

I bit down hard to prevent any more spontaneous

confessions. "There is something else that bothers me about the case."

Colin looked away from the road long enough for me to read his expression. Sometimes he did that on purpose for me to see his opinion on something I had said or done. He was displeased that I didn't want to talk about my feelings, but was going to allow me to change the topic. He turned his attention back to driving. "What's bugging you?"

"Where is Kubanov?"

"Um... I'm not sure exactly what you are asking."

My brow furrowed in annoyance at another lapse of clear communication. "In every previous case it was easy enough to spot Kubanov's influence. Apart from a lot of conjecture, there is nothing so far to directly connect him to any of this."

"But you believe that he is behind all of this?"

"Do you?" I turned in my seat, the tree-lined street forgotten.

"You know I do." His hands tightened around the steering wheel. "Those six days he had me in his basement taught me a lot about the man. One of those lessons was that he was not going to stop until he got the revenge he feels we deserve."

"The mind of a psychopath." My heart rate increased at the memories of the torture Kubanov had subjected Colin to. All because Kubanov had felt slighted when we had put a stop to his far-reaching art forgery business. From a psychology point of view I knew he was fixated on this and would not easily give up. Colin was right. "But where is the evidence that he is behind this?"

"It will come, Jenny. With an ego like his, Kubanov wouldn't tolerate us not knowing that he is pulling our strings." The corner of his mouth twitched. "Pulling strings is an expression explaining one person, the puppet master, controlling the puppets."

"Marionettes and a manipulator. A good analogy."

"Except we are much smarter than puppets and won't allow him to pull our strings for too long." Colin found a parking place close to our apartment building. He turned off the engine, but his body language indicated he had no plan to leave the vehicle. I studied him for a few seconds. He swallowed a few times, his lips compressing. He wanted to say something, but wasn't sure how to start. A heavy feeling settled in my stomach.

"I know we haven't talked about this, but you said you were still too angry with me." The tremble in my voice was barely audible, but I felt the nerves in my entire body. I didn't take time to interpret the surprise on Colin's face, but spoke even faster. "You promised not to leave me. Compared to dating neurotypical people, I know it must be extremely difficult for you to be with me. I experience a large degree of anxiety and panic when you move something out of its place. I insist on a lot of things that are clearly obsessive behaviour and am not emotionally communicative. According to studies, most men don't like the extreme emotional fluctuations of women, but you're not most men. I have never even asked you what you would prefer, mainly because I don't care. You see? I shouldn't have said that."

"Jenny. Stop." Colin took my hands and pulled me a bit closer to him. "Look at me."

I took my eyes off my trembling hands. I had been avoiding his face, not wanting to see that I was right. But Colin waited until I looked at him.

"Look." He dropped his face a little bit closer to mine. "What do you see?"

One thing invaluable to me was Colin's willingness to

patiently wait while I studied him. He never flinched away, never hid from me. I was taken aback by what I saw.

"You're confused. Why are you confused?"

"Because I don't know what brought on your lengthy explanation." His smile was gentle. "Want to tell me what's happening in your head?"

"You've been avoiding a conversation about me going with Vinnie to Hawk's warehouse. I don't know why. When you stopped here, I could see you wanted to say something you were not comfortable with—"

"—so you jumped to a conclusion."

I winced. "I did, didn't I?"

He nodded. "Yes, and it wasn't a jump, it was a huge leap. And it was in the wrong direction. I didn't want to talk about Hawk's warehouse because I was angry. I know when I debate, argue or talk with you I need to have rational arguments. While still angry, it would be difficult for me to stay calm and rational. If challenged, I would've answered, 'Because'. Not a good answer to give to you. It would only have led to senseless arguments."

"Are you still angry?"

"I'm still pissed that you went there and put yourself in danger, but not as angry as two days ago."

My throat felt thick with emotion. This was what I didn't like about being emotionally involved with someone. The vulnerability.

"Are you still looking at me?"

My face must have conveyed my incredulous response, because he nodded.

"Good. See that what I'm saying is true." He took a deep breath. "I'm nowhere near your IQ and there is a mountain of differences between us, but I'm pretty sure I know you.

And I'm pretty sure that you are trying your best to not love me, to not love anyone. But it's too late, Jenny. I see it. I see that you love me."

I started shaking my head and couldn't stop. "No. It's not true."

"What? That you love me or that you're trying not to?"

My childhood of emotionally distant caregivers, disappointed and disapproving parents came rushing to my memory. The last time I had committed emotionally to someone was at the age of five. It had been an exceptionally traumatic experience when that nanny had left like all the others, calling me a freak. What Colin was asking of me was too much.

"Aw, Jenny." He leaned back, putting distance between us. "You really don't make it easy, do you?"

"Please don't give up on me." My whisper was so soft, I was surprised he heard me.

I saw the internal struggle on his face before he moved closer to me again. The nonverbal cues of his emotions were unmistakeable. "I'm not going to give up on you, Jenny. I love you."

I couldn't help it. I gasped. No one had ever told me this and I certainly had not expected to receive this sincere gift on this specific day. It truly was a gift. I didn't know how to respond. "I need time to think about this, to catalogue this."

His smile was sad. "Ever considered not micro-analysing everything?"

I shuddered. "Not possible."

"Okay." He laughed softly, but there was no humour in it. "Then let me tell you what I was about to say before your huge confession."

"I didn't con... Sorry. I'm listening." I didn't want to add to the sadness I had already caused.

"There's a party in your apartment at the moment."

All emotions were forgotten. My apartment was being destroyed. "Who? Why? How could you agree to this?"

"Slow down." This time there was humour in his laugh. "It's your birthday party."

"You know it's my birthday?"

"We all know it's your birthday, Jenny." He leaned over and kissed me until I forgot about my emotional discomfort. I didn't forget about my apartment though. One last, chaste kiss and Colin moved back. "Happy birthday, love."

"Thank you. Who is in my apartment?"

"The usual suspects. Vinnie, Francine, Millard and Phillip. Francine is the one who started this whole thing. She wanted to go big and have a huge party, but Phillip convinced her to keep it small. They went through a lot of effort to make this surprise party for you."

"But it's no longer a surprise. You've just told me about it."

"Because I know how much you hate surprises. I thought giving you a few minutes to prepare for what was waiting for you might be better for everyone."

"Oh God. What is waiting for me?"

For some reason Colin thought my reaction was amusing. "You don't have to sound so horrified, Jenny. Vinnie baked a cake, made dinner, Francine put up some birthday decorations and, well, I don't know what Millard is doing there."

"Apart from the decorations, it sounds like a normal dinner." I lifted both shoulders. "Why is this different? We see each other every day."

"But we don't celebrate every day."

"Why would you want to celebrate my birthday? It's a strange ritual that personally I think people only use as an excuse to socialise and get drunk."

"You might very well be right, but in this case, we want to let you know that you are special to us by celebrating the day you became part of humanity."

I was stunned. In all of my thirty-five years I had never had people wanting to celebrate my existence.

"And"—Colin looked pleased with himself—"Vinnie and Millard promised me they would not pick fights with each other tonight. That might require Vinnie to stay in the kitchen all night and Millard to lock himself in the bathroom, but hey, they promised."

The thought of those two men restraining their innate need to nettle each other made me smile. "I would like to witness that."

"I thought you would." He put his hand on the car door handle. "Shall we go?"

I nodded and followed him to my apartment. He hesitated at the door, waiting for me. I took a few deep breaths, preparing myself to not react to any changes made inside. Anything out of place was only temporary and I could have a therapeutic cleaning session once everyone left. That thought was positive, one I planned to remind myself of throughout this birthday party. I unlocked the door and stepped inside.

"Surprise!" Francine jumped in front of me, shaking huge colourful pompoms. I stepped back against Colin's chest, trying my best to school my features into a pleasantly surprised look.

"Aw, Jen-girl. You really are a bad liar. That is not a surprised face." Vinnie stepped closer and pulled Francine away from me, telling her to stop scaring me. She continued shaking the pompoms with a happy smile. All I could think of was the obsessive search I would go through if the string holding the tinsel together broke. Vinnie pushed Francine behind him. "Come on. We're set up here by the sofas."

I looked to the left and saw Manny and Phillip standing in front of one of my sofas. The double doors to the balcony were open. A summer breeze cooled the interior marginally. It was a hot day. Above the doors hung a colourful banner wishing me a happy birthday. Lifting my gaze to that sign had brought the biggest form of decoration to my attention. Everywhere I looked, balloons were touching the high ceiling. They had to be filled with helium to float despite the amount of tinsel weighing them down. My apartment looked like a children's party venue.

"Happy birthday, Doc." Manny stepped forward and I leaned in further against Colin's chest. "For the love of God, missy. At least on this occasion you can let me kiss your cheek."

Colin gave my arms a squeeze, followed by a light push. His observation had been astute in the car. This party was for them. Had it been about me, I would've spent the evening blissfully alone. I didn't attempt a smile, but stepped forward and offered my cheek to Manny. The subtle woodsy scent of his cologne reached me a moment before I felt a dry, gentle kiss.

"You're one in a million, Doc." His whispered words were still registering in significance when he walked back to the sofa. "Wasn't that hard, now was it?"

"Stop harassing her, old man." Vinnie gulped visibly and looked at Colin, disappointment and contrition replacing annoyance. "Sorry, dude."

I laughed. The restraint I had been looking forward to observing had lasted all of one minute. "Don't apologise, Vinnie. I wouldn't have you any other way. You are real and I need that in my life."

"Aw, Jen-girl." Vinnie opened his arms. "Come here. Come hug big Vin. You know you want to."

I laughed again. He was outrageous. Knowing I would not be able to avoid his hug, I prepared myself and allowed him to lift me off the floor in one of his strong embraces. I admired, and envied, Vinnie's fearless approach to emotions and sharing. Thankfully, he didn't hold onto me for too long. He put me down, his smile genuine and joyful.

"I made tiramisu, a really big one. You can have that as a starter, main course and dessert if you want. It's your birthday."

Tiramisu was a guilty pleasure for me, something sweet, rich and unhealthy, yet comforting. Vinnie's tiramisu had outshone all those I'd had before. He had taken notice of my enjoyment the one time he had made it.

"Happy birthday, girlfriend." Francine pushed Vinnie away from me. "Go get the food. We want to eat and drink."

Vinnie left for the kitchen, shaking his head.

"Can I please hug you?" She knew how I detested being touched. I knew how much it would mean to her. All this touching and physical closeness so soon after all the hugs upon our return from England was stressful. I quickly called up Mozart's Symphony No. 36 in C Major as mental fortification. I nodded and was rewarded with a joyful smile. Francine was twelve centimetres taller than me, wearing high heels. She had to bend her knees to wrap her arms around me. It was a quick hug, but without inhibition. She truly liked me. "I hope you enjoy your party."

"I'm sure I will." I was going to make every attempt to honour their effort with my enjoyment.

"Well, come on then." She grabbed my hand and led me to the sofas.

Manny was sitting, but Phillip was quietly waiting for me. I pulled my hand out of Francine's hold and walked to the man who had done more for me in seven years on a personal level than my parents had during my whole life. I didn't need any prompting to hug him. He seldom showed affection, but I knew this moment would be special for him. I was right. First his eyebrows lifted in surprise as I put my arms around him, then his features went soft with affection before he gave me a solid hug. It lasted two seconds.

I sat down next to Colin on the other sofa, glad to be out of the others' touching range. Manny and Phillip got absorbed in a conversation about the new protests that had started in the Middle East. Vinnie served the *hors d'oeuvres* in the living area, then herded us to the dining room table where we enjoyed a five-course meal. By the time the tiramisu was served, we were ready to sit more comfortably in the living area.

"Time for your gifts." Vinnie had been the perfect host. In my home. "We put it in my old room, so I'll go get it."

"I don't want gifts. You have done too much already."

Vinnie made a rude noise and left for the room in the back. Colin got up and followed him.

"Oh, poo. Stop complaining and enjoy our gifts, Doc." The knot of Manny's tie was hanging halfway down his chest. I hadn't seen him this relaxed for some time. He had even smiled when Vinnie told jokes. It hadn't been a genuine smile, but he was trying. Vinnie and Colin came back carrying wrapped packages.

"Mine first." Francine jumped up and grabbed a square package from Vinnie's hands. She swung around and sat next to me. "I ordered this especially for you. Open it."

I carefully removed the sticky tape, ignoring Francine's impatient breathing and shifting. The gift was covered in two layers of wrapping, which I removed to fold later. The wooden box that was uncovered made me forget the paper.

It was a hand-carved dark wood, the carvings breathtaking. Ancient symbols flowed into each other, forming an intricate pattern.

"All these symbols have meaning, all for something you like. There's one for Mozart, one for coffee, even one for art. I'll explain them all later."

It took me three tries before I could thank her for the thoughtful gift. I was overwhelmed by her generosity and the thought she had put into something so personal. Vinnie's gift was no less meaningful. It was a collection of poetry by my favourite Russian poets, a book I had been looking for. The gift Manny thrust at me was not something I had expected. He admitted gruffly that it had reminded him of me, and he had thought I would like it.

"Oh, Manny." I opened one antique Russian doll to find another smaller one. They were not as colourful as the commercially produced souvenirs for tourists. "This is perfect. Where did you find this?"

"Some little shop when I was in England last month. The shopkeeper said these dolls were made by an apprentice of the guy who made the first dolls."

"Vasily Zvyozdochkin?" Colin leaned in to take a closer look. "Wow."

From his tone, I surmised that I was holding something of value. Manny dismissed it as little wooden figures and refused to say anything else. Phillip's gift came as no surprise. Like every year on my birthday, he gave me an antique mosaic. This year it was a pill box. It was beautiful.

"What did you give her, Frey?"

Colin ignored him and handed me a wrapped object easy to guess. "A painting?"

"Open it." He waited until I held the piece in my hands. "It's Paul Klee's Nocturnal Festivity painting."

"Did you steal that?" Manny sat up and stretched his neck to see the painting. "Or did you forge that?"

"Manny." Phillip's voice was low in warning.

"I painted this for you long before this whole cubism crap started. This week I've been worrying that it might not be appropriate to give this to you, but then I decided that everyone and everything can go screw itself. This is yours. I painted this because it made me think of you."

"I'm really glad you decided to give it to me." It was an incredibly beautiful piece of work made invaluable because Colin had painted it with me in mind. "I love Klee's work and this is… well, to my novice eye this looks exactly like the original."

Paul Klee was also a cubist painter, his paintings more colourful than Braque's, his style strongly resonating with me.

Colin pointed to the tree in the foreground. "Do you see it?"

I held the painting closer and studied the tree. I smiled. "My name. You put the letters of my name in the white touches on the tree."

"What is it with you people and cubism?" Manny asked. "And before you get all huffy, my question is real. I want to know what it is that you see in all those blocks."

"Blocks?" Colin sat up, the corner of his mouth pulled into a sneer. "Cubism is the attempt to visually describe the fourth dimension."

"You're shitting me." Manny laughed. "The fourth bloody dimension. What is that?"

"It is postulated that there is an additional dimension to length, area and volume, a special dimension." I shrugged. "There is no proof of this though."

"And cubist artists tried to paint this?"

"They painted it," Colin said. "There is something very right about looking at objects depicted in linear fashion."

"Almost like *The Matrix*." Vinnie looked unconcerned when Colin glared at him. I didn't know what matrix he was referring to.

"Like any new art form, cubism wasn't always received well."

"People don't like change," I added.

"And they usually call it evil." Colin turned the Klee reproduction for Manny to see. "Do you see any evil in this? It is not the same style as Braque or Picasso in the height of the cubist period, but it is also rather conceptual than perceptual."

"So you paint what you think you see, not what you see. That sounds like most art that is not photo-type portraits."

"You are a troglodyte," Colin said after a shocked second. He stood up, gathered some dishes and carried it to the kitchen.

"What did he just call me?" Manny asked me.

"A prehistoric cave dweller, but I think his intention was to call you unsophisticated," I said. Vinnie laughed, got up and helped Colin clear the coffee table.

"What do you see in these paintings, Doc?" Manny clearly had not received a satisfactory answer. I thought about this for a moment.

"This might have to do with me being non-neurotypical. The simplification of what the artists saw, whether people or objects, into geometrical components and planes appeals to me. That geometricity may or may not add up to how that complete object exists in the natural world, but that linear interpretation harmonizes with something inside of me."

"I don't think I can say it any better or more beautifully than that," Colin said as he walked back to the living area. "You'll just have to be happy with that, Millard."

Manny didn't acknowledge Colin's baiting. "That makes sense, Doc. Thanks."

Something said in the past few minutes was tugging at my consciousness. I knew that I had uncovered some key, possibly to this case, but it had yet to filter through from my subconscious.

"Jenny? Just tell him if you don't want to."

"Don't want to what?" I had lost the thread of the conversation.

"Can I see your Braque painting, Doc?" Manny was standing, ready to walk to my bedroom.

"Why?" I got up. "I don't mind showing it to you, but why do you want to see it?"

"Curious." He was too relaxed from the dinner and laid-back conversation to take care of his body language.

"You're lying, Manny." I walked to my bedroom, everyone following. I took a shaky breath. My bedroom was not made to entertain a house full of guests.

"This is the third reproduction of a painting that was stolen and then showed up in Hawk's house. The safe house forgery, the McCarthy forgery that Frey painted and yours. I'm trying to understand that mystery."

My bedroom filled up, everyone gathering around my bed, staring at the painting above the headboard. Manny looked at it through narrowed eyes and I wondered what he was looking for. He had no expertise to draw from. Colin and Vinnie were talking about an uninteresting topic when the change in Colin's voice caught my attention. I turned as he stopped in the middle of his sentence to step closer to the painting.

"What's wrong?" I asked. The narrowing of his eyes and the deep frown lowering his brow were telling me something was causing him great concern. He reached out and took the painting from the wall.

"This is not the original."

"Well, we know that, Frey. Doc has told us it is a reproduction."

"No." Colin shook his head and tilted the painting to the light. "This is not the original reproduction Jenny had. This is a forgery. And it looks like it was done by the same artist who did the safe house forgery."

"For reals?" Vinnie looked as astonished as I felt.

"That means he was in my bedroom." My voice was so strained, it hurt to speak.

"We're sleeping here tonight." Colin handed the painting to Phillip who was quietly holding out his hand. "Don't even think to argue, Jenny. Vinnie will sleep in his old room, but we are both sleeping here tonight."

The doorbell interrupted my attempt at coming up with a viable argument. If both men were staying over, Colin would want to sleep in my bed. I didn't know if I was ready for that decision to be taken out of my hands.

"Jenny!" Colin took my upper arms in a firm, but gentle grip. I had not been paying attention to the conversation. "Are you expecting anyone?"

"No." Reason entered before I could panic. "It wouldn't be the thief, forger or anyone like that. All the lights are on and surely he can hear us from the hallway."

"Doesn't matter. Vinnie will get it."

We left my room as swiftly as we had entered it. Vinnie was already by the front door when I followed Colin out. Francine and Phillip waited in the living area, Manny a couple of feet behind Vinnie. I had lived with fear all my life and at times rebelled against it, not always with positive results. Tonight I wasn't going to allow a doorbell to cow me. I walked with Colin to the door just as Vinnie turned around, his face contorted in anger.

"That motherfucking bastard." He held the delivery out to me. "He sent you flowers."

My gasp wasn't audible above the explosion of expletives. I wasn't listening to Vinnie and Colin vowing pain and death, or to Manny interrogating the delivery boy. My eyes were riveted on the bunch of red daffodils. I was sure if I counted them, there would be thirty-five. A flower for each year of my life. Sent by Kubanov. He had just announced his presence, his connection to this case.

Chapter SIXTEEN

The intensity of the aggressive body language this close to me was becoming overwhelming. Manny was still interrogating the now terrified delivery man. Phillip was quietly standing by, his body language mirroring Manny's. Vinnie and Colin were whispering to each other, careful to not be heard. But I didn't need to hear their words. Their nonverbal cues were speaking loud and clear. They were planning and their plans involved violence.

No one took notice when I turned away from the commotion by my front door. I cleared the last of the dishes from the coffee tables in the living area and took it to the kitchen. I had to repack the dishwasher. Vinnie's system of organising the dishes in the dishwasher was not completely unacceptable, but mine was better.

"Genevieve, I'm really sorry." Francine plucked a balloon down by the hanging tinsel and reached for the kitchen scissors. She pointed it at the door. "That bastard destroyed everything."

She cut the knot of the balloon and held onto the tinsel while the balloon deflated. It was a huge relief that she wasn't resorting to the disturbing habit of popping the balloons. I closed the dishwasher door, straightened and leaned against the kitchen counter. There had been more to her apology than commenting on Kubanov's negative character traits.

"What did he destroy?" I asked.

She grabbed more hanging tinsel and jerked another

balloon down. "This. I wanted your party to be special, and now he's gone and destroyed it."

I closed my eyes, realising the full extent of her comment. In my friendship with her, I often found myself at a loss for what to say or how to react. I searched for the best approach. "This is my second birthday party."

She looked up, confused. "You already had a party today? With whom?"

"No, not today." It wasn't easy saying this. "This is the second birthday party I've had in my whole life."

Francine lost her grip on the deflating balloon, ignoring it as it swirled around the kitchen. Her mouth was slack. "You cannot be serious. Oh my God, you are serious."

"The first party was for my fifth birthday. My parents had taken me to new doctors to fix me. These doctors told them to force me into a normal childhood, starting with social functions. They decided a birthday party would be a good start." I surprised myself by telling her this. "There were too many people, too many stimuli, and I had a meltdown, much to my parents' humiliation. The people invited had been carefully chosen to witness my parents' success, beautiful home and child. One autistic behaviour and I had destroyed their illusion of the perfect life. It was my first and last birthday party. As an adult I had never had the need nor seen the sense in it."

Her *masseter* muscles tightened her jaw, her movements stiff. "Your parents are horrible people."

"No. They are just ignorant. When people don't understand something, they are usually judgemental and unintentionally cruel."

"You can't say anything to justify their behaviour." She jerked down another balloon and cut the knot. "I still say they're idiots. Horrible idiots."

I sighed heavily. Colin and Vinnie joined us in the kitchen, listening with interest. From a sociological point of view, I understood the significance and importance of tonight. But making myself understood on an emotional level was taxing. "What I'm trying to say, quite unsuccessfully, is that this is the first time in my life someone has voluntarily wanted to celebrate my birthday with me. Nothing Kubanov does or sends will take away the value of what you have done for me."

Her eyes filled with tears. "Ooh. That is… ooh, I need to hug you."

I leaned back against the counter. There had been too much physical contact already. Francine's shoulders sagged, but then she smiled. "I'll hug you in my mind, but I'll hug Vin for real. I just need to hug someone."

She spun around and threw her arms around Vinnie. He indulged her with the forbearance observed in siblings. He patted her back with a small smile before pulling her arms away from his body. "Go cuddle the old man if you're looking for a little somethin'-somethin'."

Francine stepped back, her eyes lively with anticipation. Colin gave a tired laugh and put his hand on Francine's arm to stop her. "I don't think you should do that. Millard is volatile just now."

"We all are." Vinnie folded his arms, widening his stance. He was going to make a statement that he was not willing to negotiate on. "Jen-girl, we're staying here."

"I know." I had accepted it while packing the dishwasher.

"I think that is our cue to leave," Phillip said from the living area. The delivery man had left and Manny was nodding in agreement with Phillip.

Ten minutes later, only Colin, Vinnie and I remained in my flat. There had been threats and promises about safety, phone calls, protection and consequences. It had all been well intended, but was more stressful than comforting. It was a relief to have fewer people in my space.

Colin and Vinnie tried, but weren't able to dissuade me from restoring my apartment to its original state, so Vinnie helped. Colin tried to help, but I begged him not to. I had to fix everything after he had touched it, which was counter-productive. He disappeared into my bedroom while we finished up. It didn't take very long before everything was in its designated place and I was showered and standing next to my bed.

"Aren't you getting in?" Colin looked up from the book he was reading. "Don't over-think it, Jenny. Let's just sleep. Tomorrow we'll take this new forgery to my friend and see what he's discovered about the others."

He was right. I was micro-analysing his presence in my bedroom. I climbed in bed stiffly and had trouble getting comfortable. We had shared this bed often, but never to sleep. "I don't know how to do this."

"Close your eyes, breathe deeply and sleep."

I turned around to find him lying on his side looking at me. His book was on the bedside table, the lamp on his side off.

"You need a switch that you can flip to stop analysing everything."

I smiled. "That would definitely help."

"I make you a deal. Tonight we sleep. Tomorrow you can tell me all the reasons why I should not have slept here."

"That doesn't make sense. It's rationalising something after the fact. Totally unproductive."

"But if it will make you go to sleep, then it is a good idea." He lifted one eyebrow. "Unless you want to have wild, loud sex?"

I pushed deeper into the pillows, frowning. "Vinnie is sleeping in the next room. If you continue this trivial talk, you can sleep in your old room or one of the sofas. Or even better, you can sleep in your own bed next door."

He laughed softly, but the flash of disappointment did not escape my notice. I twisted to switch off the lamp and turned back. It was strange, but nice to lie on my side facing Colin. I didn't know if I would be able to sleep with another person in my bed, but at least I did have a complex case to think over if sleep evaded me.

It didn't. I woke up the next morning, immediately aware of arms surrounding me. For a moment, my mind recalled being drugged and abducted, followed by confusion and mild panic.

"It's me, Jenny. Relax." Colin's voice was lazy and gravelly from sleep. His arm tightened slightly around my waist and I relaxed against his back. "In case you don't know, this position is called spooning. I like to spoon. We should spoon for a few more minutes."

"What time is it?"

"Time to spoon."

I slapped his arm. "Colin."

"Half past seven."

"Oh God, we should get up." Even on Saturdays, I always got up at six. This break in my routine was most upsetting. I wrestled with his arm for a few seconds until he let me go. I stood next to the bed, looking at him. "What time are we meeting with your friend?"

"At nine." He stretched his arms above his head. His hair was mussed and he looked at ease. Blinking in surprise, I realised that I too felt relaxed and had slept well despite sharing my bed. "Did you sleep well?"

"Hmm?" I shook my head. Was this what other people

did? Asking after each other's rest? "I slept well, thank you. I'm going to have a shower."

An hour later we were in Colin's SUV, driving through the city.

"What is the purpose of these forgeries?" I asked. "And don't answer. It is a rhetorical question."

"I assumed so." Colin slowed down for a red light and glanced at me. "What do you think?"

"Something you said about cubism last night made me think. Is Kubanov focussed on Braque or on the style? Does it have to do with Braque's history, his connection to Picasso, to the war or is it cubism itself triggering Kubanov's obsession?"

"What makes you think it's cubism?"

"Those words that I emailed to myself." I leaned my head back against the headrest and closed my eyes. "In the second email I sent to myself, I put down 'hexahedron', which is a cube, and 'halo die'. I still don't know about the halo, but a die is the singular of dice."

"Few people use the word die. Most people use dice as the singular for card games and gambling."

"Could I, in my intoxicated state, have emailed those terms to myself to point to cubes?" I heard Colin's quick intake of breath. "I don't know what it means, but maybe I should check all the clients on Rousseau & Rousseau's list who have cubist paintings insured. Oh, I don't know. I can't see how that would be helpful."

"Hey, don't discard that idea. You might be on to something."

I looked at him. "You think so?"

"When cubism emerged in Europe, it was met with harsh criticism and disapproval. Picasso and Braque were reputed to have started cubism as a response against the realism in impressionism. They wanted to depict the irrationality of the human experience. At first, the critics and art snobs didn't take well to life being shown in angular shapes. The more these two guys developed it, the further away from realism it moved, until some paintings didn't resemble the original object or figure at all. For some it was an offence to aesthetic beauty. They didn't approve of this unorthodox representation of life. Kubanov is insane enough to have a similar opinion."

"Or maybe I am just desperately looking for links where there are none."

"I think we should look into that." He parked the SUV in a side street. "But we'll do that later. Right now we are meeting with the Brinius couple."

I followed him to the main street, filled with high-end stores. We entered an old building and went up to the second floor. Colin stopped in front of a large wooden door and knocked out a rhythm. The door opened wide to reveal a spacious office with high ceilings, elegantly furnished. The woman standing in the door was exceptionally beautiful with a carriage that spoke of class and very likely old money.

"Isaac Watts, you are as handsome as ever." She was talking to Colin, using one of his poet aliases, the one who was a gallery owner.

"And you are as breathtaking as ever." Even though Colin had adopted a British accent similar to Manny's, his tone and body language spoke of respect and affection. "Not a day older than the last time I saw you."

"Stop flirting with my wife and come inside, you scoundrel."

I looked around the petite woman and saw a man guiding his wheelchair to the front door. His suntanned face was filled with good humour. He was one of those people who hadn't allowed his physical limitations to stop his enjoyment of life. It was clear in the many laughter lines and the deep emotions on his face when he looked at his wife.

"And who is this lovely creature you brought with you?"

"Michael and Victoria, please meet Doctor Genevieve Lenard." Colin held out his hand towards the couple. "Jenny, these are my good friends, Michael and Victoria Brinius."

"Come in, come in." Michael held out his hand. "Doctor Lenard, it is a pleasure to meet you."

I shook his hand briefly, then Victoria's. "Please call me Genevieve."

"Are you English?" Victoria asked as she closed the door behind us.

"No, but I prefer the English pronunciation of my name."

"I have another painting for you." Colin lifted the forgery from my apartment, following Michael as he rolled his chair towards a door to the right. "What have you got for us?"

"Oh, my God, Isaac, you will pee in your pants when we show you." Victoria walked faster to catch up to Michael and rested her hand on his shoulder. Her speech was not as elegant as her bearing, which made her more approachable. Her voice raised slightly in pitch with her excitement. "I couldn't believe when Michael showed me. I've never seen anything like this."

We entered a large room, set up as an art studio. A long wooden workbench along the side wall was covered in bottles, paints, cloths, brushes and numerous other paraphernalia. I stopped and focussed on my breathing. It was beyond my comprehension how anyone could be productive in such chaos. Intellectually I understood that certain personality types felt safer surrounded by disorder. I didn't. To my thinking, a cluttered environment was a sign of an undisciplined mind.

"Oh, don't mind the mess, Genevieve." Michael stopped his chair in front of three easels set up next to the other. "I can never get Victoria to put anything in its place. Then she fights with me when she loses something. At least she hasn't misplaced me yet."

"I would never do that, you silly man." Victoria leaned down to kiss the top of his head. She straightened, looked at me, then at Colin with her head tilted. "We've been nagging you for like forever to settle down. I always knew the perfect woman would cross your path. Is she the one?"

"Victoria Gaudette Brinius." Michael sat up straighter in his chair. "That is none of our business. Sorry, Isaac. Now hit the lights, woman."

When the room lost the brightness of the artificial light, I felt relieved. The tension that had moved into Colin's body language had been confusing. I resisted the urge to try and make sense of it and focussed on the purpose of our visit. Light coming from the front room left everything dimmed, including the clutter.

"Genevieve, do you know what an underpainting is?"

"No, but from the term I conclude that it is a painting under the main painting?"

Colin stepped closer to me, narrowing his eyes at the three paintings on the easels. All three were turned around, the clear canvasses facing the front. That had been something I had noticed. Instead of the usual heavy brown paper covering the back of my bedroom painting, it was a thin, blank canvas.

"Underpaintings are more than that," Colin said. "Painters as early as High Renaissance artists used this technique. It is said that Titian pioneered it, but there are many other theories. It is an initial layer of paint that serves as a base.

Some say that it is done in monochrome, other masterpieces done by the greats have complete paintings hiding under the one exhibited in museums or galleries. Another theory is that if the underpainting is done correctly, it establishes the tonal values for the overpainting to be done perfectly."

"And loads of other theories which Isaac and I have had many arguments about. Most times the underpainting is the foundation for the overpainting. In other words, it is the same image. But there are examples in masterpieces where the underpainting is a completely different image." Michael nodded at the canvasses. "When you brought me those first two paintings, all I saw was forgeries. One good forgery and one great one—yours. But I didn't look for more until you brought me the original. I got curious what Braque might have hidden behind this famous work of his and brought in my infrared equipment."

"He was so excited to have this original in his hands. You should have seen him, Isaac. Like a kid with a new toy." Victoria was once again standing next to Michael, her hand resting on his shoulder. He covered her hand with his, a pose unconscious and I suspected second nature to this couple.

"When I took the first image, I was heartbroken when I didn't see anything spectacular under the original. A few images later, I was deeply disappointed. But, like now, the room was dark-ish, and I had turned your forgeries around to not distract me. I have no idea why I did it, but I took an image of one of the forgeries—the back of the forgery. And boy, did I get an eyeful."

Victoria handed Colin what looked like a very sophisticated digital camera.

"Take a shot so you will believe me." Michael's voice held a dramatic tone. "I still can't believe what I saw."

Colin stepped closer to the first forgery, brought the viewfinder to his eye and took a photo. He lowered the camera to look at the little display screen. He gasped. "Jesus."

"What?" I moved next to Colin and looked at the camera in his hands. On the display screen was a cubist painting. There were no colours, only stunning geometric shapes. He looked at me, looked back at the camera and shook his head. He inhaled deeply, moved to the other forgery and took a photo of it. This time a different cubist painting appeared on the display screen.

"Do you recognise any of these?" I asked Colin softly.

"No. These are very small images, but they are not from any known cubist artist I know. But it is without a doubt typical cubist style. My God, what does this mean?"

He toggled between the two images, tilting the camera for me to see. These were exquisite works of art I wouldn't mind owning. One was a cityscape and one a landscape.

The wheelchair made a soft squeaking sound as Michael rolled it closer. "Do you see how the underpaintings are almost to the edge of the frames?"

Colin made an affirmative sound. Indeed, the material used to cover the back of the paintings stretched two thirds onto the back of the frames.

"What did they paint on?" I asked.

"Looks like a thin canvas." Colin leaned in to look at the back of one of the forgeries. "Not entirely uncommon to use as a back cover, but definitely uncommon to paint on the back. And then to cover the painting with a layer of paint."

"We had actually planned to remove the paintings from the frames for further analysis," Victoria said. "When Michael saw the underpaintings, we decided to leave everything as is."

"Good thinking." Colin straightened. "Thank you."

"So, what do you think, my friend?" Michael asked.

"I think we need to do more checking." Colin looked at me. "There are a few ways to check for underpaintings. Michael has used infrared light, the most common first step. Then there is ultraviolet light and radiography."

"For this you only need good digital camera," Michael said. "My equipment is much better than that camera, but didn't show anything more than what you've just seen. A while ago a few artists produced paintings that could only be seen through the cameras of smartphones and cell phones equipped with CCD."

My mind was consumed with processing this new information. The most important element in this new development was that Kubanov was communicating. He was sending messages he wanted us—me—to interpret and act on. Looking at these underpaintings gave me no insight into what those messages might be.

"We should check this painting too." Colin helped Victoria set up an easel between the original and the other forgeries, and placed the painting from my bedroom on it, the back towards us. None of us were surprised when Colin took a photo and it revealed another underpainting.

I was still standing very close to Colin. He turned his head to look me. "Does this mean anything to you?"

"No. Should it?" I tilted my head to the side and studied the geometric shapes coming together to form a pastoral scene. This one looked more similar in style to the Klee Colin had given me for my birthday than Braque or Picasso's cubist works. "I'm not an expert in this. I don't know what this is pointing us to."

Colin grunted his acknowledgement and continued to stare at the display screen. I stood in silence, hoping for a connection to click in my mind.

"I'm not going to ask what this is about." Michael's statement broke into the quiet. His expression wasn't clear in the low light, but his tone was for the first time without levity. "Isaac, if you and Genevieve need help in anything, all you have to do is ask. Victoria and I will be here. This is not about owing anyone anything."

"Thank you, Michael." Something was off with Colin's tone. I wished there were more light. I no longer knew what the intention was behind everyone's words. As if hearing my thoughts, Victoria turned on the lights, bathing the room in bright artificial light.

Colin politely declined their offers of coffee, tea and breakfast. Victoria helped us carry the paintings to the SUV and saw us off. It was quiet in the SUV for the first few minutes. I was thinking about everything I had observed. "Why won't you accept Michael's offer of help?"

"You caught that one." His smile was quickly replaced by concern. "Do you think he got that?"

"I couldn't see his nonverbal cues clearly, but from what I saw, no."

"Good. I want to keep it like that."

"Why?"

"It's not about Michael and Victoria. They are wonderful people. It's his brother I don't trust."

"Then why did you take the paintings to him?"

"His brother is in Ireland at the moment. I knew it was safe to have the paintings there. Michael would never say anything to his brother, but that man shows up at the most inopportune times."

"What's wrong with him?"

"He's a cop." The disgust with which he said that was so unexpected, I laughed. "It's not funny, Jenny. He's a really good cop."

This made me laugh even harder.

An annoying ringtone dampened my mirth. It sounded like the music played before the wrestling matches Vinnie and Colin watched.

"It's Millard," Colin said. "You'd better get that."

"Stop changing the ringtones on my phone." I found my smartphone and swiped the screen. "Hello, Manny. You're on speakerphone."

"Frey with you?"

"Yes."

"Come to the office."

"Not even a pretty please, Millard?" Colin tilted his head towards the phone. "We're on our way home. Why do you need us at the office?"

"My guys found some paintings in Hawk's warehouse. Cubist paintings. They brought them here, and supermodel is helping me put them up in the conference room."

As Manny spoke, the pending insight into the numbers broke through. The clarity in my mind was dazzling. "Is Francine there?"

"Yes, Doc. Wait, I'll put you on speakerphone too."

"Hey, girlfriend."

"Francine, can you please locate Rousseau & Rousseau client files for me?"

"Sure, which ones?"

"Each client has a number allocated when they sign with Rousseau & Rousseau. I think the numbers on the website frames are client numbers."

"Shit. Have you told Phillip?"

"Not yet. Just get those files, please. We'll be there in another—"

"—ten minutes," Colin finished.

"Make it five, Frey." Manny disconnected the call and I put the phone back in its pocket in my handbag. Colin sped up, but stayed within the speed limit. Was my suspicion about the client files correct? If so, how was it going to connect to the rest of the case?

Chapter SEVENTEEN

Manny's voice met us as Colin and I stepped out of the elevator into Rousseau & Rousseau. I was carrying two of the paintings, Colin the other two, including the original. Around his neck, he had an expensive looking camera that he had taken from his SUV's trunk. He only smiled when I asked him why he would leave such expensive equipment in his vehicle. We followed the sound of Manny's serious tone to the large conference room at the opposite end of our floor. I seldom came here.

"About bloody time you two show up." Manny stood at the far end of the spacious room, his hands on his hips. His thumbs were pointing back, indicating an argumentative mood.

"Are these all the paintings?" Colin didn't pay attention to Manny's rudeness, immediately attracted by the new additions to the room's decor.

"There was a room behind Hawk's room in the warehouse where he kept all these." Manny waved a hand at the paintings hanging against the wall. Six months ago, when Phillip had the team room built, he had also renovated this conference room. It was now larger and set up to serve as a mini-gallery if ever the need arose. Along the wall were adjustable hooks to hang as many or as few paintings as were needed. Paintings of different sizes by different artists covered two walls.

"How many did you find?" I asked, walking to the closest painting. I recognised the work as Juan Gris' Violin and Checkerboard.

"Thirteen."

"These look like originals." Colin leaned in to a painting. "There's always a margin of error, but I'm ninety-nine percent sure this painting is an original Cézanne."

"I was afraid of that." Phillip stood in the door, his demeanour so unlike his normal professionalism that I took a step closer.

"What's wrong?"

He took a deep breath. "All these paintings are insured by Rousseau & Rousseau. I have no idea how it is possible that someone had access to this data. I pride myself in protecting my clients' confidentiality. It is what this business has been built on."

"Kubanov," Manny and Colin said at the same time. Colin turned back to inspect the paintings.

"This is a disaster." Phillip pulled out a chair and sat at the table. In the seven years I had known him, I had never seen him dejected. "Even the slightest hint of our clients' data being vulnerable and our reputation is destroyed."

"He's hitting you where it hurts." Manny sat down opposite Phillip. "He's getting to Frey on a personal level, and to you professionally. Last time he had one of the best hackers working for him, giving him access to your computers. Maybe he found somebody like that again to get into your files."

"No one has been in the system." Francine walked into the room, carrying a stack of folders. It wasn't going to get easier for Phillip. Francine put the files on the table and looked at me, the *frontalis* and *orbicularis oris* muscles in her face tight with anger. "Thirteen files for thirteen numbers."

"What's this, Genevieve?" Phillip's body tensed. He had recognised the folders.

"The numbers hidden in the frames around my photos on the website looked familiar to me. On the way here I realised why and asked Francine to see if there were client files for each of those numbers."

"Dear God." Phillip reached for the folders, but pulled his hand back.

"Manny's guys have found thirteen paintings in the warehouse. There are thirteen files here." I picked up the top file. "I think we should look for connections."

Francine and Colin also took files, the atmosphere in the conference room turning heavy with tension. It didn't take long to confirm each of the paintings on the wall belonged to one of the thirteen clients insured by Rousseau & Rousseau.

"How the hell did someone get access to these files?" Manny walked along the table where we had laid out the files, open on the page with the painting information.

"I'm the best there is, Manny." There was no arrogance in Francine's tone or body language. She was making a statement of fact. "If an unauthorised person got into this company's computer system, I would have found it. I've looked since the day Colin and Genevieve disappeared and haven't found any breach. It is no fault of Rousseau & Rousseau's."

Some of the tension left Phillip's shoulders. He upheld a high work ethic and set high standards for everyone, including himself. His integrity was paramount to his business and he saw Rousseau & Rousseau as an extension of him. It was. And that was why I could comprehend his distress.

I stood in front of a painting, thinking. Colin was on the other side of the room, taking his time with each painting. Francine was positing an unlikely theory about government espionage and Manny was becoming increasingly agitated. Something was trying to connect in my consciousness. A keyword someone had said, a clue I had observed, or a sequence of events. It could be one or all of them, but I knew when that connection clicked, I would know where and how Kubanov had gained access to Rousseau & Rousseau's database.

"These are all originals," Colin said. "Except for one."

Curious about an anomaly, I walked to stand next to him. He was looking at a familiar painting, but it was the one next to it that caught my attention.

"Oh my." My voice was a shocked whisper. "This is Braque's Man with a Guitar, the *L'homme à la guitare*. I must have seen this somewhere and that is why I included this in my email."

"It makes sense, but were we at the warehouse or did we see it somewhere else?"

"I guess we'll never know." It was most perturbing to have a gaping hole in my memory. I looked at the other Braque painting from Hawk's warehouse, the one that used to be my favourite. This brought the number of Harbour of Normandy paintings up to five, one of which was the original.

"Is this one also a forgery by the same person?" I asked.

"No." Colin pointed at the signature in the left-hand corner. "This is the artist who painted your reproduction. This is the painting that was in your bedroom, Jenny."

I took a step away from the painting. There was no doubt in my mind that this piece of art would never hang in my house again. No matter the lack of rationality, the association attached to this specific work would remind me of Kubanov every time I looked at it. The Klee Colin had given me for my birthday would be much better above my bed.

"How sure are you all the others are originals, Frey? If that one is a fake, maybe the others are also fakes." Manny was glaring at my painting.

"As I said earlier, there is always a margin of error, but this is the only non-original in this room. I would've recognised a forgery. It would take an above exceptional forger to duplicate all these paintings and not be found out."

"Someone like you?"

"You might not be as sarcastic if you see what we found out about the forgeries." Colin found a place on the second wall for the original Braque that we had brought with us. "This one should be with his brothers."

"Did your friend tell you anything about the Harbour of Normandy?" Phillip asked.

"Not about the original, no. Except that it is the original, just as I thought. Francine, can you connect my camera to the screen in here?" Colin handed Francine his camera and she got busy with the multimedia system. He pushed four conference chairs against the third wall and placed the three forged paintings and my reproduction on it, showcasing the backs. "We'll need to get easels in for these."

"I hope you plan to add a tell to your show pretty fast, Frey."

Even Phillip showed signs of impatience. Colin ignored Manny and took his camera from Francine with a nod. "If you can turn off the lights, please."

Manny and Phillip both swivelled their heads from the paintings to the screen now lowered over a part of the wall with the originals. Francine pressed the button controlling the lights and the room darkened, only the light coming from the corridor casting shadows. Colin spent some time with the digital settings on his camera before he took a photo and waited for the Bluetooth connection to transfer it to the screen. Again I was amazed at the beauty of the painting as it came up on the screen. Colin moved to take photos of the other forgeries.

"Oh my God." Francine's gasp was audible.

"What the bloody hell is that?" Manny gaped at the colourless painting on display.

"Underpaintings." Phillip gave a brief description, similar to what I had been told an hour earlier. I turned on the lights, needing to see their body language. I had hated not seeing Michael and Victoria's nonverbal cues.

"I want a life-size print of each of those paintings here." Manny pointed at the paintings resting on the chairs. "I need to see it, not look at a blank canvas or look at a slideshow on a screen."

"I'll get it done," Francine said.

"We need the other forgeries." The confusion on everyone's faces told me I had to explain. "According to Colin the forgery replacing his in the safe house and the one replacing the reproduction in my apartment were painted by the same artist. Someone had to break in to replace all the paintings. Has anyone reported a burglary?" I asked Phillip. "Have any of our clients indicated in any way that these paintings had been taken from their homes?"

"No. Ms McCarthy wouldn't have known hers had been replaced, had she not wanted to sell it."

"Looking at this, I posit that these owners all have paintings in their homes they think are originals. We should get those forgeries and check all of them for underpaintings." As I said this, more pieces clicked into place. "Once we have those paintings, I think we will have the message Kubanov is trying to send me."

"A message, Doc?"

"We are working on the theory that Kubanov wants revenge for whatever crime he perceives we have committed against him. It's not a strongly substantiated theory, but I feel comfortable using it. It fits with Kubanov's psychological profile." I had their full attention. "Through some means Kubanov knows personal information about Colin and confidential details about Rousseau & Rousseau. He has been acting on this information, killing Colin's associates and setting him up for murders. He's also using this information to discredit Phillip's business. Why Colin and Phillip? What do they have in common?'

"You," Francine said softly. "Which means that Kubanov would want to get to you too. Apart from replacing your Braque painting, what else has he done that included you?"

"He sent her those fucking daffodils." Manny sat down and looked at me through narrowed eyes. "So you're thinking that Kubanov is sending you some message with the backpaintings?"

"Underpaintings," I said. "Kubanov likes to play games. He's a strategist. Nothing he does is without purpose. I'm wondering how long he has been planning this. He would've needed to commission the artist quite some time ago to paint not only forgeries, but also underpaintings on the back of the forgeries. Then he would've needed a burglar to break into these people's homes and replace the paintings."

"But first he would've needed to know who owns which paintings, where they live and how to enter their homes." Phillip turned to Francine. "Six months ago, Kubanov got someone to get into Genevieve's computers. Could he have downloaded those client files then?"

"No. I've checked and double-checked. And I will check

again, but those files had not been accessed by anyone but those with authorisation."

"I need a list of when those files were accessed and by whom." That looming connection was gaining ground, but still out of reach. "We need those forgeries. I need to see what is behind them."

"Damn it." Phillip so seldom swore that we all looked at him in surprise. "I'll call everyone in to the office. I refuse to think that it is one of my team who betrayed me. We'll have those paintings here as soon as possible."

I needed to be in my viewing room, in my precisely arranged environment where I could allow the different components to fall into place. Any further discussion paused when Manny's smartphone rang. With an annoyed look at the device, he answered the call and left the conference room. Phillip and Colin started talking about the equipment needed to best see the underpaintings. Francine nodded towards the door in a gesture I had come to interpret as a request to follow her. We walked to the team room.

"I know you have a suspicion of someone in the company," she said. "Someone who gave Kubanov that information."

"How do you think you know this?"

"Because I have a gut feeling that you have a gut feeling." Her wide and teasing smile warned me not to fall into her trap.

I inhaled deeply. Pointing accusing fingers at someone without evidence did not feel right. I chose my words carefully. "People commit crimes for different reasons. One of those, maybe the most powerful motivator, is money. You said you were going to look deeper into the employees' finances. Did you?"

"I started a search, but there's been so much happening at the same time that I dropped it. I've been looking into Dukwicz, but now I will make this a priority."

I took a few steps to my viewing room. I didn't want to taint her search, but also didn't want her to waste time looking at the wrong people. "Start with those closest to Phillip."

"Including you?"

I turned around, nodding. "Of course. It would be a futile exercise, but without looking at me as well, your investigation would be incomplete."

"So cool," Francine said as I walked to my desk. "You are so cool."

I settled in front of my computer, closed my eyes and thought about the paintings in the conference room.

"Jenny?" I opened my eyes to find Colin in the chair next to mine. A quick glance at the clock told me I'd had only had seven minutes alone. It was not enough time. "What are you thinking?"

"Not much. I don't have time to think."

"Okay." He drew out the last syllable, something he did when I became impatient.

"Sorry." I dropped my head against the high back of my office chair. "It's just frustrating."

"It is." He stretched his legs and crossed his ankles, a sign of high comfort. "But we are getting more and more pieces of the puzzle."

"Not fast enough. Kubanov will continue killing until we stop him. The question is whether it will be individuals like your friends or whether he is planning bombs for crowds."

"Still individuals, Doc." Manny stepped into the viewing room, the corners of his mouth turned down. Reading strangers' faces was easier on an emotional level since there was no personal tie. The distress displayed on Manny's face caused my chest to constrict.

"Who's dead?"

"Tina Frazier."

Colin covered his eyes with one hand.

"Who was she?" I asked, looking at Colin. Uncharacteristically, I put my hand on Colin's and lifted it away from his face. He gripped my hand tightly, his lips thin lines of distress. "Another friend?"

"She was a good person, Jenny." His voice was low and hoarse. "One of the best goldsmiths I had worked with. She was a true artist. And she had a wicked sense of humour."

"Sorry, Frey." Manny pulled the third chair closer and fell into it. He looked exhausted.

"What happened to her?"

"Shot, like the others."

"Why is he targeting women? I have male friends as well."

"Maybe he wants Doc to think that these were all previous girlfriends and that will make her jealous. Maybe they are easier targets. I don't know."

"Kubanov won't choose anyone because they are easier targets." As I said this, evidence of the last few days caused me to reconsider. "Or maybe he did. It would not be the first time that he is contradicting his previous behaviour."

"We need to put a stop to him, Doc."

"I know. When did Tina Frazier die?"

"The local police think it happened late last night, but the autopsy will give us the exact time. Her sister found her this morning." There was little to no inflection in his tone. People did that when attempting to avoid the very personal nature of whatever they were saying. "This is another associate of Frey's, another artist."

"Wait." I recalled Manny's expression when he first

entered with the news. "You had known Tina Frazier was connected to Colin before he said it. How?"

Suspicion and anger replaced the grief on Colin's face. "Explain yourself, Millard."

"We need to include Phillip in this discussion." Manny stood up. "Doc, call him to meet us in the team room. This place is no good for meetings."

When Colin wanted to argue, I put my other hand on his and shook my head. "It will be good for Phillip to sit in."

"And prevent me from killing that arsehole." Colin waited, not letting go of my hand, while I asked Phillip to meet us in the team room. It was awkward. We got up and entered the team room at the same time as Phillip. Francine was at her computer, her fingers flying over the keys. Vinnie was already seated at the table.

"When did you come in?" I asked as Colin and I sat down.

"Two seconds ago. The old man told me we're having a meeting."

Manny cleared his throat. "Before we get onto the real reason for this meeting, I got some feedback from your convicts, Doc."

For a moment, I had no idea what Manny was talking about. I was still thinking about Colin's friend, and also wondering what Francine was finding. I blinked a few times while changing topics. "Oh, you're talking about interviewing those imprisoned killers who had used similar weapons."

"Yes. I gave the locals your list of questions. One idiot's gun exploded when he shot his victim, but he wouldn't say what gun it was or how it had exploded in his hand. Apart from the cocaine connecting these convicts, there was only one similarity in all their answers. They all said they had bought their weapons from the Printer."

"Who the fuck is that?" Vinnie asked. "I've been asking

around and no one knows someone using that street name."

"The convicts couldn't say. They had only spoken to him over the phone. All of them said he had a high-pitched voice and spoke with an Italian accent."

"It's Tall Freddy." Vinnie nodded as if he agreed with himself. "I'm willing to bet my aunt Theresa's cheesecake recipe that he also supplied them with the cocaine."

"Hawk had sent Tall Freddy five 3D printers." Pieces were beginning to fit now. "Could he have printed a few guns, sold them or given them to some of his customers? We know that 3D printing is still new and many printed guns have been reported to explode. This might have been the cause of that one killer's injuries."

The more I spoke the faster Manny was breathing. "Bleeding mother of all, Doc. Not only are you speculating, but it is a brilliant theory."

"That is not speculation." The audacity. "It's a hypothesis built on facts. The gun exploding in the one killer's hand is not physical evidence, but strong circumstantial evidence supporting my hypothesis."

"Potato, potahto. I still think it is a brilliant theory." Manny twisted around to look at Francine, who was totally consumed with what she was doing on the computer. "Supermodel, find everything you can on Tall Freddy. We need to see how he fits in with Kubanov."

Francine's fingers froze above the keyboard. She slowly looked up at Manny, blinking in the slow way she did when she flirted with the waiters during our lunches. "Handsome, but impatient. Just because I am the best in the world does not mean I am four people. Already I have five different searches running at the same time. Yours will have to take a number."

Her expressions told me she said this only to irritate

Manny. It was working. The artery on his forehead was becoming prominent, his face turning red.

"What other searches have you got?" Phillip asked.

"I'm almost done with this one, but I got a few results on my search into Dukwicz." She looked at Vinnie. "What did you find out?"

"That he's even worse than I had heard. He's a mercenary who does any kind of crime for money. Not only killing, but obviously kidnapping, burglary."

"What kind of burglary?" Colin asked. "If he stole anything of importance, I might have heard about it, but I've never heard that name."

"The kind of burglary where the dude goes in and destroys everything inside the house while the owners watch. Then he tortures them a little just for giggles before he takes all the watches."

"He only takes the watches?" Francine walked to the round table, carrying her laptop.

"Watches and clocks. Apparently, the dude has a thing for timepieces. And before you ask, most of those break-ins were never reported. Most of these burglaries were at the homes of some criminal. It was a message from some badass to a smaller badass to maintain the hierarchy of the food chain."

"Vinnie is right. I've found similar anecdotes about this Dukwicz guy. He hires himself out to organised crime bosses, all kinds of syndicates and the rich who want their competition to disappear. Basically, he is the muscle or gun for the worst of the worst."

"Why has no one ever caught him?"

"Because no one knows his full name for starters." Francine pointed at her laptop. "Not one single entry with his name other than just 'Dukwicz'."

"Did you check Interpol?" Manny asked.

"I don't have clearance to do a proper Interpol search."

"That was not my question, supermodel." Manny lowered his brow to stare at her. Clearly he had come to know her as well as I did.

"Okay, fine." Her smile was seductive. "You're so handsome when you get me. Sadly, Interpol doesn't know much about Dukwicz. Only a few rumours."

"Hmm. Doc, what do you make of this?"

"Give me a moment. Francine, can you open Susan Kadlec's crime scene report?" I gave Colin an apologetic smile. I didn't want to remind him that he had lost a good friend, but I had to make sure my suspicion was grounded.

"What are you looking for, girlfriend?" she asked a few seconds later.

"Can you put some of those crime scene photos up on the screen? If I remember correctly, her house had been devastated by whoever had killed her." The room went quiet when everyone must have realised my train of thought. Francine arranged six photos on the big screen against the wall. It looked like a tornado had gone through the living room and study. "Did the police find any watches in the house?"

"As a matter of fact, they said that it was strange to find not one single clock or watch in that house. They thought since she was a professor, she was maybe a bit nutty." Manny leaned back in his chair. "That bloody Dukwicz bastard killed her."

For a few seconds no one spoke. I had a few more things to add, but didn't know what was proper behaviour in such a situation.

"I can see that you have more, Jenny. Just say it. She's gone and nothing will bring her back."

"Dukwicz is our link between Tall Freddy and Kubanov." It felt good to finally draw a line between some of the elements in this case. "He also connects Hawk and Kubanov—"

"—which connects all of them," Manny said. "Well done, Doc."

I nodded. "We have the connections, but it still doesn't tell us what Kubanov's plan is. I want to find out what the final destination is in this game Kubanov is playing. I would also like to stop him from killing any more of Colin's friends."

Vinnie's eyebrows lifted. "Dude, who else died?"

"Tina Frazier."

"No fucking way." Vinnie swung around to look at Manny. "Is this why we're sitting here?"

"Yes." Colin let go of my hand, rested his forearms on the table and leaned towards Manny. "Millard was just going to tell us why he knew about my connection to Tina."

Manny exhibited the same agitation as before, but didn't show any insecure body language.

"Let me ask you this first, Frey." There was no antagonism visible in Manny's expression. "Apart from your work with Interpol, you have a lot of connections in the criminal world, right?"

Colin looked at him, not moving a muscle.

"Those people and the other people you have befriended along the way are not like Hawk—killers, the kind of dirt that should be cleaned off the streets."

"What's your question, Millard?"

Manny's internal struggle was visible only in his micro-expressions. Whatever he was about to say was going to require trust and he didn't want to trust Colin. Even though I believed he did.

"I have a dossier on you."

"You said so." Colin leaned back. "The one you showed to Phillip?"

"Correct." Manny inhaled deeply and spoke very fast on the exhale. "In the years I investigated you, I gathered as much intel on you as I could get my hands on. Friends, associates, connections, places you had been spotted, aliases."

I didn't want to leap to conclusions, but I anticipated Manny's next sentences.

"The people in our current case who have a connection to you all appear in my dossier. So does your Sydney Goddphin alias used for those strange purchases."

"You knew about Susan?" Colin's voice was strained. "And you didn't tell me earlier?"

"I knew very little. I only knew you visited her once a few years ago. I caught that one purely by chance. I never noticed her in your life before, or after. I didn't know the full extent of your friendship."

"What does this mean?" Vinnie asked.

"It means that someone saw his dossier, Vin." Colin didn't take his eyes off Manny. "Who did you show my dossier to, Millard?"

"Firstly, it is a paper file with clippings, printouts, photos and other paper documents connected to you. None of that was ever entered into any computer system. Secondly, you were a pet project for me, so I didn't show my bosses what I had on you."

"Not even after you arrested me and Interpol stole me from you?"

"Especially not then. I was asked if I'd had any useful information that would help them with their case against you. I gave them some stuff, the same intel I had on my computer and that was not gained by speaking to a lot of people and asking a lot of questions."

"Do you know exactly who saw this file?" I asked. Manny was avoiding a straightforward answer which made me suspicious.

"Phillip only had the bloody thing for four days. He read through everything, verified some things and gave it back to me."

"When I wasn't reading it, it was locked in the safe in my office," Phillip said.

"Sorry to tell you, my man, but that safe is piss-easy to open." Vinnie's expression fluctuated between guilt and pride. "It took me all of three minutes to get in there. Colin would've done it in under a minute."

"He has another safe, Vinnie," I said softly.

"How did you know?" Concern compressed Phillip's lips.

"Your body language changes slightly when you walk past the wooden cabinet to the left of your desk. When someone else comes close to the cabinet, the change is more visible. I never thought you were protective of the crystal glasses and expensive alcohol in there."

"Jesus, Doc. You're scary." Manny's eyes were large. "You see too much."

"Sometimes I don't see enough. If there is someone in Rousseau & Rousseau supplying Kubanov with information, why had I not caught onto that before?" My self-disgust was interrupted when Francine gave me her laptop and pointed at the screen.

"I don't need to be as good as you to see you're unhappy, Doc. What's up?"

I breathed deeply, not looking forward to the next few minutes. "I asked Francine to focus on an in-depth look into the finances of Rousseau & Rousseau employees. She found something that confirmed my earlier suspicions."

"You had suspicions and you didn't tell us?" Manny sat up. "You and your bloody dislike for speculation. Who is it? Who sold us out to Kubanov?"

I held out the laptop to Manny, but Phillip grabbed it first. He scanned the screen with an intensity not often seen until he realised what he was looking at. His face lost all colour, his hands gripping the laptop tighter than I thought wise. Manny shifted closer and squinted at the screen. I saw the exact moment he came to the same conclusion as Phillip. "That bloody bitch."

Chapter EIGHTEEN

Describing the atmosphere in the large conference room as tense would have been a gross understatement. And it had nothing to do with the paintings surrounding us. Vinnie and Francine had decided to not be part of this meeting. Francine was looking for information on Tall Freddy and Vinnie had said he needed to know more about 3D-printed guns.

Colin had insisted on sitting in on this meeting. Being tortured at the hands of Kubanov was a strong reason to confront the person handing him on a silver plate to Kubanov. I had wanted to stay behind, avoiding the impending conflict, but Phillip had insisted. My expertise would be useful as Phillip and Manny interrogated.

Sitting next to Colin, I did not feel comfortable being in such close proximity to this confrontation. Watching interviews on my monitors was safe. This wasn't. My thoughts were interrupted as Angelique walked into the conference room, carrying a tray filled with coffee and cookies. I glared at the coffee.

"Why don't you sit down for a moment, Angelique?" Phillip asked, his professional persona back in place. After Colin, he was the best at masking his emotions and thoughts.

"Sir? I thought I would make coffee for everyone else as well. They're working really hard."

"That's true, but we need your help." Phillip gestured to the chair opposite him and Manny. Colin and I were sitting a few seats away from them, the better for me to observe.

Angelique sat down, wariness written in every movement. "What can I do, sir?"

"You can tell me why." Anger briefly coloured Phillip's face before he suppressed it.

"Why what, sir?" Repetitive swallowing and her arms folded tightly, hiding her hands indicated Angelique's feeling of discomfort and possibly guilt. I suspected she already knew her secret was no longer that.

"Why you felt justified in betraying me and everything Rousseau & Rousseau stands for."

"I don't know what you are talking about, sir." She did. It was visible in the flash of recognition in her eyes and the quick intake of breath.

"You know exactly what Mr Rousseau is talking about, Angelique." Manny was using his law enforcement tone. It was strong, confident and intimidating in its push for compliance. "Answer his question."

It was almost amusing to watch her hold on to her pretence of ignorance a few seconds more. The *masseter* muscles in her jaw tightened, she looked at Manny with dislike before she turned her gaze on me. It was a look of such staggering hatred that I flinched before I could control my reaction. I hadn't been prepared for that. Her look softened marginally as she turned to Phillip.

"It was bad enough when you hired her." She nodded towards me, her last word heavy with animosity. "But when you brought in these lowlife riffraff, I knew you had lost your way. At least with her, I could avoid her. She never talked to me and when she did, she treated me as if I was beneath her, but she never did anything evil."

Her words were coming faster, her tone belligerent. "These people are evil. When you showed your support for their activities, I could no longer be loyal to you. You became a hypocrite. You gave up all those high ethics and morals you preach to us. Working with these people."

"She's lying," I said, surprising myself. I didn't want to take part in this conflict, but all eyes were on me now, Angelique's filled with hatred. "Her tone, her hands, face, every part of her body pointed to deceit as she was talking about Phillip being a hypocrite. She was telling the truth about disliking me and the others."

"Dislike?" Angelique spat out the word. "I don't dislike you, Doctor Lenard. I despise you and everything you represent."

"And what do I represent?" I asked, genuinely curious. People sharing beliefs such as Angelique's often formed factions against anything and anyone not fitting into their definition of normal. I had faced plenty of disapproval in my life. Her vitriol wasn't new to me nor was it affecting me.

The *levator labii superioris* muscles raised Angelique's top lip. Disgust. "People like you infect society with your mental deviance. You come into our lives and insist we accept you because you are ever so special, because you think your sickness makes you deserving of tolerance."

We all jumped when Phillip slammed his hands down on the table. "Enough!"

"No, Phillip," I said. "Let her talk. She's telling me much more than just the words."

Phillip looked at me as if I were a stranger. His anger was robbing him of rationality. Laypeople often referred to it as looking through the haze of rage. I knew his anger was based on offence taken on my behalf. I waited until he saw that I was not hurt or offended. His professional mask fell back into place and he nodded.

"What is her highness telling you, Doc?"

I tilted my head to the side, looking past Angelique's

vitriol. "She dislikes me, but not as much as she's pretending. I believe that she is uncomfortable around me, purely because she doesn't understand me, how I think or function. Most people don't. No, she's using this to conceal a different motivation."

"One much less noble than saving society from weird people." Manny pulled printouts from the file in front of him. He sounded bored. "Money, the age-old root of all evil. We have the evidence right here. Your financial history shows that you've been having difficulties. Your bank account is in a sorry state. But you were smart. You got your husband to open an account not connected to any of your other individual or combined accounts. Oh, don't look so surprised. We know everything about your life now. We know that in the last ten months your husband's new bank account filled up with a few handsome payments."

"Was fifty thousand Euro really worth selling your integrity, Angelique?" Phillip asked.

For a moment the Angelique I had first met showed herself. The woman with high ethics and moral values, reliable to a fault. That moment didn't last long. Her lips stretched into a sneer. "You don't understand. You never will. He did."

"Who did?" Phillip asked softly.

"He understood what it was like struggling to pay a mortgage with an unemployed husband."

"I didn't know your husband lost his job," Phillip said.

"Of course not. You were too interested in Doctor Lenard and her scum to take notice. He did. He knew how I felt about these people working here and helped me understand that it was okay to feel like it. That these people are not okay."

"When did Kubanov first contact you?"

"About ten months ago." Her immediate answer confirmed that Kubanov had been the one contacting her. I took note of the fact she had recognised his name. She didn't even realise what she had revealed. "He is a gentleman. In the last few months his voice has become even softer. He spoke to me in a tender whisper. Not like some other people."

Manny dismissed her pointed glare. I didn't pay attention to it. Something else had caught my attention. I chose my words carefully.

"As a deception expert, I know that lying over the phone is considerably easier than in person. We don't give away as much with the tone of our voices as we do with our body language. Maybe he was only creating the image of being a gentleman, making his voice soft like you said."

"You are not as smart as you think, Doctor Lenard." She lifted her chin to look at me down the length of her nose. "He didn't just speak to me on the phone. He's been visiting me. Quite a handsome man too. Not many men would look good without any hair. It really suits his kind character."

For the next twenty minutes Phillip and Manny continued to question Angelique. After a few answers, it became clear in her body language that she was not going to reveal much more. As it was, she had given me a lot of information even if I didn't know how to interpret it. Not yet.

"I quit!" Angelique stood up, her body rigid. "I will not be treated like this. I quit."

"No, Angelique." Phillip used the quiet tone he reserved for grim news. "You are fired and you will be arrested."

"Arrested?" Her voice was high.

Manny snorted. "You really think you can commit and admit to industrial espionage, data theft, and even worse, working for an international criminal and not be prosecuted for it?"

I blocked out her ranting and the two policemen who entered the room. Staring at the painting across from me, I tried to make sense of what she had said. Her dislike of me had not come as a surprise. It had been communicated in her body language from the first day I had entered these offices. I knew the names of all the employees here, but had spoken less than a dozen times to each. As much as Francine wanted to change that, I was not a social person. I saw no sense in wasting time with friends, talking about topics that didn't enrich one's knowledge or life. On a sociological level I understood the need humans had for such interaction. I didn't have that need.

But as I thought about this, I realised that by being unsociable, I had missed out on cues Angelique might have communicated. Subtle or not, I would have picked up on nonverbal cues of intention, had I looked more carefully.

"I know that look." Colin touched my arm. "This is not your fault, Jenny."

"I should've seen it. I should have noticed the change in her ten months ago." I turned to him, finding it difficult to maintain a confident posture. "Am I so self-absorbed that I don't notice the people around me?"

"No, Genevieve," Phillip said from behind me. I twisted around to see Angelique and the policemen gone. Phillip looked sad. "You see a lot. You see more than most people even realise. You are just much more selective in what you look at and look for."

"You're using your polite mediation skills on me now."

His soft laughter didn't reach his eyes. "Maybe a little. But you shouldn't feel responsible for Angelique's behaviour. It was she who listened to Kubanov, who fell into his trap, took his money and gave away our secrets. Not you. Not me. Angelique. She will pay the price for that."

"We've also been paying that price." With my left hand I gripped my right elbow in a half-hug. "She gave Kubanov all this information not just about our clients, but personal information about us. About Colin. Oh my God. That must be how Kubanov got all that detailed knowledge of Colin's visit to Russia. That is how he knew to capture him and torture him."

"Stop talking such bullshit, missy." Manny pushed Phillip out the way, his frown severe and his hands on his hips. "I thought that you of all people would be above this self-pity crap. This is not your fault. Phillip is right, it wasn't your job to see it. Why didn't I see something? I'm a bloody detective, for shit's sake. And Phillip worked with Angelique every day. Why didn't he see it? Stop being such a sissy, buck up and tell me what you think about the crap that old biddy said."

I stared at Manny, my mouth slightly agape. Never, not once in my life, had anyone told me to *not* take responsibility. I blinked a few times, realising that he was waiting for an answer, not very patiently. An unfamiliar feeling warmed my chest. It took a moment to identify it as a strong fondness.

"Um… the man she was describing is not Kubanov." I grabbed onto the topic with vigour. Analysis was safe and familiar grounds. "We have all seen Kubanov. He has a full head of hair and is vain enough to maintain that, even colouring it to not show any grey. The times I had heard him speak, there was nothing gentle about his voice and he most definitely didn't speak in a tender whisper."

"I agree with Jenny. That man doesn't have a soft voice." Colin would know. He had spent six horrid days in Kubanov's basement.

"Could it be someone acting on his behalf?" Phillip asked.

"That would be speculation." I shook my head. "All I'm willing to say is that there are two options. Either it is not

Kubanov, or it is him, but something about him has changed. It would explain the inconsistencies I've observed. And the evidence that he is taking a much more active role now. Instead of delegating as much as he had done in the past, he's showing involvement at a much earlier level."

"What do you think changed?" Manny threw his hands up when he saw my expression. "Fine, fine. You don't want to speculate. Just think about it, will you, Doc?"

Manny waited until I reluctantly nodded before he stormed out the conference room, followed by Phillip. Without speaking, Colin and I got up and walked to my viewing room. Once we were settled in front of the monitors, he sighed heavily. "You know, she was courteous towards me. She never treated me like the riffraff she said we were."

"Angelique? That venomous hostility was an exaggeration. I'm convinced she didn't like us and wasn't very comfortable with us in the office, but that performance she gave was rehearsed."

"It was really about the money?"

"Everybody has a price." I slowed down towards the end of my sentence. "Of course you would know this. The people in your world work on a price for everything."

"It's hard to believe she was the one who drugged our coffee."

Colin and I spent the rest of the day working through Hawk's computer. We found nothing else to strengthen the link between him and Kubanov. Or anything that pointed to Kubanov. I did find a few emails from Hawk's daughter. Her writing style was rife with teenage hyperbolic statements, but it spoke of an intelligent mind.

We had just finished snacking on rice cakes when Phillip brought in the last forged painting. The toll this episode had taken on us was high. But it was Phillip who was affected the most by this. His distress was visible in the deepened frown lines, his downturned mouth, and the heaviness in his shoulders when he thought no one was looking. In the last eleven hours, he had personally contacted each of the owners of the paintings recovered from the warehouse. In a manner only Phillip could, he had reassured them of the security of the rest of their valuables.

I had thought it improbable, but he had managed to retrieve all the paintings, cajoling the owners to give him access to their homes if they were out of town. As the other Rousseau & Rousseau employees brought the paintings in, Colin was checking them. Each one so far was a forgery and had an underpainting on the back.

My attention was drawn away from my monitors and thoughts by Colin's grunt as he sat down next to me.

"I don't recognise any of the underpaintings as originally painted by the masters." He kneaded the muscles in the back of his neck. "I think they're all originals."

"Painted as underpaintings? That's odd." I picked up my coffee mug only to see it empty. When had I finished another mug of strong coffee? "Here's another oddity. Rousseau & Rousseau insures pieces of high value all over Europe, all over France. Concentrating the robberies around Strasbourg makes it firstly a very targeted action, and secondly easy for us to find. What was his rationale behind it?"

"Maybe he didn't think we would find the paintings?"

An inelegant sound of disagreement escaped my mouth. "Maybe. I don't know how we would have found the paintings if we hadn't gone to the warehouse and Hawk hadn't been killed."

"Quite the elaborate setup for Kubanov to have planned."

I thought about this. "That would be in character for him.

He would've relished planning something like this, using his superior strategic planning skills. As we have studied him, he has also studied us. I'm sure Angelique freely discussed our habits, behaviour and conversations. From that alone he would have been able to obtain enough data to profile us."

"Sick and twisted," Vinnie said, leaning against the door.

"Maybe, but also very smart. My question now is what message is in those underpaintings."

"Well, let's go look at them, Jen-girl. Phillip sent me to get you. He has all the paintings set up in the conference room." A half smile eased some of the seriousness from his face. "I must say it looks super-weird to have half the room with paintings facing forward and the other half showing the backs of the paintings."

We walked into the conference room and my eyes widened. The wall to the right of the long conference table still held all the originals from Hawk's warehouse. The wall to the left was no longer empty. Seventeen paintings were neatly arranged on the wall, not one hanging off centre. Phillip was good with that, a feat I greatly appreciated. Of the seventeen paintings, four were familiar. The other thirteen were the ones Phillip had collected from the clients' homes. Under each painting was a life-size printout of its underpainting.

"You were right, Doc." Manny startled me when he spoke. I had been completely absorbed by what I was seeing and I hadn't noticed him in the room.

"I know." Being right about the originals replaced by forgeries with underpaintings didn't help solve the mystery though. "Now we need to understand this."

I made my way from the one side of the wall to the other to get an overview of the underpaintings. Colin followed me, undoubtedly seeing aspects in the art I didn't.

"These are truly exquisite pieces. This is a very talented artist."

"Apart from waxing poetic about this criminal act, what else can you tell us about the paintings, Frey?" From Manny's tone, I concluded that he was frustrated. Knowing him, it was partly because of his lack of expertise and insight, but mostly because he had to rely on Colin for said expertise and insight.

"Waxing poetic about this artist's skill is, as a matter of fact, quite important, Millard."

I was getting used to blocking their insulting arguments. I did it once again and walked along the wall a second time, looking for clues beyond the art. Colin was right. These paintings were exquisite. The painting I was in front of depicted a typical European old town. The cobbles of the streets were squares, the buildings tall, angular and squashed on top of each other. Yet it was distinctive. This was a specific street in some European town. It looked familiar to me, but I put it down to having travelled throughout Europe, mainly visiting the old towns.

I moved to the painting next to it. This was another cityscape, but of a city much more modern. It had skyscrapers and landmarks that would make it easy to identify the street portrayed. The next painting was more difficult to characterise. Only after studying it for a few minutes did I recognise what looked like a mansion next to a river. Tall trees surrounded the house, a circular driveway leading to the front door. The cubist shaping of it had obscured it into a work of beauty. Again I had a sense of familiarity. This time I didn't dismiss it. I catalogued it and moved to the other paintings.

"These are all places," I said after my third time along the wall. "Not one of these paintings is of a person or object. All these are places. Cityscapes and landscapes."

"Hmm." Colin came to stand next to me. "You're right. What does that mean?"

"That's the wrong question." I frowned in impatience. "The right question is where these places are."

"Any ideas, Frey?"

I walked to the other side of the table to put some space between me and the paintings. Often I saw things better from a distance. I stared at the paintings, recalling my feelings of recognition. What was it about those few paintings that made me feel like I knew them?

"Do you agree, Jenny?" Only when Colin touched my elbow did I realise he was talking to me.

"Sorry, I wasn't listening. What did you say?"

"I said that it is ten o'clock, we haven't eaten dinner yet, and I think we should go home."

"No." I pulled my elbow out of his hold. "There is something about these paintings. I need to figure it out."

"Frey is right, Doc." Manny pushed himself out of his chair. I hadn't even seen him sit down. "We can get back to this, bright and early tomorrow morning."

"Vinnie's made dinner." Colin infused his tone with appeal as if Vinnie's dinner was a prize most coveted. I smiled.

"Go home, Genevieve. We'll get back to this in the morning." Phillip looked exhausted. "An art restorer from the Museum of Fine Arts is loaning me his handheld x-ray machine. He'll bring it tomorrow and we'll check all the paintings with it then. He said they can't loan us their larger machines, but the handheld ones are adequate alternatives. We can use it and analyse the results tomorrow."

"You should also go home and sleep." I was concerned about the dark rings under his eyes.

"I'm sure Vinnie's made enough for you to join us." Colin's invitation was so unexpected, we all looked at him in surprise. "What? I'm being nice."

"You inviting me too, Frey?" There was a hint of good humour in Manny's tone.

"Oh God. If you really have to come, then I suppose you can. If we don't feed you, you will most likely eat another packet of those wretched shortbread cookies you keep bringing into the office." Colin sounded highly inconvenienced, but I saw past it. He was not just being polite. He had seen something that had escaped my notice. Manny's diet, anyone's diet was of no interest to me. But maybe Manny needed a good meal, as we all did after today.

Since I was outnumbered, I agreed to go home to rest, but planned to be back early morning. I needed to spend more time in front of these paintings.

Chapter **NINETEEN**

Some people needed minutes to hours for the waking process to be completed. I generally needed only five minutes to reach a state of complete wakefulness. Not now. Something wrested me out of my sleep into instant vigilance. For a moment I lay frozen, my eyes closed, wondering what had caused this. It hadn't been a dream giving me some insight into the case. It had been something more elemental, a primitive reaction to looming danger.

Since Colin had taken to sleeping in my bed, it had been noteworthy that his presence had not kept me awake, or even worse, woken me whenever he moved. His steady, deep breathing assured me that he was fast asleep and had not been the cause of my heart beating fast in anticipation. Of what I didn't know. I opened my eyes, not surprised that only the light from the city and the moon were casting a soft glow in my room. It was still night.

"You're awake. Good." A raspy voice to my left activated my adrenal glands to inject fight-or-flight hormones into my system. "Hello, Genevieve."

There was a third and more common reaction to danger: freeze. Except for swinging my head to the left, I had very little control over my muscles. I wasn't sure I could even lift my hand to fight or move my legs to flee. This paralysis I had experienced six months ago when we had saved the president's son.

Sitting on the bed next to Colin's sleeping form was a man

dressed in dark colours. The meagre light in the room revealed his bald head, but it was his features I recognised. Kubanov. And he was pronouncing my name in the French way I loathed.

"So good of you to wake up, dear. Hopefully you will be able to chat with me this time."

The last time Kubanov had made a surprise appearance next to me, I had been unable to speak, unable to warn others of his presence. I was not going to allow it to happen this time. I inhaled to wake Colin up, to call for Vinnie or to shout loud enough for the neighbours to hear.

"Ah, ah, ah." Kubanov waved a gun back and forth on each sound. On a chuckle he pointed it at Colin's head, leaving only five centimetres between Colin's temple and the end of the barrel. "Don't make a sound, Genevieve. I have no problem shooting your lover's brains out."

"Why is Colin not waking up?" I was surprised that my mouth managed to form words. I was completely numbed by fear. Unwilling to give Kubanov that kind of power over me, I sought for calm, but it was painfully difficult when concern about Colin's unresponsive state was drawing me towards panic.

"I gave him a little something. Don't worry, it is not nearly as strong as what I gave you before. This will only let him sleep really well for a few hours."

"What do you want?" My voice was stronger even though my anxiety for Colin grew. How many times a week could one body effectively deal with being drugged like this? I took a deep breath and switched on Mozart's Horn Concerto No. 3 in E Flat Minor in the back of my mind. As background music to this newest trial, it might serve to give me the presence of mind I would need to retain as much as I could. Giving myself the goal of observing, absorbing and cataloguing put me in control. This was what I was good at. Even when I was limited by bad lighting.

"What I want, my dear Genevieve, is for you to suffer like me." His laugh was wheezy and manic. A painful cough stopped that disturbing sound and it took a few minutes for him to recover. "How delightful that I managed to sound like a clichéd Hollywood baddie."

"Why are you here?" I narrowed my eyes, my focus solely on him. A few things registered at the same time. Firstly, his bald head. Kubanov's profile would not have predicted him shaving his head. I wondered if there was another reason for the change. Secondly, his posture. He was sitting at an angle on the bed as if he truly were visiting with us, but something looked off. The lack of proper lighting was debilitating and fast becoming frustrating. I couldn't see the smaller muscle movements in his face. Nor could I see his other hand disappearing onto his thigh and covered in shadows.

"I'm here for many reasons." He adopted a wistful tone. "But mostly, I just want to have a little chat with my favourite person."

"Who's that?"

Again he laughed until he coughed. "Priceless. My favourite person is you, Genevieve. I'm hurt that you don't know this."

His hand holding the gun to Colin's head was outlined enough for me to notice the slight tremor. Kubanov was not nervous. He was sick. My eyes were drawn to the weapon in his hand. Again I loathed the low light for not affording me a good enough view.

I didn't answer his absurd statement. Not because I didn't know what to say, but because I was concerned about the steadiness of the weapon in his hand.

"Really? You have nothing to say to my compliment? I'm

devastated." His hoarse whisper drew my eyes away from the slightly trembling gun to his face. "Oh well, have it your way. Tell me how you liked your body art."

"It was simplistic." I chose my words with great consideration. Kubanov would not take an insult to his intelligence well. "Too easy to decrypt. As was the website. Too easy."

Success. His body stiffened, his head pulled back and there was an audible quick intake of air. "You think you are so smart, Genevieve. There is so much more to that tattoo than what you think. Have you not learned that there are always layers on top of layers on top of layers of everything?"

"Like the forged paintings?"

"Yes, of course. You found them." A minute change in his tone made me look really hard at his expression. I didn't know if I imagined the *risorius* muscles lift his mouth into a smirk. What was he feeling smug about? "I was a little bit disappointed, if I have to tell you the truth. It had been a lot of fun replacing all those paintings, leaving those rich idiots none the wiser."

"Of course you got only the best to replace those paintings for you."

"You think Hawk did that?" The cough resulting from his laughter was so strong this time, his hand holding the gun started shaking. My mouth went instantly dry with fear for Colin. "For someone so smart, you can sometimes be really naïve. Hawk was a terrible thief. He was only good at one thing and that was importing illegal goods. And storing things. Those were the qualities I used him for. Not for his cat burglar skills. He soon became redundant."

"And then you killed him." This time I did see his reaction. "Okay, so you had him killed. You wouldn't get your hands dirty, not with someone like Hawk."

"I would've preferred that he had stayed useful a little longer." He lifted one shoulder in a half shrug, not believing his own words. "I also would've preferred that you had not found those paintings so soon. But you found them and now you're wondering about the underpaintings, aren't you?"

"They are beautiful." I knew from Angelique's comments that this would antagonise Kubanov. I infused awe in my tone. "Not only the original paintings, but even the underpaintings are such exquisite pieces, I wouldn't mind having them in my home."

By the time I finished he was shifting on the bed. "That is not beauty. That is perversion. Putting whatever you see into squares and calling it art is a deviance. No brain sees things like that. Any artist claiming that cubism is a different perspective of vision is wrong! Brains like that are sick."

I almost smiled. "And you think I have a sick brain."

"Of course you do. I won't deny enjoying your intellect. It is quite a challenge, but you're sick. You are a weakness and a sickness in society. And you people are the weaker of the species. If we were in our basest, primal nature, you would never have survived. Only the strongest survive."

"Just like you are the strongest and are surviving?"

He jumped up and pushed the gun against Colin's head, his movements stiff and unsteady. I had pushed too far. Another rush of adrenaline spread through my body, adding to my fear and desire to escape into the safety of Mozart and my mind.

"Continue mocking me, Genevieve. I will splatter your boyfriend's brain matter all over you and this room."

"I wasn't mocking. I was asking." Despite my best effort, I couldn't keep the fear out of my voice. I needed to change his focus. "I have another question for you. How did you get in? Oh, make that two questions. Have you also drugged Vinnie?"

"Your big gorilla bodyguard? No, he left." His posture relaxed marginally as he turned his head to the bedroom door. "Dukwicz! Come in here, would you?"

I wasn't able to stop the gasp that escaped me. Soft footsteps sounded across my living space before a large male body filled the doorway. It was Dukwicz, the scarred man from the warehouse video, the man who had kidnapped and punched me. The light coming from my living room caught the side of his face, highlighting the raised scar on his jaw. The hypertrophic scar.

I was confident in my assessment that Kubanov would not hurt me. He needed me alive and well to continue playing his mind game until it had reached its conclusion. But Dukwicz? He would enjoy hurting me. Fear of having them in my home gave way to deep terror. I knew the darkness at my periphery was not from the night. It was from panic rolling in to take over.

With strength I hadn't known I possessed, I fought back the fear. Having Colin unconscious next to me had the same effect as the last time we had been in a similar situation. I felt the irrational need to protect him. I turned up the volume of my mental Mozart playing and slowed my breathing.

"Good day, Doctor Lenard. Such a pity I didn't get to beat you up again when I offed Hawk." Dukwicz's smile was malicious, his voice deep and steady as if breaking into my apartment was an everyday event. "You should really spruce up your security. It's as bad as that little cottage in England. Too easy."

I saw the deception cues as he laughed softly at the ease of breaking through Vinnie and Colin's security measures. But there was also triumph. He had enjoyed taking on the challenge and winning. Dukwicz nodded once when I didn't say anything and disappeared into my apartment again. I was going to clean every single centimetre to remove their presence.

"Dukwicz has been watching your little love nest for some time now. He loves your decor, especially your clocks. And he knows your gorilla quite well, he says."

"His name is Vinnie."

"When your *gorilla* left on some rendezvous an hour ago, Dukwicz phoned me to make use of this opportunity. He had been watching you going in and out of your apartment, so it took him only two minutes to get me inside. Some security system you have here, Genevieve." Kubanov couldn't possibly have known how much the French pronunciation of my name agitated me. His continuous use of it fed into my annoyance, pushing back some of the fear. I grabbed onto it. Anger was a powerful motivator.

"Not only is Dukwicz really good at disposing of redundant things, he is very gifted at entering places." He looked at the gun and then at me. "I have something to give to you, but you must promise to behave. Else I will get Dukwicz to dismantle lover boy."

"I won't move or scream." I assumed that was what he had meant by behave.

"Good." He put the gun in a holster on his belt and called Dukwicz again. "Bring me the stuff."

Only the knowledge that Kubanov would ruthlessly execute his threat kept me from placing my hand on Colin's chest to feel the steadiness of his heartbeat. His touch always calmed me and I wondered if me touching him would have the same effect. That thought was immediately forgotten when Dukwicz walked into my bedroom and handed Kubanov a large bouquet of flowers. I felt sick to my stomach. I didn't need any light to know the flowers in the crystal vase were red daffodils.

"I can't say I was surprised that you didn't accept my birthday gift. Having something delivered is terribly impersonal. That was why I brought these—to make sure you don't feel that I'm neglecting you. I'll put it over here." He walked to the large wooden chest of drawers, moved a Peruvian statue out the way and carefully placed the flowers in the middle. He stepped back. "Ah, beautiful."

"Flowers are usually given for a reason. Either to celebrate, to commiserate, to apologise, to thank or to connect. I know my birthday isn't the real reason. Why are you giving me those flowers?"

"I would say it is a little of all those reasons. It is just a little token before the other gift."

"You have more gifts for me?" I was horrified.

"Not here and not now, but soon. It will be my way of saying you're special, but not nearly as clever as you think you are."

"Are you planning to hurt only me? What about your other enemies? Surely a man of your calibre has plenty of people who might be more an enemy to you than I am."

"But you're not my enemy, Genevieve." He took a step closer to the bed. "You are the closest I've ever had to an equal. Everyone else has always been too easy to outwit, outplan and oust."

"In your tone I hear genuine respect and in your body language I see no deception. If what you are saying is true, why target me?"

He walked slowly to my side of the bed, his gait halted as if hiding great discomfort, pain. He stopped by my side and placed an object on the duvet covering my chest.

"You can look at it when I'm gone." He tilted his head to

the side, his face completely in the shadows. "You are a worthy adversary, Genevieve. You asked me earlier what I want. The truth is that what I want is no longer available to me. Lacking that option, I've had the last few months to come up with alternatives. Outthinking, outplaying and outsmarting you seemed like a delightful challenge to go straight to the top of my list. Twice you have beaten me. There will not be a third time."

I only had his silhouette and the tone of his voice to use for understanding his words. It was the slight modulation in his tone that made me take special note and catalogue that for later analysis.

"Before you go, please tell me what you gave Colin." I needed to know what to tell the paramedics.

"Only a little Diazepam. Really, Genevieve. Your fascination with him disappoints me. It makes me feel more justified in the actions I've taken and will take." He turned and walked to the door. "Don't bother phoning the police. We'll be gone long before they even get here. Spend the time enjoying my gifts."

The weight of the object he had placed on my chest held me in place as if it weighed much more than it actually did. Kubanov walked through the doorway on unsteady legs. I watched him disappear into the next room and listened to his shuffling footsteps and a softer footfall going towards my front door. He and Dukwicz had the audacity to leave through my front door, closing it hard enough for me to hear. I didn't know what to do. Were they truly gone? Was Kubanov waiting on the other side of my room until I got up to come back inside and shoot Colin?

I didn't know how long I lay frozen in my bed, fighting off the panic that relentlessly pulled at me. The first movement I allowed myself was to let my hand travel under the covers to touch Colin. Relief made me exhale sharply as my hand came in contact with the warm skin of his side. He wore only pyjama bottoms to bed, something for which I was irrationally happy. I placed my hand palm down on his chest and waited. The first heartbeat I felt under my hand calmed me much more than I had expected. Feeling my hand lift as he inhaled was an equal reassurance.

I pushed the weight off my chest and scrambled onto my knees next to Colin, not taking my hand off his chest. "Colin? Wake up. Please. Wake up."

It had been Kubanov's dismissive tone that had made me believe him. He had not drugged Colin to prove a point, to make him suffer or to kill him. Colin was merely an inconvenience he had taken care of to reach his true target. Me. I sat looking down into Colin's face until I felt bolstered enough to reach over him and turn on the bedside lamp.

My eyes had grown accustomed to the dark and the soft light was so bright, I squinted for almost a minute. It didn't stop me from looking Colin over for signs of blood or other indication that he might have been hurt more than just an injection. My eyes adjusted and the healthy colour in his face told me he was indeed in a drugged sleep. At least I hoped so.

I got out of bed and ran to Vinnie's room, calling out to him all the way. His room was empty. Kubanov had been right. Vinnie had gone out. I ran to the dining room table, jerked my handbag from the chair it was hanging from and took out my smartphone. My hands were shaking, but I was much more in control than in Hawk's house. It took three swipes, one tap and three rings to have Manny on the line.

"What's wrong, Doc?" Alert and professional.

"Kubanov was here. He drugged Colin. He was here. In my bedroom."

"Where's Vinnie?"

"He's not here. Colin is drugged." My voice was unsteady and I couldn't help repeating myself.

"I'll call the paramedics to meet me at your flat. I'll be there in a jiffy, Doc."

"Does that mean soon?"

"Very soon." His voice had the quality of someone on the move. "Are you sure Kubanov is gone? Will he be back?"

"No, they're gone."

"They?" He lost the calm professionalism, raising his voice.

"Dukwicz was here too, but they left. I don't think they'll come back."

"Where's Frey?"

"In my bed."

"Oh bloody hell." It sounded like he was in his car. "Lock yourself in your bedroom with Frey and don't open to anyone until you hear my voice."

"I have a steel-reinforced door to my bedroom," I said as I hurried back to my room.

"I know, Doc. Lock yourself in there. I'm on my way."

The line went dead and I took the phone with me into the bedroom. I only breathed easily when I locked the heavy door separating my bedroom from the rest of my apartment. Ideally I would have preferred to move to my bathroom. It too had a steel-reinforced door. But I couldn't leave Colin alone in bed.

I stood next to the bed looking at him sleeping peacefully. It was really hard to not give in to the strong compulsion to shake him until he woke up, then strip the bed and dispose of all the bedding. It didn't matter that Kubanov had only sat on the duvet. Everything seemed contaminated. I got back onto my side of the bed, kneeling next to Colin. I placed both my palms on his chest as I called up Mozart's Piano Concerto No. 24 in C minor.

In my mind I flattened a sheet of music paper, appreciating the beauty of five lines equally spaced to form a musical staff. The staves filled the page to create linear beauty, pleasing to my eye. I carefully drew a line down the sides of two staves, combining them for the first line for the piano of the first movement of the concerto. Drawing the G-clef always made me smile. In one movement of the hand, curl upon curl, an artful symbol emerged. For a few minutes I gave myself over to the solace of writing note after note.

Not much time could have passed when I opened my eyes. Manny wasn't here yet. Within a few minutes my apartment was going to be filled with people, and I didn't want to feel as vulnerable as I did. Already I felt more in control after mentally writing a few bars of Mozart. Getting dressed would add to that.

As fast as I could, I put on a comfortable pair of jeans and a top I felt confident in. Shoes inside my apartment would be inappropriate, but light socks added to my sense of shielding. Body language was not the only way we communicated nonverbally. Our clothes told volumes about us, our character, mood and intention. My intention was to create an impenetrable buffer around myself.

My gaze constantly strayed to Colin. Despite Kubanov's reassurances, and Colin's steady breathing and good colour, I was still concerned. Deeply concerned. As I got back onto my side of the bed, fully dressed, my knee bumped into something hard. Kubanov's second gift.

At first, I pushed it out the way to put my hand again on Colin's warm chest, simply to console myself. After feeling a few regular heartbeats under my palm, I looked down and picked up a statue that should have weighed much more than it did. My knowledge of artworks mostly extended to paintings, but I recognised this piece. It was a Costa Rican stone Sukia figure.

I twisted it around and studied it with my untrained eye, to which it looked like an exact replica. I looked closer, because it was made of a material I could not identify, most definitely not marble or any other medium usually used for statues. It felt like plastic.

3D-printed plastic.

Chapter TWENTY

"Oh, for the love of Pete, missy." Manny sighed for the eighth time since he had ordered me to sit at the dining room table and allow the crime scene unit to check my bedroom for evidence. "Frey will be fine. He's a hardy thief."

I glanced at my bedroom door and saw a white-suited figure move to the other side of my bedroom. As much as I disliked this invasion, there was no malevolent intent. I could accept the presence of strangers in my home if it were to aid us putting an end to Kubanov's taunting.

"That's it. I give up." Manny pushed himself up with his hands on my dark wood dining room table. The marks his hands left behind didn't bother me as much as usual. I was going to clean my entire apartment in any case. I looked up to see Manny glowering down at me. "Come on, Doc. You're so worried about Frey, I can't get a word out of you."

He was right. I hadn't said much since I had allowed him, two paramedics and three crime scene unit members into my bedroom. That space was too small for all those bodies, and Manny had quickly escorted me out. But I wanted to be in my bedroom, making sure Colin was still breathing. The paramedics had assured me that his vital readings were normal, as if he was in a deep sleep. They had injected him with a mild stimulant and had taken another ten minutes reassuring me that he was going to wake up soon. I wanted to be there, so I followed Manny into my bedroom.

"Are you guys going to be much longer?" Manny asked the figure kneeling next to the bed.

A woman got up, her eyes wide. "I don't know what you want us to look for. This place is immaculate. There isn't even a speck of dust. It's really amazing. Clean. Even under the bed. I could eat dinner there."

On any other day, I might have thanked her for the compliment and dissuaded her from eating dinner under my bed. Not now. I walked straight to Colin and climbed on the bed again. I placed my hand on his chest and held my breath until I felt his heart beating under my palm.

"You should take the flowers," I said without looking away from Colin. "Kubanov brought them in that vase. I don't think it's anything but flowers and water, but you should test it."

"He brought you flowers?"

"And Dukwicz took all my clocks." I had walked through my apartment on Manny's request while the paramedics had been looking at Colin. The three clocks I had bought at separate auctions were the only items missing from my apartment. None of them were significantly valuable, but they had been mine. When I had seen the first one missing, I had known Dukwicz had given in to his obsession with timepieces.

"We'll get them back for you, Doc." Manny walked closer and glanced at Colin. "It just looks like he's sleeping."

"He is in a drug-induced sleep. That's not the same."

"I know, Doc. Tell me about the flowers."

"He brought me those flowers and this." The statue was on the bed where I had left it. I handed it to Manny, but he didn't touch it. The crime scene investigator took it into her gloved hands and showed it to Manny.

"What the hell is this?"

"A Costa Rican stone Sukia figure."

"What does it mean? Why did he give this to you?" Manny turned the investigator's hand to look at the statue from different angles. He gave an impatient grunt. "I don't know what I'm looking at. Take this with you to the lab."

"Yes, sir."

"Doc, did Kubanov touch anything else? Should these guys look for anything else?"

"No. I told you it was a waste of time to have the crime scene unit here."

"They can take this and analyse it." He looked at the investigator. "I don't care what you have to do, but I want a complete analysis by noon. You have been sitting on the other statue as well. I need that ASAP."

"Yes, sir." She put the statue in an evidence bag. "If there isn't anything else?"

"No."

"Yes," I said, gaining their attention. "Could you please take photos of the statue from as many angles as possible and email it to me?"

"Send it to me. I'll forward it to Doc. You guys can clear out since there isn't much else to find here."

"Yes, sir." She gave me a quick smile and left.

"Let me see them out and then we'll talk. You need to talk to me, Doc." He lowered his head to emphasise his words.

"I'll tell you everything."

"Good." He left and soon all the voices in my apartment moved towards the front door. I jumped from fright when the front door slammed open with a loud noise. There was a moment of shocked silence.

"What the fuck is going on?" Vinnie was back. The aggression in his voice told me he was ready to attack. "Where is Jen-girl? Jen-girl! Colin!"

"In here, Vinnie." I heard a grunt and assumed he had pushed someone out of his way. No sooner had I answered than he rushed into the room, a gun in his hand. I didn't like it. "Why do you have that?"

He glanced at his hand and quickly holstered the gun under his t-shirt, at his back. "I thought I might need it. What happened? Are you okay? What's up with Colin?"

"Kubanov was here. He drugged Colin so he could talk to me."

Vinnie's head jerked away from studying Colin to look at me. His eyes were wide, his mouth downturned. "What the fuck? Did he hurt you?"

"No, he gave me gifts."

Manny came into the room carrying a dining room chair. He put it next to the bedside table at Colin's side and fell into it. He glared at Vinnie. "Stop hovering like a mother hen and sit down."

Vinnie dismissed him with a quick frown and leaned closer to Colin. "Is he okay?"

"The paramedics said he'll wake up soon. He's just sleeping." I cleared my throat. "Vinnie?"

He looked up quickly at my soft tone. "What do you need, Jen-girl?"

"Would you please sit there?" I pointed at the exact spot Kubanov had been. If Vinnie sat there, he might replace the negative memories with his overpowering and caring presence. He sat down immediately. And he didn't ask me why. It made me feel weak with gratitude.

"Where the bleeding hell were you?" Manny leaned forward, resting his elbows on his knees.

"Out." The expression on Vinnie's face as he turned his attention to me was pure contrition. "I should have been here. This shouldn't have happened. I'm sorry, Jen-girl."

"It's not your fault." I shook my head. "Kubanov brought Dukwicz with him."

Manny sat up, rubbed both hands over his face. "Okay, Doc. Start from the beginning."

I told them everything that had happened. It took me less than ten minutes.

"Okay, let me get this straight." Manny was back to leaning his elbows on his knees. "You think Kubanov is sick, maybe terminally so."

"Yes. I think he has cancer. The little I saw, he moved with difficulty as if he was in pain. He's also lost weight. Angelique was right. He was bald, but I think it might be from chemotherapy."

"Holy hell. This is not good at all."

"Why not?" Vinnie asked. "Nature will take care of our problem for us."

"Maybe, but on a psychological level I agree with Manny. It is a worrisome situation."

"Why?"

"Because he has nothing to lose." The thought made me feel cold inside. "That is the worst situation for him to be in. If he no longer cares about living to old age, he will become more careless in his action."

"So? We can catch him easier."

"Not necessarily. He might become careless, but he is still highly intelligent and systematic. The biggest problem is predicting his next steps. Our profiling didn't account for that, which in hindsight explains the anomalies I had noticed."

"Yeah, I can see how this is not good." Vinnie shook Colin's leg. "Wake up, dude. Come on."

Colin didn't react, but Vinnie persisted. He gave up after

half a minute, concern contracting the *orbicularis oculi* muscles around his eyes.

"Tell me more about what he said, Doc."

"I already told you everything word for word."

"You did." He nodded once. "Now tell me what you read into that."

"Not much. I couldn't see him very well." The impatient look that flashed across Manny's face made me talk faster. "But I heard changes in his voice as he spoke. Inflections not related to discomfort or pain, but rather emotion."

"You can hear those?"

"I prefer to read expressions, but if I have no option other than speaking on a telephone, I need something else to understand hidden meanings. Our tone gives away the emotion motivating the words. To answer your question, yes."

"What did you hear?" Manny waved his hand in an impatient gesture for me to speak faster.

"The first time I bested Kubanov, he lost a lucrative art forgery ring. He also lost face, his connections in Eurocorps—"

"—and the Russian House," Manny said. The Russian House was a mansion in Strasbourg where I had first met Kubanov. It had been emptied by the authorities and locked down a year ago. "Last I heard, it was sold to a local developer and was set to be demolished. They had asked the city permission to build a small apartment complex. But that's not important now. Continue."

"Six months ago, we foiled his extremely well-strategized revenge plan. It was a lifelong dream of his to take a loved one from the president, just as he believed the president had taken from him."

"Do you have a point, Doc?"

"I believe this time there will be no big far-reaching plot.

In both the previous cases, the victims and intended victims had been numerous."

"What are you saying, Jen-girl? Is Kubanov targeting you?"

"No. Yes. No." I took a deep breath. "His voice carried very strong emotions when he talked about outthinking, outplaying and outsmarting me. Yes, I am his ultimate target. No, he will not kill me. He's having too much fun giving me gifts and playing games with me. But I don't know what or who his intended target is—who he's going to use to get to me."

"Oh, bloody hell, Doc. Not even a non-speculating speculation?"

"There is no such thing, but I understand your intention. No, I don't know. Not yet. I do know that we are all in danger, but that was a safe conclusion from the beginning."

"We'll all be more careful from here on out." Manny looked at Colin for a few seconds. "And what is it with Kubanov giving you that statue? Does it have any personal meaning?"

I took a moment to consider my answer. "Nothing I can think of. I'll ask Colin when he wakes up. Maybe he has some personal connection or experience with the statue. Like the symbolic meaning of the statue from his safe house."

All attention turned to Colin as his breathing increased and he groaned. It took him ten minutes to wake up sufficiently to make sense of his surroundings. I insisted on moving to the living area. It no longer felt right having this many people in my bedroom. Colin was a bit unsteady on his feet, but made it to the sofa by himself, Vinnie hovering nearby and Manny frowning in irritation. It took another ten minutes to update Colin on everything that had taken place.

"And you are sure it was the Costa Rican Sukia?" he

asked. His voice was becoming clearer the longer we spoke. The initial slowness of his speech was gone.

"Yes, but the material it was made of was strange."

"Here." Manny shoved his smartphone into Colin's hand. "I took photos of it. The crime lab will send us better shots, but this will give you an idea."

I was yet again impressed by Manny's thinking. Often he portrayed the image of someone not paying attention and definitely not thinking ahead. That was not true. He had known Colin would want to see the statue.

"Yes, this is the Sukia figure." Colin tossed the phone to Manny, who caught it with an annoyed grunt. "The statue he gave me had significance. What is the association with this statue?"

"You don't have any connection to it?" I asked.

"Nope. I've never even been close to the original. This is an amazing piece of pre-Columbian art, but not very valuable. Tell me more about the feel of the statue."

"I wasn't paying a lot of attention to the statue." I had been too worried about him, and about the fact that Kubanov had been in my bedroom. "But it wasn't heavy like a marble or bronze statue of that size would be."

"Maybe plaster?"

"No, it felt more like plastic, but I didn't get the sense it was hollow." I looked at Manny. "You should tell the crime lab those statues might have been printed."

"What is it with all this 3D-printed crap?" Manny asked. "Aren't these printers supposed to be quite temperamental?"

"Very," Vinnie said. "It is technology with great potential, but often an object being printed goes belly up... um... terribly wrong. The result is a big mess of plastic strings. One guy calls it plastic pasta. Depending on the design, the printed objects can be very fragile while in production.

Sometimes the print head might touch an already printed part while readjusting and knock it out of place. That means hours of printing lost. And a lot of plastic."

"How long does it take to print, say, that Suk-something statue?" Manny asked.

"Anything up to twelve hours." Vinnie had kept his word about finding out more about 3D printing. "It's printed by putting layer upon layer. The design is of utmost importance. If the blueprint is off by a millimetre, it is a disaster."

"Blueprints!" My heart was racing when that one word clicked a few elements into place. "Vinnie, you said that photo of the blueprint I emailed myself was for a gun. Could that be a blueprint for the 3D guns? The guns that were used to kill all these people?"

My outburst brought a shocked silence. Manny spoke first. "Holy hell."

"The question now is where you saw that blueprint to photograph it," Colin said. "It had to be in England since that was where you had access to the phone."

"It could've been anywhere. In Dukwicz's car or anywhere else they might have taken us." I sighed. I wanted to get to my viewing room to have access to my computers and all the information on it. It would be easier to show them the conclusions I had reached. Without my computer, I had to order my thoughts so I could give a clear explanation. "On Hawk's computer we found that shipment of five 3D printers to Tall Freddy. Can it be that Hawk also sent Tall Freddy blueprints of guns? As we already suspected, he could then have used that to print and sell the guns used by the killers, who said they had bought their guns from the Printer who had an Italian accent."

"Oh, mother of all that is holy." Even Manny's lips had lost colour. "We should've looked into this much earlier."

"We've been overwhelmed with incoming information," I said. "There is never a guarantee that the clue one pursues would be the one yielding key results."

Colin sat up. "What about that large shipment of unnamed electronic devices that Hawk received two months ago? Did your guys find it in the warehouse, Millard?"

Manny shook his head. "How would they know what that shipment was?"

"I think we can safely presume it was 3D printers." Colin sounded confident. I thought it to be speculation.

"They didn't list any 3D printers on the report I got from them. I actually looked for it when it was first mentioned."

"Let's work with my presumption." Colin smiled at me. I frowned. "Do we know how big that shipment was, Jenny?"

"Whatever he had ordered, there were a thousand five hundred units of it." I was not willing to commit myself to Colin's theory, but taken into the context of the last week, it did make sense.

"If each unit can print a gun a day, the European market will see more than ten thousand untraceable guns a week, most of which are single-use."

Manny and Vinnie spent three minutes swearing in the vilest of manners about how grim this situation was. I agreed with them and quietly waited for them to calm down. Manny was the first to take a deep breath. "Okay, Doc. First things first. We need to find that shipment. Dear mother of all that is pure, I hope it is still in storage somewhere."

Colin tensed. "Nobody needs to look into anything right now. It's half past two in the morning. We should be sleeping."

"Colin is right," I said. "We need to find that shipment, but we also need to sleep."

Colin leaned back a little and stared at me, his eyebrows raised, his eyes wide. I had surprised him. My concern was for him. I knew he would not let me work alone and would join me. His body needed time to recover from being drugged. Again. And this was more important.

I couldn't really blame him for assuming I would immediately want to start working. My obsessive behaviour had formed a distinct pattern. It gave me unexpected pleasure to be unpredictable. This one time.

"And that is me being told I've overstayed my welcome." Manny got up and walked to the front door. "Be in the team room eight sharp. I know it's Sunday, but we're working against the clock here. And Doc, get that super brain of yours ready to make other connections. We need to put this monster to bed."

I also got up and followed him to the door as he opened it. "Manny."

He turned and waited.

"I wasn't asking you to leave. You know I would say it if I didn't want you here."

He relaxed a little. "I know, Doc. We are all tired. I am tired."

"I... uh..." I pulled at my sleeves and immediately stopped when I realised what I was doing. "Thank you for always picking up the phone and coming every time I need you."

A softness that Manny seldom showed settled around his eyes. He leaned towards me. "For you, Doc? Anytime."

I thought he was going to kiss me on my forehead, but he pulled back when Vinnie asked mockingly if Manny would come if he phoned. Manny sighed, looked at me, sighed again and left.

Chapter **TWENTY-ONE**

"Okay, so which one of you mastermind criminals is going to tell me everything I need to know about 3D-printed guns?" Manny looked around the table in the team room. Everyone was seated at the round table, coffee and croissants in the centre, surrounded by papers, laptops and tablets.

Manny had been in the office before any of us, working on his computer. The speed with which he typed using only his index fingers never ceased to amuse Francine. Her teasing had chased away his tired look. The alertness in his eyes did not show any signs of his lack of sleep, rushing to my aid in the small hours of the morning. "Anyone? I need to know more than I do."

"The most common gun printed at the moment was the one some idiot uploaded the blueprints for on the internet," Francine said. "Anyone and his psychotic brother could've downloaded it. And most likely did. By the time the big shots got it removed from the internet, over sixty thousand blueprints had already been downloaded. That gun is printed with ABS plastic and has sixteen parts, fifteen plastic and the firing pin."

"How is it that you know all this, supermodel?"

Francine tapped him on the nose with a manicured finger. Her nails were dark brown today. "Always on a witch-hunt. Don't you get tired of it sometimes, super-cop?"

Vinnie snorted a laugh and even Phillip smiled. I had to admit that Manny's longsuffering expression was entertaining.

"Stop farting around, supermodel, and tell me what else you know."

"That funny-looking handgun is not the only weapon that can be printed. Any gun, even a semi-automatic, can be printed, but at a great risk. Without any reinforcement and only made of plastic, the printed gun cannot handle much stress. It is quite flimsy. If the printer head moves a tiny little bit while printing the layers, it won't handle the pressure of a bullet travelling through the barrel at crazy speeds. As we already know, quite a few have exploded in the shooter's hand."

Vinnie nodded his agreement. "That is why not many hardcore criminals want to take the risk of printing guns, even though it is totally untraceable. Today anyone can buy a 3D printer. Even though those blueprints were taken offline pretty quickly, they are still available if you know where to look. You can even choose the colour plastic you want to print your gun with. Anything printed by a 3D printer would have to be pressure-washed to remove a waxy coating and then it must be doused in alcohol."

"Which again coincides with the ballistic reports." Most of what they had said was new to me. My knowledge had been as limited as Manny's. I had never considered 3D printers or 3D-printed guns to be a threat worth watching out for. I had been naïve.

Francine straightened in her chair. "My lip-reading guy got back to me."

"Is this for the video clips of Genevieve and Colin being kidnapped?" Phillip asked.

"Yes, it is." She tapped on her tablet and the large screen against the wall sprang to life. My association with this video was not that I was being abducted, but rather that it was evidence of my meltdown. Francine started the video, but stopped it after the first two seconds. "Oh yes, the whole conversation was in Russian. My guy so happens to have a Russian roommate who translated this stuff for him."

"Christ, supermodel. Are these people trustworthy? You're just handing out sensitive stuff all over the place."

Francine laughed. It was a laugh not communicating mirth or amusement, but rather anticipation. "Let them just try to double-cross me. They know their balls are on the line here."

I had learned in the last year of our friendship that Francine frequently threatened men's genitals. It got her good results. Not that it surprised me. There was never a trace of deception in her threats. Rather worrying.

"Also, some of the conversation was said with their heads turned, so obviously we didn't catch that, but here goes." She tapped the tablet again and the figures on the large screen began moving. I watched myself trying to get out of Dukwicz's grip. It was a relief when Francine started talking, focussing my attention on the men's mouths rather than the image of my squirming body. "There he says that this bitch needs to calm down. Sorry, Genevieve."

"You didn't say that. You don't need to apologise."

She smiled, quickly looking back to the action. "Ooh, there the other guy is saying that with Dukwicz being such a big hotshot and all, he doesn't understand why they still have to do this dirty work. That should mean they can get others to do this. He asks again why they have to do this."

At that exact moment Dukwicz slapped me in the face. My breath caught and Colin's hand closed over mine.

"Dukwicz says that he's doing it because he enjoys it. Doing that butler was especially pleasurable. He always wanted to do one of those rich servants. But he also liked doing the VIP's. Like the professor and this one." Strain had entered Francine's tone. We watched Dukwicz punch me in the stomach. "Here he's saying that you are important to the plan, and that he didn't want to give someone else this pleasure. He is the best there is."

This was the point in the video where Dukwicz pushed me into the car and turned to the other man, still holding Colin. "This is a really bad part where my guy couldn't get a clear shot of their mouths no matter what he did with the video. All he got here was that Dukwicz said he wanted it big. We don't know what 'it' is. Then the other guy responds by saying that of course the Printer has to something, something. Sorry. We missed a few words there when he turned."

We watched a little while longer, but the men were either not talking or their mouths were obscured.

"Was that all you got?" I asked.

"Unfortunately, yes."

"It is not quite so unfortunate," Vinnie said. "We have him on video admitting to murdering the butler and Susan Kadlec."

"He admitted to 'doing' a butler." It wasn't easy for me to be so realistic. I want this video to exonerate Colin from any suspicion. "He didn't say he killed Susan or Kathleen McCarthy's butler."

"She's right." Manny sank deeper into his chair. "I'll find a way to nail this guy, don't you worry."

Francine changed windows and brought up a document that looked like an order form.

"What are we looking at now?" Manny asked.

"You remember that large shipment of unnamed electronics that were delivered two months ago? Well I know what it is." There was triumph in her voice. "These days you can't be a successful criminal unless you can outdo the best hackers, or if you go old school. If criminals communicated and did business without any electronic trail, it would be much harder to catch them. That's why the Russians are back to using old typewriters. The moment something is entered into a computer system, you're screwed. And I will find you."

"Well, congratulations on being the best hacker out there." Sarcasm. It gave me immeasurable pleasure to recognise it from Manny's tone and expression. "Could you now please tell us what you found, supermodel?"

"It took some time, but I traced the order to its origins." She pointed at the monitor. "This document tells me that one thousand five hundred 3D printers were delivered to Hawk's warehouse."

Manny squinted at the monitor. "I don't see anything saying it's printers. Where do you see that?"

"It's in the number given in the product description. I traced that number to the stock this supplier had and those are Halo 3D printers."

"One thousand five hundred." This number had been bothering me since last night. Data my mind had registered somewhere along the line were coming to the fore. This number had significance, but I couldn't place it.

"A lot of printers, right?" Francine said. "Why would he need this many printers?"

"Shit. Frey, you were right."

Colin laughed. "Did that hurt, Millard?"

Manny ignored Colin. "Supermodel, we need to find those printers."

"What makes you think Hawk or Kubanov or whichever shithead hasn't already handed them out like candy?" Vinnie asked.

"The number of murders with ballistic evidence pointing to 3D-printed guns," I said.

"Doc is right. If other scumbags had printed guns, we would be looking at hundreds of cases, not tens."

"Halo." I pressed my palm hard against my sternum the moment this connection clicked in my mind. "That was one of the words I emailed to myself."

"Halo as in the Austrian producer of electronics," Francine said. "Then these 3D printers are definitely connected to this craziness."

The number one thousand five hundred was still an itch in the back of my mind. Absorbed by what I thought might be the clue I had been waiting for, I got up and walked to my viewing room. A few minutes later, I had the necessary document open and stared at it, waiting for that moment where everything became clear. I didn't close my eyes to mentally write Mozart, but continued to stare at the columns in front of me. The moment of clarity came when I finished doing a few calculations. This was it.

"What is it, Jenny?"

"Where's Francine?"

A slight frown told me Colin had not expected me to ask for someone else.

"What do you need, girlfriend?" Francine was standing in the open door to the team room, Manny next to her and Phillip behind them. I was sure Vinnie was lingering behind the wall, listening in. It appeared they had been waiting in suspense for me.

"Did you check this document?" I nodded at the monitor.

"I did. All those names belong to organised crime leaders, gang leaders and other more prominent criminals around Europe."

Manny walked closer. "That list of who's who in the criminal world in Europe. What did you find, Doc?"

"I was wondering what the purpose was for Hawk to have this list."

"I thought he had this list to keep track of his competition, his enemies or his potential clients. Whatever you prefer to call them," Francine said.

"Possibly, but look at the column next to their names."

"It has a number." Manny leaned closer. "Each number is different."

"There are three hundred and fifteen names. When I added the numbers next to each name, it came to one thousand four hundred and eighty-nine. Almost one thousand five hundred."

"Holy freaking hell." Manny stepped away from the monitors. "Okay, let me get this clear, Doc. You are telling me we have proof that Kubanov or Hawk or Tall Freddy ordered fifteen hundred printers to send a bunch to each of these violent criminals?"

"I'm not telling you that. I'm telling you that I'm suspecting that." There was a big difference even though Manny's expression didn't agree with me. "If each of those violent criminal received their allocated number of printers they can distribute, it will arm a lot of people across Europe."

"What about plastic cartridges to print this crap?"

I pointed to another monitor, showing a document also opened from Hawk's computer. It was a spreadsheet with four columns only showing numbers. "The first column is the date delivered. He ordered a lot of cartridges. The second column's numbers correspond with the number next to the names on the printer delivery form. The third column is a number I'm not sure of. If Francine can check, it might be the number of guns that can be produced with all this plastic."

"Why would Kubanov do this? Or Hawk? Or Tall Freddy?" Francine asked.

"Kubanov would do this despite what Hawk or Tall Freddy wanted," I said. "If he is as ill as I think he is, he would do this simply to leave Europe in chaos. Sending complimentary equipment to produce guns to all these violent criminals would be a disaster for law enforcement. The idea of this would be greatly pleasing to Kubanov."

Silence fell in my viewing room for a few seconds. Manny was the first to break it. "I have a shitload of phone calls to make. This is… this is… I don't know what this is."

"I'll leave you to it, as well." Phillip pulled at his cuffs. "I still have a few concerned clients to calm down. I tried, but couldn't keep the thefts quiet. Now I have people with one little painting phoning me in panic."

I watched them leave, followed by Francine and Vinnie. My mind was consumed with all the unclear elements. "Why did I send myself that email about the frame of reference? I really believe it has a bigger meaning than you being framed for the butler's murder."

"The murder could just be a distraction. Something to send us looking in the wrong direction."

"Possibly." I grunted and slumped in my chair. "What are you going to do now?"

"If you don't need me, I'm going to look at all the puzzle pieces we have. An analogy," he said quickly when I frowned. "We have all these bits and pieces, so it's like a puzzle that needs to be built."

"Using your analogy, we've built quite a bit of this puzzle already. But you are right. It will be good to look at it again from the beginning. Let me know if you find something." I turned back to stare at the monitors, wondering where next to look. It might be a good idea to also look at the evidence we had accumulated in chronological order instead of in discovery order. It took me an hour to run through the information we had, to no avail.

I got up and left through the door leading to the hall. Walking through the team room would attract attention and possible questions. Sometimes their interest was difficult to process and categorise as such when it felt so intrusive. I stood in the hall for a few seconds, deciding where to go. It didn't take long for me to realise where I needed to be and I walked to the conference room.

The sunken ceiling lights were switched on and I decided it provided adequate light. It was a reprieve from the strong artificial glare everywhere else in the office. I closed the door and immediately enjoyed the sense of isolation. The spacious room felt like a reprieve from the continuous accompaniment of the last few days. I allowed myself a deep sigh and walked slowly along the wall, looking at the printouts of the underpaintings. It was interesting how every painting extended onto the back of the frames. I stopped in front of a particularly beautiful work and wondered about the significance of painting on the frames.

"What are these?" The young voice behind me made me jump and grab at my chest. For a micro-second I had thought Kubanov had found me, but it had not been his voice. I calmed myself enough to turn around. There was no one behind me. I frowned and looked deeper into the room. In the far corner of the room was a huddled figure on the floor.

"Who are you?"

"Nikki." Her eyes were wide in what looked like uncertainty, her dark hair tied up in a messy ponytail. She stared at me. "Who are you?"

I walked a bit closer. "Doctor Genevieve Lenard."

"Like a medical doctor or a clever doctor?"

"Often medical doctors are clever, but I'm not a medical doctor. I am, however, very intelligent." I pulled out two chairs. "Please sit down."

"I like it here." Her jaw jutted, her arms folding tighter around her.

"How old are you?" Her small frame and huddled posture made it difficult to ascertain her age. She could be anything between fourteen and nineteen. I rested my posterior on the edge of the table, trying to adopt a more approachable posture.

"How old are *you*?"

"I turned thirty-five two days ago." I didn't know if I was communicating correctly. How did one speak to a young adult? I had not spoken to a young person like her in the last fifteen years.

"That's old."

"Not really. With today's medical technology, my lifestyle and genes, I am likely to live to eighty, even ninety. That means I haven't yet passed the halfway mark of the average lifespan. I have reached the top of my field internationally, but I aim to improve my skills all the time."

"You're weird." Her body language shifted from defiance to interest.

"You mean that as a compliment. Thank you."

We sat in silence for a few minutes. She seemed comfortable with it. I was.

"Why were you looking at those printed paintings? And why do they look like that?"

I glanced behind me. "They are called underpaintings. An artist paints a basis for his final work and paints over it. In this case, the underpaintings are the final product."

"Why?"

"It's a message."

"For who?"

"Whom. For whom is the correct form of the question." I sighed at my digression. "The message is for me."

"So what does it say?" She got up and took a few steps to the painting closest to me.

"I don't know yet."

"I thought you said you were clever." She turned to me, the frown on her face. Despite her current expression, she had all the markers of becoming a beautiful woman. Now she was underweight, had dark circles under her eyes, and her body language communicated a prolonged period of stress. It was the slight tilt of her head and her cheekbones that brought recognition. I had seen that before on a photo. There she had been younger and happier.

"You're Monique, Hawk's daughter."

Her head whipped up and she took a step towards me. "You know my dad? Do you know what happened to him?"

I didn't know what to do. All indicators warned me this young woman was on the brink of a breakdown. I wanted to run out the room and call Phillip. He would know how to deal with this young person. I barely managed to communicate with adults. How was I going to walk through this maze of talking to a girl whose father had died while my hands were covered in his blood?

"Doctor G? What happened to him?" She was standing right in front of me now. Unbearable pain was etched around her eyes and mouth. "Mister Manny wouldn't tell me anything except that there was an accident. He thinks I'm stupid. I'm not. I know my dad was a criminal. I know he did bad things. But he loved me. He wanted a better life for me. That was why he sent me away. Do you also think I'm stupid or will you tell me what happened?"

I studied her dispassionately as if she was on one of the monitors in my viewing room. She studied me back. I didn't know what she saw, but what I saw was an intelligent young woman asking for answers adults wouldn't give her. It resonated within me. I had been where she was.

"I was with him when he died. I had been drugged and left lying next to him, but he was alive when I woke up." My voice softened as I watched silent tears ran down her face. "He had lost a lot of blood when I woke up. He knew he was dying and he spent his last energy talking about you."

"What did he say?" Her *mentalis* muscle caused her chin to tremble.

"He said you are a good person. That you are better than him." And he made me promise to look after you. It was hard to not say this to her, but I didn't know if it would do more harm than good. As it was, I watched her demeanour crumble.

She looked at me and I saw myself in her. A youth misunderstood by society, buckling under the expectations of her family and those associated with her family. I wondered how my life, how I, would have been different had there been someone to reach out to me. I could not allow myself to let her feel the isolation I saw on her face, the isolation I had experienced at her age. With uncommon determination, I set aside my dislikes and typical behaviours. I opened my arms.

She fell against my chest with a loud sob, clutching me around my back. I swallowed hard at the desire to scrub clean the wet tears running down my neck. Nobody had been willing to sacrifice for me as a child. I had grown, trained and developed enough to do it for this young person. Having read about the power of human touch, and having experienced the calming power of it from Colin, I closed my arms around her. I rubbed slow circles on her back, not saying anything. Instead I wrote Mozart's Symphony No. 36 in C Major to keep from pushing her away.

That was how they found us.

The door opened and I heard a loud gasp. Then I heard my mother's voice.

Chapter TWENTY-TWO

"What have you done to that child?" My mother's voice carried the same disapproving tone I had heard when I had last seen her four years ago. It was the same tone I had heard throughout my childhood. Nikki stiffened in my arms, clutching me even tighter. I took a deep breath and called back Mozart's symphony to play softly in my mind. I would need all the calming I could get.

"Do something." The *depressor anguli oris* muscle brought the familiar look of disdain around my mother's mouth as she spoke to my father. "Don't just stand there. Get the poor child away from her."

My parents took a few steps into the conference room. I was grateful for its spaciousness, leaving my parents at a safe distance. Nikki's sobs had quieted. I felt her muscles tense under my hands as she fought to regain her composure.

"Don't come any closer." The strength in my voice stopped my father from taking another step. My mother moved slightly behind him. It was almost amusing to watch my father's expression. That flash of fear was of me, not for the young girl in my embrace. I thought of Colin and the rest of the team, my friends. None of them had ever had that specific expression in relation to me.

I had left my parents' home and financial care as soon as I had been able to. Even in my much more emotionally unstable teenage years, I had known I was more than my parents' opinion of me. Hawk's daughter knew her father had loved her. I didn't have that luxury. On the other hand, I didn't have the legacy of a father who was a violent criminal, possibly leaving a lot of people behind seeking revenge for different reasons. It made me concerned for Nikki's safety.

She took a trembling breath and sniffed loudly against my shoulder. My stomach roiled in reaction to the sound. I was going to put this outfit through a double washing cycle tonight when I got home. My parents were watching us closely. They looked ready to leap and defend Nikki physically if the need were to arise. My attention shifted to Nikki as she leaned away slightly. I dropped my arms, but she didn't step away from me.

She sniffed again and glanced at my parents. "Who are they?"

I pushed away from the table and stood straight. Nikki stayed so close to my side we brushed against each other with the slightest movement. I turned up the volume of my mental Mozart Symphony. "Monique—"

"Nikki." She pushed against my side. "My name is Nikki."

I nodded. If that was her preference I would respect that. My parents had insisted on pronouncing my name in the French manner, which I to this day found offensive and unsuited to me. "Nikki, these are my parents, Gerard Lenard and Charlotte Lenard."

"Well, isn't this total awesome-sauce? Meeting the family is cool." Vinnie walked into the conference room, followed closely by Francine. She wasn't as successful as Vinnie at masking his concern as insincere familiarity. He walked to them, his hand outstretched. "Howdy, folks. I'm Vinnie, Jen-girl's best friend."

"Vin, I'm her best friend." Francine pushed him out the way to reach my parents first. "I'm Francine."

Francine had not succeeded in catching their attention.

They were looking at Vinnie in horror, their eyes focussed on the large scar running down his face. Fear warred with contempt for dominance in their expressions.

"Ah, they're shy." Vinnie turned away from my parents and walked to me. Nikki moved closer to me, tucking herself half behind me. Francine had my mother's attention now, introducing herself, keeping them from following Vinnie's progression to us. He stopped in front of me and looked at me as if to make sure I was well. He must have seen my parents' presence wasn't causing me distress. "Colin is coming. He ran out for some food, but I phoned him as soon as I heard your folks were here."

"How did you know they're here?"

"Francine has this whole place under surveillance, remember?" He looked down to my side, addressing me. "Who's the little punk?"

Nikki inhaled sharply and took a small step to my side, still touching me. "The little punk is Nikki, you big punk. Who are you?"

Vinnie laughed. "I like you, punk. I'm Vinnie."

"Genevieve?" My mother's voice froze Vinnie's laughter and made me feel like sighing. "Who are all these people? I thought this was a reputable establishment. I should've known this was too good to be true."

"Listen, lady." Vinnie stepped forward, placing himself in front of me and Nikki. Our protector.

I took one step to be at Vinnie's side. Immediately Nikki's body pressed against mine. I focussed on the situation rather than the overwhelming desire to lock myself in my viewing room. Alone. "Vinnie, don't. No matter how rational or factual your argument, they won't hear it."

"Hmm, they're those kind of people," Francine said softly as she moved to stand behind us.

My parents were standing in the same place, a few feet away from the door. The long conference table separated us, but there was a much larger psychological space between us. My mother's one foot was pointed towards the door, her weight resting on that leg. Our bodies lead where our minds want to go. My father's body language was more aggressive, his feet planted apart, his hands on his hips, thumbs pointed to the back. Argumentative.

"What are you doing here?" I had only once told them where I worked, but had not expected them to ever show any interest. "It's Sunday. Why did you come to my office on a Sunday?"

"You invited us here, Genevieve." My father frowned at Vinnie. "Else we wouldn't be where we clearly don't belong."

As if conjured by my wish for his presence, Phillip came into the conference room. I had to concentrate to not allow my body to sag in relief. Especially when Colin followed Phillip into the room, ignoring my parents and walking straight to me.

Phillip introduced himself to my parents, his charm uncanny in its effectiveness. Daily he worked with people like my parents. Entitled, pretentious, self-important. Visibly, my parents relaxed, their social smiles back in place.

"Are you all right?" Colin asked as he stopped in front of me.

I nodded. Feeling crowded in the dimly lit room lost importance compared to what my father had revealed. Colin stared into my eyes for another second before he looked to my side. "I'm Colin, who are you?"

"Nikki. What's going on here?"

"I think this is another gift," I said. "It's part of his message."

"Like from the paintings?" Nikki asked. Her voice was stronger, clearer. She was losing her reserve.

"You seem to know more than I do, young lady." Phillip walked towards us, his hand outstretched. There were too many people around me. I knew I couldn't ask Nikki to leave. Not when she was starting to relax. I looked at Colin while Phillip introduced himself to Nikki.

"What's wrong?" he asked in a low whisper before I could say anything.

"Too many people." No sooner had I said this than Vinnie and Francine walked to the other side of the table. Vinnie made sure I saw his reassuring expression. Francine just looked concerned. Colin took a step away from me, leaving me with only Nikki against my side.

"Is she okay?" he asked, again in a low whisper.

"I think so." But I didn't want to push her away from me. Maybe I could explain to her later how strongly I disliked physical closeness. Later. Now there was another much more pressing issue. Phillip was asking Nikki if she would like something to eat. I didn't wait for her to answer him. "Did you invite my parents?"

Phillip straightened and frowned at me. "No. Why would I? Did someone invite them?"

"You did." My mother's eyes supported her accusing tone. "You sent us that embossed invitation with those horrid red daffodils."

Adrenaline rushed through my body, instantly making my hands cold. I turned away from my parents, my focus on Colin. My mouth felt dry and I cleared my throat. "Kubanov."

He nodded. Vinnie and Francine moved closer to the table to be part of our conversation.

"Why would he want my parents here?"

"I thought you wanted to show us where you worked," my father said. I glanced at him. My mother had lost interest and was looking at the underpaintings. "The invitation was for five o'clock this afternoon, but we decided to come this morning. We're meeting with old friends for an early dinner before a concert this evening. We didn't want to cancel our plans to merely see your workplace. Now I'm glad we didn't."

I looked at them, not seeing the people who were biologically connected to me. I was processing everything my father just told me, trying to make sense of this. "Did you tell anyone you were going for dinner and a concert?"

"No, why would I?"

"I put it on my Facebook page." My mother looked away from the underpainting she was studying. "I even got fifteen likes when I last checked. It seems everyone liked the fact that we had won those concert tickets."

Even though I had heard my mother scoff at social media as being plebeian, I wasn't surprised that she couldn't resist the temptation of being a mini-celebrity. It would be the perfect platform for her to build an image of much higher social standing and activity than was real.

"I know this place." My mother pointed at the second underpainting from the left. "It's our street in Marseille. It was your elementary school years. That was when we started homeschooling you. This is quite a good cubist rendition of it."

This I had not expected. I took a moment to school my thoughts and tone. "Do you recognise any of the other places?"

"Why, yes I do. Come look here, Gerard." She waited for my dad to join her. "This is Toulouse. We had that big country house where you were homeschooled before you matriculated."

I watched them as they walked along the wall with the underpaintings. My mother didn't identify any of the other paintings. A deep dread was sending more shots of adrenaline through my system, making my stomach feel heavy. I didn't like where my thoughts were taking me. "How did you win the concert tickets? I don't remember you ever approving of competitions."

The *orbicularis oris* muscle around my mother's mouth pursed her lips. "It was a giveaway at a recent gala event we attended, if you have to know. I was just lucky that my number was chosen. It even paid for the trip here and our accommodation. Five-star, thank goodness."

"Maybe now you could tell us who all these people are to you, Genevieve." My father looked at Colin, who had taken my hand in his. I hadn't noticed.

"I'm her employer," Phillip said. "This is a specialised team she works with in her art crime investigation cases."

"They are also my friends." I wasn't going to hide behind Phillip's diplomacy. "Francine and Vinnie are my best friends. And Colin is—"

I didn't know how to finish the sentence. What was he to me?

"—your boyfriend?" Nikki elbowed me in my side. Vinnie snorted a laugh and Colin lifted both eyebrows.

This was far beyond my purview of social interaction. I stood frozen, not knowing how to address the expectation in Colin's eyes. My mind raced, reaching for a path out of this quagmire.

"You need to leave here now." Desperate to escape the current topic, I allowed my tone to become a bit too harsh.

"Well, you don't need to be rude." My mother put her

hand on my father's arm. "She hasn't changed a bit."

"No, really." I stepped forward, my suspicions becoming stronger by the second. "You need to leave. Now."

Phillip looked at me for a moment before he escorted my parents from the conference room.

"What's up, Jen-girl?" Vinnie walked around the table, but stayed close to the door, not invading my space.

"Kubanov would only invite them here for a reason. He doesn't do things without a purpose. My question is what is that reason? And what does he have planned for five o'clock?"

"What makes you think he has something planned for five o'clock?"

"He's been investigating us. He knew things about Colin that no one else knew. Undoubtedly he investigated me and must have found out about the lack of any relationship between me and my parents. My mother didn't win those tickets. Somehow Kubanov set it up for her to win that trip here. He also knew she would be at the concert at five."

"How did he know they would come earlier?" Francine asked. "And how did he know we—you—would be in the office today?"

"That I don't know. Maybe he's been watching them and came to the conclusion that based on prior behaviour there is a large probability they would come earlier. The same with us working today."

"Five o'clock?" Colin asked.

"He easily could've predicted I would challenge my parents' presence and find out about the invitation. That would give me the time."

"For what?"

My shoulders dropped a bit. "I don't know. It's here, but I don't know what I'm looking at."

"You said his illness could've changed Kubanov. Maybe he just did this to fuck with your mind."

Francine slapped Vinnie hard on his arm. "Language. There's an impressionable person in the room."

I was startled that I had completely forgotten about the young body pressed against mine. Nikki's presence, her proximity was non-intrusive. Until she snorted. It was very unladylike and unsuitable for a person her age. "That is not the worst word I've ever heard."

"It doesn't matter, young lady." Francine gave Nikki a stern look. "Around here we talk like ladies."

Vinnie and Colin laughed, relieving some of the anxiety in the room.

"We have less than six hours until five o'clock," I said when the laughter had died down, and before Francine could argue with Vinnie about her ladylike behaviour. "I need to figure out what Kubanov has planned."

"Got it." Francine grabbed Vinnie's arm. "Come on, big guy. Let's leave Genevieve to do her thing."

Vinnie allowed her to pull him to the door, but he turned back, a serious look on his face. "Those people aren't your family, Jen-girl. We are."

"She's going to say something about blood and genetics and biology." Francine pointed a shiny brown nail at me. "Don't you dare say that. Blood isn't thicker than water. We are your family. Capiche?"

"The density of blood really is thicker than water, Francine. You should know... Is this an expression?"

"You bet your ass it is." Vinnie winced when Francine slapped him again. "Sorry, punk. Jen-girl, you're ours. Deal with it."

Francine blew me a kiss and winked at Nikki, then pulled Vinnie out the conference room.

"They're right, you know?" Nikki eased away from me, enough to still feel her body heat, but no longer in full contact. The tension in my muscles decreased significantly.

"About what?" I asked, distracted by the unidentified underpaintings.

"The old guy, the big punk and the model treat you like family. Your parents don't. I think the big punk is right." She lifted one slender shoulder.

"How do you know how families treat each other?" I asked.

Colin stiffened next to me. "Jenny, um, maybe—"

"I spent a lot of time with my friends in America." Nikki didn't look uncomfortable with the question, despite Colin's concern. "I'm an only child and my father is—was—a big-time criminal, so I had to watch them to know what a family is like. They're like you guys. Except you're weird and they're not."

Colin chuckled. "What are you doing here?"

"Mister Manny told me to wait here."

Things had been happening so fast, I hadn't had time to consider all the questions around Nikki's presence. "How long had you been waiting in here before I came in?"

"Only a few minutes. Some police-type people fetched me yesterday and put me on a plane to come here. No one told me anything." Any trace of light-heartedness disappeared, sadness taking its place. "Until you did. Thank you."

Colin looked at me. "Jenny, is this—"

"—Monique, Hawk's daughter."

"Jesus." He shook his head. I didn't know if it was to erase his swearing, express his disbelief or to show his understanding of the complexity of this new development.

"Do you want me to leave now?" Nikki's question was soft and hesitant, as if not wanting an answer. Her eyes were on Colin and she moved back to be in full contact with me again. "I promise I'll be quiet. You won't even know I'm here. I won't even move."

"That's not possible." I saw her expression and it took me less than a second to understand her disappointment. "I mean it is not possible to not move. You'll move, but it's okay. If you sit quietly somewhere and don't disturb me while I think, I don't mind."

"You sure, Jenny?"

I nodded, already walking towards the paintings. In the background I heard Colin offer Nikki food, her voice eager when she accepted. At some point I heard Phillip's deep voice, but I was too focussed on the underpaintings and what they could mean. These places had significance. Kubanov had researched not only me and Colin, but also my parents. He knew where I had been born and where I had been schooled. Then he had commissioned an artist to paint scenes from those places. Were the remaining paintings someone else's residential history? If so, was it Colin's? Someone else's? I needed to check my suspicions.

"Can I go with you?" Nikki's voice stopped me at the door. I had forgotten about her.

"Yes." I walked to my office and heard her hurried footsteps following me. I swiped my key card to open the door to my viewing room.

"Wow. This is supercool." Nikki walked past me and turned in a circle, taking in the detail of my room. "You work here?"

"This is my viewing room." I sat down at the computer and opened an internet search engine.

"Can I sit here?"

I turned and saw Nikki at Colin's desk. Her eyes kept wandering to a large sketchpad.

"It's Colin's desk. You have to ask him."

"Where is he?"

"I don't know." I was wasting time answering her questions. "Oh, just come and sit here next to me."

From a drawer under my desk, I took a notepad and a pack of newly sharpened pencils and gave it to her as she settled in the office chair next to me. She looked small in the large chair. Her eyes widened when she took the notepad and pencils. "Awesome. Thanks."

About ten minutes later, I had confirmed my suspicion only fifty percent. That wasn't confirmation. The glass door to the team room opened and Colin walked in. He stopped and looked in surprise at Nikki quietly drawing. His eyes narrowed when he focussed on the notepad and he walked closer.

"This is really good."

"Oh, thanks." Nikki gave him a quick smile and returned to the notepad.

"I need Francine." I got up and walked to the team room, Colin following me. "Actually, I need everyone."

"What have you got?"

"I think I know the message behind the underpaintings."

Francine stopped typing on her keyboard. "What is it?"

"I don't have enough data to support my suspicion, but I think Kubanov is targeting all of us."

"Where is she?" Manny walked into the team room and looked around. "Is Monique here?"

"Nikki, and she is in my viewing room."

His posture relaxed a bit. "Oh, good. I was worried she ran away."

"Why would she do that?" I hadn't observed any such intentional cues.

"Why? Because she threatened to do it all the way from the airport. The officers who brought her here considered putting cuffs on her."

"They were total ass-wipes." Nikki stood in the open door to my viewing room. She looked tense, her eyes shifting to me constantly.

"Watch your language, young lady." Francine looked at Nikki from under her brow, negating her severe look with a wink. "Come stand here and watch me work magic on the computer. What do you need, Genevieve?"

"I need all of you to come with me to the conference room." I walked to the door, not waiting for their responses. I knew they would follow me.

"Do you need Phillip as well?" Francine asked as I stepped into the conference room.

"Yes."

"I'll get him," Manny said. "Don't start without us."

While I was waiting for Manny and Phillip to join us, I studied each underpainting with my newfound suspicions. I felt cold when I recognised another painting.

"Okay, what did I miss?" Manny was standing at the far end of the conference table, next to Phillip. I quickly told him about my parents' visit.

"And you now think something is going to happen at five o'clock today?" Manny's question came out forceful in its displeasure.

"Yes. I also have a suspicion that these underpaintings are our history."

"What do you mean?" Vinnie asked, glaring at the paintings.

"Three of these paintings show my life history." I pointed at the first underpainting my mother identified. "This one is where I spent my elementary school years. That one is my high school years and that one is where I lived when I studied in Oxford. It is a cubist view of the street my apartment was in."

"Oh shit." Francine walked along the wall. "What about the other fourteen paintings?"

"There are five of you. I think each person has two or three underpaintings showing parts of your life." I walked to a painting that I particularly liked. "From Manny's biography on Interpol, I know he was born in Birmingham. In this painting you can see the Joseph Chamberlain Memorial Clock Tower."

"Holy hell." Manny walked closer in long, angry strides. "That was my university."

"I know. I need you to look for buildings or landscapes that were part of your childhood or life in these paintings. I think there are two for each of you." I was still speaking when everyone starting walked around the room, stopping at the paintings. None of the body language I observed was relaxed. I pulled out a chair and as soon as I sat down, Nikki was sitting next to me.

"You won't know I'm here."

"I know now you're here. Your reasoning is flawed."

She leaned a bit closer to me. "You're like totally weird, you know. But in like a really cool way."

"High praise coming from a teenager." Colin sat down. He tried to disguise it, but I saw concern unlike any I'd observed before. "There are three paintings with places from my life. How did he get this, Jenny?"

"That fucker is dead." Vinnie sat down, but stood up again to pace along the length of the room. "He's got my Aunt Theresa's street there. I lived with her for some time when I was a kid. How the fuck did he know this?"

Francine wasn't correcting Vinnie's use of swear words.

She was pale as she stood in front of a painting. "This is my dad's church."

One by one, everyone identified paintings depicting parts of their lives. Manny and Phillip had two paintings each, the rest of us had three. I didn't know if that had meaning.

"Okay, so now we know this sicko is after us. But we've known this all along." Vinnie eventually calmed enough to sit down. He was still shifting a lot in his chair. "We also know something is going to happen at five. What would that be?"

"I don't know yet." I felt powerless. The people in this room needed to be protected and I didn't know from what. A ringtone sounded loudly in the room.

Manny took his smartphone from his jacket pocket. "It's the results from the two statues. They were both printed. The lab says they could actually see the layers once they knew what to look for."

"Two statues?" Phillip asked. "I thought there was only the one from Colin's safe house."

"Kubanov gave Jenny a Costa Rican Sukia figure."

Phillip drew a sharp breath. "Can I see it?"

"Here." Manny handed him his phone after finding the photos he took in my apartment.

Phillip's brows lifted high on his forehead. "This is the statue I bought for my parents the week before they died. I buried it with them. And I might have mentioned it to Angelique once."

"That bitch," Francine muttered, scowling. "That was how Kubanov knew about this."

"When was that?" I asked softly. The pain on Phillip's face was hurting me.

"Twenty-three years ago. They died in a freak yachting accident."

Francine put her hand on Phillip's arm and smiled sadly when he looked at her. "I'm sorry for your loss, Phillip."

Nothing else was said for a long time. I could clearly see everyone was overwhelmed by the knowledge that Kubanov knew so much about us.

"Back to work." Manny slapped both hands on the table. "We will not let this arsehole scare us. We're going to find out where that shipment is, Doc is going to Mozart her way into finding out Kubanov's endgame and we're going to put him away for life."

He stood up and waited until everyone was standing before he nodded and walked out the room.

"Mozart is not a verb," I said as I followed Colin out the conference room. "I wish people would stop using it as such."

"What do you guys do here? Are you like art cops?" Nikki asked from behind me. I looked around and saw her carrying her notepad. Had she been drawing even in the bad light of the conference room?

"Something like that." Colin nodded at her notepad. "I suggest you pretend that you don't hear anything we say here."

I watched the expressions on her face. Young people seldom had well-developed skills at deception and masking their emotions. On Nikki's face I saw understanding of the situation. I wondered how many times Hawk had told her to pretend to not hear anything. How many times she had overheard crimes being planned. She nodded once as we entered my viewing room. I watched her sit down on the floor between two of my cabinets. She pulled a pencil from her ponytail and started drawing.

"Something about the woodwork doesn't make sense." I

turned to Colin sitting next to me. "Why would Hawk have a workshop in his warehouse?"

"My dad hated woodwork." Nikki lifted her shoulders up to her ears in a classic tortoise posture, trying to disappear when we turned around to look at her. "Sorry, sorry. I'm not here. I don't hear anything."

"No, wait. Have you been to your dad's warehouse?" I asked.

"Many times. There was never a workshop there."

"When is the last time you were there?"

"The last time I was in the country. Nine months ago."

I looked at Colin. "It is possible that he had that installed more recently. To what end?"

We turned back to face the monitors and discussed a few ideas, but none of them were viable. Either they were too farfetched to be considered as options or they didn't fit Kubanov's previous behaviour.

Nikki had said something that brought even more confusion to the case. If Hawk didn't enjoy woodwork and he didn't sell any wood products, what was all that equipment doing in his warehouse? We sorely lacked information on Tall Freddy and Dukwicz, and Francine couldn't find a trace of the thousand five hundred printers. Added to that was the list of unconnected things bought with Colin's credit card. Five o'clock was coming closer and I was running out of time to make sense of these disconnected pieces of information.

Chapter TWENTY-THREE

Three hours later I had gone over the case in my mind three times and still wasn't any closer to answers. Nikki was still drawing quietly between the two cabinets. Colin was in the team room working with Vinnie and Francine, trying to locate the 3D printers. I didn't like that I had started to doubt my conclusion that something was going to take place at five o'clock.

There was something in those paintings I had not yet seen. I had no reason to be so convinced of it, and refused to call it a gut feeling. I needed the focus Mozart brought to my mind. It took me a few seconds to find the right track on my computer and another second for Mozart's Symphony No. 40 in G minor to fill the viewing room with its dark beginning.

Five bars into the symphony, I remembered Phillip had sent me an email. I opened it to a five-line email informing me that Phillip's museum contact had brought the handheld x-ray machine. It was in the conference room and had a simple instruction leaflet next to it. The museum contact hadn't been interested in sacrificing another minute of his weekend to show Phillip how to operate it. Phillip, on the other hand, was too busy with clients to concern himself with it.

Without second thought, I got up and walked to the conference room. Again I switched on only the sunken ceiling lights, reasoning that one did not need a darkened room to see x-ray images.

On the table was a device that looked like a strange video camera. It had a screen that swivelled away from the body of the device just like a video camera. I picked up the leaflet, sat down and started reading. Operating it was surprisingly simple. I touched the machine and thought how far we had come in technology. The leaflet also claimed the benefits of using it in warzones, on site at car accidents and many more places. It even listed statistics on the safety of the radiation exposure. I felt safe.

Following the instructions, I turned the x-ray machine on, changed the settings and aimed it at my hand. I couldn't help the smile when I saw the bones joining my thumb to the rest of my hand. This technology was amazing. I moved it up to capture my wrist, but stopped there. There wasn't time to play. I walked to the nearest painting, curious what I would discover.

I aimed the x-ray device at the painting, but was too close. I took a step back and tried again, capturing a section of the bottom left hand corner. This time I saw an x-ray image of the painting on the screen, but that was not what caught my attention. It was the frame. I took another three images of the frame in different places.

I didn't want to believe what my eyes were seeing. My mouth lost all its moisture and my hands turned cold. I called up the Mozart symphony I had earlier listened to in my viewing room. It was imperative for me to not shut down.

To confirm what I saw, I walked stiffly to the next painting. The strange purchases with the fake credit cards in Colin's alias name made sense. My incoherent email about a frame of reference made sense. The wood glue, wires, duct tape and seventeen pagers made sense. The underpaintings going to the edges of the frames and preventing us from removing the frames made sense. As did the workshop with all the woodwork equipment in Hawk's warehouse.

An involuntary whimper escaped when the next painting showed me the same as the previous one. Even to my untrained eye, it was shockingly obvious what I was looking at. With every new image, my muscles became more frozen, my mouth drying. Blackness pushed in from my peripheral view, but stayed there as I focussed harder on the first movement of Mozart's symphony. With this work Mozart had set a new precedent, first using the accompaniment before introducing the theme. Later it was to become a favourite amongst Romantic composers.

As if from a far distance, I heard Nikki call me, asking me if I was okay. I hadn't known she was in the conference room with me. I couldn't answer. It would take me away from Mozart and push me into the black void calling me. I heard her leave the conference room shouting for help. She sounded scared. I wanted to tell her to listen to Mozart. It would make her feel safe.

"Jenny?" Colin's hand on my arm was warm. I aimed all my attention on that warmth, forced my eyes away from the little screen I was staring at to look at his strong hand on my forearm. His grip was firm, his thumb rubbing gently. "Jenny, are you with me?"

I nodded my head, but my stiff muscles turned it into a jerky movement. "Bombs. They are all bombs."

"What are all bombs?"

I took a deep breath, looking only at Colin. I knew Vinnie and Francine were also in the conference room, but I couldn't deal with them right now. The safe familiarity of Colin's face was a good combination with Mozart. Even if he used a name as a verb. I pointed the x-ray device at a painting and swivelled the screen towards him.

"The woodwork equipment was used to make specialised frames. Those frames are filled with what I suspect to be C4, maybe another explosive. No, it would have to be C4, because of the traces found in the warehouse by the woodwork equipment. Look at the wires and the small electronic device at the bottom of each frame. To me it looks like a pager. I don't know how it will be set off, but I'm sure they are bombs."

"Are you saying all the paintings *here* are bombs?" Francine's tone did not hold its usual sultry, relaxed quality.

I nodded to confirm her repetition of what I had said.

"Motherfucker." Vinnie ran out of the room after a quick apology to Nikki.

"We have to leave." Colin got up. "Come on, Jenny. We're leaving this place right now. Francine, take Nikki and get out of here. We'll meet you at the cars."

"Someone has to tell Edward." I allowed Colin to push me towards the door, thinking that Manny would have the bomb technician's contact details.

"I'm not leaving without Doc G." Nikki's voice was soft, but stubborn.

"Not now, Nikki." Colin lowered himself a little to be closer to her height. "I'm getting Jenny out of here. You go with Francine. We will not leave you alone. We stick together. Got it?"

Nikki looked at me, fear in her eyes.

"Go with Francine. I'll be out soon." Why was this girl connecting with me? On top of everything else, I couldn't carry that responsibility as well. I was relieved when she nodded once and left with Francine, who was talking on her phone, her tablet tucked under her arm.

"What are you doing?" Colin held his hand out to me. "Let's go."

I was walking towards the offices where I knew a few employees were working today. "We need to evacuate the whole building. Maybe even the street. I don't know the projections of the damage if all those explosives were to be detonated."

"Vinnie's gone to tell Phillip. They will take care of the office. Edward will take care of the rest. Come on, Jenny." The urgency in his voice sent another blast of adrenaline through my body, this time fuelling my muscles. It took us three minutes to take the stairs down and meet Francine and Nikki on the other side of the street, next to Colin's SUV. We joined them on the far side of the vehicle and Nikki immediately moved to my side, not quite touching me, but very close.

I took a deep, calming breath. "Where's Vinnie?"

"There." Colin pointed at the front door of the building. Vinnie was walking towards us with long strides, holding a smartphone ahead of him as if it was leading him. He had a laptop in his other hand.

"Take this." He shoved the phone in my hands. "The old man wants to talk to you."

"Put it on speakerphone," Colin said as Francine moved closer. She took the laptop from Vinnie with a nod. There were too many people surrounding me. I put up my hand holding the phone.

"Please give me some space."

Nikki moved behind me, her logic amusing. If I couldn't see her, I wouldn't feel crowded. I still felt her body heat against my back, but didn't say anything. Francine and Vinnie took a step back and the tightness around my throat and chest eased. I pressed the speakerphone button on the touchscreen.

"Manny, we're all here and you're on speakerphone."

"What the bloody hell is going on, Doc? Phillip tells me there is a frigging bomb in the office?"

"Make that seventeen bombs, Millard." Colin leaned a bit closer to the smartphone in my hand. "Hawk used that woodwork equipment to make frames that he filled with C4 and pagers. All the forged paintings in the conference room have them. Jenny saw it on the x-ray images."

"Holy fucking hell."

"Nikki is here, Manny." Francine was overly concerned about the use of strong language in front of Nikki. I would have to ask her about this.

"Where are you?" I asked Manny instead. This was more important.

"On my way back to you. I was in a meeting with the bigwigs. Doc, are you sure about what you saw?"

"Yes."

"I also saw it, Millard. Those are bombs."

"Hellfire." He cleared his throat. "Okay, Edward is on his way. He should be there soon. Doc, I want you get in your car and drive to the bottom of the street."

"Only me?"

He grunted loudly. "No, take all the criminals with you. And keep this bloody phone close to you in case I need to speak to you again."

The phone went quiet and I looked up. Colin had the back door open and was gesturing at Nikki to get in. Only when I opened the passenger door and got in did she get into the back. Vinnie got in on one side of her, Francine on the other. They had scarcely closed the doors when Colin drove down the street.

He double-parked next to a white sedan, the SUV still running.

"This doesn't make sense." I pulled at the seatbelt across my chest.

"What doesn't make sense?" Colin shifted in his seat to look at me.

"The bombs explain all those things bought with your credit cards. It's another way of setting you up. It also explains the workshop in Hawk's warehouse."

"But?" Colin asked when I stopped speaking. I needed to think. There was a thread through all this and I needed to find it.

"Those bombs had no guarantee to kill all of us. Manny went to a meeting. What if Colin had gone out again for food, or Vinnie had gone to meet one of his contacts? What if none of us were in the office? That plan is flawed."

No one spoke. They were giving me the silence I needed to reach into my mind for that elusive piece of information. I closed my eyes and allowed Mozart's energetic fifth symphony to blast through my mental barriers at full volume.

"The numbers!" I bounced in my seat, pushed my sleeve up my arm and showed it to Colin. "He told me that there was more to the tattoo. That there were layers to uncover."

"It gave us that website, rousseaus.hin.org."

I had made the mistake of stopping at that revelation, not looking for another layer of information. Mozart's symphony had brought it to my consciousness. "If you take the .org away and scramble the letters, it gives us two words: Russian House."

"No fucking way."

"Vinnie!" Francine's reprimand went with a loud slap.

"Sorry, punk." He didn't sound contrite.

Colin pulled into the street as the sound of sirens came closer. "Are you saying he is organising all this in the place where it started? Rather poetic."

"I don't see poetry in that." Only psychology. "That was the first place he was faced with me, with us. If still true to his profile, he would have seen that as an unacceptable humiliation and it is the place he would want to right the balance."

"You should be telling Manny this," Francine said from the back. She was right. I phoned Manny and put him on speakerphone.

"What's up, Doc?" Manny answered after the first ring. I didn't know why Vinnie and Nikki snickered at his greeting.

I told him my discovery. "Do you know who the developer is who bought the Russian House?"

Manny gave a name amidst a lot of swearing.

"This developer was registered two years ago by another company which is one of Hawk's lesser-known companies," Francine said. I twisted around and saw her working on her laptop, while Nikki was holding the tablet at an angle for Francine to see.

The tablet trembled in Nikki's hand. I looked up and saw her face drained of colour. Someone was going to have to give this child guidance through the unorthodox double world her father had lived in. His role as a father had been significantly more benign than any other role he had taken on.

Colin was driving increasingly faster. I turned back to face the front, wanting to be under the full protection of my safety belt and the airbag.

"We'll be there in about three minutes," Colin said as he took a corner skilfully, but very fast. I gripped the side of my seat with my free hand.

"I'm five minutes out," Manny said. "Wait for me. And for the love of Pete, don't do anything stupid."

Chapter TWENTY-FOUR

I stared at the stately mansion in front of us. The Russian House. The walls were a brilliant white against the afternoon summer sun, the once carefully landscaped gardens neglected and overgrown with weeds. The windows were dark and empty. An abandoned atmosphere clung to the house. I huffed inwardly at my irrational thoughts. I was imprinting my knowledge on what I was seeing. Just because I was told the house had been empty didn't mean it was.

Being here brought back a flood of frightening memories from a year ago. It had been three hundred and forty-seven days since the night I entered this house to catch a man working for Kubanov, killing students all over Europe. My mouth was dry and my throat tight.

We were standing outside the car at the entrance gate, waiting for Manny. The sound of a racing car engine announced his arrival. As soon as he stopped and turned off the car, he jumped out. "Move back, people."

It took a few threats before we were all stationed on the other side of the street, the vehicles a barrier between us and the house. Manny was still berating us for being so close to a possible bomb site when GIPN arrived in three black vehicles. They were an emergency response unit, the equivalent of a SWAT team. Officers dressed in black uniforms exited the vehicles with military efficiency. I recognised the team leader, Daniel, from our last case and nodded when he greeted me. I didn't want to be here.

GIPN went into immediate action, trained to almost choreographed perfection. They set up surveillance, analysed heat signatures from inside the house and sent in two teams when they determined no one was inside. All the while, I was trying to understand this new development unfolding in front of me. I had the added challenge of Nikki staying close to my side at all times. Fortunately, she didn't speak.

"The house is clear, guys." Daniel walked across the street an hour later, unfastening his helmet strap. "We've checked every nook and cranny of that house. There's no one there. We've also checked for explosives. Our dogs picked up nothing."

"Is there something inside the house? Furniture? Paintings?" Maybe Kubanov had left a message for me.

"There is one painting in the ballroom, but that's it. Nothing else. It's a ghost house."

"Can we go inside?" I needed to see that painting.

"Sure." Daniel waved two of his team members over. "We'll accompany you."

"Have you checked the painting for explosives and wires?" I was thinking not only of the bombs in the office, but also when Kubanov had fitted bombs to paintings six months ago, once nearly killing me and another time injuring Manny.

"Checked and cleared, Doctor Lenard."

"Genevieve," I said absently. When I took my first step to follow Daniel, I became aware of Nikki right next to me. I stopped and looked at her.

"I don't want to stay here alone," she said. I continued to look at her, but she didn't waver. She stared back. "Don't leave me."

"I'm not leaving you. I want you safe. There are a lot of police here to protect you. If you go inside, I will be distracted and I might miss something important. Please wait here for me. I will come back."

"Promise me."

There wasn't time to argue with her, and there was definitely no time to ask her why she had chosen me to become attached to. I nodded stiffly. "I promise. Now please wait inside the car."

Relief relaxed all the muscles in her face when I gave her my word. She believed me, and I knew she would wait in the car. Without checking to see if she went to the SUV, I turned and walked with Colin to the front door. The thirty metres it took us to get there I used preparing myself. I didn't want to spend time and energy analysing the expressions I had seen on Colin's face observing Nikki and me interacting.

Daniel and the others had already entered through the front door. I hesitated. Dread of what I might find inside settled in my chest like a growing rock. Colin's hand closed around my elbow and immediately I felt grounded, no longer as terrified. His hand moved down to cover my fist. He waited until I opened my hand and intertwined his fingers with mine. He was with me.

We walked through the door, the view spectacular with a winding staircase leading to a landing overlooking the foyer. Dust dulled the previously shiny surfaces and I spotted a few spider webs. I looked away from the accumulated dirt with a shudder and followed the sound of voices towards the back of the house.

As I remembered, there were seven large rooms downstairs. This house was perfect for entertaining, but was now an empty husk. Our footsteps echoed through the house, Manny's voice bouncing off the walls as he spoke to Daniel about the search. From Daniel's response, they had systematically gone through the house. There was no faulting their technique and I felt comfortable he was telling the truth.

If Kubanov wasn't here, why the five o'clock message? Why the clue leading us to the Russian House?

We entered the largest room on the ground floor, the ballroom. Objectively speaking, it would be a pity for a house of such beauty to be demolished. It was spacious, elegant and reminded me of a black and white movie Vinnie had watched on my large-screen television. Yet the irrational emotions in me insisted demolishing this house sounded like a good idea.

"What do you make of this, Doc?" Manny was standing in front of a painting. He moved to the side and presented the painting with an extravagant hand gesture. "Another bloody Braque painting."

On the wall was another reproduction, another forgery, of Braque's Harbour of Normandy. I never wanted to see that painting again for as long as I lived. I stepped closer, pulling Colin with me. "Is it a forgery by the same artist who forged the paintings in your safe house and my apartment?"

Colin leaned in and nodded. "Yup, looks like the same work."

"Can we remove it from the wall?" I asked.

"Sure. I'll do it." Daniel carefully lifted the painting away from the wall and checked the back. "Nothing here."

Colin held out his hand and took the painting, turning it around. "It has brown paper at the back. No canvas, no painting. Vin, could you go get my camera from the SUV?"

"Done. I'll check on the little punk as well."

I had forgotten about Nikki and was glad Vinnie hadn't. I returned my attention to the painting in Colin's hands. "Do you think there is an underpainting on the painting itself?"

"I have no idea. We'll check."

Daniel's radio crackled and he left the room. Colin tore

the brown paper from the back, revealing nothing strange. He hung the painting back on the wall with an annoyed sigh. I took a step back from the painting, tilted my head and looked for anything out of the ordinary.

"Do you see something strange?" Francine asked. "Because I really don't."

"It's an exact replica. Not a brilliant one, but exact." Colin folded his arms. Before he could say anything else, Daniel stepped back into the room.

"We have a hostage situation downtown. Do you guys still need us here?"

"I've got it from here," Manny said. "You go ahead and do your job."

"I'll leave two uniforms to keep watch from the gate until you are ready to leave. The other team is on standby if you need anything." Daniel was already walking out the room. "Call and they'll be where you need them."

"Thanks, Daniel."

I didn't think Daniel heard Manny. His face told me he was already analysing the hostage situation. I looked at the painting again. "There has to be something here."

"Here's the light, dude." Vinnie walked into the room, holding out the digital camera. "I brought the little punk with me. Hope it's okay with you, Jen-girl."

"I know you know I'm here, but I'll be so quiet, you'll forget." Nikki walked to the window and leaned against the low windowsill. I looked at her for a few seconds. When I could see no fear or indicators of distress, I nodded and turned back to the painting. Outside GIPN's vehicles started up and raced away.

"There's too much light in this room to take a good photo." Colin tilted the camera in his hand. At half past six in summer the sun was still high enough to provide a lot of natural light. In this case it was not welcomed.

"We can close the shutters." Nikki raised her shoulders towards her ears when we looked at her. "Sorry. I'm not here."

"She's right. The shutters are operated from here." Francine pointed at the switches by the door frame. I had assumed they were all for the lights. "Let's check if it will work."

A whirring sound brought a smile to Francine's face when she flipped one of the switches. The shutters closed slowly, gradually casting the room into shadow, adding an eerie atmosphere to the empty space. Colin waited until the shutters were completely closed, the room in semi-darkness before aiming the camera at the painting to take a photo. Confusion was on his face when he looked at the display screen.

"Nothing. Huh." He took the painting from the wall, turned it around and took another photo. "Again, nothing."

"Then why are we here and why is the painting here?" Francine flipped the switches to open the shutters. Late afternoon light streamed back into the room, showing the dirt on the floor and dead insects on the windowsills. Except for Nikki pretending to not be here, everyone turned to the painting. Studied and tense silence filled the room.

"Isn't it nice to have you all gathered here," a familiar raspy voice said from the door to the hallway. Adrenaline flushed my system, making my hands and feet cold, drying my mouth and bringing black panic into my peripheral view. Kubanov was here. He chuckled. "Just as I hoped."

As one, Manny and Vinnie reached for their weapons. At the same moment Colin pushed me behind him, placing himself between me and Kubanov.

"Ah, ah, ah." Kubanov's warning reminded me of when he was in my bedroom. I looked around Colin to see what

Kubanov was doing. He had a handgun in each hand, waving them for emphasis. He pointed one gun at Manny and one at Vinnie. "Drop those guns and kick them towards me."

Manny and Vinnie hesitated. They were a few steps away from me, closer to Kubanov. I was looking at their backs and had no idea what was going on in their minds.

"Now!" Kubanov's order echoed through the empty house. Nikki whimpered. She was standing frozen by the window. Alone. Kubanov stepped into the room. "Do it now or he gets it."

He delivered his threat with a backwards nod, and Dukwicz walked into the room, pushing Phillip ahead of him. Dukwicz held a handgun in one hand, a semi-automatic machine gun slung over his shoulder. Phillip looked terrible. His bespoke suit jacket was missing a sleeve, his cheek was cut and his white shirt bloody from the wound still oozing a thin stream of blood down his jaw and neck. Oddly, his silk tie was still perfectly positioned. I had given that tie to Phillip on my first Christmas working for him.

Two loud clangs on the floor jerked my attention away from the tie. Manny and Vinnie kicked their guns towards Kubanov. He walked closer and kicked the guns to the far side of the room. "Okay, now you will all play nice with me. I want your phones. All mobile devices. On the floor and kick them towards me."

My smartphone was still in my handbag in my viewing room, but all the others had brought theirs. One after the other smartphones fell to the floor and slid across the room towards Kubanov.

The shaking started in my hands. Then it moved up my arms, down my legs, through my torso. I had to bite down hard on my jaw to prevent my teeth from chattering.

Kubanov tilted his head to one side. "Genevieve?"

I hated the way he pronounced my name.

"She didn't bring her phone," Colin said.

"Did I ask you?" Kubanov asked, then turned around and hit Phillip across the face with the butt of the gun. A gash opened up on Phillip's other cheek, blood running down his face. He grunted, but stood stiffly upright. Kubanov turned back to us, his guns trained on Manny and Colin. "No one speaks unless I ask them to. No one moves unless I instruct them to. Tell them what will happen, Dukwicz."

"I will strangle this nice old man with his fancy tie." Dukwicz's *risorius* muscles stretched his lips into a cruel sneer. It lifted the already raised skin of his scar, filling his expression with malice. "I will do it slowly so you can watch every expression, Doctor Lenard. You like watching expressions, don't you?"

Darkness closed in on me. I couldn't afford to close my eyes, finding calm in Mozart. Phillip needed me. He looked at me, his expressions unguarded. He let me see his anger, his determination and his pride. That was enough for me to fight back the darkness to the very edges of my vision. I didn't know what to do, but I would not let him down.

Kubanov had threatened Phillip's life if anyone talked, but I needed Kubanov to talk. I needed to study his expressions. The little that I noticed through my haze of panic didn't make sense. I also needed him to communicate so I could find a way to talk him out of executing whatever plan he had made.

"Stop thinking so hard, Genevieve. The two cops outside are sleeping nicely on the front lawn, so screaming for help is pointless. All the bushes, trees and large garden? The neighbours won't hear you either. And GIPN is nicely occupied with their hostage situation. There is also a second situation—a bank robbery." His smile didn't look right. "Oh, don't worry. It is a real hostage situation and a real bank robbery. I think one hostage has already been killed. You see, I've been planning this carefully. I didn't want any interruptions."

Again Kubanov waved his guns. "Let's get this started. Everyone except Genevieve and the little girl turn around and slowly walk backwards towards me. If you try anything, Dukwicz will shoot Phillip and strangle Genevieve with his blood-soaked tie."

I had a view of everyone's backs. The stiffening of their muscles told me no one agreed with this option. I couldn't see any way around it. It was clear that Kubanov was applying a battle tactic—divide and conquer. He wanted me separated from everyone else. I didn't want Phillip to be killed because my friends were trying to protect me.

"Genevieve." Kubanov waited until I was completely focussed on him. "You know I will do it. And I will enjoy it. Tell your friends to do as they are told."

"Do it." My voice came out as a whisper so soft, I had to clear my throat. "Do what he says. Please."

"Jenny." Colin spoke softly through his teeth, but the sound travelled through the empty room. Kubanov immediately responded by elbowing Phillip in the stomach. I whimpered.

"This is the very last warning." Kubanov's calm demeanour as he faced us was more frightening than the cruelty evident on Dukwicz's face.

"Please do what he says," I whispered. Phillip was gasping for air as he pulled himself up. I couldn't bear making him suffer any more than this.

Slowly, the four people in front of me, my friends, turned around to face me and walked backwards. The dominant expression on their faces was rage. I didn't think they were only angry with Kubanov. Being powerless would make these strong personalities go on immediate offense. The problem was they couldn't do anything, not without knowing what was happening behind them.

"That's enough." Kubanov said when they were about a metre and a half from him. "Now get onto your knees. On your knees! Now!"

My mind was simultaneously bombarded with information and distracted by intense emotional distress. I couldn't believe I had just asked my friends to go towards their own execution. The emotions crossing their faces were too many to process. In total contrast, Kubanov's face rendered very little information. He was moving with difficulty, yet I saw no indicators of pain.

I watched my friends slowly lower themselves onto their knees. Despite their positions, there was not one nonverbal cue of surrender or submission to be seen. Not even on Francine's pale features. On Kubanov's face there was no glee, no anger, no disgust, no rage, nothing. It didn't make sense.

"Join them." Kubanov waved one of his guns at Phillip, pointing to the others. "On your knees next to them. Dukwicz, you know what to do."

Until a year ago, I had only studied white-collar criminals. My exposure to malice, murderous intent and psychosis had been purely academic. In a textbook of abnormal criminal psychology, I had once seen a smile as vicious as the one on Dukwicz's face. He pushed Phillip hard enough to make him stumble forward and fall onto his knees next to Manny. Phillip straightened slowly with as much dignity as he could. He was in pain.

"You." Kubanov pointed his gun at Nikki, who gasped. "Go join Genevieve."

Nikki didn't need a second invitation. She ran to my side and plastered herself against me. The physical contact was distracting, but it also grounded me in a peculiar manner. I moved slightly to put myself in front of her.

"Now isn't this cosy." Kubanov moved to the side, giving Dukwicz space. The scarred man was holding the semi-automatic machine gun in his other hand. My five friends had four guns, one of which could shoot dozens of bullets per minute, aimed at their heads. As loud and powerful as I could, I mentally started playing Mozart's Flute Concerto No. 2 in D Major. I needed as much calming and clarity as I could muster. This concerto gave me both.

"It's me you want. Let them go." My voice was stronger than I felt.

"No, my dear Genevieve." He pointed the gun at Vinnie's head. I noticed the different-looking surface of a common SIG Sauer. "What I want is not to let you die. I want you to watch your friends die. Then you can live the rest of your life with that image in your mind. You can spend hours listening to your beloved Mozart, wondering how you did not see that I was setting this up for you to come to me. How you did not figure out that I was going to fuck with your genius little head by erasing the only people in your life you care about. How you will be the reason they are all dead."

"Why do you want me to suffer?"

"Why not?" He laughed and unsurprisingly started coughing. His throat sounded raw. I wished for Manny's experience, Phillip's wisdom and Colin's charm. I had none of that. All I had was my skills and those were failing me. I couldn't read Kubanov's expressions. He smiled, but the muscle movement was not right. He caught his breath and wiped his mouth with the back of his hand. "I had myself a little treat this morning. Want to know how I spoiled myself?"

The change in his voice told me that there was more to the word 'spoiled' than a luxury activity. He was waiting for my answer.

"How did you spoil yourself?"

"I went for a rather expensive cosmetic treatment. The woman was quite confused why I wanted Botox injected all over my face." He tilted his head and gave another strange smile. I couldn't interpret it. "I spoiled myself for you. You can't read me. You see how well I know you? I also know that you don't have a relationship with your parents, so doing something wicked to them wasn't going to touch you. But these… these people? Well, them you like. Maybe you even love them. I don't know why you would, but I've seen the way you look at them. They are your weakness. These people and your mind."

I felt paralysed. Not from my inability to read him, but from fear for my friends. Kubanov moved away from Vinnie, but both the guns in his hands were still pointed at the kneeling people facing me. Their expressions I could easily read, but I didn't want to. I had seen the trust on all of their faces and it was too much responsibility to carry. Narrowing my focus on Kubanov alone made the situation marginally more bearable.

"Yes," he continued, glee in his voice, but not on his face. "I knew taking away your only weapon would turn you into a non-equal. You can't read my face and that is making you suffer. You don't know what to do, do you?"

"No, I don't. You're right. I have nothing without my skills. At this moment, I only understand your words." When my lie came out weak and believable, I almost cried.

People think they only communicate with facial expressions and hand gestures. They forget about the rest of their bodies. A lot of people learn to control the typical folding of arms or putting of hands on hips, but no one can control innate gestures. Tiny cues that were telling me Kubanov was really planning on killing my friends. Changing my focus from his face to the rest of his body empowered me. It gave me irrational hope that I could turn this situation around.

"Your body is dying, and you would like to blame someone else for this. I am an easy, convenient target." I ignored Manny's soft, but sharp intake of air. "What cancer do you have?"

"Esophageal cancer, stage four. It has spread."

"Prognosis?"

"I have a few months at most." His laugh was wheezy, painful. "I knew I wouldn't live forever, but I expected to die at the hand of someone else. Some young upstart killing me to take over from me. Not my body turning against me."

"I am—"

"No. Enough psychobabble from you. Your intellect makes you fun to talk to, but you distract me from my true purpose." He pushed the gun in his right hand against the back of Colin's head. "Who cares what little bits of information you want from me? I'm not going to confess all my sins to you, Genevieve. No. I'm going to kill your friends one by one and you are going to tell me which one to start with."

I didn't know if the trembling I felt was from Nikki moving further behind me or from my own body bowing under the mental stress. Kubanov had found the perfect plan to not only torment me, but very possibly break my fragile mind. I could never make a decision such as he expected and live with that. No amount of rationalisation would ever heal the wounds inflicted. Darkness beckoned me to its safe comfort.

"Genevieve!" Kubanov was pointing his gun at Francine's head now. I had not seen him move. Whether strength or fear, I didn't know, but I managed to push away the panic, pull back my shoulders and look at Kubanov. He stroked Francine's hair with the gun barrel. "This one first? She's a good hacker, but apart from that she's pretty useless. Did you know she changed her last will and testament to include you?"

He waited until I shook my head. I dared a look at Francine's face. Once she had told me that she was not scared of dying. I didn't see fear. I saw anger, determination and trust. I didn't want her to die.

"Or shall we start with Phillip?" He slowly walked past my friends. "Vinnie? Maybe Manfred Millard would be a good start. I understand he's always shouting at you. Hmm. No. I think we should maybe start with your lover. I'm still deeply disappointed that you coupled up with him. It would be a great joy for me to kill him first. I will finish the work I wasn't able to when he visited me. But I will leave the choice up to you, Genevieve. Who shall I kill first?"

My breathing was shallow and staggered. Gone was my ability to observe situations objectively, process the information, analyse it and make clearheaded decisions. All I could think of was how these people kneeling and looking at me with trust had changed my life. They had given me acceptance. They had given me friendship. They had given me a birthday party.

"Genevieve?" He pointed the guns from one to the next head. "Tell me who I should kill first. Choose."

I shook my head. I wanted this to end so we could all go to my apartment. Vinnie would cook and argue with Francine about spices. Manny would insult Colin and discuss politics with Phillip, and I would fret about fingerprints on my pristine surfaces. I wanted to go home and tell Colin how much I trusted him, how much I needed him. That I loved him.

It was that knowledge, that desire to tell Colin that brought clarity to my thinking. In Kubanov's sad desperation, he was attempting to take back control of his life. Cancer had taken his future from him, also his power. By forcing me to decide which friend was to die first, he was regaining a form of power. I didn't want to give him that. I didn't want him to know exactly how terrified I was at this moment. If I denied him that pleasure, the only power he had left was his guns.

"Choose!" Kubanov pushed the gun hard against Colin's skull, moving his head forward.

"No." The word came out barely audible. I didn't know if I could act on my assessment. I might deny him the psychological power he wanted over me, but he still had a gun—a gun that could kill my friends. My breath stuttered. I swallowed. "I won't... I will not choose. I refuse."

"You refuse?" His hands were shaking from the effort of aiming the two weapons for an extended period. He was the one who was weak—physically, but especially psychologically. He took two steps back, his guns aimed at Colin and Phillip. Dukwicz stepped to the side and back, placing him in the doorway. His body was communicating cues that he was planning to leave. I didn't have time to think about that. Kubanov took another step back. "Hmm. This is a good distance, I think. Now I won't get any brain matter on my shoes."

There was no warning contraction of the *orbicularis oculi* muscles under his eyes, no facial indicators, no other nonverbal cues. He just readjusted and pulled both triggers.

An inhuman scream tore from my throat as darkness

rushed in at me. I fought it back so I could protect my other friends. I wouldn't let Kubanov kill more people. Not the ones I cared for. It took me only a heartbeat or two to regain control. When I was able to refocus, the scene in front of me was confusing.

No one was on their knees anymore. Vinnie and Colin were on top of Kubanov, who was lying on the floor screaming. Francine had dropped and rolled to the side, and Phillip was sitting on his heels, cradling his arm. Dukwicz was gone, Manny too.

They were all alive. How that happened, I didn't know. All I knew was that I had failed them. My analysis, my actions had nearly got them killed. The guilt combined with the relief of seeing everyone still alive took all the power from my legs. I sank to the floor, my entire body shaking. I could feel the blackness, the rocking and keening looming, but I didn't want to take my eyes off my friends. My alive friends. A millisecond before the blackness won, I irrationally wished for one of Vinnie's breakfasts.

Chapter TWENTY-FIVE

"Jenny. Love, we're safe."

It was a scene that had played out many times before. Colin was rubbing my arms, calling me out of the warm, comforting darkness. I opened my eyes to movement and chaos around me. My breath caught and my heart sped up.

"Hey. Don't worry about them. Just focus on me."

I tore my eyes away from all the black-uniformed figures moving in and out the ballroom. Colin was sitting against the wall of the room. I was on his lap, cradled against his chest. My throat was hurting as if I had been keening loudly for an extended period. I sat up and wrapped my arms around my torso in a full self-hug. I cleared my throat. "How long?"

"You've been out for two hours."

"You're alive." I looked him over, but couldn't see any injuries apart from the bruising he had acquired fighting with Vinnie. "How is that possible?"

"Kubanov had two printed guns." Colin's smile was genuine. And malicious. "The piece of shit printed guns for himself, one of which exploded in his hand. He lost most of his fingers on that hand."

"And the bullets? Where did they go?" I was feeling awkward trying to see Colin's face while sitting on his lap. "Um, can we stand?"

"If you feel up to it."

I nodded and got up. Only if I was in a shutdown would I sit on a floor this dirty. Even though my legs felt unsteady, I preferred to stand. "The bullets?"

"The one aimed at me hit the wall over there." He stood up with ease and pointed at a wall between two tall windows. "He shot at me first. That was the gun that exploded in his hand. The shock made him pull the other trigger in reflex, or so Vinnie and Millard think. The gun was aimed at Phillip, but the shot went wide and nicked his arm. It's only a superficial scratch. The paramedics already got him sorted out."

The fortuitous turnout of that event was hard to comprehend. "Where is Kubanov?"

"Under heavy guard in hospital. Manny vowed to make sure he gets out of hospital and into a solitary confinement cell as soon as possible." He took both my hands in his and pressed them against his heart. "I'm sorry you had to go through this, love. Are you okay?"

I didn't know. Watching two of the most important people in my life being shot, thinking they were going to die, was not something I had thought to ever deal with. How did one process such an experience?

"Are you sure Kubanov is under guard?"

"There's no way in bloody hell he's getting away, Doc," Manny said from behind me. I turned. On his face was not only concern, but his usual expression lines were more pronounced.

"If Kubanov is locked up, I will be okay." I hoped. The movement around us was distracting. Something about the body language of the people in the room caught my attention. "What or who are they looking for? Oh wait, where is Dukwicz?"

The lines around Manny's mouth deepened. "The bastard is gone. And he took a bunch of printers with him."

"When Kubanov's gun exploded, Dukwicz ran out,"

Colin explained. "Millard followed him into a hidden passageway—"

"—which GIPN obviously didn't find." Manny grunted. "It was a door behind a door going to a tunnel parallel to the basement. To top it off, the tunnel is lined with a layer of glass that makes it impossible to catch their heat signatures while they are there. Bloody Russians and their secret tunnels."

"Why didn't you catch him or shoot him?" It was hard to believe I was asking questions containing such violent action.

"My little revolver was like a fart against his submachine gun thunder." He nodded when I smiled at his analogy. It was amusing in a dark way. "He got away from me, jumped in a van packed with boxes and raced away. I phoned Daniel, who got GIPN back here. Dukwicz disappeared. There is a continent-wide alert out on him, but if they couldn't find a trace of him with all the cameras in this city, then I'm not holding out much hope."

"What was in the boxes? Did you see?"

"Oh yes, I saw, Doc." His lowered brow and flaring nostrils indicated anger. "Bloody 3D printers. The tunnel leads to the house across the street. In the basement are the printers we've been looking for. The problem is there are only a thousand two hundred and something printers. Dukwicz can't have fitted more than one hundred printers in that van, so we don't know where the other two hundred-odd printers are."

"This is not good."

"No, Doc, it isn't. A killer-for-hire possibly now has the tools to print at least one hundred single-use guns a day. That is not good at all."

"Can we go now?" a soft voice asked from behind Colin. I looked past him and down. Not far from where we had been, Nikki hugged her knees to her chest, a small figure on the floor.

"Why is she still here?" As soon as I asked this, Nikki's expression told me that my tone had been too harsh. I inhaled deeply. "I'm wondering why no one took you to a safer, more comfortable place."

"She refused to leave." Colin moved to stand next to me, holding one of my hands in a tight grip. He was smiling at Nikki. It was genuine, warm. "Not even Vinnie could convince her to go help him cook. She kept me company. We had a really nice chat."

I looked at Nikki, not sure what to think. Even though there was a wealth of growth in the pre-frontal cortex of the teenage brain, it was hugely underdeveloped. Adolescents were not astute in weighing outcomes, forming judgements and controlling impulses and emotions. Yet from the little I had observed in Nikki, I didn't think she was a typical teenager. That was partly what confounded me. The other part was the trust written in her nonverbal cues when she looked at me.

"Yeah, but now I'm really hungry." She stood up. "And I would like to leave this place. It's creepy and it bites, like big time."

I didn't understand all of her wording, but the meaning was clear. "Vinnie is cooking?"

"And Francine has gone to help him," Colin said with a smile. "Phillip went home to change, but he'll meet us for dinner. Vinnie and Francine didn't appreciate being in such close proximity to dozens of law enforcement officers. They left as soon as they felt everything was under control."

Manny grunted and mumbled something under his breath. "Well then, let's go. Nikki is not the only one who's hungry. That criminal had better have made enough food."

They didn't give me time for any more questions, or to greet and thank Daniel. Manny stalked ahead of us out the house to his car. Colin had an unbreakable grip on my hand, leading me out of the mansion and waiting impatiently for me to get into his SUV. Nikki followed us silently and was in the backseat before I got in the vehicle.

On the way home, Colin told me how quickly GIPN and the paramedics had arrived. I smiled when he told me Francine had insisted that the paramedics leave Kubanov to bleed to death. Apparently she had cursed a lot without once apologising to Nikki. That elicited a derisive snort from the backseat.

It was a feeling of great relief that settled over me when we stopped in front of my apartment building. Manny parked behind us and we went up to my apartment together. It was a novel experience to have Manny and Colin this close and not exchanging insults.

"You've got to be kidding me," Manny said as we walked into my apartment. He scowled at the food Vinnie was putting on my dining room table. "It's bloody half past nine at night."

"If you want to eat something else, go somewhere else, old man." Vinnie put a serving plate with cheeses on the table. I didn't know how he had known, but Vinnie was busy cooking breakfast. He smiled at me. "Good to see you, Jen-girl."

"Hey girlfriend," Francine called from the kitchen. "I'm making tea. I don't think we need coffee or any more stimulation."

Phillip was seated at the table. With the exception of his injuries, not a hair was out of place. I walked to him, studying his face. "Are you well?"

"I might have a few more grey hairs, but I'm fine." His

smile turned into a wince when his muscle movement jolted the cuts on his cheeks. Small butterfly plasters covered both wounds, bruises already starting to show. He lowered his head. "I'm really fine, Genevieve. Are you?"

I sat down in the chair opposite his and dropped my face into my hands. Not only did I want to hide my expressions from their concerned looks, but I didn't want to cry in front of them. They seemed so strong, so normal. Having everyone in my apartment brought home how dire the situation had been. How different the outcome could have been. How my actions had almost caused their deaths. I seldom indulged in hypothesizing possible and probable outcomes, but this moment was too overwhelming.

A chair was moved closer to mine and familiar arms pulled me closer. I buried my face in Colin's chest, my whole body shaking with silent sobs. It took a few minutes and a whole page of Mozart's Flute Concerto in D Major to feel ready to face everyone. After a few shaky breaths, I straightened.

"What do you need from us?" Colin asked quietly, wiping a stray tear from my cheek.

"Normality." I needed my routines. I needed to know these people were safe, no matter how annoying their behaviour was at times. I looked at Colin. "I need you."

"You have all of us, Jenny." A soft smile smoothed out the tense lines around his eyes and mouth. He leaned closer. "And you have me. Always. I'm not going anywhere."

"Oh hell. Just kiss her and get it over with, Frey." The discomfort in Manny's voice chased away the last of my tears. I shifted in my chair, moving away from Colin. Manny shook his head. "No? Well then, let's eat."

The normality of sharing a meal in my apartment with them settled my turbulent emotions. I knew it would take some time for me to work through the impact of the last year, this week, and especially this day's events.

"So Doc, what do you think?" Manny looked at me and I saw he knew I had not been listening. He was going to have to repeat his question. "Putting those bombs in the frames was smart, but having those underpaintings wasn't. What if we had looked at the underpaintings with x-rays from the very beginning? We would have caught on to his plan much sooner."

"There are a lot of what-ifs, Manny." Phillip only spoke that slowly when he was warning me to think before I spoke. This time his warning was directed at Manny. "There is no sense in blaming anyone."

"I'm not blaming anyone. I'm asking Doc why Kubanov would have done something so stupid."

I considered my answer before I spoke. "Either he did it in the hope that we would find it. He would've gotten pleasure from our fear alone. It also would've served as another clue in the game he was playing with us."

"Or?"

"Or he became careless. Over the course of this case, there were a few instances when I thought him to have been surprisingly negligent. But even that could've been strategic."

Manny pushed out his bottom lip, nodding slowly. He put a croissant on his plate with jerky movements. "To make us think he was changing or losing his mind when he wasn't. Not that I care anymore. He's going to be alone until his cancer kills him. I will make sure he has no access to media. He will not be able to enjoy any coverage his case is going to get."

"Good." Dying in obscurity would be true punishment for Kubanov. I also reached for a croissant, and wondered where Vinnie found fresh croissants at this time of the night.

He came from the kitchen with another basket of croissants and a jar of juice. He sat down next to Nikki, and winked at her. Surrounded by this many alpha personalities, she was quiet and watchful.

"Doc?" Manny looked annoyed. "I'm not a face-reader like you, but are you feeling guilty?"

I couldn't control the shiver that went down my spine.

"You are!" Manny leaned forward and shook a knife at me. "For someone so smart, you can be really daft sometimes."

"Manny." Phillip's voice was low.

"No, she needs to listen carefully to me. I've been in this a lot longer than you. I'm the expert here. And I know that Kubanov would've pulled those triggers no matter what you said. You also know this. It is not your fault, Doc. None of us are to blame. He is just a sick fucker that is now going to die alone."

It was quiet in my flat. I considered Manny's words and knew them to be true. Yet I knew that I was going to analyse this whole case to see if I could have done anything differently. I had to agree that the only person to blame was Kubanov. I stopped rubbing my upper arms as if I was cold and looked at Manny. "Thank you for saying that."

"He's right, Jenny."

"I know. I just wish your lives were never in danger." I didn't know if I would ever get the image of my friends on their knees out of my mind.

"I spoke to the president tonight." Manny's change of topic stopped my train of thought. "He personally wanted to thank me—thank us—for catching Kubanov, and so eliminating a threat to him and his wife personally."

"And his son," I said.

"Yes, his whole family. Well, the president was so impressed with our work that he called in the head of Interpol. They agreed that we should remain a team." All eyes were on Manny as he took a bite of toast and egg. He chewed a few times and swallowed the food down with some orange juice. Someone should tell him about the dangers of not chewing one's food properly.

"Goodie for them." Francine leaned back in her chair and folded her arms. "They may agree all they want. It doesn't mean we agree."

"Back down, supermodel." Manny sighed. "We will still be working like we did before, looking into art crimes. The difference is we will be at the president's disposal whenever he needs us. Previously, he had thought this arrangement only to last until we got Kubanov, but he wants us to continue. It will be a joint operation with GIPN, Interpol and the president's office. Our next assignment will be to find Dukwicz."

"I will not be party to some grand scheme to violate citizens' rights, collecting all kinds of data on them." Francine shifted her folded arms as emphasis.

"You hack into people's computers and collect all kinds of data every day," I said. "How is that different from what you just said? Oh, it doesn't matter. It's off topic."

More arguments exploded around the table. Francine hated the idea of anything more than a tentative working relationship with any government. Vinnie refused to be under anyone's authority. Colin scoffed at the notion of being subordinate to Manny. Things escalated until Francine slapped both hands on the table. "Would you please watch your language, people. We have a young person here."

"I'm not that young, you know." It was the first time Nikki spoke since we had entered my apartment. "My dad was a criminal. The people I grew up with used words much worse than that."

"But these are adult words." Francine's concern was interesting.

"In four months I will be an adult." She looked at Manny. "That also means if you think of putting me in some kind of system, I will disappear for the next four months."

"You are still a minor, Nikki." Manny tempered his tone, but residual anger in his voice from his argument with Francine and Vinnie caused Nikki to tuck her elbows into her body and lean deeper into her chair.

"You can't make me do something I don't want to." Her answer communicated more than the words. Had she been a willing participant in her life and education in the United States? Or had all decisions pertaining to her life been made regardless of her desires?

"What do you want to do?" I asked.

She blinked a few times, her micro-expressions telling me she had not expected to be asked for her opinion. "I want to stay with you."

My *masseter* muscles responded to my shock, lowering my jaw to an open-mouthed expression.

"Um, Nikki and I chatted a lot." Colin winked at her. He liked her. All his nonverbal cues told me that. "She wants to move back to France, but doesn't want to go into the system."

"What are you saying?" There was too much communication in his expression.

"I won't mind if Nikki stays with us until she goes to university."

"With us?"

"I promise I won't touch anything." Nikki's eyes were wide with expectation.

"That would be impossible." I saw the devastation on her face. Again I had not phrased my thoughts correctly. "I mean it would be physically impossible to not touch anything."

"I don't think anyone has to make any decisions tonight." Phillip's calm voice penetrated the building panic in me. Colin put his hand over both my hands gripping my left knee, and squeezed.

"If it's okay with Jenny, you can stay here tonight. Once we've all slept enough and are able to take a step away from our emotions, we'll talk about this again. Okay?"

Nikki looked at me until I nodded stiffly. Her torso collapsed slightly as she exhaled deeply. She smiled and started eating again.

I worried about having another guest in my home. Vinnie and Francine started arguing again about being in a team with Manny. That led to insults being thrown around, Phillip watching with amused interest. A year ago I would never have entertained the thought of being comfortable with a house full of arguing people. Now it caused a warm feeling. Was this what people felt when they talked about home with a wealth of emotion in their voices?

I watched Francine flirt with Manny until he was red in his face from annoyance and embarrassment, Nikki telling Phillip about her university plans, and Vinnie adding to Manny's annoyance. Colin was leaning back in his chair, his arm draped over the back of mine. I was too tired to see any significance in this domestic scene other than a growing concern about the arguments after a day of such emotional intensity.

I turned my hands around and interlaced my fingers with Colin's. His other hand cupped my shoulder and squeezed lightly. Without giving logic time to interfere with what I knew needed to be said, I looked at Colin. "If you still want to, we can break through the wall."

His eyes widened and his mouth went slack as he blinked a

few times. It had gone quiet around the table, but I didn't want to look away from Colin's expression. I needed to know that his reaction was true.

"Well." He cleared his throat.

I resisted the desire to fold into myself. "Should I not have said this?"

"You should absolutely have said this." He pulled me closer and lowered his face until we were almost nose to nose. "I love you too."

"I didn't say that."

"You did."

"You are reading nuances into my words." I leaned a bit back to look at his expression. As always he waited for me to look my fill. He truly believed that with my agreement to joining our apartments, I had declared my love for him. My mouth was dry, my voice hoarse. "You're right. I love you."

"Maybe we should continue this discussion later." He didn't show discomfort for being overheard. I saw desire.

"He wants you to be alone, so he ca—"

"Nikki." Francine voice was heavy with warning.

I still didn't look at anyone but Colin. "I'm sorry. I will say this later."

"Bloody hell." Manny threw his napkin on the table. "Do you want us to leave?"

Colin rested his forehead against mine and chuckled before he turned back to the table. "No, Millard. Finish your food."

"Well, I kind of lost my appetite."

"Ooh, more for me." Francine leaned over to take a piece of toast from Manny's plate, but he tapped her hand with his fork. She teased him about sharing a lazy breakfast with him some day in the future, his cheeks coloured and again teasing, arguments and insults were exchanged.

I sat back, comforted by Colin's touch. I liked that we were going to remain a team. Despite the incessant arguing, we worked well together. At least, as far as I understood team dynamics. I decided to invest in a few books on this topic for further research. This thought gave way to another type of research awaiting us if we were to find Dukwicz. We didn't even know his first name. I also fretted about the missing 3D printers, about Nikki and my promise to Hawk.

In the last year I had lived on the edges of panic more often than before. The immediate future didn't seem to offer a reprieve. Not only had I publicly declared my emotional vulnerability towards Colin, but I had agreed to join our apartments. Add to that the possibility of Nikki moving in and my breathing became shallow, my heart racing. Convinced that the next few months were going to be challenging, I mentally flattened an empty music sheet. A notable difference was the lack of emotional and social isolation I felt as I started writing Mozart's Clarinet Concerto in A Major.

~ ~ ~ ~ ~

Be first to find out when Genevieve's next adventure will be published. Sign up for the newsletter at
http://estelleryan.com/contact.html

~ ~ ~ ~ ~

Listen to the Mozart pieces,
look at the paintings from this book
and read more about 3D printed guns,
Cubism and Braque at:
http://estelleryan.com/the-braque-connection.html

The Flinck Connection
Fourth in the Genevieve Lenard series

A murdered politician. An unsolved art heist. An international conspiracy.

A cryptic online message leads nonverbal communications expert Doctor Genevieve Lenard to the body of a brutally murdered politician. Despite being ordered not to investigate, Genevieve and her team look into this vicious crime. More online messages follow, leading them down a path lined with corruption, a sadistic assassin, an oil scandal and one of the biggest heists in history—the still unsolved 1990 Boston museum art theft worth $500m.

The deeper they delve, the more evidence they unearth of a conspiracy implicating someone close to them, someone they hold in high regard. With a deadline looming, Genevieve has to cope with past and present dangers, an attack on one of her team members and her own limitations if she is to expose the real threat and protect those in her inner circle.

The Flinck Connection *is available as paperback and ebook.*

The Flinck Connection
Fourth in the Genevieve Lenard series

Excerpt

Chapter ONE

"And I will always love you." The melodramatic, yet oddly memorable song jerked me out of a restful sleep. It took me a mere second to go from a state of relaxation to utter annoyance. I grabbed my smartphone from the bedside table where it had been perfectly aligned to the corners. As I sat up, a few things registered in my mind, the face flashing on my smartphone's screen being the most vexing. I swiped the screen.

"You changed my ringtone. Again." I hated when Colin did that. He had started this unacceptable behaviour the first time I'd met him eighteen months ago.

"Jenny, you need—"

"—to have my old ringtone back. You know how much I hate it when you do this. Why do you continue doing this? Will you ever stop being a thief and stealing into my smartphone?"

"Jenny!" The urgency in his tone not only stopped my annoyance, but also triggered a shot of adrenaline to enter my bloodstream. "You need to phone Millard."

"Why? What's wrong?" It wasn't just his tone that alerted me to a problem. For the last seven weeks, Colin and Colonel Manny Millard had been at odds.

Colin Frey was a thief, reappropriating art that had been taken during conflicts or illegally obtained. He did this to return these artworks to their rightful owners.

Even after knowing him for eighteen months and being

romantically involved with him for eleven months, I still felt conflicted accepting his profession. The fact that he was secretly employed by Interpol did nothing to aid my discomfort. Before he had entered my life, everything had been much simpler. I had successfully divided everything in black and white categories. Things had been either right or wrong. Colin had taught me that life consisted of grey areas.

One of those areas was his cooperation with Manfred Millard. An Interpol agent and lifelong law enforcement officer, Manny headed our team of five as we investigated art crimes. Our team existed on the order of the president of France, and the probes into art illegalities were second priority to any case the president requested us to look into. This position was well suited for Manny, but it was a daily conflict for him working with the rest of the team, especially Colin.

They shared a turbulent past and it often seemed they took pleasure in antagonising each other. Something had happened seven weeks ago between Manny and Colin that had caused renewed hostility between them. Neither one was willing to talk about it. Colin had stubbornly refused to talk to Manny. The current state of their relationship would not allow Colin to ask for Manny's assistance. That was why Colin's request for me to contact Manny was a surprise.

"Jenny, are you listening?" He wasn't as patient as usual when I got lost in my thoughts. There was an unfamiliar sharpness to his tone.

"I'm listening. Why do you want me to phone Manny? Why don't you phone him?"

"I'm standing in Claude Savreux's home office, looking at his dead body."

"Oh my God, did you… No, of course you didn't kill him. Why are you there? What are you stealing? Are you talking about Monsieur Claude Savreux, the Minister of Defence and Veteran Affairs? Why do you want to steal from him?"

"Jenny." His voice was low, the tone he took when he needed me to focus. "Phone Millard, tell him to get people he trusts and a warrant or something that will get him into this house."

I took a moment to think this over. "Are you sure he's dead?"

"Very."

"Then I'm not going to phone Manny until you tell me why you are there."

A few hard breaths sounded through the connection. "Wake Nikki up and ask her. I have to leave. I don't want to overstay my welcome here."

"Nikki?" My voice raised a pitch and a few decibels. "You're involving Nikki in your crimes?"

Nikki was an eighteen-year-old student who had come into our lives five months ago. She was the daughter of the late Hawk, a notorious arms trader. When he had died, Nikki had been seventeen, not yet an adult. She had refused to be placed in the government system and threatened to run away. We had become her foster parents until she came of age three months ago, yet she was still staying with us.

"Jenny." He sighed. "Just wake her up and let her tell you. I've got to go. I'll keep an eye on the house until Millard arrives, but I'm leaving now."

Before I could give more voice to my outrage, he gave me the address and promptly hung up on me.

I trusted Colin with my life. I even loved him, despite his life being shadowed by unclear moral and ethical lines. He was also the only person whose physical touch and closeness I could bear. Time and again he had proven himself to be a man of integrity. That was the reason I swiped my smartphone's screen and tapped on Manny's number.

"What's wrong, Doctor Face-reader?" Manny's voice was gruff from being woken up.

"Colin is in Minister Claude Savreux's house and he's dead."

"What? Who's dead? The minister?" His voice was decidedly clearer and louder. "Did Frey kill him?"

"Colin didn't kill him. I don't know any details. Colin phoned me to tell you to get to Minister Savreux's house as soon as possible. With a search warrant."

"Bloody hell." A grunt came through the connection. "Do you know what the time is?"

"Of course I do." What an inane question. "It's fourteen minutes past two."

"Exactly."

"Oh, and Colin asked that you get people you trust for this. I don't know why he would say this, but his tone implied that this was particularly important." I didn't want to tell him about Nikki's involvement yet, particularly since I didn't know how she had become entangled in this. With her unfailingly cheerful disposition, she had won the hearts of everyone, including Manny's. He was overly protective of her, hence my reticence in telling him.

"Oh, for the love of Pete," Manny said after a few quiet seconds. "Give me the address and let me see what I can do, Doc. I'll phone you in a bit and you had better have more information for me by then."

"How long is a bit?"

"A bit?" He groaned. "I will phone you in twenty minutes, Doc."

The Flinck Connection *is available as paperback and ebook.*

Other books in the Genevieve Lenard Series:

Book 1: The Gauguin Connection

Book 2: The Dante Connection

Book 3: The Braque Connection

Book 4: The Flinck Connection

Book 5: The Courbet Connection

Book 6: The Pucelle Connection

Book 7: The Léger Connection

Book 8: The Morisot Connection

Book 9: The Vecellio Connection

and more…

Find out more about Estelle at
www.estelleryan.com
Or visit her facebook page to chat with her:
www.facebook.com/EstelleRyanAuthor